The Jam Factory Girls Fight Back

Mary Wood was born in Maidstone, Kent, and brought up in Claybrooke, Leicestershire. Born one of fifteen children to a middle-class mother and an East End barrow boy, Mary's family were poor but rich in love. This encouraged her to develop a natural empathy with the less fortunate and a fascination with social history. In 1989 Mary was inspired to pen her first novel and she is now a full-time novelist.

Mary welcomes interaction with readers and invites you to subscribe to her website where you can contact her, receive regular newsletters and follow links to meet her on Facebook and Twitter: www.authormarywood.com

BY MARY WOOD

The Breckton series

To Catch a Dream
An Unbreakable Bond
Tomorrow Brings Sorrow
Time Passes Time

The Generation War saga

All I Have to Give
In Their Mother's Footsteps

The Girls Who Went to War series

The Forgotten Daughter
The Abandoned Daughter
The Wronged Daughter
The Brave Daughters

The Jam Factory series

The Jam Factory Girls
Secrets of the Jam Factory Girls
The Jam Factory Girls Fight Back

Stand-alone novels

Proud of You
Brighter Days Ahead
The Street Orphans

The Jam Factory Girls Fight Back

Mary Wood

PAN BOOKS

First published 2021 by Pan Books
an imprint of Pan Macmillan
The Smithson, 6 Briset Street, London EC1M 5NR
EU representative: Macmillan Publishers Ireland Ltd, 1st Floor,
The Liffey Trust Centre, 117–126 Sheriff Street Upper,
Dublin 1, D01 YC43
Associated companies throughout the world
www.panmacmillan.com

ISBN 978-1-5290-3349-6

1 3 5 7 9 8 6 4 2

A CIP catalogue record for this book is available from the British Library.

Typeset by Palimpsest Book Production Ltd, Falkirk, Stirlingshire
Printed and bound by CPI Group (UK) Ltd, Croydon, CR0 4YY

MIX
Paper from
responsible sources
FSC® C116313

To Betty Swift and in loving memory of her late, much-loved mother- and father-in-law, Maud and Jim Swift.

Betty's daughter, Jilly, contacted me after her mum had enjoyed reading *The Jam Factory Girls* to tell me that Maud and Jim Swift had worked together for many years in Hartley's Jam Factory.

It's a coincidence that I called Millie's jam factory Swift's, but an honour to hear of this connection to Betty and her parents-in-law and to dedicate this book to them all with my love.

Chapter One

Millie

Millie closed the box she'd been packing and sealed it. 'That's the last of the boxes, Ruby. I can't tell you what a relief it is.'

'Aye, and sommat as you shouldn't have tackled, with you about to have your babby.'

'What else could I do? Mama and Wilf aren't due back from their cruise until next week, and the new owners of Raven Hall want to take over the week after that.'

'Eeh, Millie, lass, how all our lives have changed, eh? This time last year I was still your maid in your London house, you were happily trying to settle your new-found half-sister, Elsie, into your home, and the pair of you were making a grand job of running the jam factory. Your ma lived here and was picking up the pieces of her life, and you were looking forward to being married.'

Millie walked over to the window. So much of what Ruby said brought pain to her.

The view she looked down on showed her the vast expanse of the beautiful Raven Park in Leeds. Memories assailed her of herself as a little girl running down the slope, tumbling

1

and rolling, her giggles filling the air, and her then-beloved papa pretending to chase her – catching her and tickling her until she screamed out for him to stop.

A tear slid a silvery path down her cheek as her hand went to her bulge and she gently massaged the baby inside her. *Will I be able to give you a happy childhood, my baby? Will I even be able to keep you with me?*

The pain of this thought made her gasp.

'What is it, Millie, lass? Eeh, I shouldn't have brought such things up – I'm sorry.'

Ruby ran over to her with her arms open, and Millie went gratefully into her hug. *Dear Ruby, how often she's been here for me in the past.*

'Don't get into the doldrums, lass, it's naw good for your unborn. I knaw you have a lot to contend with, but you're strong and you can get through this. Selling this house and the estate has set you up, and you said you've a buyer for the London house. And here you are, all settled with a place in The Blue of Bermondsey – not that I ever thought you'd live there, lass. I didn't think of it as a place for the likes of you, but you seem happy enough.'

'I am, Ruby. I'm near to Elsie and Jim and feel protected by them. And Cess works on his market stall in the street below us, so I can chat with him whenever I want to.'

'How is he? It beggars belief that he's still only a young 'un of nineteen. He's got the head of a much older man and has been through more than most. Yet he's picked himself up and is getting on with life. Eeh, he's a good 'un.'

'I take a lot of strength from him. He's like a brother to me. He makes me feel that if he can come out the other side of losing lovely Dot and carry on, then I can cope too. But . . . Oh, Ruby, I can't stop worrying about Len and what revenge he's planning. Not just on me, but on Elsie and Jim too. Because he'll never take the responsibility of it being his own actions that caused me to leave him, but blames Elsie.'

'Aye, it's a worry. That Len's a nasty piece of work. But Jim and Elsie are strong. They'll be all right. And, like I said, you are too, Millie. Together you're a force to be reckoned with, and the likes of Len'll not find it easy to break you.'

Millie sighed.

'Eeh, lass, don't take on. I'll give Rose a shout, eh? She's going to be your maid, so she can start now and make us a pot of tea. I'm ready for a cuppa meself. And then we can sit and have a chinwag. You can tell me exactly what you fear. Get it all off your chest, as you knaw what they say: a trouble shared is a trouble halved.'

Millie didn't see her problems being halved, not even by crying on the trusted Ruby's shoulder, but knew it would be good to talk them through. Ruby had been her maid, and for a long time she had been the only dependable person in her life – a friend more than a servant. When Ruby had married her Tom and decided to settle back here in her native Leeds, Millie had felt bereft – everything had changed. Life had gone from being a simple struggle against her mama's desire to elevate her to the upper classes, to a devastating discovery of long-held secrets.

It was a time when she'd found that her father wasn't the man she'd believed him to be. He'd owned Swift's Jam Factory in Bermondsey, she'd adored and looked up to him, but all the time he was taking advantage of his workers – having affairs with the vulnerable, who he charmed into believing he loved them. The only good thing to come out of his dalliances was discovering that she had two half-sisters: Elsie and the sadly now-late Dot. Dot had looked the most

3

like herself, with the same dark hair and dark eyes, whereas, although Elsie had the same features and dark eyes, she took her glorious red hair from her mother.

Ruby cut into her thoughts. 'Eeh, lass, think on. Len left you broke, which gave him a good hand of cards, but you've overcome that one. So what's really bothering you, eh?'

'Well, yes, money-wise I'll be fine now, with the generous gift of the proceeds of this house from Mama. But, oh, Ruby, the letter that was waiting here for me when I arrived from London has shattered me.'

'I knew it had dealt you a blow. You were that happy when you arrived, and I'd said to me ma, "Nowt can keep my Millie down for long." And it won't, lass. Letter or naw letter.'

Millie smiled. She loved Ruby, who always stood for good sense and was a much wiser being than herself, even though she was only three years older.

'Well, this blow will take some getting over. The letter was from Len. He says he has seen a lawyer and has been advised that he has a right to the custody of our child . . . Oh, Ruby, I couldn't bear it.'

'That bloody swine! By, I could wring his neck for him. Can he do that? Has he really got the right to take your child or is he bluffing?'

'I have Jordan and Issy working on it – they are a husband and wife team and are my new solicitors. They have been like a rock to me. Completely in my corner, not like the double-crossing Gutheridge, my father's old solicitor, who was working with Len behind my back. Also, I'm going to talk to Wilf when he and Mama get back from the first leg of their honeymoon next week. Do you remember how he helped Elsie and Dot that time? I know he's retired now, but he was the top lawyer in the country. Wilf's son and his wife took over the practice and are excellent lawyers. They are working on trying to prove that Len duped me out of the factory and my property portfolio. They haven't come up with anything that would stand up in court yet, though.'

'But we all knew he did – he only married you to get it.'

'I know.'

Though Millie said this, and knew that it was a large part of why Len had wooed her, she also knew that deep down he did love her and still wanted her. He'd begged her to go back to him and then, when she'd refused, he'd tried using emotional blackmail. When that failed, he used threats. These took the form of him saying he could legally take any proceeds she gained from the sale of this land and estate, because capital gains acquired after a woman married belonged to her husband. And now this latest devastating news that he intended to take custody of their child. *Maybe I should just go back to him. It would solve so many problems. But no, I could never live with the man who raped my dear Elsie.*

'Surely these lawyers can stop him, lass?'

'They will try. But Len and his father are influential men. They move in all the right circles; they are well respected and have powerful connections. With Len owning the main bank in Bermondsey and soon to become a partner in the largest bank in England – and now owning what was my jam factory, and my sizeable property portfolio – people such as lawyers, solicitors, judges and magistrates jump when he tells them to. I, on the other hand, am laughed at – the daughter of a man who was constantly gambling, who cheated in business and in life, a self-made man who tried to jump up above his station, and was only tolerated by society because of my mama's background.'

Spelling it all out hit Millie with the enormity of what she would be fighting against. Suddenly she felt that losing her child to Len was a certainty.

'Eeh, lass, I don't knaw what to say. Is there naw hope?'

At this moment Millie didn't think there was. She felt weary of it all. When she looked up, she saw a tear running down Ruby's face. 'Oh, Ruby, I'm sorry. I didn't mean to upset you. Oh, my dear.' Rising, she went to crouch at her friend's knee. 'I'll fight him, Ruby, I will. I shouldn't have shown despair like that. This is my child and I won't give it up. Everything will be all right. Don't upset yourself. Oh, Ruby, Ruby . . .'

Ruby was sobbing now. Her body was heaving, her hands trembling in Millie's.

'What is it, Ruby, love? Is there something you're not telling me? Are you and Tom all right?'

'Aye, we are. I were so happy. I – I wanted it to be . . . a . . . nice thing to tell you, but now it seems all is coming good for me, and you're so desolate. I – I'm sorry, lass, so sorry.'

'Ruby, love, how can anything that makes you happy affect me any other way than to make me happy too? Come on, out with it, and cheer me up, eh?'

'But . . . I'm to have what you might lose, Millie.'

'A baby! Oh, but Ruby, that's wonderful. Wonderful! I feel like skipping around the room. When? How long have you known? What does Tom think?'

Ruby gave a tearful giggle. 'You don't mind? It don't hurt you to knaw that I'll have a child, when yours might be taken? Eeh, lass.'

'No, I think it the best news I've had in a long time. Oh, Ruby. Tell me all about it . . . well, not – you know . . .'

They burst out laughing, which lifted Millie's spirits. Even more so as she listened to how Ruby was in her fourth month, and how she and her ma had done a dance with Tom when she broke the news to them.

'Ruby, changing the subject, how does your ma really feel about me selling this house? And the other staff too? Have they any worries they're telling you that they're not sharing with me?'

'Naw. Ma's happy for you, and for your ma. She got on really well with the lady who will be her new mistress and liked her very much. She'll be fine. Nowt can daunt me ma, now she's back in her beloved Leeds. And because she's happy, the rest of the staff are, an' all. And those who've been here a long time are happy that there will be children around the place again. They're allus talking of when you were a youngster.'

'That's nice of them. And I'm so glad. You know, I never thought my mama would give this place to me or encourage me to sell it, as she really loved it and looked on it as her sanctuary.'

'Well, things move on, and she's found the happiness she deserves. We could all see that when she came to stay and gave a party for us before her wedding. We were that happy for her, and accepted Raven Hall was to be sold.'

Millie stood. She looked around the drawing room they were in. What she saw didn't conjure up any emotions – the memories were now in crates, to be stored until Mama and Wilf came home. Everything was to be taken to Wilf's house in Knightsbridge and marked according to the list Mama had left, as to which room each crate should go into.

Wilf had tried to sell his house and had sold most of his furniture, thinking to buy another, which he and Mama could choose together when their world tour came to an end. But their plans had changed with the predicament Millie found herself in, and they had cut short the tour for now. Wilf's household staff were all still in place and would see to everything being set out as Mama wanted it to be.

Oh, how I wish Mama was here now. I so need the comfort she would offer, and the help and advice that Wilf could give me.

A tap on the door hailed Rose coming into the room. 'I've been sent to tell you, ma'am, that the removal men are here.'

'Thank you, Rose . . . Oh and Rose, are you ready for our journey?'

'I am, and I'm that excited. I can't imagine what London will be like. I feel it's the change I need after losing me ma and . . . well, everything.'

Millie knew Rose was referring to her husband's death, which happened shortly after they'd met her. For a moment she felt awkward as to whether to mention it or not, as she understood from Ruby that not all had been well with the marriage. But still, she felt she had to say something.

'I was sorry to hear of your losses, Rose, it must have been very difficult. I hope you will be happy in your new position.'

'Eeh, I knaw I will. And it'll be good to see Elsie again – we made friends at Ruby's wedding.'

'Yes, I remember, you looked after my sister when she thought she could drink two glasses of sherry, but found her stomach couldn't.'

'I felt sorry for her, ma'am. She shouldn't have been taken advantage of— I mean, eeh, I'm sorry, me tongue wags away with itself at times.'

'It does an' all, Rose. I hope Millie will get used to that about you. You're a lovely lass, but you can say more than is necessary.'

'Ha! You sounded just like your ma then, Ruby. Don't think any more about it, Rose. There isn't much that went on that I don't know about now. My sister wasn't to blame for any of it, so, although I don't want to talk about it all, if you slip up, it's not the end of the world.'

'Ta, ma'am.'

'And once we leave here there is no need to stand on ceremony, either. You can call me Millie. I know it's not conventional, but you won't be a maid in the strict sense of the word, you will be my assistant and will look after my child when I have to be elsewhere.'

'Aye, that's the bit I'm looking forward to the most. I was a trained nanny before I became a maid. I loved the work. When I finished me training, I was looking for a post but couldn't find one. I took this job to tide me over. I liked it here, so I stayed.'

'But that's wonderful, I never knew that. You don't know what an asset you will be to me. Do you have any written, formal papers to tell of your training?'

'Aye, I do.'

Rose then amazed them both by telling them, in a far different voice, 'And I can speak in a very posh voice when called upon to do so. I have only spoken in my accent since I took the post of maid. But my elocution is second to none, when I am required to appear to be a young lady of breeding, who has fallen on hard times and is now a nanny.'

Millie laughed, 'Well, what a transformation!'

Ruby, who'd sat open-mouthed, joined in the laughter.

As did Rose as she asked, 'So, will I do?'

'You will – you will do very well indeed.'

'I'm so glad, as this move is sommat I really need. Anyroad, I'll get back to me chores, or your ma'll have me guts for garters, Ruby.'

They both laughed once Rose had left them. 'She's a card, I'll tell you, Millie. She'll be a tonic to you. But I'll miss her.'

'But you won't carry on working, will you? Not now.'

'Naw. It's never gone down well with Tom that I carried on after we were wed. I had a fight on me hands, and it weren't sommat I wanted to do, but they were short-handed here and I just sort of slipped back into it. Now I don't have to be loyal to the new folk, so I'm leaving at the end of this week, before they are in residence.'

'I'm glad, Ruby. It's hard work being pregnant. Are you over the sickness stage?'

'Aye, I am. Anyroad, we'd better shift ourselves. I'm to help with supervising the sending of this lot in the right direction. We need to put your things onto the van first, then by the time they unload your mama's, you'll have arrived home to receive them.'

'Don't worry too much. My flat is already filled with my furniture from our old London house in Burgess Place, so it won't hurt if any of it lands at Wilf's.'

'Well then, are you set to go?'

'Yes, I'm ready. Tom is going to take me and Rose to the station in a couple of hours. I need to rest before then . . . Oh, Ruby, it's been lovely spending these last two weeks with you. I miss you so much.'

'I knaw. I miss you an' all. Will you write often? I'll be worried about you.'

'I will. And you must keep me informed of every step of my little godchild's journey into being.'

'Eeh, who said you're going to be godmother, then?'

'Me. And you and Elsie are going to be godparents to my child – it's all settled.'

'Ha, you're a one, Miss Millie! Allus were, and I hope you allus will be. I'd have nawbody but you stand for me babby, you knaw that.'

'Nor would I. I do love you, Ruby.'

With this, they hugged. Millie's heart felt heavy – weighted with worries, and now with saying goodbye to Ruby.

'We went through a lot together, didn't we, Ruby? Thank you for always taking care of me.'

'The best job I ever had, lass . . . You knaw, I've allus meant to ask, are you still friendly with that girl from school called Bunty?'

'No. She asked me to her house once. I was thrilled, but when I got there, it was only so that I could be looked over as a potential wife for her brother. Her family had run out of money and saw me as a provider, and thought I would sell myself to gain a title – or, at least, that my mama would sell me.'

'Your mama has changed, lass.'

'No, not changed.' Millie tried to explain. 'Mama always was a kind, loving mother, only she wanted a different life for me than she'd had to put up with from my father, and she was misguided in how she thought she could accomplish that. Hence her pushing me into those upper circles, which exposed me to insults and loneliness. She regrets it now. And she shows me the love she has for me – oh, and the funny side of her, which I never knew as it had been buried under her unhappiness. At times she makes me split my sides. But now I wonder if she was right to look for a husband for me, as I've made a hash of my own choice . . . Anyway, I have

11

to scoot or I won't have time to lie down, and I feel so weary. Little one has been kicking me all morning. He really didn't like what I was doing and wanted me to stop and sit down.'

'He? You think you're having a boy, then?'

'That's what Ada, one of the women who works at the factory, thinks. Elsie and I have been helping her to be rehoused. She has so many children, and she said that she can tell what she is having by her shape. I'm carrying more at the front, and apparently that means a boy – I don't know myself, as I can't see the size of my rear, and don't want to at the moment.'

They laughed at this as they left the drawing room, with Millie feeling more hopeful about her situation. *Surely if I can show I have a qualified nanny to look after my child, that will put me in a better position in any fight over his custody?*

It would show that the baby was being looked after in the same way that Len would look after him, and that he was being given the same standing he would have with his father. To make his future seem all the more secure, she could now prove she was of independent financial means, and could book him into a good school as soon as he was born. Len's case could only be built on the stigma that might result from his child being bought up by a mother on her own. Not a strong case surely, now that she had a nanny?

Feeling relaxed and rested, Millie sat back in the comfortable seat of the first-class carriage and smiled to herself at the title of the book Rose was engrossed in: *Baby's First Year*, a dog-eared copy that looked as though it had been read many times.

The countryside whizzed by as she mulled over all the

possible outcomes of her coming plight, at times feeling despair, and then finding some hope to cling on to.

Her child, seeming to sense her agitation, wriggled about in protest. Putting her hand on her bump to soothe him, Millie told him in her mind, *I'll take care of you, my little one, I promise. You're coming into a different world from the one I came into, but you have me to fight for you – and I will. I'll get back the jam factory that should rightfully be mine, and I'll bring you up to know the proper, decent folk of this world, not the climbing middle class or the snooty upper class, but good old cockneys – salt-of-the-earth, decent folk. And you'll start with your Aunt Elsie and her brothers. There's Cess, who you'll know as Uncle Cess. And Bert, who's too young at seven years old to be called uncle, but I know he will be the best mate you could wish for.*

You see, the cockneys call each other 'mate', little one . . . Oh, but I mustn't forget little Kitty, Cess's daughter and your proper cousin – her mum, your lovely Aunty Dot, was my half-sister, as Elsie is. I'll tell you now, darling, Kitty gives us all the runaround and has us at her beck and call, even though she's only just turned one. So you watch out – she'll be the boss of you.

Now, I have one more of those I love to tell you about, Rene. Rene's a sort of aunt to Elsie, and a real character – a bit of a shock to the system at first, but when you get to know her, you will love her as I do.

You'll love them all, I'm sure. All my family and friends, as they have come to mean so much to me.

Elsie's husband Jim is a dear friend. You'll never meet a better man than him. He's not cockney. He's more of your father's standing, but nothing like your father. Jim will teach you music. You'd like that, wouldn't you? Oh, and there's Dai. I don't know Dai very well. He's Welsh and he's Cess's friend and his partner in business, but what I do know of him, I like. He's gentle and he understands what it's like to suffer. I have a cottage in Barmouth in Wales, little one. I'll take you to it. It's a peaceful haven.

As she closed her eyes, Millie found herself transported to Wales. For a little while she felt its tranquillity and could hear the sound of the sea breaking gentle waves onto the pebbly beach and feel the breeze playing with her hair. *Thank God I didn't give it to Len along with everything else – or, rather, have it blackmailed out of me, as my factory and property portfolio were.*

But I will keep my pledge, and one day Elsie and I will walk back into the jam factory as the owners once more, and we'll give back to the workers what Len has taken – their rights, the better conditions that Elsie and I had put into place, and their dignity.

Chapter Two

Elsie

Elsie paced the room.

Rene sighed. 'Give over, will you, mate? Millie will get 'ere whenever she does. You can't hurry her.'

Elsie laughed. 'I know, Rene. But it isn't just Millie – it's Rose too. It'll be lovely to see her again. And then I'm expecting Jim home as well. He was to have a meeting with Len today, so I'm on tenterhooks about that.'

'Why? Is he finally giving in his notice, then?'

'Yes, at last. These last months have been hell, with Jim having to continue working for Len after all that happened, but we think we can now manage on our earnings from teaching music. Me customers who want to learn to play by ear, how me gran taught me to, are bringing in a fair bit, and Jim's proper music classes are growing steadily.'

Going to the window, Elsie looked down on the busy street of The Blue in Bermondsey. Her flat was on the second floor, above Rene's dressmaker's shop on the corner of Blue Anchor Lane. She could see the tops of people's heads as they went about their business, and her brother Cess as he sold swathes of material from his market stall. Cess and Dai owned two stalls. The other, a bric-a-brac stall on Petticoat Lane, was run by Dai.

As Cess looked up, he spotted her and waved his hand. Elsie grinned and waved back, but it was then that she caught sight of Jim striding along. She went to wave to him, but something about his stance stopped her. His face looked like thunder. She'd only ever seen him look like that once before – just before he'd hit Len.

Elsie dropped her head and turned away from the window. Whatever Rene had been saying had gone over her head, but she brought her attention back to her friend.

'I tell you, girl, I hope Jim's told that Len where to shove 'imself. Yer need to get on with yer lives. No one's going to do it for you – nor can they. You and Jim need to get out of his rotten clutches.'

'Rene, he's coming. Jim's walking down the street. Can you make yourself scarce, mate, as he don't look like he needs to see anyone but me at this moment.'

Rene didn't object. After she slipped out of the flat, Elsie heard her running down the stairs. She held her breath, afraid that Rene would trip and fall in her heeled boots. Although she was slowly building up the dressmaking business that Millie had helped her to set up, Rene still dressed the part of an East End prostitute, despite having long given up that profession. Her ample breasts were always exposed to just above the nipple and wobbled with her every movement. Elsie had the feeling they would pop out one day. And although Rene's dark hair was pulled back tightly into a bun, it seemed she couldn't help but release a few tantalizing ringlets from the hairband and let them play around her face. But to Elsie, she was just Rene. She loved her and felt loved by her, and always had done. And at times, since the murder of her mum, Elsie didn't know what she'd have done without Rene. Nothing pleased her more than to see her friend gaining work, such as being commissioned to make some of the costumes for the production of a new musical that was due to show at the Vic next year.

As the tendrils of smoke from Rene's newly lit fag filtered up to her, Elsie thought of her mum and could almost see her and Rene standing outside the tenement block where they'd lived on Long Lane, smoking a Woodbine. Elsie would be sitting at her mum's feet on the step of their flat, and Jimmy – her lovely, late brother Jimmy – would be trying to teach Bert how to kick a ball into the makeshift goal made from two coats on the tarmac. And Cess would come along the lane, whistling and holding hands with Dot.

Pain shot through Elsie. How she longed to go back. To have her mum still alive, and Jimmy, and dear Dot – her best friend, who'd been like a sister to her from when they were born. But oh, how she wished they'd never found out that they were true half-sisters, fathered by Millie's dad. Everything had changed in their lives after that, and not everything for the good – except for Millie, of course. She'd never regret meeting Millie. She loved Millie with all her heart.

There was no time to dwell on it all further, as Jim came through the door. His greeting to Rene wasn't at all like him – a curt 'hello', and even his hurried footsteps on the stairs sounded angry.

Elsie ran to the door to meet him as he leapt up the last few steps. 'Jim? Has something happened, love?'

'It has, Elsie.'

She went into his open arms, felt his body tremble and then heave. With this, Elsie felt her world become unsteady as she realized that her lovely Jim was crying.

'Jim, Jim, love. What's to do? Come inside.'

Closing the door behind them, Elsie had a feeling that what she'd feared – the crumbling of the fragile happiness they had – was about to happen.

She'd been so easily lured by her deep love for Jim, and by him making her his own, into feeling secure and thinking they could weather everything, even all that was unresolved in their lives. But now she instinctively knew that wasn't to be.

They sat on the larger of their two rose-coloured sofas. But the softness of the feather cushions didn't offer the usual comfort to Elsie's tense nerves.

The flat had been furnished to her taste before Jim moved in, and although he liked it, he thought it had a feminine look, with the flora-patterned centre of the grey carpet being picked out by the floral curtains. To tone this down and make him feel more welcome, they'd made a few changes. The curtains had gone, replaced by plain grey velvet ones, and they'd stripped the floral border from the walls and painted them cream.

Most of the furniture had been replaced too, as the originals had come from Elsie's mum's old home and had been the worse for wear, although she hadn't been able to part with the cabinet, as her mum had bought it not long before her life was taken and had been so proud of it.

Jim leaned forward and rested his elbows on his knees. 'My assault on Len is coming back to bite us, Else.'

'How? Why? You did as Len said. You've run the jam factory for all these months and he dropped the charges, so how can it now be a problem? Surely he didn't think it was going to be a lifetime commitment, after what he did to us?'

'Apparently he does expect to own me, for life. He was showing me the plans for the new factory he'd always planned, and he admitted that he was never going to keep Swift's open when he took possession of it.' Jim shook his head. 'He had it all worked out, sure in the knowledge that he would take the factory from Millie before she could get a chance to complete the legalities for you to become an equal owner.'

'Not keep the factory open! But what about the workers? They depend on their wages.'

'He doesn't care about that. Len's plans are well advanced. The new location for the factory is in Kent. He discussed this as being my opportunity. I told him that I wasn't prepared to move there. That when Swift's closed, that would be a parting of the ways for us. He was shocked and went mad, Else. He shouted. Can you imagine anyone shouting in the men's club?'

Elsie couldn't even imagine what a men's club looked like, let alone anyone shouting in one. Such places weren't for the likes of cockneys like her. That side of Jim's life was alien to her. She still wondered what he saw in her, knowing that she came from a poverty-stricken background and that her mum had been a prostitute.

Jim had been brought up in a well-to-do family, thinking he would take over his father's jam-making business in due course. Only his father had lost it all through bad decision-making and Jim had been left beholden to his friends – and Len had been one of those. Or, rather, he hadn't.

Len was a user. He used Jim to get a foot into Millie's factory. He'd introduced Jim to Millie as someone needing a job and an expert in all matters to do with jam-making. Len had achieved this by using the fact that Millie was a woman and pointing out her inexperience in the business. He convinced her that she needed a manager like Jim to help her and advise her, in order for her to succeed. Jim had turned out to be excellent at his job. And besides that, a lovely man, who had stolen Elsie's heart and won Millie's deep friendship.

She listened in shock, without interrupting Jim as he went on to tell her that during his rage, Len had told him he would be finished if he didn't do as he was asked.

'I managed to quieten him and get him to discuss everything calmly and stop drawing attention to us. But then Len became menacing. He told me that although he had told the police he no longer wanted the charge against me for assaulting him to go ahead, he'd had his lawyers prepare a civil case against me for grievous bodily harm. Apparently his doctor will testify to the fact that Len has been left with long-term defects – memory and coordination impairment – and is now on a short fuse, after being a very placid, even-tempered man.'

'A what? Len was never that. And as for his memory, that has always worked to suit himself. But oh, Jim, is it really possible this will happen? What will it mean if he wins?'

'Then they will file for compensation, even though I haven't got much, but it seems they can take everything we own. Your possessions too. As we are husband and wife, you will be liable for my debts. He also said . . . Oh, Elsie.'

Jim's despair increased. His head drooped and a tear plopped onto his knee.

'Jim, don't. Please, Jim, we can beat this – we can. We'll tell of what Len did.'

'We've been pipped to the post on that one, as it seems he is prepared to include what will look like more injury done by us, as he has cited you as being responsible for the breakdown of his marriage by – as he puts it – coming on to him and luring him into having sex. There is also an allegation that we duped him and . . . I – I can't believe this, but he told me he has evidence that I have falsified the amounts of jam produced, the hours the women worked and the ledgers I sent to his accountant.'

'How? I mean, how are you supposed to have done that, and what would you gain?'

'He says that I put more hours down than the women had worked, embezzling up to fifty pounds a week.'

'Oh God, how can he do that? You haven't, so he can't have proof that you did.'

'He says he can prove that the clocking-in and -out machine was tampered with.'

'That's ridiculous.'

'It's not, darling. It can be done. *I* haven't done it, but it can be done – and on top of that, Len says he can show that the amounts I got from the accountant were more than the women received. He suspected I might do what he called "the dirty" on him and had prepared everything, just in case. Even to having someone check the women's envelopes as they went home last Friday. The amount that they had in total was fifty pounds short of the amount I ordered to pay them with, which means he must have the accountant in his pocket somehow, if he can produce evidence of this.'

'Oh, Jim. Len's a bastard. Rene never calls him anything other than that and she's right – he is.'

'How are we going to deal with it all? He has tallies on the jam stocks that make it look as if I have booked in less than what we produced, and an outlet where I sold it cheaply – he named several of my father's old customers in the Liverpool area.' Jim shook his head. 'It all beggars belief, Elsie. The elaborate methods he must have gone to – there must have been men in the factory at night taking stock out, and others making new stock sheets to replace mine, and I never noticed. I just took the last figure as the one I had been working from – only it wasn't mine. It was Len's, as he prepared to bring me down if I refused to work for him any longer.'

Elsie felt at a loss. It was all above her how such a thing could be achieved, or even thought of, but then it wouldn't be by anyone normal – they were dealing with Len. The man who had blighted their lives, devastated Millie's and was about to do that again to her and Jim. A madman out for revenge. How could they stop him? How?

'Did he offer you a way out of all this, Jim?'

'Yes, but I – I can't take it. It will mean leaving you, Elsie, and going to Kent to set up his new factory. And living in his father's house where, apparently, there's plenty of room and his father rarely visits. He tried to sell the idea to me as if it was a wonderful alternative to what he called the "low life" you had dragged me down to. I would have full use of the stables, and staff at my disposal, and he'd introduce me to local society, so that I could take my rightful place in life again – meet fellow-minded men and beautiful women of my own standing. He dared to call you a whore, my darling. My fists clenched at this and I only just stopped myself from thumping him again, but I knew that would only add to our troubles.'

Elsie couldn't take it in. What would it mean for them? Their chances of making their own way in the world, with the music school they'd planned, now lay in tatters – even having a life together seemed impossible. There was no solution, just two options – Jim went to prison for

22

embezzlement and debt, or Jim left her. Options given and directed by the hateful, spiteful Len. How could she ever have thought herself in love with such a vile creature, as she had done when she'd first met him?

Guilt washed over her as she thought about how she'd found it hard to resist Len's kiss. How stupid she'd been to think it was really her that Len loved – the kiss was just part of his evil plan to ensnare her, to make her give up her part ownership of the jam factory. And his rape of her was his punishment for her not giving in.

She would never have told Millie about the rape – she couldn't have hurt her in that way and she'd begged Jim not to. But when Len's tricks had defrauded her of her right to half of Millie's inheritance, Jim had snapped. Poor Millie heard the truth, and Len ended up in hospital. But it didn't suit Len to press charges then and have Jim charged. Oh no, he needed Jim. Needed his knowledge of running a jam factory. And this was the result – his revenge for what he thought had wrecked his marriage, something he didn't recognize as being his own fault, although he did recognize how to turn everything to his own advantage.

At this moment Len seemed to hold all the cards, but there must be something they could do. 'Jim, there'll be a way of stopping Len. There must be! What about the night-watchman? Wouldn't he have seen things going on?'

'Well, if my theory is right, he must have. But no doubt he has been bribed or threatened.'

'What if we offered him more, to be a witness for you?'

'I don't know if we can – it depends on what he was given.'

'And your father's old customers, do you know them all? Would they help us by telling us who actually sold them the jam? And what are you supposed to have done with the money?

We can prove we haven't had more than your wages and the allowance Millie makes me, from me so-called father's estate. We can show bank statements.'

'Yes, we can. I hadn't thought of that. And I could try to find out which of Father's customers have been buying the stock, and tackle them. But will Len have thought of that and made sure they believed they were doing the deal with me? And his lawyers may argue that I wouldn't be stupid enough to put whatever money I got from the embezzlement into my bank, but must have made some other arrangement to stash it away. Because there would be no cheques taken for the produce. No one buys stolen goods with anything other than cash.'

'Is it a large amount of money?'

'From what Len says, it's in the hundreds.'

Elsie gasped. 'That's a lot of jam, so . . . how? I mean, wouldn't you notice all that going out of the factory?'

'He must have been doing it for months, bit by bit – from the very first day I agreed to carry on working for him. Oh, I wish I hadn't done so now.'

'He left you no bleedin' choice, darlin'. It was a case of carry on doing so or he'd press charges for assaulting him, and that would have meant prison anyway. It's me who was at fault for ever telling you about Len raping me.'

'No, none of this is your fault, Else, none of it. It's all at Len's door – his door and his father's, and the vengeance they want to bring down on us all; or at least on Millie. And we're the tools they're using to do it.'

'And all for something her – our – father did. Even from the grave, Richard Hawkesfield is ruining my life.'

'I'm sorry to say, darling, but there's more. Len . . . well, he used a further tactic. He told me he intends to put Rene's rent up by the fifty per cent discount that she was given on the going rate by Millie, when Millie owned all the properties, if I don't do as he asks.'

'No! The bloody pig! Rene won't be able to afford it. Can he do that? Doesn't Rene have a contract?'

'I tackled him on that, and he said the contract isn't worth the paper it's written on because it was an agreement with his ex-wife, who no longer owns the property. Not only that, but the contract runs out in its present form after twelve months. The granting of a new one will then be subject to negotiations.'

'Yes, that's right. Millie gave Rene a huge reduction in rent to help her build her business, but they agreed that they would review it, to see if Rene was able to pay more for her second year. But Millie wouldn't have put Rene's payments up by that much.'

Jim hung his head in despair. Elsie leaned towards him. 'We'll fight this, Jim, we will. We have to, as all the options we've been given are unthinkable.'

Jim lifted his head. 'Thank you, darling, for staying strong. If you were to break, I don't know what we would do. I'll look out my father's contact book. It's in the chest upstairs that I brought here with me. I'll make a start by telephoning all his contacts.'

'Oh, Jim, I hope you find the ones who've been involved and they can help us to prove it wasn't you, mate.'

'Actually I'm more likely to get help from any of those who were offered the jam cheaply, but who refused, as the others may fear what might happen to them. I think I know a couple who might have turned the offer down. Wainwright's Food Warehouse in Liverpool is one. It supplies small corner shops. And Bestways Produce, which specializes in shipping abroad. Both of the owners of these concerns are God-fearing.

Wainwright is an upstanding figure in the Baptist Church, and the other, MacDonald, was instrumental in setting up a Presbyterian congregation and the building of a church in Liverpool.'

'And would they know who you are?'

'Yes, I had close dealings with them both. They are meticulous businessmen, and I had to show them around our factory and satisfy them about our best practices in order to do all the deals we did with them. We'll just have to hope they can help.'

Elsie felt her stomach muscles clench when Jim came down the stairs. The book he'd spoken of, and now clutched in his hand, was more like a huge ledger. She wondered at a factory having so many customers and still going out of business, but Jim had never spoken in depth about how that happened, saying only that his father lost their Liverpool-based jam factory and that he'd been left with next to nothing.

She knew too that when Len had called upon Jim to work in Millie's factory as a manager, the job had been a lifesaver to him, as his own means were running out and he'd been desperate to find work. Jim hadn't known then that he was going to be a part of Len Lefton's elaborate scheme to take all that was ever owned by Richard Hawkesfield, in revenge for a double-cross that had cost Len – and his just-as-hateful father, Howard Lefton – a great deal of money.

She held her breath as she heard him speak into the receiver. 'May I speak to Mr MacDonald, please? It's Jim Ellington.' After a pause Jim went on, 'That wasn't me – it was someone impersonating me. Please tell Mr MacDonald that I am being set up for a fraud, and ask him to speak to me as I need his help . . . Thank you, I will hold on.'

Elsie could see the beads of sweat glistening on Jim's forehead. With his free hand he twisted his wax moustache, making it even more pointed.

'Mr MacDonald, thank you for speaking to me.'

Elsie listened while Jim explained why he was ringing. After a few minutes he put the telephone down. His dejected and shocked expression told that all wasn't well.

'He said he hadn't wanted to be a party to my scheme, and now he doesn't want to be a party to me getting off the hook. He's never heard of such unchristian behaviour, and is appalled that I even considered ringing him with such a scam in the first place. He ended with "Like father, like son".'

Elsie didn't know what to say. She took Jim's hand in hers and led him back to the sofa. Sitting with him, she laid her head on his shoulder. 'We won't give up, Jim. We have to prove your innocence. I can't bear either of the alternatives.'

'No, neither can I, but Len wants an answer. If I don't give him one, he will start proceedings.'

'Millie will be here any moment, me darlin'. She might have a solution.'

'There's only one answer to it all, Elsie. I have to buy time. I'm going to have to tell Len that I will go with him.' At her gasp, he said, 'It will only be a pretence. Just to stop me from being arrested – and maybe put behind bars to await a trial. If that happened, I wouldn't be able to do anything to help myself. Please stand by me in this, my darling.'

Elsie nodded. The action spilled her tears.

Jim took her into the fold of his arms, but she felt none of the usual comfort – her fear of the future was too great for that.

Chapter Three

Cess

Cess looked up from straightening the roll of material he'd just been flaring out to show a customer when he caught sight of Millie and Rose.

He remembered Rose from Ruby's wedding. He raised his hand. Millie gave her lovely smile, but that didn't stop the concern for her that rose up in Cess. To him she looked so different from the carefree girl they'd first met, and he felt the guilt of that. It wasn't his fault how their lives had all turned out to be linked, but it seemed to him that Millie meeting his sister Elsie and his lovely late wife, Dot, was the start of a downward turn in Millie's life. And yet he was glad it had happened, as he couldn't imagine his life without Millie in it.

As she crossed over the street towards him, Millie held her arms out. Cess went willingly into them, although her bulge prevented him from holding her as close as he wanted.

'How are you, Cess? How's Elsie, Jim and Rene? Oh, I've missed you all.'

'Ha, you've only been gone two weeks, mate. Hello, Rose, nice to see yer again. Hopefully you won't have to rescue any of us this time.'

Rose smiled up at him. 'Aw, it's good to be here, and I'd rescue you all if I could. Eeh, I haven't been listening in or owt, Millie. I – I, well, the staff talk . . .'

Cess was thankful when Millie helped Rose out of whatever hole she thought she'd dug for herself. 'Whatever the staff may, or may not, have told you, Rose, don't worry, as you were soon to hear it all from the horse's mouth. You can't help but know everything here – cockneys are honest folk who tell it all as it is.'

Cess laughed. 'Well, that's a summing-up of us, but we ain't gossipers, just straight talkers. And like Millie said, we're honest – ha, or at least we'll make you think so! Now the lady who just left me stall truly believes this is the finest Indian silk, but it was made up north in one of the mills.'

They all laughed. Rose's laugh surprised him; it was a hearty sound that caused a few heads to turn in their direction.

When they sobered, Cess told Millie, 'Elsie's been on tenterhooks watching for you coming, Millie, luv. But I ain't sure all's well now. Jim came home a bit ago and he looked like thunder. He didn't even glance in me direction, which isn't normal.'

'Oh? I wonder what's happened?'

'No doubt it's something to do with Len. Jim had a meeting with him today and he was going to finally hand in his notice. I don't think it a good idea to go up there yet, at least . . . well, I don't want to appear rude, but not with Rose.'

'You cockneys do say it how it is.' Rose was grinning as she turned to Millie. 'I'll stay with Cess. I can tell folk that he's a cheat, and that his stuff ain't from India after all.'

'Ha! Most of it is. But this imitation stuff isn't and, if they want cheap, then they get it with a fib attached.'

Millie was laughing as she left them.

'So, Rose, you've come to stay, then? Elsie'll be glad to see you when the time's right, but as much as I'll enjoy your company, you'll get cold standing here. I'll tell you what, I'll shut up shop for ten minutes and we'll go and have a Rosy Lee in Aggie's place.'

'A Rosy Lee? What's one of them, when it's at home?'

'A cup of tea – ha, you northerners!'

'Well, at least we're hardy. It ain't cold. By, you southerners are a load of softies.'

'Bloomin' 'eck. I think of an excuse for a break and you shoot me down. But we can stay out here and have a warming drink, as I've got a flask here.'

They stood clutching their tin mugs, blowing away the steam, when Rose said, 'I reckon I'm going to enjoy living down here. I loved Elsie when I met her, even though she were the worse for wear, and I'm finding you're all right an' all.'

'Ta, that's a compliment. But our Elsie never drinks normally. It was being at a posh do that unnerved her, and she had a lot going on.'

'Aye, I knaw, and that day's now come to bite her on the bum. Poor Elsie. I really am hoping I can be a help to her. To you all, as I knaw you've been through the mill, Cess, and I knaw what that feels like . . . Anyroad, how're you coping?'

Cess didn't press Rose on what she'd been through, as he sensed she didn't want to talk about it, but he found himself telling her about Dot, and how they'd had to run away together because of her vindictive ma. And about Dot's illness and how she died, and his little daughter, Kitty. 'You'll love her – she's a cheeky little thing.'

'I love all children. I'm a trained nanny. So who cares for Kitty while you work, Cess? And, well, is Cess your real name?'

'No, I'm Cecil. And as for Kitty, she has the best ever person to look after her – Gertrude.' He told her how he met Gertie when Dot was taken into an asylum. 'She's a trained nurse. She lives in, with me and Dai. She's nanny to Kitty, but a sort of ma to me and Dai. I bless the day I met her; she's turned out to be a darlin'.'

'Dai?'

'Daffyd – he's Welsh. He likes to be called Dai . . . Speak of the devil and he's sure to appear.'

Dai came up to the stall.

'Dai, this is Rose, who I told you about.'

'Pleased to meet you, Rose.'

Cess felt something unseen pass between Dai and Rose. They both had an expression of surprise mixed with something he couldn't determine. Rose looked away first, and Cess could see her cheeks were flushed. *Well, well, am I seeing the start of something flourishing here? I hope so. Poor Dai's still lost after the tragedy of losing his wife and son at the child's birth. But then, I know the feeling of loss.*

'That were a sigh and a half, Cess. If I'm in the way, you will tell me, won't you?'

'You're not in the way, Rose. It was just me thoughts. Telling you everything has made me revisit it all, but has helped too, in a way. Me and Dai talk a lot, but it was good to say it all to someone different. Anyway, Dai, what brings you here, mate?'

'I came for company. It's dead in the Lane. And you know how fatal it is to me to be standing around on my own.'

Rose linked arms with him. 'I sense you have troubles an'

31

all, lad. By, they're rife here. Cess here's been trying to get rid of me, so how about you and me go and have what he calls a Rosy Lee? And I hope it's better than the ditch-water he tried to make me drink out of his flask!' Rose winked at him.

Cess felt warmed by the gesture and he felt too that to have Rose in their midst was going to be a big help.

'Good idea, Dai. Let Rose take you under her wing. She's a witch and can change your mood with the nod of her head.'

'Aye, well, you wait till I wave me wand – I'll sort you all out then. I'll whisk you all off to a happy land on me broomstick.'

Cess had a good feeling as he saw a rare thing – Dai put his head back and laughed out loud. But as he watched them cross the road, that changed. Suddenly he felt alone in the world as they laughed together. Dai, a tall man, looked down at Rose, and she looked up at him, and Cess felt a moment of being shut out of their world. His heart pinched with a familiar pain. *Oh, Dot, Dot, I miss you so much, me little darlin'.*

Unable to stand the heavy ache that burned him, Cess called out, 'Watch me stall a mo, Alf, while I fetch me van, will you? I'm calling it a day. How's your day been? You seem to have had a few punters, mate.'

Alf, the stallholder next to him, threw his fag down and ground it into the tarmac. 'I ain't had a bad un', but I'll be glad when the winter's over. It seems a long one this year.'

Cess nodded. For him, every day without Dot was a year on its own.

When he arrived back at his stall, Millie came out of Elsie's and crossed over to him. 'Cess, I can see you're getting ready to go home, but I think you should come up and see Elsie and Jim before you do. Something has happened.'

'What? Oh, Millie, haven't we all had enough?'

'We have, Cess. But it isn't over yet. Where's Rose? I'd like to get home now. I feel whacked out. If you see her, will you tell her I've gone on up to my apartment?' As she said this, her body swayed.

Cess put out his arms to catch her. 'Millie, luv, are yer all right?' His answer was a flood of water from Millie, wetting his trousers and soaking his boots. 'We'd better get you home, Millie. Can you walk, luv?'

'Oh, Cess, my baby isn't due for some weeks. It can't happen now. My mama . . .'

'Babies don't wait for mothers.' Cess looked around, frantic for Rose and Dai to appear, but they weren't in sight. He looked up at Elsie's window, willing her to look out at that moment, but a moan from Millie brought his attention back to her.

'Help me, Cess.'

'I've got yer, luv . . . Alf, run over to Aggie's and fetch Rose, the young lady that were talking to me and went off with Dai. Tell her to get to Millie's as fast as she can.'

'Cess! Cess!' His name was almost a scream.

Lifting Millie, Cess ran with her to her flat in the building adjoining Elsie's and kicked open the door. The stairs felt like climbing a mountain with a huge weight.

Millie gasped and cried out. 'It's coming. My baby's coming.'

'Hold on, luv, you're all right. Rose will be here any minute. Have you got your key?'

'My bag . . . Oooh, Cess! Cess – hurry.'

'Get the key, Millie. I can't, unless I put you down. Do it, Millie!'

Millie got the key and leaned down to unlock the door.

When it opened, despite the anguish he felt, Cess still marvelled, as he did every time he entered Millie's flat, at how she had managed to make the humble five rooms above a shop in the thick of Bermondsey into what looked like a palace, with the rich furnishings she'd brought from her huge house off the Old Kent Road, not far from where he now lived. And always he was struck by the thought that it didn't seem believable that he – a boy from the tenements on Long Lane – and her, from the higher classes, seemed to be changing places, both in where they lived and in their fortunes.

'Oooh, Cess, it's coming, it's coming. Get me to my bed, please, Cess!' Cess had only just laid Millie down when she cried, 'Take my undergarments off . . . Oooh, help me-ee-ee!'

Without thinking, Cess lifted Millie's skirt and tugged at her knickers. As he did so, a head appeared. Millie contorted, an animal-like prolonged growl came from her and a babby slid from her onto the bed.

Cess was taken with emotion. Tears streamed down his face as he grabbed a small blanket that had been draped over the bottom of the bed and laid it over the child.

'Make my baby cry, Cess. Hurry!'

At this command he gently rubbed the child, then stepped back as a yell louder than any his Kitty had ever made at the same age came from the tiny bloodied figure, and its body began to turn pink. 'Oh my God!'

'My baby – I want to hold him. Is it a boy, Cess?'

Cess carefully removed the blanket, then put to one side what he knew to be the cord. 'It is. Oh, Millie, you've got a son. And my golly, he's letting us know he's here, darlin'. Ain't yer, little man?'

Millie giggled. 'Pass him to me, Cess, but be careful of his cord.'

34

As Cess placed the little boy on Millie's chest, he was struck by the beauty of what he saw. Millie, though sweating and with her eyes bulging, looked a picture of loveliness as she looked at her child and then up at him. He took the hand she offered.

'Thank you, Cess. Say hello to Cecil Two.'

'What? You're calling him after me? Oh, Millie.'

'None better. You're like the brother I never had, and a tower of strength to me. Though you'll have to stop picking me up off the side of the road.' Another lovely smile and Cess felt a surge of love for Millie and her son. Thinking about it, he had had this feeling for a long time towards Millie – a kind of family love, even back when the first incident that she had referred to happened.

'Well, it was your horse that plonked you down, the last time I picked you up. And now it's another Cecil – me little namesake. So what do we do now?'

'You need to ring for my doctor. His number is on a pad next to my phone . . . Oh, Cess, I've made a mess all over you, I'm sorry.'

'Never be sorry, Millie. You can never do anything to me that you need be sorry for.'

Her eyes opened wide and held his. A look of shock passed over her face, before she looked down at her child once more.

The feeling that went through Cess trickled shame through him, as his Dot came into his mind, but then a strange thing happened. Dot's funny little laugh filled him, and he fancied that he saw her and heard her say, 'Me Cess, me lovely Cess, be happy.' The weighted feeling that had clouded his life since Dot had died lifted a little, and he smiled back as her image faded.

The call made, Cess returned to Millie. 'Can I do anything for you, Millie? The doctor said he'll be here as soon as he can.'

'I feel shivery, Cess. Not cold, but I can't keep my limbs still.'

He became aware of her trembling all over. 'Where can I find a blanket, Millie? I daren't move you, to get one from under you, while the baby is still attached to you.'

At Millie's direction, Cess hurried over to the large chest at the end of the bed and pulled out a soft pink blanket. Laying it gently over Millie and the now-quiet baby, he joked, 'It's the wrong colour, but it'll do,' before sitting down on the edge of the bed, as worry for her flooded through him. 'Let me hold you to me, Millie – it might help.' As he held her in his arms, he gently rubbed her back. 'Is that helping, Millie?'

She looked up at him, her face making little jerking movements, but her eyes wide and holding a look of wonder as she nodded.

Cess felt his heart in his throat. 'Millie, I—'

Rose coming in at that moment stopped what he was going to say. 'Eeh, Cess, what happened?'

'She's all right, Rose, only she's shaking all over.'

'Right, out with you now, lad, I'll take care of her. You go to Dai, he's in the kitchen. He needs you, as this has upset him.'

Cess nodded at Rose. He knew exactly how Dai felt, as the same intense grief had visited him. And yet something more powerful had happened to him too, and he was glad to get away from whatever it was that had gripped him when he'd looked down into Millie's eyes. *God, I nearly said something to her that would have her kicking me out of her life. What's happening to me?*

Taking a deep breath, Cess expected to feel an all-consuming guilt, but nothing happened. It was as if Dot had set him free. But did he want to be? He missed Dot with every part of him. At times even his bones ached for her.

He found Dai outside, standing with his foot against the wall. 'The doctor's just arrived, Cess.'

'Right. Hello, Doctor Fletcher, how are you?'

'Cess! Haven't seen you in a while – it's a family affair, then?'

'Yes. Though Elsie isn't here yet, but I dare say she won't be a mo.' Then proudly he announced, 'I delivered the baby, Doc, but Rose, the new maid, is with Millie now.'

'Yes, I can see you were in the thick of it. Well, I'd better get up there. Well done, Cess. I remember you rescuing Millie once before – it's becoming a habit.'

Dr Fletcher nodded at Dai before disappearing through the door.

Cess turned back to Dai. 'Are you all right, Dai, mate?'

'I am. I came over a bit funny – it was the thought of it. I felt afraid too. The baby's all right, isn't he?'

'He's fine. A strong little chap with a good pair of lungs – demanding, a bit like his da, but Millie will sort him out and make a gentleman of him no doubt. So, how did it go with Rose? I reckon she took a shine to you, Dai. She had you by the arm. And marching you away the moment she met you.'

'She's lovely. She really helped me, and then this happened. But I'll be fine – it brought it back, that's all. Is Millie all right?'

'She is. Everyone's doing great. Well, not sure about meself, mind. I've had a funny turn.' Cess could tell Dai anything.

He'd been able to since the moment they met when, after Dot died, Cess had gone with Elsie and Bert and his little baby girl, Kitty, for a break at Millie's cottage in Barmouth. They'd gone to the little churchyard where their brother Jimmy was buried, and there was Dai, standing over his wife and child's grave. They all got talking, and Cess and Dai had found common ground when they spent a week together after that, consoling each other and talking for hours on end. This led to them becoming partners in business and sharing a house together, and Dai had since become like an older brother to him. Though he was only young, Cess felt as if he'd lived a whole lifetime in such a short period. Not many of his age had loved and lost and been left with a baby. Without Dai, he didn't know how he would have got through everything.

As he thought this, he looked up the street and his mood lifted. 'Hey up, look who's coming – trouble. Hello, Bert, had a good day at school, then?'

Cess opened his arms and his seven-year-old brother ran into them and hugged him. 'What're you doing here, Cess? And why have you blood all over your shirt? Has your stall closed? I was going to help you when I got home.'

'Slow down, mate, one question at a time. Stuff's been happening here, that's all. There's a new member of our family' – it came so naturally to call Millie 'family'. He ruffled Bert's hair; he loved this young brother of his. 'We've got another Cecil, mate. Millie's little chap has arrived.'

Bert looked wide-eyed. 'How did that happen? Am I his uncle too? Cos I don't know if I can cope with another one – not after Kitty.'

'Ha! You buggerlugs, you. Call me daughter difficult, would you?'

'No, sorry, Cess. I love Kitty, but she can be a handful for me. What if this Cecil is like that?'

'Don't worry. You're not an uncle to Millie's little chap, but I hope you'll care for him like you do Kitty. All babies need that.'

'I will. I'll love him and show him how to go on. I just don't want him to be a lot for me to cope with, and chuck his toys at me like Kitty does, so I have to dodge them.'

Cess looked at Dai and saw how he was bursting to laugh out loud. Bert was like an old man in a lad's body. 'I tell you, Dai, he could cheer up the devil on a bad day when his fires won't light.'

Dai burst out laughing then. Cess grinned. It was good to see Dai back to normal. 'Well, Bert, I suppose you want something to eat, eh? Here.' Cess fished in his pocket. 'Go and get yourself one of them pies from Aggie's. And sit in her cafe and eat it. And while you're gone, maybe the doctor will be finished here and you can go and say hello to the new baby when you get back.'

'Ta, Cess. I'm starving, but won't Else have the tea on?'

'Nothing will be normal tonight, mate. Off you trot.'

Cess had been thinking about Elsie, and wondering why she hadn't yet turned up. 'Dai, I'll go and check that Elsie knows. Did you and Rose go and tell her?'

'We asked Rene to, then we came straight here.'

'Right, I'll be back in a mo.'

When he reached the shop, Rene looked up from a customer she was dealing with and shook her head. Taking the stairs to Elsie's flat two at a time, Cess knocked on the door and opened it. Elsie turned from the window and gasped. 'What on earth . . . Cess, you're covered in blood!'

'I am, and for good reason – I only went and delivered Millie's son!'

'What! Millie! When?'

Jim, who hadn't spoken, jumped up from the settee. Elsie looked from him back to Cess.

Cess could feel an atmosphere like none he'd experienced between these two, but decided to ignore it for now. 'It happened about ten to fifteen minutes ago, when me and Millie were alone.' He told Elsie what he had had to do. 'The doc was with Millie when I left, but I know that as soon as he's gone, she's going to want you, Else, luv.'

'I'll get me coat. Are you coming, Jim?'

'I am. Try to keep me back. Huh, you delivered him, Cess? Well I never.'

'Many talents, me, Jim. Now I can add midwife.' They laughed together, and Cess felt he could ask a question. 'Is everything all right, Jim?'

Jim shook his head. 'But there's too much to tell you at the moment. We need to go to Millie.'

'We do. Millie was a star, but, well, that can change with new mums.'

Jim tapped his shoulder. The gesture was one of understanding, and comfort. Something Jim was good at giving, only this time Cess could sense that he needed help himself.

'Anything I can do, Jim, you've only to ask.'

'I know, Cess. And we are going to need you. Elsie more than me.'

Elsie came back down the stairs at that moment. Cess thought she looked near to tears, but he didn't remark on it. 'Come on, Else, you've a nephew to meet – and guess what? He's called Cecil.'

Elsie cheered up immediately and clapped her hands.

40

'Couldn't be called after a better person, Cess. I can't wait to meet him. How's Millie? What size is the baby? Does he look like Millie?'

'Ha, you'll find out everything in a mo. Go on, get going.'

As Cess closed the door behind him, Rene appeared at the bottom of the steps. 'Bleedin' woman, she took hours going over this and that, and then left without ordering a bleedin' thing . . . I'm sorry, Elsie, me darlin', I couldn't get away to tell you about Millie. That Rose popped her 'ead in me door, told me who she was and what had happened.'

'Don't worry, Rene. Come with us, luv. I know Millie will love to see you.'

As Cess followed them all back to Millie's, he felt a shyness come over him. He didn't know how to face Millie. It was as if she'd suddenly become a different person. She was no longer just Millie to him. She was something far more. And he couldn't understand it.

Chapter Four

Millie

Millie looked around at the sea of faces surrounding her, avoiding making eye contact with Cess as she felt strangely shy with him after what had happened, and not just because of his involvement with her giving birth. But she was being silly. Cess was like a brother – and a younger brother at that. She was two years older than him. She must stop this ridiculous notion.

Holding little Cecil to her, she looked down at him and then up into the loving eyes of Elsie bending over her. Millie returned the love with all her heart. Yes, life had changed since discovering they were half-sisters, but despite all that had happened, it was for the better, for having Elsie in her life. But now Elsie once again faced heartache.

Millie touched Elsie's face and whispered, 'It will all be all right. We'll make it so. With Len selling up and moving the business, this is our chance to get the jam factory back. We can do it, Elsie, we can.'

Elsie seemed to cheer up, but her smile didn't touch her eyes as she nodded her head. 'We can, luv. My, he's a lovely boy. Hello, Cecil, I'm your Aunty Elsie. Ooh, look, he smiled

. . . Well, I know it's only wind, but it was lovely. Ooh, I love you, little Cecil, darlin'.'

Rene made clucking sounds as she smiled down at the baby. 'He's a darlin', Millie, luv, and he didn't hang around, did he?'

'No, he didn't, Rene. He gave me no notice.'

'That's bleedin' men for yer. Whoops, 'ark at me swearing.' Rene spoke to little Cess then. 'Sorry, mate, but yer may as well get used to me.'

Millie laughed. 'Yes, that was Rene for you, son.' But the giggle did lift the feeling of despair that she felt as she worried about what it was that Elsie and Jim faced. Nor could she erase her own fears, as the expressions of love for little Cecil didn't touch the surface of how she felt about him. During his minuscule slice of life he'd captured her heart and splintered her, all at the same time, as the possibility of Len taking him from her loomed. *Please God, don't let it happen.*

'Eeh, Millie, is that a tear I saw? You're tired, lass. I think you need a rest now.'

Millie seized on this as an excuse. 'Yes, I do feel tired, Rose, but it's all right.'

'I'll get off, Millie, love. I've an awkward customer who's coming back when she's thought about what she wants. Take care, love – see you soon.'

'Bye, Rene, thanks.'

'Well, I think everyone should go now. You need your rest, Millie.'

Rose sounded very stern, but Millie put it down to her caring about her. 'No, Rose, not yet. Honestly, I'll be all right. I want to be with everyone.' Why did she want to add, 'Especially Cess'? *What is this feeling that's taken me over?* She glanced past Elsie and directly into Cess's eyes.

He held her gaze, and for a moment it was as if only they existed.

Embarrassed, she looked away. *It must be because he helped me in my most vulnerable moment. Oh God, did he really see all of that happening? Did he really take my knickers off and see to the baby between my gaping legs?* Her colour deepened.

'Well, not for long, then . . . By, you're clinging on to your babby as if your life depends on it, lass. Let someone hold him for a while, eh? You can lie back and relax then.'

Again there was something in the tone of Rose's voice. Millie obeyed this time and handed little Cecil to Elsie. As she did so, she felt bereft.

'He's so beautiful, Millie.'

'He is, Elsie.'

'And you calling him after Cess too. That's an honour.'

'Well, Cess is the nearest I have to a brother. I look on him in that way, so . . .'

Cess turned and went towards the door. She knew she'd hurt him. Knew, from the look they had exchanged, how he felt. But it had to be this way. She couldn't start a relationship with anyone, not for a long time. If she did, Len would stop at nothing to destroy them.

'It's going to be confusing with two Cecils.' Elsie turned and looked surprised. 'Oh, are you going, Cess?'

'Yes, I need to get back to Kitty.'

'Now there's a thing. I wonder what Kitty will make of Cecil.'

It was Bert who answered this. 'She'll love him, just like I do, Else. Look how tiny he is. Was Kitty that small?'

'She was, Bert, but you soon forget, because you always think of her as little. She'll look like a giant by the side of little Cecil, mate.'

44

'She acts like one sometimes, Elsie.'

Millie smiled at this. Bert could always lift her mood. But he hadn't completely managed that this time. She lay her head back on the pillow, but didn't miss Jim stepping forward and putting his hand on Elsie's shoulder. She willed Elsie to accept the loving gesture, but Elsie visibly stiffened. Jim withdrew his hand. Millie felt so sorry. She could understand both of their points of view and, at this moment, she hated the vile Len with an intensity she'd never felt before. How dare he play God and split these two up? But, like Jim, she didn't see an alternative. A free Jim had the chance to fight for himself – caged and on remand, he wouldn't stand a chance.

Suddenly little Cecil let out a yell that startled them all.

Rose jumped up. 'He's hungry. Time to leave mother and babby to feeding time, and then I must insist that you rest, Millie. You've been through a lot and you'll have night feeds to contend with an' all.'

They stood to leave, and for the first time Millie noticed that Dai wasn't still in the room. He must have followed Cess out. While thinking of Cess, she had an overwhelming need to talk to Elsie about what was happening to her, where Cess was concerned, and have Elsie put a practical light on things – tell her she was being silly. 'Don't you go, Elsie. Stay a while with me.'

'I will, if Rose thinks it's all right, luv. She's in charge till you're stronger.'

'Aye, that'd be grand, Elsie. I'd be glad if you would. You've had plenty of practice with young 'uns. Besides, I'm whacked after the journey and want to unpack and get to knaw me room.'

When Rose left, Jim hovered for a moment, as if unsure

what to do. Millie needed him to go before she made her first attempt at feeding her now-screaming baby. 'Oh, before you go, Jim, can I ask you to kindly let Len know that his son is born?'

Elsie shot round. 'Don't say anything about your decision yet, Jim. We need to talk for a bit longer about it.'

This was said in a cold, demanding way. Jim shrugged. He looked appealingly at Elsie before telling Millie he would do as she asked. 'What shall I say if he wants to come and see his son?'

'Tell him to telephone me first and we'll make arrangements. Thanks, Jim.' As Elsie was now taken up with bobbing little Cecil up and down, Millie took the opportunity to try to convey to Jim that she would talk to Elsie. He seemed to understand, as he took Bert by the hand and they left the room.

'Well, hand him over, Elsie. Let's have a go at pacifying him.'

It took them both to get little Cecil to suckle, but when he was doing so, Millie felt an overwhelming surge of motherly love for him and a longing for her own mother to be here. But that was still five days away. She knew Mama would be as upset at missing the birth of her first grandchild as she was herself at not having her here to share this moment.

Elsie interrupted these thoughts. 'What does that feel like, Millie?'

'Wonderful, if a little strange. Maybe it won't be too long before you know the feeling yourself?'

'Well, nothing has happened yet, and may never happen. Maybe I can't have—'

'Of course you can, Elsie, darling. I think it's just all that has been going on since you got married. Everything's all right, isn't it? I mean . . . with you and Jim, is it still difficult because of what happened to you?'

'No, it's all amazing. Rene helped me. She's got tricks you've never dreamed of.'

Millie smiled as Elsie blushed and tried to retract this.

'I – I mean, well, Jim's nothing like that disgusting Chambers. I hope the noose really hurt him and kept him dangling for ages before he died. Nor does Jim do what . . . you know, Len—'

Millie cringed at the mention of Len and what he'd done to Elsie. She knew first-hand how it felt to suffer rape at Len's hands but, she thought, it was a measure of how hurt Elsie was feeling in general for her to mention Len's violation of her. It was an even bigger indication of how upset Elsie was, to have spoken of the capital punishment that had been Chambers's fate for the murder of Elsie's mum. That was a subject they both avoided at all costs.

Feeling there was nothing she could say, Millie just squeezed Elsie's hand.

'Oh, Millie, what did we do to deserve it all?'

'Nothing. We're not to blame. Look, Elsie, tell me to mind my own, if you like, but about Jim's decision . . . I mean, what do *you* want him to do? Poor chap's been given Hobson's choice. None of us would know what to do in the same circumstances, but the choice he has made is, to me, the most sensible.'

'Well, whatever Hobson's choice is, I can't bear either of the options Len has left Jim with. I feel Jim should let Len think he is considering his offer, and then get on quickly with trying to prove his innocence. But it feels to me as if Jim's giving in. I'm scared, Millie. I don't want Jim to leave me.'

'Hobson's choice is when you're left with no – or very little – alternative. I think the original story was about a man who made his customers buy the horse in the first stable box or not have a horse at all. But don't quote me on that. Anyway, maybe if Jim can stall for a week, Mama and Wilf will be home. I know Wilf has retired, but he can advise both Jim and me . . . Oh, Elsie, I'm desperate to find a way to block Len from taking my child. I couldn't bear it.'

'Will our troubles ever end, Millie?'

Millie sighed. 'Not unless we can rid ourselves of Len and his father. I never thought I would ever meet people like them, or even that such people existed. And as for ever falling in love with Len, I must have been out of my mind.'

'We were all taken in by him, luv.'

They fell silent. Into the silence came gentle sucking noises, and Millie became aware of the soreness of her nipple. She took her hand from Elsie's to try to ease her baby off her breast for a moment.

'He's doing well for a newborn, Millie. Not that your milk will be in fully yet, luv.'

Millie kissed her sleepy son. Her heart brimmed over with love for him. 'Yes, I read that in one of Rose's books.'

'I think he should go to your left breast now, with a little break to wind him – not that I've had a lot of experience with breastfeeding. Ma couldn't do it, and so I used to bottle-feed the lads. I did that with Kitty an' all, after . . . Oh, Millie, I miss Dot so much.'

A guilty feeling took Millie as she thought of the new feelings she had for Cess. She made her mind up that she shouldn't discuss how she felt with Elsie. Things might change. Wasn't it too soon for him – for either of them? They were two lonely souls, hurt by the love they had given to others – Cess by losing his Dot, and she herself by the treatment she'd received from Len. It would be natural to reach out to each other now, but as time went by they might end up hurt again, if their feelings were only based on seeking comfort.

She gently rubbed little Cecil's back. He immediately burped as his little head flopped to one side. Millie heard Elsie giggle. The sound seemed so normal that Millie felt a longing to get back to that normality. To leave the world of selling the only homes she'd ever lived in, of thinking about how she could put everyone's future right, of battling with the insanely revengeful Leftons. To just be the carefree girl she used to be. And more than that – to find happiness again.

As she went to put her baby onto her left breast, the incessant ringing of her doorbell set an alarm going inside her. She felt Elsie stiffen. She heard Rose scurry along the landing and down the stairs. And then the voice she dreaded. 'Rose! What are you doing here?'

Millie looked at Elsie. 'How does Len know Rose, Elsie?'

'I don't know. They may have met at the wedding when I . . . Oh, Millie, I'm still ashamed of how I behaved at your wedding.'

Millie patted her hand, hoping the gesture reassured Elsie as Rose's voice drifted up to them. 'I'm maid and nanny to Mrs Lefton, sir.'

'That's a turn-up.' Len said something they couldn't hear then. Millie couldn't think what it might have been, because afterwards he sounded like his normal pompous self. 'Well, you'd better start acting like a maid and take me to my wife at once.'

'I will ask Mrs Lefton if she will receive you, sir.'

'Out of my way! Receive me? In this dump? Don't be so

ridiculous. This isn't the kind of establishment where anyone is *received*. And I wouldn't even lower myself to visit, if it wasn't to collect my son.'

The strange exchange between Rose and Len now forgotten, Millie implored Elsie, 'Oh God! Elsie, don't let him take Cecil, please.'

'Over my dead body, mate.' Elsie looked around her, then leapt off the bed and grabbed the small wooden footstool that stood in front of Millie's nursing chair. She took hold of the legs, wielding the stool like a weapon as Len barged in.

'Just you try to take the baby, Len Lefton, and I'll smash your head in.'

Len looked astonished. His glance went from Elsie to Millie, his expression changing to one of anger. 'You can't stop me, you whore. And if you try, I'll have you locked up! I warned you before that I would file for custody of my child. Well, now he is born, the papers are being drawn up at this very moment to give me temporary custody of my son, while formal documents are being prepared for a court hearing to make it absolute.'

He turned to Millie. Never had she felt such fear, such despair.

'If you want to stay with your baby, it's time for you to behave in the proper manner and come back to me – your husband. And to take your rightful place by my side. To sever the influence that these lowlifes have over you and start behaving in the manner you were brought up to.' He looked around the room. 'All this finery, from the life you're used to, doesn't lift your status in this slum, Millie. What on earth are you thinking to live in such an area? And in the midst of the scum of the earth?'

'We ain't scum, Len. You are, and that bleedin' father of yours. In fact, "scum" is too good a word for what you are – you wrecker of lives. You bastard rapist. You—'

'Shut up! Shut up with your filthy lies. You're the one who wrecks lives. You're just like your mother. Didn't she wreck Millie's family life? Didn't she entice a decent man from being faithful to his wife – and even bear his child? Now you are carrying on the tradition. You know how you behaved towards me, even on my own wedding day. Throwing yourself at me. Rose can verify that. You were clawing at me in your drunken way, telling me you loved me. You're disgusting! And now you have your claws into my wife. Well, she isn't going to be the rich benefactor that you think she is.'

He turned to Millie, who cowered beneath his evil glare.

'Just you remember, Millie, that the money you have from your mother's estate, you gained after our marriage and so I have a legal right to take the lot.'

Millie gasped in horror.

Elsie leapt forward. The stool was held high above Len's head.

Millie wanted to scream out to her to do it. To kill him! But reason held her back. 'No. No, Elsie, don't.'

Len turned, his fist clenched. His vicious swipe caught Elsie and sent her reeling backwards.

'Stop it. For God's sake, stop it!' Millie's scream assaulted her own ears. Her baby jumped. His body stiffened, then screwed up as his cry split the still air.

This held them all suspended. Elsie lying on her back, Len looking down on her as if he would attack her again, and little Cecil distressed beyond what any newborn should ever be.

Cuddling him to her, Millie rocked him backwards and forwards. 'Leave, Len. Please leave now!'

'Not without my son. Or, preferably, with you and my son – *our* son. Millie, please see sense. Please unravel yourself from the clutches of this . . . this whore, and come home with me. Take your rightful place in society. No one knows where you are, or how you have slipped so far down from your standing. They all think you are up in Leeds, staying in your mother's mansion. They know there's trouble between us, but not the nature of it. Not how you have been deceived – taken in by people who are not fit to lick your boots. Your father's bastards!'

He stepped forward, placed his hands on the bedstead and leaned towards her.

'Please, Millie. I'm begging you. You should be with me, your husband. I love you. I will take care of you and our son. The home my father has given to me is beautiful and, as you know, is in the best part of London. You will be happy there. You'll have everything you want. We can take time to get back what we had when we first married. The love. The closeness. All you have to do is see these people for what they are. Wake up to how this slut ruined everything with her whoring ways. Yes, I was weak. But she got me to that stage. She'd offered herself to me on a number of occasions.' He bent his head. 'Oh God, why wasn't I strong enough to resist her? How could I have hurt you so badly?' He lifted his head. Tears were streaming down his cheeks. 'I love you, Millie. I'll never hurt you again. You can stop all of this. If you come back to me, I'll forget them all. We both will. And I hope Jim will come with us and put them all behind him too.'

'Neither Jim nor I wants to go with you, Len. We both

hate you.' As she said this, it occurred to Millie that she did hold some power, where Len was concerned – power that she could bargain with. 'However, it may be possible for you to redeem yourself to me. If you let Jim go. Stop your blackmail of him.'

'What do you mean, blackmail? I am trying to save him.'

'By framing him? By giving him the choice of prison or working for you and leaving his wife? I think that is blackmail of the first order.'

'You listen to, and believe, every lie told to you, Millie. It's time you listened to, and sided with, your husband. I haven't framed Jim. Jim has behaved in a criminal way, but I believe him when he says it is the influence of this lot.' He pointed down towards Elsie. 'So I am merely giving him a chance to once and for all get out of their clutches. They will have made him do what he did. I know that. I am offering him a way out. As I am you, Millie.'

Len really seemed to believe what he was saying. How could she fight that? But she would. For her sister Elsie's sake, she would.

'I will listen to you, once you start to show compassion for my family. They lived the life they did because of my father . . . No! You listen to me now, Len. I – I will come back to you, on the condition that you release them all from your vendetta. That I settle on Elsie her rightful due, from her father's and my father's estate. That you release Jim from all threats, and you accept that I will keep a close relationship with my sister.'

'What? Are you mad?'

Millie didn't cringe under his glare. Cecil wriggled in her arms. The thought came to her that Len hadn't even acknowledged his son, or bothered to look at him. *Oh God! Am I doing the right thing? Can I bear to be with Len? Have him lie with me, take me again – even father another child borne by me?* She looked over at Elsie, who was broken, hardly possessing the strength to rise up off the floor, and knew that she could, for her beloved sister's sake. She could.

'They are my terms. You either accept them or don't. If you don't, I will fight for the rest of my life to keep my son away from you, and to discredit you in the eyes of the world.'

'Ha! You really believe you can do that, don't you? Well, let me tell you, Millie. My lawyers have now gained a temporary order based on the safety of the child – no one of our standing can even think of bringing a child up in this area amongst such people. The lawyers are incensed on my behalf.'

'I thought you said no one knew?'

'They don't. Only my legal team. They had to know my reasons for claiming custody. And although I can give them many, just where you intend to live, and the people you intend to bring up my heir with, was enough to convince them to file the papers and for the judge to grant the order. And don't forget, they know you, Millie. They know how easily you are led. You didn't do yourself any favours when you sacked the family solicitor, the man who had served your father for many years.'

'And don't *you* forget who my mother is married to. Wilf was – and now his son is – the top lawyer in this country. Wilf's son is working on an injunction to stop you taking my son. I am expecting the papers today. If you truly want me back, you have one course open to you, and one course only, Len. Let Jim out of your clutches and abide by my other stipulations. And I mean completely. Remove all the blackmailing tricks you tried, including the threat to double Rene's rent.'

'Good God. You are mad! I told you in the beginning that the rent for that shop in this prime location for retail business was far too low. And I have told you many times that you let your heart rule your head. But tell me, what if I do all you ask – what kind of wife will I be getting? One who is compliant to her husband's wishes? One who will make me happy in every way? Who will grace my life? Be a congenial hostess? Give me the children I desire to have? Be loving, kind and faithful? Or will I be getting the petulant, stubborn, embarrassing specimen that you have proved to be from the start?'

'Millie, please don't do this. Please, Millie. There'll be another way. There will, mate.'

'Huh! Listen to the begging from the gutter.' Len turned and looked down to where Elsie was trying to rise. 'You can see your meal ticket disappearing, can't you, Whore?'

Millie looked at Elsie as she turned her head towards her – saw the desperate appeal in Elsie's eyes, but knew what she had to do. 'I have no choice, Elsie. I cannot give up my son. And I so want to save you and Jim.'

'Save them? Save them from what? Themselves? Their lying and cheating ways? You can't do that, Millie, unless you acknowledge their behaviour. Once you do, you will cut yourself off from them. I don't want to sever ties with Jim. He's one of us. I can't abandon him to the clutches of that whore. I need him . . .'

'That's it, isn't it, Len? Jim's useful to you. He's the best in the jam-making business. Without him, you doubt your new venture will flourish, and it has to, doesn't it? It's your baby. That's all you care about – making money, being seen as a powerful figure, rising to the ranks of the elite. But don't you see? The elite don't want you.'

'That's ridiculous. I'm different from you. You're just the daughter of a self-made man. I am from money, position, power. I am accepted in the right circles. I can buy and sell the lot of the so-called "old money" folk, and they know it. I can take decisions within the banking system that would affect them, and the paltry pennies they are hanging on to. I can call in loans and bankrupt their rambling, ramshackle estates. They not only want me, they need me.'

'You're pathetic, Len. Elsie is right. I won't come back to you. I'll fight you. We all will.'

Elsie had made it to her feet. Her movements were unsteady, but she teetered over to the bed to be beside Millie. Her voice steadied as she spat out, 'And you just bleedin' try taking this child and, between us, we'll kill you!'

Len's anger emanated from him. He glared at them, before turning and storming out of the room. 'I'll be back, and with legal force that will enable me to take *my* child!'

Millie clung to Elsie, while holding her darling baby to her. Her fear tightened every muscle in her body, but she spoke bravely. 'I won't let him win, Elsie, I won't.'

Chapter Five

Elsie

As she sat on the bed holding Millie's shivering body, Elsie felt her own fear deep in the pit of her stomach, not only for Millie, but for herself. When Len had knocked her over, for a moment he'd held her eyes, his yearning plain for her to see, despite the vitriolic words he'd spat out at her. She'd seen that look before. *Oh God, don't let him get it into his head to try to rape me again.*

'Elsie, we'll be all right. You're trembling too. I know you fear him. He is hateful, spiteful and difficult for us to beat, but we will win – we will.'

'I'll have to give in and let Jim go, won't I, Millie?'

'Yes, I think you should. The sacrifice will be immense, but you will be giving Jim time, and that's what he needs, Elsie. Look, let me put Cecil to my breast. He's very distressed. It might help him. Then we can talk.'

In her anguish, Elsie had almost forgotten the baby, despite his crying, but her instincts took over and she picked up the child. 'Get yourself into a comfy position, Millie, luv. You look as though you've slithered down the bed.'

When Millie held her child once more and he was suckling,

Elsie slid off the bed and stood watching as she dried her tears and controlled her fear. 'There's no lovelier sight, Millie.'

'I cannot bear to lose him, Elsie, or to think of a wet nurse feeding him – because that's what Len would have to do: employ a wet nurse.'

'We must stop it happening, Millie, luv. We can, mate, if we give it some thought. Do yer reckon the papers you spoke of will be here in time to stop him?'

'I don't know. I was bluffing, as I think Len must have been.'

'Then we're to think of a way to delay him. Does Len know exactly where in Wales your holiday cottage is?'

'I'm not sure, but I think so. Yes, I'm sure I told him it was in Barmouth . . . But I see what you're getting at, Elsie. And you're right, that's the answer! I disappear with Cecil while my solicitor and lawyer sort everything out. They can keep in touch with me by telephone.'

'But you won't tell them where you are, will you? They may tell Len.'

'No, that won't happen. My solicitors are completely loyal to me, and Wilf and his son will then have more time to help me fight the case Len is preparing.'

'Yes, but if it becomes a legal requirement, they will be forced to reveal where you are, mate.'

'Yes, they will. Oh, Elsie. I had hope for a moment then.'

'Don't give up, luv. It could still work for you. You'll get to be with little Cecil, without being harassed by Len. I know you'll have the worry of it all hanging over you, but you will both be safe and out of Len's clutches. Look how he tried to convince you that he was allowed to take your baby. If he really had been, he'd have done it, but he didn't.'

'You're right. Oh, it would be so lovely to feel safe. I

could go to Southampton and be at the dockside when Mama's ship comes into dock. That would be lovely.'

'Oh, Millie, I wish I could come with you. But you will have Rose, and I have to think of Bert's schooling.'

'You have to come too, Elsie. I would be afraid to leave you. Len will blame you, and we don't know what that will lead him to do. Our stay may only be for a short while, but if prolonged we can see that he is schooled by a tutor. Or maybe he could stay with Cess, and then Gertie could look after him?'

'No. I want him with me. He's had enough to contend with in his short life, and he depends on me . . . and on Jim. Poor boy will be lost as it is, with Jim going.' To Elsie, just saying this made her realize the truth of what was happening – her Jim was to leave her. Could she bear it?

Millie's hand tightened in hers and she knew that she must.

'Millie, can Len take the money your mother has given you?'

'I'm not sure. I don't think so. I think he was bluffing again. Women don't have a right of ownership on all such matters, but . . . Oh, it's all such a mess. Please get Rose to come and see to Cecil for me, Elsie. I'm so tired. But before I rest, I'll ring my solicitor.'

'But you can't get out of bed, Millie!'

'I can, and I will. I'm not an invalid. Besides, I'll have to, if we're to travel.'

Elsie wasn't so sure about this. She'd envisaged either Cess or Jim carrying Millie down to the car, not her walking. As she understood it, recovering mothers had to stay in bed for at least fourteen days.

She found that Rose agreed with her, and the two of them

persuaded Millie of the folly of doing any more than getting off the bed to sit on the commode.

'I'll telephone whoever you want me to, Millie. Or, better still, take a letter round to them for you,' Elsie told her.

'Yes, a letter would be the answer. These legal bods are sticklers for not talking to anyone but their client. Bring me my writing box, please, Rose.'

With the letter safely tucked into her blouse pocket, Elsie pulled her shawl around her against the bitter wind and ran next door to her flat. Rene called out to her from her shop, but she just shouted out that she couldn't stop, she was in a hurry.

When she opened her door she found Jim sitting on the sofa, his head in his hands. Bert, she could hear, was upstairs practising his piano chords – Bert was never happier than when he was learning his scales. Jim had said many times that he was talented and could go far in the music world. It was something that made Elsie feel proud, and seemed to her to be a legacy from their dear gran, who had played the music halls in her day.

'Jim. Oh, Jim, I'm sorry. I've been so selfish, mate.'

He rose and came to her. Hope lit up his face, but was then dispelled as he saw the bruise on her cheek.

'My God! Elsie, what happened?'

'Len – he . . . Oh, Jim, I have to hurry.'

Jim was by her side now. He opened his arms. Inside the circle of them, Elsie found the strength she needed.

She told him as quickly as she could what had taken place. 'But you mustn't do anything about this, Jim. You have to be strong. Stronger than Len is. Don't give him another stick to beat you with.'

'I know. But one day, my God, one day will be mine, and I will make him pay. But for now we have to fight him on his own terms, Elsie, and we have to be stronger than he is. You and Millie going into hiding is the best thing I've heard. I'll take the letter, my darling. You begin to pack and get yourself and Bert ready. You say that Rose is already doing that for Millie?'

'Yes, they're getting ready right now. We'll go and stay in a hotel for now, but if this is long-term, then I expect we'll look at renting a furnished place.'

'Oh, Elsie. Everything will come right, my darling. I'll make it be so, and then we'll be back together again and nothing will ever part us.'

'Will you call on Len? What will you tell him?'

Jim thought for a moment. 'I don't know. I have to convince him this isn't a plot, or the moment you disappear he's going to suspect me, then use further blackmail to make me tell where you are. God, he's evil. Always was and always will be. I'll get my coat.'

Elsie paced up and down the room while she waited for Jim to come back down the stairs.

This flat wasn't like the others, but was made up of two storeys, as she had rented both of the floors above Rene's shop.

The upstairs contained the bedrooms and a music room, where she had been giving free lessons to the cockney women. She was teaching them to play some of the good old London songs. Her talent had turned many occasions into a riot of fun, laughter and dancing. She'd wanted to give what she could to others. Most had a piano in their Sunday-best room that took pride of place, was polished till it gleamed, but never had its lid opened or its ivories tinkled. She wanted to change that. To have families enjoy a sing-song together, just like she used to with her gran and her mum.

When Jim came back, he found her staring out of the window. Tears stung her eyes. Times were hard back then, but she'd give the world to go back to them.

Jim's arm came around her waist. 'Darling, everything will come right, I promise. I have written a letter, which I will send to a number of my father's ex-clients, once I know the address where I will be staying.'

She lay her head on his shoulder. 'I am worried that you will go before I can give you my address, and then we'll not even know where each other is! Oh, I know you will be in Kent, but where?'

'I don't think my going will be immediate. But if that happens, then we'll both use Cess as our contact – you let him know where you are, and so will I. We won't lose touch, darling. Wait a minute . . . an idea just occurred to me. I won't call on Len. I'll wait until you have gone. Then I'll go to him, frantic to find out where you are. Tell him that you disappeared during the night without a word. I'll play the distraught husband, then the embittered one who has been dumped, and so I might as well go along with his plan as there's nothing left for me in London.'

'It's brilliant, Jim. Exactly the sort of planning that he would cook up himself. And that's how we have to be to beat him – play him at his own game. But, oh, Jim, how am I going to live without you?'

They were silent for a moment. Jim held her to him. 'I love you, Elsie. How we're to get through this, I don't know.' His voice held that husky note of desire. Then he abruptly let her go. 'I'll be as quick as I can, darling, as we must get your journey under way. We have to act quickly.'

Elsie clung to him for a moment, then released him, turned from him and ran up the stairs. In her room she flung herself on her bed and wept.

A little hand rubbed her back. 'Else? Else, don't cry. I feel me tummy sinking when you're sad.'

Sitting up, she gathered Bert into her arms. 'I'm all right, Bert. Don't fret, but I do have something to tell you.' Deciding that she must protect him at all costs, she made herself brighten. 'We're going on holiday, mate. To the seaside!'

'What? When?'

'Now! We're going with Millie, Rose and little Cecil. You'll like Rose, when you get to know her.'

'I like her already. She made all us kids laugh at the wedding and brought us some lemonade when we were playing outside. But why are we going away? What about school? And Cess and Kitty? And is Jim coming?'

'You're just having a short school holiday.' She told him about the idea of a tutor. 'And no, Cess and Jim aren't coming, as they have to work. And Cess would miss Kitty too much if we took her with us. But they'll write to us, and maybe talk to us on the telephone.'

'Is that why you were crying, Else, because we're leaving them all behind? I feel like crying. I don't want a holiday, or a tutor.'

'Yes. I will miss Jim, and everyone.'

'Let's not go then, cos I'll miss them too. I'd rather stay here, Else.'

'We have to go. I can't explain, but don't you worry, the tutor will be nice – everything will be all right, buggerlugs, I promise.'

As she held him, she felt his little body shiver. Poor little mite. As his big sister, she was supposed to make his world happy and carefree, but she couldn't. The forces at work against her made that impossible, but she would shield him as much as she could.

Digging into her cockney spirit, she ruffled his hair. 'Right, buggerlugs, get back on the piano and play "It's a Long Way to Tipperary". We'll sing as we get ready – this is a holiday, and here we are behaving like a couple of wet weekends.'

Bert turned from her and went towards the music room. His head hung, his walk showed his unhappiness and yet he didn't argue further. In his young life he'd learned that most kids from around Bermondsey had to take whatever life dealt them, and often that wasn't a good slice of the cake.

When the first note sounded, Elsie took a deep breath and made her voice sound joyful and excited as she called on another talent she had – writing lyrics – and made up a verse to fit the music:

'We're going to the seaside
We're going to have some fun
We'll take a long, long ride to get there
And there won't be that much sun.

But we'll savour the fish 'n' chips
The whelks and jellied eels
And we'll watch the folk come off the ships
And will wonder how that feels.

Oh, we're going to the seaside . . .'

By the time she belted out the second chorus, Bert was joining in with her. His voice was giggly and held a note of excitement. But although this lifted her heart, Elsie wondered how she was to get through the next few weeks – or months, even. For who knew how long it would take before everything came right in their lives.

Cess returned with Jim, who told Elsie he'd thought at the last moment to tell Cess what was happening. Cess gathered Bert in his arms, but before he could unwittingly dampen Bert's mood, Elsie burst into the chorus of her made-up song once more.

Bert pulled back from Cess and joined in, making both Cess and Jim smile.

Cess got the hint. 'Well, mate, aren't you the lucky one, eh?'

'There'll be big ships there, Cess, and jellied eels, and it might be a bit cold, but I'll still go on the beach. I'll wear me wellies.'

'And I'll come down to see you, mate. One weekend I'll get in me car and take the long, long road to Souffampton.'

Bert laughed out loud. 'Souffampton? Haha, I didn't know that was its name.'

'That's the cockney name for it. And don't you forget, you're a cockney, born and bred, Bert. Our big sis talks a bit posher these days, unless she's riled, but me and you can be cockneys all we like – it suits the market trade.'

Elsie took this as an affront. 'I can be as bladdy cockney as you, mate!'

They all burst out laughing and the mood lightened.

'Go and do your teeth, Bert. You can use that free sample of Ribbon Dental Cream; you'll like that better than the powdered one.'

Bert went towards the bathroom, then stopped. When he turned, his face had dropped. 'But, Else, I haven't read *The Jungle Pow-Wow* book to Kitty yet.'

Elsie was taken aback for a moment, but then remembered the book that had come with the free sample of toothpaste – that's if you could call it free, when she'd had to enclose a tuppenny stamp to get it. Thinking quickly, she said, 'Well, that'll be a treat for her when we get back, eh? You can practise making the animal noises to make her giggle.'

Cess helped again by doing an impression of a monkey's gait and arm movements, while making the sound the animal makes as he chased after Bert. Bert's squeals of laughter, mixed with a little trepidation, rang out and the moment passed.

'Poor Bert, Jim. It's such a shame for him.'

'No, darling. Lucky Bert. He has the most caring sister and brother in the world, and all a child needs is love.'

Remembering that Jim had had all the privileges that money could buy as a child, but no love, she knew he would recognize this as a truth. She crossed over to him. 'Not only a child, Jim. We all need love, and you now have all the love anyone could give a man.'

'Oh, Elsie.'

They clung together. Elsie heard the bathroom door open and then close again, and then more giggles from Bert. And she knew that, no matter what age you were, everyone needed love. 'Our love'll grow stronger while we're apart, Jim.'

'It will, darling. And I promise you, I will contact you as often as I can – I might even make it down to see you. After all, Len's not going to be down in Kent. Well, not often, so he won't know what my movements are.'

With this, hope soared through Elsie. 'Oh, Jim, that would be wonderful. Really? You think that you could come and see me?'

'I do, and as often as it is safe to do so, darling.' He snuggled his head into her neck. 'So make sure you have a room with a double bed, as you'll never know when I'll be creeping in beside you.'

Once more his voice had deepened and a kindred flame lit in Elsie. She held him even tighter and felt his desire. Taking his hand, she pulled him towards the stairs as she called out, 'Me and Jim are just going to finish my packing – we'll be down shortly.' Then she smiled as Cess called back, 'Take your time, sis.' And laughed out loud as he shouted, 'Make memories to take with you.'

Jim chuckled as they hurried up to their room, but once there, he became serious as his desire overwhelmed him. Even in his eagerness, Jim was a gentle lover, taking time to undress her whilst planting kisses on her neck, in her hair and running his fingers down her spine.

Elsie gasped with the pleasure he gave as he laid her down and explored every part of her, taking her nipple and gently massaging it between his fingers, then putting his mouth to it. The action made her cry out with the thrill of it, but then an intense yearning assailed her as the thought came to her that she so wanted to have a baby do this to her, her own and Jim's baby. With that thought came a trickle of despair. *Why haven't I become pregnant before now? Why?*

Sensing her anguish, Jim lifted his head and looked down at her. Mistaking her feeling for fear of their coming parting, he said, 'I'll visit often, darling. This won't be our last for a long time, but I want to make love to you as if it is.'

When he entered her, the feeling this gave took all negative thoughts from her as she drowned in the ecstasy of his splintering of her, into a crescendo of feelings that took her out of all the sorrow.

With Jim's love to sustain her, Elsie knew she would cope.

Chapter Six

Cess

Hearing the noises coming through the ceiling, Cess grinned, despite the loneliness and longing that gripped him. 'Right, buggerlugs, do your teeth quickly and we'll go round to Millie's. We'll leave a note for Elsie to come to us when she's finished packing.'

'They're making enough noise about it, Cess. I reckon they're at it.'

'Bert! When did you learn to be crude, little brovver? You shouldn't be saying things like that.'

'Oh, me mate at school told me all sorts. I know all about stuff now.'

Cess ruffled his hair. 'Well, we don't talk about it. Not until you're a man, right? Boys' talk is boys' talk, but you keep it for when you're with your mates, otherwise you'll embarrass folk.'

'I felt embarrassed at first, but you soon get used to it.'

'Ha! Come on, you. But remember not to talk like that in front of ladies.'

*

Rose let them in. She looked at Cess expectantly. 'Naw Dai?'

'No. I just came to say goodbye to you both. Elsie will be here in a moment.'

'Oh, come in, me lads. I'm busy, busy, but you can keep Millie company. She's awake now and I've dressed her. I'll check that she's all right with having you sit with her.'

When she came back, Rose told them Millie was really pleased he'd called and would he come through. Then to Bert she said, 'You can come with me, if you like, Bert. I could use some help.'

'I'm a good helper, Rose, and me mum told me a good turn has to be paid back.'

'That's a noble thing to live by, lad, but I ain't done you a good turn, have I?'

'You were kind to me at the wedding that time.'

'Ha. Come on then.' Rose looked over at Cess.

Cess couldn't believe what he'd heard – Bert mentioning their mum in passing meant that he'd made a big stride forward. But thinking it best not to mention it, he just said, 'Be a good boy for Rose, Bert. Don't pester her, and don't hinder her.'

'I won't, Cess.' The look of complete trust and love that Bert gave him brought a lump to Cess's throat.

Millie looked lovely sitting in the glow of the fire. 'So you're going then?'

'It's our only way, Cess. I don't want to. I want to get on with sorting my life out, but I'm left with no choice.'

'You should employ Rene to sort things for yer – she has some useful friends.' He laughed as he said this, showing her that he didn't mean it and was only trying to keep the mood light, as he took the chair to her right.

'Talking of Rene, will you watch out for her, Cess? I wish

I could go and see her, but I shouldn't really be out of bed. Anyway I don't know if Elsie told you . . .'

He listened with disgust at what Len intended to do to get Rene evicted. Once she'd started, Millie poured out everything Len had said.

'He's an evil bastard – excuse me swearing, but he's the kind that makes you. But look, don't worry about Rene, mate. I'll find her a new shop.'

'But that means Elsie's home will go too.'

'Else won't bother about that. I'll sort it. I'll find a place that will take them all and I'll see to the move.' The enormity of this task daunted him a bit, though he didn't show it. But exasperation at all he'd heard, and at him having to tackle it, made him angry. 'Is there no end to that man's evil? How come he has so much power over you, Millie?'

'Because I gave it to him. Oh, I was so stupid to give in and sign everything over to him. And now my mother's gift to me, to help me to stand on my own two feet, is in danger too.'

Cess felt at a loss as to what to say. He wanted so much to give comfort to Millie, but didn't know how to.

'But I do have my solicitor working on that for me. I know the law changed years ago as regards a woman keeping her own assets, and I think it now includes us keeping all we own, whether it came to us after marriage or not.'

'If it doesn't, it should. So you're forced to go into hiding, then?'

Millie's head bowed.

'I'm sorry, I – I'll . . . Anyway, if there's anything I can do, other than look after Rene, I will. I owe you a few debts.'

'No, you don't. We're family . . . well, almost – I mean . . . Anyway, "almost is as good as is", Ruby used to say.'

Cess wanted to say that he didn't want to be looked on as a brother, but he didn't understand these new feelings he had for Millie, and didn't want to express them. He had to think that it could just be his loneliness that was prompting them. If not, then why now? He'd known Millie for over two years and had never felt anything like this for her. He'd always liked her – loved her, in a brotherly way – but this was deeper and was disturbing him. Perhaps it was just as well that she was going away. Give him time to come to his senses, although the thought of her going tore at him.

The silence between them seemed charged with unspoken feelings. Millie broke it. 'I wanted to thank you again for earlier. I . . . well, I should be feeling embarrassed, but having you with me seemed the most natural thing.'

'It did to me too.'

Their eyes held for a moment, before Millie looked down again. 'I'll miss you, Cess.'

He felt his heart jolt. Millie looked so desolate, so beautiful and so . . . *Stop this, Cess. Think of Dot. Me lovely Dot. She's not been gone a year yet. Dot was me life.*

But forcing these thoughts didn't stop him wanting to go to Millie, to take her in his arms and make her feel safe. Before he could stop himself, he said, 'I'll miss you, Millie. I feel—'

A tap on the door, and Rose entering, stopped Cess mid-sentence and gave him a sense of relief. He'd nearly told her. He'd nearly let both Dot and Millie down. Millie looked on him as a brother and would be mortified to think of him seeing her in any way other than as a brother would look upon a sister. Maybe it really was as well that she was going.

'Eeh, it's warm in here. Like an oven. You southerners

71

are a cold-blooded lot. You should live in the North for a while – you'd soon toughen up.'

Millie gave a little laugh. The unbearable atmosphere was broken with the sound, and Cess felt saved from himself.

'Anyroad, I came to tell you that Elsie and Jim are here, Millie. Shall I bring them in?'

'Of course. There's no need to stand on ceremony with my family, Rose.'

Elsie and Jim looked a lot happier now, and Cess was glad to see it. Elsie ran over to Millie. 'Are you ready, luv?'

Millie looked unsure for a moment. 'I think so. Are we, Rose?'

'Aye, but I've packed the minimum that we'll need for the journey, as I were thinking about the room in the car to get us to the station. And then if we can't find a porter to help us, we'll have to lug it about, with two young 'uns to manage an' all.'

'Well, that's good thinking. And we can just buy what we need when we arrive.'

'Millie, do you have to go this evening? We don't know if there are any trains, and I can't take you, in case Len finds out.'

'I do have to, Jim. I cannot risk Len actually getting the papers that he pretended to have and returning with them.'

'What if there isn't a connection to get you to Southampton?'

Cess saw Millie's hesitation, as Jim came back with this. He hadn't thought of any of these practicalities, but now saw a chance to be with them all a bit longer – especially Millie. 'Why don't I drive you all? Not that I could get all of your luggage in.'

Jim jumped on this. 'That's a good idea, Cess. Excellent.

You girls can pool some of your things into a small case that will fit into Cess's car, and then put the rest into a large valise. We can put that on a train for you, once we know where you are.'

'But, Jim, if Len does return here and forces his way in, he'll see the luggage. We've nowhere to hide it.'

Cess intervened, 'Jim, can you get your car? We'll load yours with all of their luggage. The girls can get in with me, with their overnight bag, then we'll take the extra to my house and I'll have it shipped to them from there. That way, this place can be locked up and left. And then, if Len does resort to having the door broken down, he won't find any trace of you.'

The look of relief on Millie's face was a sight that gladdened Cess.

Within minutes everyone was scurrying around sorting out the luggage, with Jim carrying one item down at a time, as it was declared ready to take to Cess's house.

To Cess, there seemed an air of fear as this went on, and he marvelled at how one man could cause all of this trouble and how they had no way of stopping him.

The drive went well, and after two hours and a few stops because Millie was uncomfortable, or the baby needed tending to, all was quiet. Cess looked to his left to where Millie was sleeping. He could just see her outline in the moonlight. Her face was squashed against the door window.

The moonlight worried him as the car felt cold and, with as many bodies as it had, it shouldn't have done. Bright nights like this one usually hailed frost or even snow.

When he saw a sign saying Guildford, he made up his mind to stop there for the night. He was running short of petrol anyway as he'd used up his spare cans, so would need to get more in the morning.

Besides, it was the safest option and the best for them all, particularly for Millie, who he knew would be uncomfortable beyond soothing when she woke up. He remembered the extreme tiredness and messiness in the aftermath of Dot giving birth to Kitty.

Ahead he could see a street lamp illuminating the sign of an inn. When he reached it, it was brightly lit and had a 'Rooms vacant' sign.

'Wakey, wakey, everyone. Time to eat and then to bed.'

'Are we here?' Millie yawned this out.

'No, but we are as far as we're going. You all need a bed – especially you, Millie.'

'Oh? How far have we come?'

'We're in Guildford. You're safe, luv. All of you, get your-selves awake while I go in and ask for rooms.'

As it worked out, the inn had two vacant rooms. One with three beds in and a single room. They didn't have a cot, and the landlord frowned when Cess asked if the room had a chest of drawers.

'It does, but that's a funny question, I might say.'

'Not where we're from, mate. We often use a large drawer to make a cot for a baby. If you would be kind enough to supply a blanket that we could fold to make a mattress, then I'm sure the baby's nanny has shawls and stuff to keep him warm.'

'Well I never! Yes, I can do that. And there's a fireplace in the big room. Will you be partaking of a jug of ale and a bite to eat? I can get the fire going while you do and I can warm the room up for you too.'

'Thanks, mate. The jug of ale will be welcome, and I'll

order suppers to be taken up to the ladies when they're ready, as they're whacked out and won't want to come down to eat. How much?'

'Two shillings to a cockney like you, and that includes supper taken upstairs to the ladies. But you pay for your ale as you get it.'

Cess smiled and guessed this was the landlord's stock answer, wherever you came from. 'Does that include having a bath?'

'No, I've not got the facility for a bath. You can have a jug of piping-hot water for each room, but that's me lot.'

'Ta. You can take both jugs to the bigger room. Me and me brovver'll manage, but the ladies need plenty.'

Elsie joined Cess in a jug of ale, and Bert tucked into a glass of lemonade, while Rose took Millie to the ladies' powder room and then up to their bedroom. The mood was subdued, despite Elsie's attempt at being cheerful. 'Well, we do see life since we met Millie, Cess. We seem to be in one mess after another.'

'It's hardly her fault, mate.'

'Oh, I'm not saying that. It's just that sometimes I long to be back in the tenements in Long Lane. Life was tough, but it had an even rhythm to it. We knew what to expect.'

'I know what you mean, sis. Ha, look at Bert – his eyelids won't stay open. Poor nipper, he's had enough.'

'I'll take him up to your room. Will you be long?'

Cess sighed and looked around him. For all the world he could order another ale, then another, but knew that would be daft. 'No. I'll come up. I'll borrow the landlord's newspaper and bring it up with me – that's if there's enough oil in the lamp to see the pages. It seems everything's on a budget here.'

Elsie suddenly leaned forward and kissed his forehead,

always the mother figure to them. He smiled up at her and saw her drawn, tired face. He stood and took her into a hug. 'It won't be so bad, sis. You said that Jim'll visit secretly when he can, and I'm thinking of trying to as well. We'll find a way to cope with it all. We always do.'

As she left his arms Elsie sighed deeply, 'We do, mate.'

The anguish in her voice left Cess wishing he could do more. His thoughts turned to Millie. If he and Elsie felt down like this, how did she feel? Used to the best in life, this inn – though clean and having what they needed – must feel to Millie as though she'd been dragged into the gutter. *If only I could make her feel safe, and happy again.*

Elsie turned as they reached the door. 'Keep your chin up, luv.'

Cess nodded. He knew he must do that for all of their sakes – especially Millie's.

They reached Southampton mid-afternoon the next day. The newborn had been fractious for most of the way and Cess had to admit to having a headache, which had caused him to lose his concentration several times and resulted in him taking a wrong turn. They ended up going miles out of their way.

'Well, we're here at last . . . so what now, Millie?'

'Find a decent hotel, I think, Cess. One we can stay in until my mama and Wilf dock and advise us what to do. We could start by finding a Thomas Cook shop and letting them make the arrangements for us while we have tea?'

Cess hadn't thought of this way of doing things. He would have driven around till he saw something decent and plumped for it.

When he came out of Thomas Cook's, Cess was smiling.

'We have rooms – in The Dolphin, where none other than Jane Austen held her eighteenth birthday and Queen Victoria stayed!'

Elsie smiled, but Cess could see her concern as she asked, 'Are you all right, mate? Wasn't she the author of the book that gave you and Dot the idea to elope?'

Cess nodded. He knew why Elsie felt apprehensive for him, when every small thing connected with Dot had, until now, given him a jolt and sent him into misery. This comment hadn't, and he couldn't understand why. He hadn't missed the reference, when told of Jane Austen's connection to The Dolphin Hotel, but it hadn't made him feel sad. *What's happening to me? Less than a year ago I lost the love of my life, and yet nothing of the misery and despair I went through is touching me now.*

He nodded at Elsie. 'The very one. And I've read her book *Pride and Prejudice* from cover to cover. I feel excitement at staying in a place Jane Austen set foot in.'

'I'm glad, Cess.'

'Eeh, it'd be grand as owt – as Ruby and Rose would say.'

They all laughed at Millie, and Cess's moment of pondering the past left him.

Rose pulled them all up. 'Nowt will be as grand as owt if we don't get these young 'uns settled and fed. Especially poor Bert, as he's flagging an' all.'

'Go on, then,' Cess told her. 'You ladies go inside – the porter will show you to your rooms now. Ha, it's a bit different from the inn last night.'

Rose grinned as she went to retrieve the bag that she'd nursed on her knee the whole journey. She'd insisted on bringing it, and they'd all agreed when she told them it contained all she needed for the baby.

True to form, a porter stepped forward and took the bag from her and collected their overnight bags. Millie thanked him.

'This way, ma'am.'

As Cess got into the car to park it, he saw Millie following the porter. She looked regal to him – as she was, and should be, in her natural surroundings. He sighed. Although he knew her well and had done for two years, he knew their worlds were different – the way they'd been brought up, their expectations of life and of others. To Millie, it was natural that someone carried her bag, whereas for him, you carried your own. And oh, so many other things – some of them small, but others putting a huge gulf between them, such as the education she'd had, while he'd been put to work at a very young age. Could he ever come up to her standards? He doubted it. Sighing, he revved the engine and pulled away from the kerb.

What must you think of me, Dot? Here I am, thinking about Millie, and you not long gone. I love you, Dot, and I always will, girl. You were everything to me – my life.

As before when he'd thought these thoughts, a peace settled in him. It was as if Dot knew that, and would continue to know it, whatever happened in the future.

Chapter Seven

Cess and Elsie

'Will we have to stay here forever, Cess?'

'No, mate.' Cess had opened the door to the twin-bedded room that he and Bert were to share for the night. 'Just for a couple of weeks or so, but I'm going to have to leave you tomorrow.'

'But I don't like it here. It don't feel right.'

Cess sat on the bed and put his arm round Bert. 'Too posh, you mean? I thought you were used to living like this. When you and Elsie lived with Millie, you had your own room and a tutor, no less. You were one of the toffs then, mate.'

'No, it's not too posh here – it's weird.'

Cess hadn't a clue what Bert was referring to, but felt his body quiver as he lay on the bed beside him, so he held him closer. 'You seem afraid, buggerlugs, but you've no need to be. Your every wish will be the staff's command. You're going to have a great time. Once you've had a rest you'll feel better.'

'I won't sleep here when you've gone. You won't make me, will you, Cess?' A tear seeped out of the corner of Bert's eye.

'Hey, mate, what's wrong?'

'I don't know, I just don't like this room.'

Cess looked around him. To him it was a lovely room, with printed wallpaper, a cream carpet and beautiful, embroidered silk quilts draping the beds. They were of the same ruby-red colour as the velvet curtains.

'Come on, let's get a wash and brush-up and then go in search of something to eat, eh? We might find some jellied eels – you'd like that, wouldn't yer?'

When they were ready, they went along to the room the girls were sharing. At his knock on the door, Rose opened it. 'No entry for men, Cess. Eeh, you should knaw, lad, that we have a new mother in here and she's in bed.'

Millie's voice called out, 'Let them in, Rose. They've seen me in bed before.'

To Cess's relief, Millie looked a lot better. Her strained, drawn look had gone and her cheeks had the shiny look of having just been washed. But more than this, she had a calmness about her.

'I take it you're feeling better, Millie?'

'I am, Cess. I wasn't comfortable for the last hour of the journey, but Rose and Elsie have sorted me out.'

He wanted to go to her, to hold her and tell her that everything would be all right, but instead, he told them what he and Bert planned.

Bert left his side and ran to Elsie. Seeing Elsie wrap Bert in her arms, Cess's heart lurched. They looked so lost. He wanted to make everything right for them too, but knew that he couldn't put their lives back to how they were.

Bert burst into tears. To Elsie's enquiring look, Cess said, 'He's bound to feel a bit unsure of everything.' Crossing the room, he went down on his haunches. 'Now then, Bert. All's going to be all right, mate, I promise you. You'll be back in

Bermondsey before you know it. I thought we were going for those jellied eels?'

'I want to stay with Elsie.'

Mystified, Cess shrugged his shoulders in a gesture to convey to Elsie that he couldn't fathom Bert.

'I'd say you're more tired than hungry, buggerlugs. Let's get you onto my bed and you can stay here with us, eh?'

'Even when Cess has gone home?'

'Yes, you can sleep in my bed with me. It's only just through that connecting door.'

Bert visibly cheered. 'I don't like being on me own in a strange place, Elsie.'

'I know, luv. But even if I'm not in there with you, I can leave the door ajar and I'll be in here and with you in a tick if you need me, though you mustn't come barging in. You must always call out and ask if you can come in. Ladies need privacy sometimes, mate.'

With this exchange, Cess felt a sense of relief. He'd have been worried sick about Bert, but now he knew he'd be all right. Especially when Bert got off Elsie's knee and gave him a hug. 'Sorry I can't come for a walk, Cess.'

'Don't you worry, mate, I'll see you later.' As Elsie took Bert through the connecting door, he turned and waved to Cess, who felt overwhelmed with love for his little brother. It weighed heavily on him that once more Bert's and Elsie's lives were being disrupted.

Turning towards Millie didn't help to lift this feeling of being helpless to make things right for everyone, but he didn't voice this. 'Well, what's everyone doing about eating? I'm starving.'

'Rose has ordered a tray for me and herself, but Elsie wanted to see what you and Bert were doing first.'

'I think I'll stick to me plan. I feel like a walk to stretch me legs. I'll see what there is to eat down by the sea front.'

As Elsie came back in, she told him, 'I'll come with you, Cess. Bert said he wouldn't mind if I did, as he knows that Rose and Millie are through here . . . That's if it's all right with you both?'

'Of course, Elsie, darling. I'm fine and if Bert does get hungry, I'm sure there'll be plenty on our tray for him.'

'Hold on a mo while I get me wrap, Cess, and I'll give Bert a kiss goodbye.'

Elsie was only gone a few moments, but in that time Rose had taken something through to what Cess assumed was the bathroom of this suite and had left him and Millie alone. Their eyes met and held.

'Cess, I . . . We need to talk. But not now. Maybe you could come and visit sometime?'

Finding it hard to speak, Cess croaked out, 'I will, I promise.' A noise to the side of him told him that Elsie was coming back in. He coughed to clear his throat. 'And if you need anything from the flat, then if you give me a key, I can sneak in and get it for you without anyone knowing. I learned some crafty tricks as a kid.'

They both laughed and the tension broke.

'What's amused you two, then?'

'Nothing, Else. Come on, let's get going before me stomach thinks me throat's been cut.'

'Oh, you, Cess, could eat a three-course meal when you'd just finished a banquet. Come on then.'

When they stepped outside, Elsie linked arms with him. Apart from a few passing remarks, they walked in silence until they reached the promenade and then stood taking it all in. The boats bobbed in the fresh-looking choppy water, surrounding a ship that was bigger than any Cess had seen bringing freight into the dock in Bermondsey. White and regal, it looked magnificent. But the seagulls were the same as those that pestered the dockers. He watched them as they ducked and swerved around a fishing boat, their squawking filling the air as they squabbled over the pickings.

'It all looks idyllic. Wouldn't you just love to be one of the passengers on that liner?'

'I would, Cess. With me Jim and little Bert, and you and Kitty and . . . Oh, if only we could turn the clocks back.'

Cess knew she was going to say 'Dot', and took this as a good time to broach what was troubling him. 'Else, I've something to talk over with you, but I don't know how you'll take it.'

Elsie looked up at him. 'Depends what it is, Cess. I can't take any more troubles, mate.'

'Well, there's two things, but we have to talk about one. Millie told me about what Len intends to do to Rene.'

'Rene? Oh God, yes. Oh, Cess, I forgot about that, with all that's going on!'

'I can fix it, Elsie. It's no big deal, as long as you're all right with what I suggest.'

'But how? Her shop . . . her dreams.'

'I have a plan and I want to know what you think. I can do everything, if you're all right with it. I'll find a shop with two flats above. One for her and one for you, Jim and Bert. I can have it all settled by the time Millie feels safe and you can all come back. I can't promise it will be in The Blue, but I'll do me best to get it as close as possible.'

Elsie was quiet for a moment, and when she spoke Cess was glad to hear her agree.

'As long as Rene's all right with that, then it'll be a relief, to tell the truth, Cess. I don't want to be anywhere near anything owned by that bastard. I don't want him having any hold over me.'

'Good. Leave it with me, Else . . . Ooh, look, a stall. Let's hope they're selling jellied eels.'

The stall sold hot spuds, but anything was welcome to Cess. As they walked away, juggling the hot potato wrapped in newspaper, Elsie asked, 'What was the second thing, or is it that that's going to cause me more anguish?'

'Let's sit on that wall and I'll tell you.'

They sat on the wall surrounding the quayside, but before they could talk, a squall of wind played havoc with them, whipping off Elsie's bonnet and dancing with it along the cobbles. And yet it lightened their mood, as Elsie fell about laughing, watching Cess's antics as he tried to stay the bonnet's progress, only to have it snatched away just as he was about to put his foot on it. At last a passer-by grabbed it and handed it to him.

Back with her, Cess smiled. 'It gladdens me heart seeing them laughter-tears, Else.' With this, he plonked the bonnet firmly back on her head and sat back down, putting his arm around her. She looked into his face, trying to see if there was anything troubling him, but if there was, his smile hid it as he told her, 'When you laugh, Elsie, it makes me feel good, as it always did when we were kids.'

Something in Elsie wanted him to have good memories and to wipe out the bad. 'Did we laugh often enough, Cess?'

'We did – we had our fun despite everything.' His wink as he sank his teeth into the spud, and melted butter dribbled down his chin, warmed her.

'Ha, you're just as messy as then, little brother. Here, let me wipe you.'

He shrank back. 'No, not with spit on the hanky, Else. That's the one thing I'm glad to have left behind, mate.'

'Well, you needed plenty of it, you scruffy ragamuffin, you.'

They were laughing again and it felt good to Elsie, though she did worry what the second thing Cess wanted to say would bring. She tucked into her own spud and allowed the delicious taste to block everything out, while she battled with keeping the butter from trickling down her own chin.

Once they'd eaten and screwed the newspaper up into balls, they giggled as they tried to hit the bin next to the stall and both of them missed. Cess went to retrieve their rubbish and deposit it safely. When he returned, his manner showed that the moment was upon him. He sat back down next to her.

'Now, come on, Cess. No matter what it is that you've got to share, share it now.'

His deep intake of breath increased her concern. But she waited, letting him take his time.

'It . . . it's about me feelings, Else. I mean, not those of grief that you're used to me having. I don't feel those any more, and I have some guilt over that, but not as much as I should do. I'm guilty of not feeling guilty.'

'What on earth are you on about, mate?'

'I don't feel the loss of Dot as I think I should . . . as I did. I mean, I – I, well, I have feelings for . . . for Millie. And it's daft, but I think she may feel the same. But it's all too soon for us. And anyway, her being from bread and honey, it ain't right.'

Elsie didn't know what to say. She'd had no idea of any feelings between Cess and Millie. It wasn't their different backgrounds that worried her, because although Millie was from money, as Cess had said, she wasn't affected by it and had never shown that she thought herself better than them. But was this just Cess clutching at anything to heal his broken heart? If it was and he didn't recognize it as such, he might end up embarrassing both himself and Millie.

Despite Cess having been through such a lot, and it making a man of him before his time, he wasn't yet twenty and must still retain some of the impetuousness of his true age.

'Say something, Else, even if it's to tell me off.'

'I don't want you hurt again, Cess, luv. Give it time, eh?'

'You're not mad at me? I mean, am I insulting Dot? I still love her, Else, but it . . . Oh, I don't know, I just suddenly feel that I could get on with me life. That Dot's telling me it's all right to do so.'

'That's how it should be, but it's too soon, mate. You need to be sure this ain't you clutching at straws. You and Millie shared a moment yer never should have – a profound moment of a new life being born. That don't happen to many men. It's had an effect on yer. It's bound to have. I've never seen a baby born, let alone helped to deliver one, but I can imagine it's a special moment.'

'It was. I can't describe it. I was scared and, well, a bit embarrassed – for Millie, more than me, but it was special.'

'There, you see. And Millie probably feels that too. She's scared, and feels Len could take her precious child away from her. She's gone from living the life of a rich girl with her every whim pampered to, to losing everything – then regaining her means, only to have to run away to protect herself and her baby. She's in a very emotional state and probably sees you as her hero. You were there to help her at her most vulnerable, and are still helping her. But when

86

reality hits you both, then you'll see this for what it is, I'm sure of that, mate.'

'Ta, Else. I'll do as you say. I'll get back home tomorrow. And don't worry about anything. I'll be all right. I have Dai to talk to. He understands everything. Well, we seem to go through the same things at the same time – losing our missus, the grief of that, and now he's experiencing the same thing. He's found himself attracted to Rose.'

'Rose! But that would be wonderful! I love Rose, and Dai's a great fella. Oh, Cess, wouldn't it be great for them to get together?'

'Well, that got your approval. Yer don't reckon it's too soon for Dai, then?'

'Oh, Cess, don't take it like that, mate. The circumstances are different. Can't yer see that? Millie's me half-sister, and you're me brovver. And I love yer both dearly and I'm trying to protect you both. If this is real and you do love each other, nothing would make me happier, but I'm afraid for yer both. Why now? Neither of you has seen the other as anything but good friends before.'

'Wasn't it like that for you and Jim?'

Elsie let out a deep sigh. He was right.

'I'm sorry, Else. I know that were different. I know what you're saying, and daft as it sounds, it's what I'm thinking. But it's hard to accept it, feeling how I do. I'll try. I'll go back up to London tomorrow and get on with things.'

'That's the best way, mate. But I ain't saying this thing yer have for Millie can never be. I'm just telling yer that you'd be best to give yourself and Millie time to step back from it and make sure it's not a fleeting feeling, stirred up by other stuff that's going on in your lives – like, well, you both maybe clutching at hope.'

'I know you're right. You're more than a sister to me. You've been mum and dad too, at times. A rock of strength that helped me through me childhood and stood by me through everything.' His arm came around her again, 'I love you, sis.'

Elsie pulled her head back on her shoulders and gave him a look that said he was losing his marbles, 'Blimey, mate, what made you so soppy in yer old age?'

'Ha, I'm going soft, sis.' He kissed her on the cheek.

She pushed him away. 'Gerroff, you daft sod.'

They both laughed as they slid off the wall and he took her hand. 'Race you to the end of the road, and winner gets out of the washing up.'

Elsie put her head back and laughed out loud at this childhood memory they'd played so often – usually at her prompting, as she knew he'd win and it would be a way of letting him off his chores without looking as if she had. Then he would go out and play with his mates, which was something she'd loved to see.

'I know. It's soppy, but I do love yer, sis, and will always be there for you.'

'I know. And I love you, yer big oaf. Come on, let's get back.'

Despite everything that had happened to them, they'd made it through and would continue to do so. Elsie knew that. *Well, as long as I have Cess and Bert by my side, I will. If only I could have Jimmy too. But I know he's safe with Mum, in heaven.*

She thought of her Jim then. *More than any of them, I need you by me side, me darlin' Jim.* At this, hate welled up in her for Len Lefton, but so did a determination to get the better of him. *And I will.* With this thought, it flashed into her mind how Len looked at her, and she realized that maybe she could use his desire for her to take him on at his own game. *Use him . . . could I stoop so low?*

To get her Jim back, save Millie from heartache and protect little Bert – him more than anyone – Elsie she knew that she could.

Chapter Eight

Millie

They'd been in the hotel for three days and Millie hadn't been able to get Cess out of her mind.

Tomorrow her mama and papa would be docking, and her excitement and hope were brimming over.

She was supposed to be resting and, to that end, Elsie had taken Bert out for a walk and Rose had taken little Cecil, wrapping him up against the elements as if they were in arctic conditions, and yet the weather was quite pleasant for early spring.

Rose's books cautioned not to take a young baby outside until it was at least two weeks old, but although she followed their advice to the letter in other things, she ignored this. It was as if she needed to go out herself on some sort of mission, and taking the baby gave her an excuse to do so.

Millie shook the thought from her: *what on earth am I thinking? What possible reason could Rose have, to want to go out on an errand?* Telling herself that she was letting her fear and imagination run away with her, she turned her thoughts to the jam factory and her plans to buy it back. She wished she could tell the workers of this, so as to put their minds at rest, but everything was so up in the air and she still didn't know for sure if Len could ruin it all once more.

The telephone ringing cut into her thoughts. Taking a deep breath to calm herself, she lifted the receiver. But when the receptionist asked if she wanted a call putting through from a Mr Cecil Makin, her heart missed a beat and a warm glow swept over her body. Keeping her voice steady, she agreed to take the call.

Within seconds his voice came to her. 'Hello?'

Millie's throat tightened. 'Hello, Cess.'

'Millie! I hoped you would answer. I mean, how is everyone?'

'They're all out – sorry, you've missed Elsie and Bert, they've gone for a walk.'

'Don't be sorry, Millie . . . Millie, I—'

Wanting him to say it, and yet not wanting him to, Millie cut into his sentence. 'How are you, Cess?'

He cleared his throat. 'I'm all right. I was worried about you all. I thought Elsie would have rung me.'

'She meant to, but Bert's taken all her time. This move has really upset him.'

'Poor mite. He was just settling well at school and was meeting new mates; he's bound to feel it.'

'I feel so guilty, Cess. Everything that has happened to you all has stemmed from meeting me.'

'No. Don't say that. You made things better for us all . . . just knowing you. I – I mean, I'd never want you out of me life, Millie. I – I . . . well, I know Elsie feels the same. Your father had done wrong by her long before she met you. None of it's your fault, and you're a victim as much as us.'

Hearing this increased the way Millie felt. Her father had

started it, but by marrying Len and giving in to him, she had perpetuated their problems.

'Millie? Are you still there, Millie?'

'Yes.'

'Oh, Millie, I can't stop thinking about you.'

There was a silence. The unspoken had been spoken and Millie's heart soared. But was this right?

'Millie. I'm sorry. You can forget I said that. I wasn't going to, but . . . Oh, I don't know – I just don't know what's happening to me. What I feel is so strong . . . stronger than . . . Well, I feel terrible and it adds to me guilt, but I feel something stronger than I've ever felt before. Everything pales beside it. Forgive me, Millie. I won't mention it again. We can carry on as we were. I—'

'No, Cess, we can't. I – I feel it too. It's incredible and I keep questioning how I feel, and why, and telling myself I shouldn't. That it's wrong and—'

'Millie, oh, Millie. It ain't wrong, not if we both feel it. I love you, Millie. With everything that I am – which I know ain't much, compared to what you're used to, but I do. I have never felt such a deep and consuming love, and that is the only thing that makes me feel bad, because I did love Dot. I did.'

'Oh, Cess. I love you that way too. I can't understand it. I can't bring any logic to it. I just do.'

There came a sound like a sob, and Millie realized that Cess was crying, and then that she was too.

'Cess. It's all right. I mean, well, Cess, don't feel guilty about Dot. You were so young and Dot was so lovely. I miss her every day. She was still my half-sister, my blood. My father fathered her. But I know Dot wouldn't begrudge us finding happiness. But Len will, if he finds out . . . Oh God, what a mess.'

'I'm all right. Don't cry, Millie. It tears my heart out to hear you cry. I'm sorry. You're right, though. I can feel Dot's approval, and her telling me to find happiness. And I've been talking to Dai about it all. He's made me see that what I had for Dot was a deep love and caring, built up over the years of needing each other. Because of all that we suffered as kids. He thinks that if she'd lived, I'd have been as happy as Larry, taking care of her, trying to make her happy and having a houseful of kids. But that wasn't to be, and a man can love twice, as Dai is beginning to realize.'

'Oh?'

'Yes. But it's not for me to tell you. And I haven't forgotten your matchmaking traits – you'd be in your element and would push things too soon.'

'I'm intrigued. But I think Dai is right about you and Dot, as I know you loved her. I felt the same for Len in the beginning, but now I know it wasn't the real thing – not real love, because now I feel like I have been hit by a great force. Am I making sense?'

'You are, me darlin'. You're making sense and causing bells to ring, and giving me such happiness that I don't know how to cope. I can't bear not being with you, and yet I don't know how I can be with you. I love you, Millie, I love yer so much that it's driving me insane.'

This last sounded desperate, but it matched how she felt herself. 'There will be a way, there has to be, Cess. I'm meeting Mama and Wilf tomorrow. Once they've settled into the hotel and rested, I'll talk everything over with them. Be patient, my darling.'

'Oh, Millie. Millie, I don't know what's going to be harder: how it was when I yearned to tell you and hoped you felt the same, or now that we both do feel the same. I will come down to see you as soon as I can. Give my love to Elsie and Bert. By the way, will you tell Elsie how you feel about me?'

'How do you think she'll take it?'

'I have told her how I feel and she cautioned me to take me time. I meant to, but just hearing your voice . . .'

'Oh, Cess. She wasn't against it then?'

'No, she said she would be happy if we both felt the same, but she was worried that I wasn't thinking straight. I told her I thought you felt the same, and she said that would be because of us having the baby together . . . I mean—'

'You knew? You knew how I felt. Oh, Cess . . . And yes, it does feel like I had your baby. I know that's idiotic, but I can't stop thinking like that. Little Cecil feels more yours than he does Len's.'

'I would love him to be. I felt a surge of love for him when he was born into my hands and I held him. That same moment was when my feelings for you surfaced, and yet I feel now that I have had them forever.'

'Dear Cess, I do love you. I want so much to be held by you. I feel my world would come right then.' Saying this came so naturally to Millie. In her mind, she could see his sandy hair and his lovely hazel eyes. How tall he was, and how muscular from all the training he'd done as a lad, wanting to be a boxer – big and strong enough to protect Elsie, Dot, Bert and poor little Jimmy. Tears prickled Millie's eyes as she thought all this. 'Are you still there, Cess?'

'Yes. Sorry, I choked up when you said that. I want nothing more than to put your world right, Millie darlin', but I can only try to keep it so once the legal bods have sorted everything out for you. But, Millie, remember, darlin', that even if everything goes the wrong way for yer, I'll be there for yer, I promise. I'll take care of yer, and you'll want for nothin'. Remember that, Millie.'

'I will, Cess. I will. I feel safer already.'

'You sound tired, darlin'.'

'I am. I think it's the peace you've brought me. Hurry down to see me, Cess. Try to get here when Mama's here.'

'What will she think?'

'She loves you already and will be very happy for us. Ha, you might have to give up half your stall to her, as she's still hankering to run a market stall.'

Cess laughed as he remembered Millie's mother's love of the markets, and of Petticoat Lane in particular. And how she had imitated the cockney slang once, giving a rendition as good as any born within the sound of Bow Bells, as she'd hollered out to her imagined punters.

'She can come and work with me any day. But isn't she going to cruise the other half of the world, once she's met her grandson and made sure you're all right?'

'She is. She and Wilf plan to set off again as soon as they can. I can't wait to see them and hear all about this first leg, besides having them help and support me.'

'I can't wait for that, either. As soon as they are with you, I feel this will all get better, and each thing that gets sorted will bring us closer together.'

'It will, my darling, it will . . . I still can't believe this, Cess – me and you.'

'I know. I was a ragged-arsed kid who thought he was a man when you met me. But I am one now, Millie. And I know my own mind. You won't be persuaded from yours, will you?'

'That would be impossible, Cess. My feelings dictate

95

everything and they are very, very strong. Oh, Cess, I wish you were here. Right here with me.'

'I am, Millie, me darlin'. I'm there in me spirit, and in the love that I have for yer.'

'I know. I feel you here. I only have to think of you and I feel you near. It's all incredible, and yet it's made me incredibly happy.'

A key turned in the door and the knob turned.

'They're all back now, Cess. At least someone is . . . Ah, yes, it is all of them. Do you want to talk to Elsie and Bert?'

'I do, but I don't want to stop talking to you to do so.'

Millie laughed. 'We can do all the talking in the world when you get here. Make it soon.'

'And not just talk, but hold each other, Millie, me darlin'.'

His voice took on a lower, gruffer note, which thrilled Millie. She just had time to whisper, 'Yes. I want that. I want that so much.'

'What do yer want, Millie? Did I hear you ask if they wanted to speak to me and Bert? Is it Cess?'

Millie felt her colour rise. Elsie looked at her, then ran over to her and flung her arms around her. 'Oh, Millie, I'm so glad, so glad.'

Rose looked astonished. 'Eeh, what's going on? I haven't a clue what's made you all happy. But I'm glad of it.'

'And me. I don't like it when everyone's sad. Where's Cess, Elsie?'

'He's on the phone, buggerlugs, and with good news for us.' Elsie leaned over to the bedside cabinet and picked up the phone. 'Hello, Cess. I've guessed, darlin', that your feelings are returned. And, oh, Cess, I'm so happy for yer.'

Millie rolled over to the other side of the bed and swung her legs over the edge. She felt like crying and laughing all at the same time. She hugged herself, unable to believe the happiness she felt. She couldn't understand it, but that didn't matter. Another saying of Ruby's came to her: 'It is as it is.'

She'd never felt surer of anything that this was so right for her. Cess, the boy-now-man she'd first met two years ago, was in love with her! *And I love him – I love him so, and now it feels like I always did, like I was waiting for him to happen in my life and, on the day that he helped me bring my son into the world, he did!*

'Oh, Millie, luv.' Elsie glowed with happiness as she looked at Millie. 'I've not heard such good news for a long time. That brovver of mine made me half-sister Dot a sister-in-law to me, and now it looks like one day he'll do the same with us. I know he'll make you happy, Millie.'

'He has already, Elsie. I feel . . . well, as if my life is about to change.' On saying this, a little doubt crept into Millie, as she knew her life might change in more than one direction. But for now, the hug she found herself in more than made up for the fears she felt.

Millie stood excitedly on the dock the next day. The *Virginian* liner was offloading passengers, but as yet she hadn't spotted her mama and Wilf.

'I can see them, Millie – look, there!'

'You've got good eyes, Elsie. I can't . . . Oh, yes. Oh, Mama! Mama!'

'Millie, please don't rush forward, luv. You're still meant to be confined to bed for another week.'

'Eeh, there's naw good telling her that, Elsie. I try, but in the end all we can hope is that she doesn't live to rue the day.'

Millie laughed at them both, as they were like mother

hens. Well, nothing was going to stop her. This was the moment she'd been waiting for. Holding little Cecil to her, she ran towards the gangplank.

When she got there, the voice she'd longed to hear cried out, 'Millie! Millie . . . how? I mean, what are you doing here? Oh, my darling, you've had the baby – you didn't wait!'

Millie laughed. 'Ha, he wouldn't let me.'

'He? Oh, you clever girl, Millie.'

Mama's arms were open. Millie went into them and felt her troubles halve. 'Oh, Mama. Mama.'

'I hope those tears are tears of joy, darling?'

'A mixture. I have so much to tell you, Mama. Hello, Wilf. Lovely to see you . . . Oh, I've longed for this moment.'

'I detect that something is terribly wrong, darling. We weren't expecting you to be here, let alone here with your child. Let me peep . . . Oh, he's adorable – my love is surging towards him. Hello, my lovely grandson. I'm so pleased to meet you, little darling.'

Wilf bent over Cecil. His face lit up as he told Millie, 'He looks just like you, my dear.'

'Thank you. He's such a good boy. Oh, Wilf, I've so needed to speak to you.'

'Yes, I think your mama and I have deduced that, my dear.' Wilf put his arm around her mama. 'Well, I think we'd better book ourselves into a hotel, my dear, as it seems we won't be taking our onward journey right away.'

'I've sorted that out for you. I have a suite in The Dolphin, and I booked one for you too. I took it for two nights, to give us time to sort out what to do about my situation . . . I'm so sorry. I didn't want to cause you problems, but I so need your help, Wilf.'

Mama freed herself from Wilf and took hold of Millie, who wanted to crumble into her arms and sob her heart out. She was filled with relief and love, and yet she still held fears.

'Oh dear, poor Millie.' She felt Wilf's hand gently patting her back. 'I'm sure we will sort everything.' He spoke to her mama then. 'Darling, you go with Millie and ask Rose to hail a taxi for us, while I go and arrange for our luggage to be sent to The Dolphin.'

Mama took little Cecil in her arms. 'Oh, Millie, thank you – thank you for my little grandson. What are we to call him?'

On hearing the baby's name, Mama looked at her. Her expression held curiosity. 'No doubt you will tell me why, though I do approve of you calling him after such a lovely man as Cecil. But that can't have gone down well in certain corners?'

'Len doesn't know. He didn't ask. He didn't even look at him, but he's—'

'Save it all for now, darling, till we can have a proper talk later . . . Elsie! Oh, and Rose and Bert! Hello, young man, I think you've grown an inch while I've been gone.'

Bert beamed. 'Yes, I have. I was up to your elbow last time, and now I'm on me way to your shoulder.'

They all laughed. Mama wasn't very tall, so this didn't make Bert a big lad. Always small for his age, the look of pride on his face was a joy to see as he stood to his full height.

'Well, well, so you are. I go away and when I come back, you not only have a niece, but a nephew too. You'll have an entourage soon.'

Bert giggled, but his look said that he wasn't sure what Mama meant. Mama looked from one to the other. 'Anyway, we're all together now. And yes, you do have a lot to tell me, Millie. I can't think why you are all here, but I'm very glad to see you all, my dears.'

As Rose did a little curtsy and took the baby from her, Mama shivered. 'Brrr, it's cold. I should have put my wrap on.'

'Here, have mine, Mrs Hawkesfield . . . Oh, I mean, Mrs Hepplethwaite. I have a thick cardigan on and was just thinking how warm I was.'

'That's very kind of you, Elsie. Ha, all these new names take a bit of getting used to. All of us except Rose have had a new one in the last year. Oh, dear, I feel that a lot has gone on, and not all of it good.'

Millie smiled. 'It has, Mama and, like you say, not all of it pleasant, though some of it will greatly surprise you.'

As they piled into a taxi, Millie felt sad to have so much to put onto her mama's shoulders, and wondered what she would make of her new-found love for Cecil. But she was so very glad that she was here. She could feel the benefit of her support already as she chatted gaily away, keeping the mood light and telling them little snippets about the first leg of their Grand Tour.

After settling Mama and Wilf into their suite, Millie went to her own room with Elsie and Rose. 'I need to talk alone to Mama and Wilf – it will be easier. Are you both all right with that?'

'Of course, mate. You take your time, and I'll be rooting for you. Me and buggerlugs'll go for a walk.'

'And I'll settle baby down for his afternoon nap.'

'Oh, I think I'd better take him with me, Rose. Mama will be mortified if I don't. I can lay him on their bed. And besides, he may need another feed.'

'Eeh, in that case, I'll have a little walk meself.'

Once in her mother's suite, and as the story poured out of her, Millie couldn't stop the tears from cascading down her face. 'How can anyone be so evil, Mama? Poor Elsie. And . . . I – I couldn't bear losing my child.'

'My poor darling.'

To be held by her mama felt so good.

'Let's sit down, my dear. I'll hold my darling grandson and you can squat in front of me, how you always used to.'

As she did this and Mama stroked her hair with her free hand, Wilf, who had stood listening, sat down in the chair opposite. He cleared his throat. Millie had the feeling that he was covering up his emotions, and this was confirmed as his voice trembled when he spoke. 'My dear, nothing is as bad as it seems. There is a lot that Len has threatened that he'll find isn't lawful. For instance, you are entitled to your own money. You do have it in a different bank from the one he owns, I take it?'

Millie nodded, holding her breath and wondering what the verdict would be on Len claiming custody.

'As far as Jim's situation is concerned, that's a lot trickier. Len has compiled evidence that he can use in a court, and it does sound as though it would all stand up. The only course I see there is what Jim intends – getting evidence to the contrary. Someone must have seen something. We could get a private detective on to that. There's a man we have used a couple of times. He has no real credentials, just a knack of finding things out that are very useful. But . . . well, my dear, I am very sorry to have to say that Len is entitled to file a case to take custody of your son. And circumstances may weigh in his favour – a woman bringing a child up single-handed, the affordability of good schools, a nanny, her housing . . .'

'The nanny I have. Rose is qualified.'

Mama looked shocked. 'Rose? A qualified nanny?'

'Yes, but her status in life and speaking in an accent made it difficult for her to get a job. She did take elocution lessons and can speak the King's English, but with no connections, it was almost impossible to get employment as a nanny, so she gave the idea up and became a maid, then found that she was happy and so left it at that.'

'Well, having a nanny will help. But, my dear, as bad as it sounds, where you have chosen to live and bring up the child of a respected and very rich banker will be frowned upon. And . . . I have to warn you, the Leftons carry a lot of weight in the right circles. If they are not entirely accepted, they are well respected and needed. That is, in the sense of holding the purse strings. There are many who couldn't live without the overdrafts afforded by them. They include judges, magistrates and many top lawyers. Most of them have a grudge that they still hold against your late father, and they may see this as their chance to avenge the wrongs your father did to them.'

'Oh God! Are . . . are you saying that losing the custody case is a possibility? No. No, it can't happen!'

'I promise you that I – well, my son and I – will do all we can to stop it, but you have to prepare yourself, Millie.'

'My darling girl. I'm so sorry.' A tear fell onto Millie's forehead as she looked up into the silently weeping face of her mama.

At that moment reality hit and panic gripped her. 'Don't let it happen, Mama . . . don't.'

Silence descended on them like a cloak – a heavy, cloying cloak that Millie felt would suffocate her.

Mama dabbed her eyes. 'Is there nothing we can do, Wilf?'

'There are a few things Millie could do to try to improve things. Moving to a better area, for one.'

This shocked Millie, and yet it made sense.

'It's just that . . . well, the area you live in, Millie, isn't perceived as being a good area, and could very much go against you.'

'I – I understand. I love it there, so near to Elsie, but her life is changing. Cess is looking for somewhere for her to live, and for a new shop for Rene. So moving won't be a difficult thing for me to do. I'll do anything – anything.'

'Good. Second, you need Rose to act at all times in the manner of a nanny. I don't want to sound condescending, but if she can speak well, then she must do so at all times. Don't get me wrong, there is nothing about Rose that offends me, but a nanny who's obviously from a lower class won't help your case. She needs to be distant, and in charge only of the child's welfare – not treated like a friend. You need to show that your child has the care that those who will judge you will look upon as acceptable. And your child needs to have his name down at a good school. Yes, they need to see that he is loved by a caring mother, but these other things are more important, on the scale of a well-brought-up child with prospects being prepared to take his proper standing in life. What you are giving him is far outweighed by what Lefton can offer him.'

Millie felt a sense of despair, and yet her spirit was strong. She'd said she'd do everything she could, and she would. With this thought a new strength came into her and her heart didn't thump so heavily as she listened to Wilf's calming tones.

'I advise you too to give your child another name – I know that Cecil is like a brother to you, but I'm sorry, calling Len's son after him will give Len another stick to beat you with. Cecil isn't your brother, nor is he . . . Oh dear, this is so awkward and is making me say things that are so alien to how I feel, but I am trying to show you how you have to be seen to be going along with convention, my dear. Have you registered the birth yet?'

'No, but . . .'

'Well, I think you should register him very soon, or that will look like another lapse on your part, as children are meant to be registered in the first week of their birth. Now I also think you should stay in hiding for another couple of weeks while your mother and I get all of these things in place for you. Your mother is still looked upon in a good light, in view of her own family background . . . I know, it is all so false and snobbish, but it's important to some people – the people who will matter in your fight against Len. So I suggest that you move into my Knightsbridge house with us, as it is big enough for us all to live together. We do have to open it up, though, before you can come. And make sure everything has been done according to your mother's instructions, and refurbish my son's old nursery and the nanny's sitting room next to it.'

'Thank you so much, Wilf. But please don't go to any expense. I have furniture in my flat that can fit out both of those rooms.'

'That's good. This will be a very sound arrangement for you, my dear, and I am so pleased you are in agreement. Living with your mother takes away that mother-alone status that will go against you. And it will also elevate your position if you are seen to be under my protection.'

Millie felt so grateful for this offer. She'd suddenly felt alone in the world, and now knew a lessening of that. 'Thank you. Thank you so much, Wilf.'

Mama was looking at Wilf as if she would drown in his love. 'Oh, Wilf, my darling. This is so very kind of you. And we won't be able to go on the next leg of our tour until everything is settled. Will you be all right with that?'

'I will, my darling. I know that if Millie is unhappy, then you will be. And I know that in just this short time you feel a love for your grandchild and it will break your heart to lose him. I cannot allow that, although even with these measures, we won't be completely sure.'

'What possible reasons could Len still have for claiming custody?'

'It doesn't always take a reason – these are the Leftons we're dealing with. That could mean bribery, blackmail, discrediting Millie in some way . . . anything. Millie, is there anything at all that you can think of that Lefton could use against you?'

Hating herself for even thinking that lovely Cess could be a reason, she nodded her head, then looked up at her mama. 'I don't know how you're going to take this, Mama.'

Mama gave a little laugh. 'Darling, life with you is like riding a merry-go-round, but not always with the "merry" bit. I don't think that anything concerning you, my darling, can shock me.'

Millie smiled. 'It's something that has brought happiness to me, Mama, but which the people Wilf has been talking about won't approve of. And it will incense Len, who will see it as a slight against him. But . . . I have fallen in love with Cecil.'

There was a silence. Wilf looked bemused, but then would he even know Cess – other than what he'd been told? Millie couldn't think that he would. Even with his involvement in the case that he'd taken on when Elsie and Dot had been accused of murder, he wouldn't have come into contact with Cess.

'Mama?'

'I – I don't know what to say. I – I, well, isn't it only a few months since his wife – your other half-sister – died?'

Millie took from this that her mama didn't approve, though she hoped it was the shock that had taken her aback.

'I know. But we both feel that Dot will always be with us, not against us. We will always love and respect her. But . . . well, we didn't plan this. You see, Cess delivered my son and—'

'What? Good God, Millie!'

If it wasn't so serious, Millie would have laughed. Her mama's face was a picture. And yet she didn't get the feeling that she altogether opposed the idea. But then, to Millie, no opposition could stop her feelings for Cess. She could, and would, put them on hold for the sake of her son, but they would be there for the rest of her life.

Chapter Nine

Cess and Millie

As Cess drove towards Southampton he mulled over the plans that had been set out for Millie. The thought of them was hurting his heart every minute of the day and keeping him awake at night. How cruel was it of Wilf to ask them to shelve the love that he and Millie had only just found? But at the same time he understood and was willing to do anything for her.

It hurt too that she'd had to rename her child. Cecil was now Daniel Thomas, after Millie's and Len's respective grandfathers – Wilf had researched the names to make sure they got them right. It was all a ploy not to displease the hateful Len.

Wilf had found out that, unlike his Lefton descendants, Thomas had been an honourable man and a hero, who had been cited for great acts of bravery in the Crimean War, and this had made Millie feel better about the name.

Cess yawned. It had been a long day, working on the market till three and then a long drive. He'd had to stop twice to top up with petrol from the cans he carried. He shook his head to try to clear the feelings of sorrow that clawed at him.

Although this trip was to pick up Elsie and Bert and take them to his home, he hadn't yet been able to secure a place for Rene, because only three weeks had passed since everything had happened. But it was his last chance for a long time to be with Millie as he wanted to be. As he'd never been. To hold her, kiss her and to have her hold him. To hear her tell of her love for him.

Despite everything, the thought cheered him, causing him to put his foot down on the accelerator to try to get to Southampton sooner.

Although other feelings arose in him, he knew he would have to deny them. He wouldn't insult his lovely Dot's memory, or treat Millie with less than the respect she deserved. But, oh, how he longed to lie with Millie. To give himself completely to her, and to feel her wrapped around him in the union of their love.

These thoughts were having an effect on him – heightening his need of Millie, and making his despair surface once more, as he remembered loving Dot in that way. *Ours was first love, me darlin'. Beautiful, fraught with problems, but something that will stay with me forever. But how I wish that all this business with Len was resolved, and me and Millie could be free to be together.*

At last he was in Southampton. So near. His aching heart raced as he slowed down to a crawl and wound down his window. Peering at the buildings ahead of him, he spotted the hotel. Under the gas light in front of the entrance a group of women stood. From their pose, he could tell these were ladies of the night. As he prepared to pull up, one walked towards him and came up to his car. She placed her hand on his protruding elbow as she walked alongside him. 'Looking for a good time, love?'

Cess laughed. 'No, ta, darlin', just me destination, and I'm here – The Dolphin Hotel.'

'Crikey, you're a turn-up for the books. A bloke crawling along the kerb and not wanting a shag.'

He wanted to yell out his sorrow at what this girl had to do, as he thought of how his own mother had done the same. But knowing he couldn't change things, he sighed, then smiled up at the woman. 'I wasn't crawling in that sense, just looking for the hotel in the darkness. My family are inside waiting for me.'

The woman stepped backwards, but then tripped and fell. The action almost looked like a circus trick, but Cess jumped out of his car. As he helped her up, he asked if she was all right, though he was sure she was and that this was some kind of ploy to take advantage of him.

Her voice shook as she said, 'Yes, ta.' She kept hold of his hand. 'Only . . . well, you ain't got any fags on yer, have yer? I'm dying for a smoke.'

'I don't smoke, but I can give you enough money to buy some. Ain't yer cold out here, dressed like that?'

The girl was scrawny-looking and although she wore a long skirt, her flimsy blouse hardly covered her bosom and wasn't a match for the chilling sea breeze.

'Used to it, mate.'

As Cess got his wallet out, a shove in his back sent him off-balance. He landed heavily on the ground. Someone jumped on top of him, pushing the breath from his lungs. A voice with a triumphant ring to it shouted, 'You're nicked, mate.' Then, in a softer tone, it said, 'Well done, Daisy. That'll earn you a bit of respite from our lads for a while. But watch yourself, as our mission is to clear the streets of you prossies.'

Cess stiffened with fear and shock.

'Don't even try to resist, fella. You're under arrest. You'll more than likely go to jail for kerb-crawling with the intention to procure sex.'

Cess couldn't believe this was happening, 'Blimey, mate, I – I didn't do that. I—'

'We watched yer. Yer haven't a leg to stand on. You were approached and chatted for a minute – no doubt discussing what was on offer. Then you got out of your car and pulled your wallet out of your back pocket, obviously with the intention of paying for whatever services you'd decided to have. Yer scum. Yer come down 'ere from London with one intention. Well, why don't yer get it from yer own end of the world – yer've enough prossies there to keep yer going. Or were yer looking for something different, eh?'

'I'm down to visit me family, they're—'

'Shurrup. Save it for back at the station.'

The shame of his situation washed over Cess. Would anyone believe him? It all looked so bad for him. He appealed to the girl. 'Tell him. Please, I beg of yer, luv. Tell him I was just giving yer some money for fags.'

The girl spat on the floor, turned and walked back to her mates.

As the policeman shoved Cess into the Black Maria, the girl's cackling laughter split the still air. Cess knew that the sound would stay with him forever. They'd sold him. Tricked him and then traded him for the freedom to trade for a few days longer, without being bothered by the police.

The cold seeped into his body as the movement of the van rocked him from side to side. A tear plopped onto his cheek. But even in his despair, part of him understood. He had so many memories of seeing his mum distraught at being warned off the streets, and at times being taken away from them for a few days and locked in the cells. He hoped she'd never been party to such trickery to help the police, just to earn herself some respite.

Millie came to his mind. *Oh God, what will she think of me? And Else and Bert? Will they believe me? Oh God, help me.* His body began to tremble. His mind dipped into a nightmare that he hardly dared to acknowledge. *Prison – God, no! Don't let that happen to me. But above all, please let Millie believe me. Please.*

Millie felt increasingly anxious. Cess's estimated time to arrive had passed an hour ago. She looked over at Elsie and saw the concern in her expression.

Rose moved busily backwards and forwards as she packed Millie's and baby Daniel's case.

Oh, how hard it is to think of my little Cecil as Daniel, but I must. I mustn't slip up.

The plan was that the day after tomorrow Wilf would return to fetch her, Daniel and Rose and take them to his home, which was now ready for them. Cess was to transport Elsie and Bert, but was to come a day early and had booked a room.

Millie was longing for him to arrive so that they could spend the evening together, and then tomorrow – their last chance for they didn't know how long. They'd vowed not to see each other until everything concerning Daniel's custody and her divorce was finalized. She hadn't done anything yet about divorcing Len, but she knew she must. It was just that she only had his rape of Elsie that she could cite that held her up.

Elsie had been adamant that she should proceed, telling her that she didn't care about the cost to herself or her reputation. She knew that Len's rape of her, and his

111

counter-claims, would be dragged into the public eye. But they knew the truth, and that's all that mattered. She just didn't want Millie to suffer any more, or for it not to be possible for her to marry Cess.

Millie so wanted it to be possible to marry Cess. She had no doubts about their future together, but she did worry about putting Elsie through so much when her life was already in turmoil.

Another hour passed. Millie and Elsie were distraught. Millie prayed over and over: *Please, God, let him be safe. Bring him to me – don't let anything have happened to him. I couldn't bear it.*

They had rung the local hospital and had learned nothing. Now they sat in silence, the loud ticking of the clock on the wall the only sound.

Rose broke the silence. 'By, you're imagining the worst, the pair of you. Calm down. Cess has more than likely had a flat tyre, or his car has broken down or even run out of petrol. He'll be here. Eeh, let's order a hot drink and some biscuits, eh? I allus fill me belly when I'm worried.'

Millie nodded, but didn't think she could stomach anything. *Oh, where are you, Cess?*

The internal phone by her bed rang before Rose could reach it to place her order.

Millie stiffened as she watched Rose lift the receiver. She turned, her expression unreadable. 'Reception wants to speak to you, Elsie. They say it's urgent.'

'No!'

This from Elsie was a hushed, shocked sound that held all the fear Millie felt.

'Hello . . . Yes, this is Mrs Ellington speaking. Oh? Can . . . can he come up, or shall I come down? Yes . . . that's all right. Ta.'

112

Millie jumped up the second the receiver went back on its cradle. 'What? Oh, Elsie, please say Cess is all right.'

'I don't know. There's a policeman coming to see me. He's coming up here . . . Oh, Millie!'

Millie felt her body propelled towards Elsie without her seeming to make the decision to move. When she reached her, they clung together and stared at the door. They both jumped when the knock came, even though they were expecting it. Millie didn't want it to happen, didn't want to hear what she felt sure was a truth – that something had happened to Cess . . . *Don't let it be that Cess is dead. Dear God, please don't let it be that.*

Rose opened the door. The policeman standing there had his helmet under his arm. His shock of red hair glinted in the light of the many chandeliers that lit the corridor, and looked an almost identical colour to Elsie's.

'Mrs Elsie Ellington?'

'Naw, this is—'

'I – I'm Elsie Ellington . . . Is it me brovver? Is he hurt?'

'No. Well, he may be a bit bruised, and his pride's hurt. But may I speak with you alone?'

'You can speak in front of me half-sister and me friend. What's happened to Cess? Bruises, why? And why should his pride be hurt? Where is he?'

'Your brother, Mr Cecil Makin, has been arrested for attempting to procure sexual favours from a prostitute.'

Millie jumped to Cess's defence before Elsie could close her dropped jaw. 'That's ridiculous, officer, totally and utterly ludicrous! Cess? No! Cess is an honourable man. He wouldn't dream of doing such a thing. How on earth did this happen?'

'And you are?'

'Mrs Lefton. Millie Lefton. Cess is my . . .' Suddenly what

she was going to voice about who Cess was to her sounded sordid, even to her own ears – her, a married woman, proclaiming that another man was soon to be her fiancé. '. . . my half-sister's brother and therefore mine too, in a roundabout way. But his relationship to me doesn't matter, as I know Cess very well, and I know he is not capable of doing what you say.'

'Well, I'm sorry, but he was caught red-handed.'

Millie felt shocked to the core of her. *Cess? No, not my Cess, it's impossible.*

Elsie hadn't spoken since being told, but now she blurted out, 'That's a lie. Me brovver would never do anything like you say he has. Never!'

'The police do not frame anyone, Mrs Ellington. Your brother was observed slowly driving along the High Street. He then caught sight of three known prostitutes. When one approached, he stopped the car to talk to her.'

'Oh? And what did he say to her?'

'We don't know, Mrs Lefton. He wasn't overheard.'

'So, for all you know, he could have been asking the directions to get here.'

'Men don't usually ask anything of a prostitute and then pay her for telling him.'

Elsie jumped in again, her voice sounding almost hysterical, 'So, what does Cess say he was talking to her about – he has a side to this as well, you know. You can't go assuming the obvious, as it might not be that. I know me brovver would never . . . never seek the services of a prostitute. Never!'

'Look, I understand you're upset, but it don't change anything. None of us would like to think our brothers would do such a thing.'

As she'd listened to this exchange, Millie had imagined

114

the scene. 'He would have been looking for the hotel. The prostitute must have mistaken that for him looking for one of them.'

'His car had arrived at the hotel, Mrs Lefton.'

This shocked Millie and Elsie into silence.

'Look, we have carried out preliminary enquiries. After hearing his side of the story, we pulled the prostitute in and she is willing to make a full and signed statement to the fact that Mr Makin stopped his car at the kerb edge and beckoned her over. That he asked her a number of questions about what favours she gave, and how much for each. She said he told her to step away from the car so that he could get out and see her properly. When she did, she fell. When he lifted her, he said that she would do, as he'd had a glimpse of what she was offering. He then reached for his wallet. At that point we intervened.'

Millie's voice was sarcastic as she said, 'How convenient that you were on the scene, officer.'

'That is as may be – our officers are patrolling the area at all times.'

'Oh, and you allow prostitutes to operate on your route?'

The policeman's attitude changed. She was no longer 'Mrs Lefton', but was addressed formally. 'Madam, I did not come here to discuss the ins and outs of a criminal case with you, or our detection of and fight against crime on our streets. You may want to spend your time phoning a solicitor, rather than arguing the whys and wherefores with me.' He unbuttoned his top pocket. 'I have the names here of a few who work after hours, and who you can make arrangements with. Your brother will have to face an interrogation in the morning when our detectives come on duty. That will happen at around eight a.m. It would be better for him if he had a solicitor present. I am only here to tell you this and to inform of your brother's whereabouts, not to receive the third degree. I'll take my leave now, goodnight.'

As he left, closing the door with a bang, Elsie turned to Millie. 'Oh, Millie, when will it ever end? Could Len have had a hand in this? Poor Cess, he's been framed, I know he has.'

'You're right, but I can't possibly see how Len could have anything to do with it. He doesn't even know where we are.'

'But what if he's found out? And what if he knew Cess was coming here tonight? What if he knew how things were for you and Cess, and paid for this whole set-up?'

'But why would Cess even talk to these women, and why offer them money? How could Len know he would do that? Oh, Cess, Cess. Why didn't he just come inside?'

'You're not saying—'

'No! Never. I was just expressing my frustration at him being so close to here and stopping to talk to those girls – then offering to help them. Such women are always trouble.'

'Me and Cess know that ain't true. Some can't help themselves in any other way. If they approached him and asked him for money for a cup of tea or something, he would give it to them.'

'Oh, I'm sorry, Elsie . . . Oh, God, why didn't I think of that? Of course he would help them. He'd be thinking of the past and would want to give them something. That's all this is.'

'Is it? Millie, how convenient is it that these girls were standing near this hotel tonight? The very night Cess is expected?'

'I know what you're thinking, but no. In the first instance, Len cannot possibly know that Cess and I are in love. Second,

116

if by any remote chance he has found out, I still don't think this is his doing at all. If Len plans any kind of revenge, he gets every detail right. He doesn't rely on chance. I would say that the police were watching the prostitutes – trying to catch them in the act of touting for business – and Cess, because of his kindness, got caught in the trap.'

'But the policeman didn't say this was some kind of trap for the prostitutes, nor did he say that the woman had been arrested for her part.'

'So how do you think Len could find out about us? And not only about me, but the details of Cess's journey and the time he would be expected to arrive? And how would he arrange it all? For the girls to be in the right place, for Cess to be crawling along at the right moment, and for the police to be in position too?'

'I don't know, Millie, but I just have this feeling. Could it happen that Wilf or his son has said anything?'

'No. Impossible. They both move in the same circles . . . but no, ethics would prevent them, even if they weren't loyal to Mama, and to me, their firm's client. And they are well practised in not indulging in careless talk.'

But although she said all this, Millie had begun to wonder. A sinking feeling in the pit of her stomach told her that Elsie might be right and that this could be the work of Len. But how?

Gathering her thoughts, she crossed over to the telephone. Wilf answered. 'Oh, Wilf, I need your help even more.'

But even as she said the words, she wondered if anyone could help her win through against the massive odds of beating Len, for the more she thought about it, the more she became convinced that somehow he had had a hand in what had befallen her beloved Cess.

Chapter Ten

Elsie

As she stood in the police station, memories assailed Elsie, as she saw in her mind's eye herself and Dot, frightened as she was now and falsely accused of murder, with seemingly no one to help them, until Millie intervened.

A lot had happened since she'd met Millie – most of it terrible to bear – but she'd never change knowing that she was Millie's half-sister, nor would she ever want to be parted from her.

'How can we help you, madam?'

Elsie marvelled at how the first impression she gave nowadays was that of a young lady – dressed as she was in the nice clothing she could now afford.

'I've come to enquire after Cecil Makin. I'm his sister.'

'Oh? Enquire about what exactly?'

'I – I wondered if he was all right, and if the solicitor that we engaged had made contact and . . . well, if I could see him?'

'We don't have visiting hours, and neither do we give out information, but I'll have a word with my sarge. Wait there a moment.'

Elsie sat on the hard wooden bench that stood against the wall. A cold draught whipped around her from the door, which was wedged open. Inside, she felt alone – more alone than she'd ever been. *Oh, Cess, me lovely brother, how did this happen to you?*

At this moment she so wanted Jim by her side, and Millie too. But on hearing what had happened, Wilf had immediately sent a car for Millie, Rose and Daniel, saying it was imperative that Millie distance herself from what was happening here.

Elsie had agreed. If they were to save little Daniel from Lefton's clutches, Millie had to thwart any plans he had of showing her in a bad light – for as yesterday evening had worn on, Millie too had become convinced that all that was happening was somehow down to Len.

Elsie was glad Millie had gone. Not for any other reason than to know she was safe and that it would now be so difficult for Len to take Daniel, or to accuse Millie of having anything to do with Cess other than them being good friends. The policeman who'd called at the hotel could vouch that Millie hadn't seen him, and it could be shown that she left soon afterwards.

But although Elsie knew this was the best way to handle everything, she also knew she was going to miss Millie and Rose so much. She could have gone with them, but she was determined to stay down here until Cess was freed or . . . *No! I mustn't think of there being an alternative. He must be freed. I know, without a shadow of doubt, that he didn't do this awful thing.*

The policeman coming back shook her out of these thoughts. 'The sarge said you can have five minutes, madam. Come through.' He held up the hinged part of the counter to let her pass. 'Nice hair, miss.'

Elsie looked up at him, shocked to hear his lowered voice and the tone he'd used.

'A cockney done good for herself, eh? Staying at The Dolphin, hmm – nice.' His face came nearer to hers. 'Very nice.'

Elsie shuddered. She pushed by him. His laugh held a mockery of her. How did he know that she hadn't always had nice clothes and been able to afford to stay in smart hotels? Her mind raced over the possibilities and came back to one person – Len! But how? How would Len get information about where they were, and their own and Cess's movements?

Shown into a small, whitewashed room that was almost bare, but for two chairs and a table, Elsie sat waiting, feeling anxious and yet relieved that she was going to see Cess.

As the minutes ticked by, her mind was a turmoil of thinking that this person and that had betrayed them. But the worst thought of all was that it could have been Jim. Jim had telephoned her the day before, and she'd told him that Cess was coming. He'd asked what time she expected him and when they would set off for home. Were these just general questions of the type they exchanged in all of their conversations? Please God, let them have been. *But more than that, help us. Me and Jim. Make everything right in our lives.*

There was no time for more prayers as Cess, looking broken, slid into the chair opposite her. His eyes stared out of sunken sockets and were swollen and bloodshot with the tears she knew he'd shed. When she put out her hand to him, he took it in both of his.

'Oh, Cess.'

'I didn't do it, Else. I was driving slowly, as I was coming up to the hotel and getting ready to stop. Please believe me, Else.'

'I never considered it for a minute, mate – not for one second did we believe it.'

'*We?* You mean Millie don't, either? Where is she, Else? I thought . . . No, I was just being daft.'

'She's gone back to London, to her mum and Wilf . . . It's the best thing, Cess.'

Cess nodded. 'So where's Bert, who's looking after him?' Although this made it sound as though everything was fine, and he wanted to change the subject, she knew he must be hurting badly, with all that had happened and with missing his last chance, for a long time, of being with Millie.

'Bert's all right. He doesn't know anything yet, mate. We told him that your car had broken down and you couldn't make it. He cried, but we talked him round. He's made a friend of a boy who is staying at the hotel with his parents and his nanny. He's with them until I get back. I told him I was going to arrange for us to get back to London. He's looking forward to living at yours with you, Cess.'

'I don't think that will happen, Else. Not me going back to London.' His eyes filled with tears. 'The evidence against me looks bad.'

'I know it does, luv.' Despite the policeman's presence, Elsie needed to reassure Cess, so she told him, 'We think this is you-know-who's doing. We don't know how, but it smacks of his dirty work.'

Cess looked as though a light had turned on for him. 'God! I never thought of that. But it does, sis. It all seemed like it was set up. The woman's actions – everything. But how?'

'We don't know. Someone must be feeding him informa-tion. What was the solicitor like, did he believe you?'

'He was all right, but I got the impression he didn't really care.'

'Well, we'll sort that. Wilf will get the right one to take on your case. But in the meantime we have to find out if there is information getting through about us. I'm scared, Cess . . . I'm scared it might be Jim.'

'Don't be daft, sis. Jim? Never in a million years.'

'But who else? I mean, Jim knows everything. I told him about you and Millie, and when you were coming.'

'Oh, Else, I can't believe you're saying this about Jim. I thought it was all right between you now, but if you don't trust him, you've nothing, mate. Len could have a private investigator on to us all. They can find out anything they want to know. And Jim isn't here, to have been able to set all this up, is he? Nor would he. He'd never sell any of us down the river, Else. Jim's a victim. Try to remember that. He doesn't want to be away from you. He broke his heart to me about it. Stop condemning him for trying his best to save himself, and your lives together. Support him, and do all you can to help him get through. I can't understand yer, Else. This ain't like you.'

Elsie knew that Cess was right. Jim going had set her world reeling. It had made her imagine all sorts about the man she loved dearly, despite his own and everyone else's reassurance that the way he'd chosen was the only way.

'I know. I'm sorry. I've been so down since all of this started, and now this. How can we ever beat an evil force like the one we are fighting, Cess?'

'We will, because we have right on our side. We've done nothing wrong, sis. Hold on to the strength I know you have.'

The policeman coughed. Elsie looked round at him. A man in his forties, he had a kindly face and was looking apologetic. 'I'm sorry, miss. But your time's up.'

'Oh no. Oh, Cess. I will stay strong. I will do all you say. But you must too. We'll prove your innocence.'

They stood up. Elsie could hold herself back no longer. She took Cess in her arms. They hugged as if they would never let each other go.

The policeman didn't object, but after a moment he said, 'Now come on, you don't want to get me into trouble, do you?'

When she pulled out of Cess's arms, she told him, 'I'll prove your innocence. I will. But just one thing. What did the woman look like?'

'She had long scraggly hair – blonde. Oh, I don't know. She was called Daisy.'

Again the policeman coughed. 'Begging your pardon, miss, but don't think of contacting a witness in your brother's case. It will go against him and get you into trouble.'

Elsie had the feeling that this officer was on their side. 'I won't, officer. Look, I don't know if you'll believe me or not, but we have an enemy who will do anything to hurt us.' She quickly explained about Len and how he would do anything to hurt Millie, and discredit her, to take their child.

'Well, that's a tale and a half. But I believe you, miss. You strike me as an honest person, and so does your brother. I know of a lot that goes on around here – I can't talk of it or I'd be hounded out of me job, but just to say that what you suspect could happen.'

'You mean there are those in this station who could be bribed?'

'I'm not saying that or anything else, miss. Now it's time you left. I have to get your brother back to his cell.'

'Ta, officer, you don't have to say more.'

As Elsie stepped outside the police station, she felt there was hope. She didn't yet know how it would materialize, but she would have to find a way to make it do so.

As she walked along, she thought how quiet the streets were for noon on a Saturday. In Bermondsey it would be heaving in The Blue. A figure was walking towards her. A gentleman. But other than him – apart from the odd carriage and horses, and a family on the other side of the street – it was almost deserted. A bitter wind cut off the sea and whipped around her. Elsie put her head down against its onslaught, but then jumped when a dearly loved voice asked, 'Can I keep you warm, Elsie, my darling?'

Astonished, she looked up. 'Jim? JIM!' Picking up her long skirt, she raced towards him and he to her. When they collided, all her pain left her and her world came right as his arms encircled her and he held her close. Laughing and crying, she clung to him as she told him, 'Oh, Jim, I'm sorry. I'm so sorry.'

'Hey, what's all this? You haven't found someone else, have you?'

'No, Jim, never . . . never. Hold me.'

'Oh, my darling, I've missed you. I can't believe I've run into you like this. I lost my bearings while looking for the hotel where you are staying. Where's Bert? And how's Cess? I—'

'Why are you here, Jim? I – I should have been leaving; you knew that.' Alarm bells were clanging in Elsie's head.

'Elsie? Don't look at me like that. Millie rang me late last night. She told me everything, and what you all suspect too.

I got up very early and caught a train to be with you. I booked into a hotel near the estuary. I didn't want whoever was informing Len to know I am here. You don't think . . . Oh God, Elsie, have I gone so far down in your estimation?'

Shame washed over Elsie. 'Oh, Jim, forgive me. I just don't know what to think. I feel like a trapped mouse with a huge cat waiting to eat me and, if I turn from it, there's a trap waiting to snap down on me. I'm lost, Jim. Len has done this to me – to all of us.'

'Don't let him, Elsie, or you will be truly lost, my darling. That is how he will win. By breaking us and making us mistrust everyone, and each other. I came to be with you, to support you, my darling. I've missed you so much. I never expected to bump into you. I was going to come to the hotel and leave a message at reception to tell you where to meet me. I thought The Dolphin being the largest hotel, there would be so many comings and goings that I wouldn't be noticed.'

'I don't know what to say, Jim. I'm falling apart, little by little.'

'No, you're not. Not my strong, brave Elsie. You – we – we'll all win in the end, believe me. We will.'

'Take me back to your hotel, Jim. I needn't . . . well, I mean, Bert's all right where he is for a while.'

'My darling. I want you so much.' His kiss told her how much, and fully awoke in Elsie her love and need for Jim.

'I'll have to book you in too, Elsie, otherwise I won't be able to take you to my room . . . Oh, Elsie. Could you fetch Bert later and both stay with me tonight?'

'But I don't think anyone at the hotel could possibly be informing Len. . . Unless Cess is right. He wondered about a private investigator.'

'Yes, I wondered that. And if there is one, he may be watching the hotel, as Len still suspects I'm in touch with you, even though I denied ever wanting to see you again and told him I had been a fool to have trusted you.'

'Ta for that!' She hit him playfully.

'Ha, that's the spirit. That's my Elsie.'

They were walking in the direction of the promenade, holding hands and seeming carefree, when Elsie had a sudden thought. 'If there is someone watching The Dolphin, I can't come to stay with you, Jim. They will know and will let Len know, and then the nightmare of the accusation against you will flare up again.'

'Oh, Elsie, that's only us speculating. There might not be anyone watching. I am beginning to think that, because surely they would have followed you today, but I didn't see anyone other than a few families. And there's no one around now. Although I'm not surprised in this cold. I'm freezing.' As they turned the corner onto the promenade, Jim said, 'There it is, the Ocean View Hotel.'

For the next few paces Elsie forgot about men sneaking around watching her moves, as a feeling of joy surged through her with the expectation of what was to come – at last she was going to be with her Jim as they should be.

The hotel was not as grand as The Dolphin, but was nice and welcoming. Jim's room had a view over the water and the bobbing boats, and Elsie noticed that there was a lot more hustle and bustle here in the street below than she'd seen before.

'Well, darling, have you only come to look at the view?'

Turning, she ran into his arms. His kisses thrilled and frightened her with the intensity of his desire. And yet she showed no resistance as her own feelings deepened and inflamed and she became lost in her love for him, drinking in the sensations that splintered her into a thousand pieces and then built her up again, to shatter her fragility once more, as she lay drowning in his love for her.

Afterwards they lay without speaking. In their silence was all the love they had for one another, and a completion of them both.

After a moment Jim rolled towards her and looked down at her. 'My Elsie, my darling wife, I'll put everything right, I promise.'

Elsie held his eyes. 'You have already. My darling, you have mended me. I feel strong now. I love you and will never doubt you again.'

As he held her to his naked, damp body, he told her, 'Never. Never even think that I would harm you, my Elsie. If you do, you are letting Len win.'

'Can we stop him?'

'We have to show him that whatever he does to us, we can beat him. I have news on that front, as it happens, and apart from knowing that you were in trouble, it is what spurred me on to make this journey, despite the risks.' Jim sat up and then swung his legs over the side of the bed. 'Get dressed while I tell you about it, darling.'

Elsie got up and walked over to the bowl and jug that stood on a washstand in the corner of the room. The jug was full, but pouring it over her hands made her shiver. 'It's freezing!'

Jim laughed at her antics as she braved washing herself in cold water. How quickly she'd forgotten what it was like.

Her mind went back for a moment to the tenements on Long Lane, but she shook the thoughts away from her.

'Ha! I've never seen anyone dress as quickly as that – you ladies usually take hours.'

'Us ladies? How many have you watched getting dressed, then?'

'Oh dear, I'd not dare to watch any while you're my wife. That flash of temper you display in an instant frightens the life out of me.'

'Good! I intend to keep yer in line, and to have yer all to meself.'

'You've got me, and I'm honoured. Now, let me tell you my news.'

Worried about Bert, Elsie suggested that he did so as they walked to her hotel.

'But isn't that dangerous, darling?'

'Yes, but I don't care any more. Let Len do his worst. I'm not letting you go again, Jim.'

'But, Elsie, please – we must. You know what Len is like. Please, Elsie, just a little longer.'

Elsie didn't want to part from Jim. She felt safe, strong and able to cope, with him by her side. It was agony when he was away. But she agreed. 'Let's at least go to the cafe next door for a cup of tea then, luv. And we have to think of a way to meet up later with Bert. I can't let yer go just like that.'

'Oh, darling, I know it's hard, but we have to do it. Come on. Let's hurry.'

In the cafe, with their tea and buttered scones in front of them, Jim told her his news. It was all music to her ears. 'Really! You've found someone to help you? Oh, Jim.'

'Yes, a Miss Jenkins. She is secretary to the company director of Bestways Produce. She remembers me and my father, and the dealings we had with her. She didn't know how to get hold of me, but was suspicious when the consignment they bought was delivered, as she asked the driver how I was, and he didn't know me. She said she described me to him and he said he'd never seen me in the factory, but then he only worked nights. When she said, "But surely someone must mention Mr Ellington, as he is the manager of the factory", he said she must be mistaken, and mentioned that a Mr Riley was the manager.'

'Reginald Riley, the night-watchman? So he's involved.'

'Yes. Didn't you know him when you were younger, Elsie?'

'I did. It was me who suggested he should be offered the job when we took over the factory, after the previous night-watchman retired. Riley used to live in the tenements. His wife is Beatie, who works on the line with Ada . . . Oh my God. When we were helping Ada to move from Salisbury Street, she told us that Beatie had moved into a flat on the other side of the Thames. From what she described, these flats were far superior to the tenements. It seemed, from what Beatie had told Ada, that Reg Riley had come into a bit of money from an uncle who'd been at sea all his life and had not married.'

'Well, it all falls into place, although I know Beatie doesn't seem a likely person to be involved.'

'No, she isn't. Beatie's a lovely woman – sort of harmless, kind and very quiet. To think of her plotting against us, well, I can't believe it. I don't think she knows the truth. Reg was probably paid a certain amount and made up the story.'

'Then maybe there's hope there if you could speak to her, though she may be loyal to her husband.'

'Maybe, but I don't think there's much love lost. Reg often beat the living daylights out of her on a Friday night.

The problem is that even if she did know what he was up to, she'd be afraid to say, but I'll try. I think I could take Beatie into me confidence about Len's plot against you, and that would sway her to help us. Would this Miss Jenkins be willing to help us, do you think, Jim?'

'Yes, she would. She doesn't know everything. I only told her that a scam had been carried out in my name, and that I was trying to find those who'd been taken in, to warn them. It was then that she told me that the supply had dried up. She ordered more jam, but she had a letter telling her the company hadn't found it viable to deliver so far afield.'

'Oh? Doesn't that help your case too?'

'No, quite the opposite, as now it looks like it all stopped when I left.'

The hope that Elsie had felt bubbling up inside her died. But then a thought came to her. 'What about this driver – can we find him? Surely his testimony to the fact that he was told Riley was the manager will help. I mean, he never took an order from you or a consignment delivery address, and didn't even know you existed.'

'Yes, that's exactly what will help. But how do we find him? We don't have a name, or a clue as to where he came from. Miss Jenkins said his van had some writing on the door, but she didn't note it down.'

'Someone will know something. I didn't have any time to do anything before we had to leave, but I will when I get back. I'll do everything I can to find someone to help us.'

'Oh, darling, that's what's needed. For us to ask questions and find out the truth. But what about Cess? How are we going to help him?'

'I am putting my trust in Wilf. He'll get Cess cleared of this charge, I'm sure of it.'

'I hope so, darling, I really hope so.'

Elsie was quiet for a moment. The enormity of it all weighed her down, but then some of her old spirit entered her and she took hold of Jim's hand. 'We can do this, Jim, we can. I'll go and get Bert and bring him out for a walk. Can you hang on here? I know it will do him the world of good to see you, darlin'.'

'And me to see him. And you're right, Elsie. We will get through this. Stay strong, darling. Never doubt me, no matter what happens. Promise me.'

'I promise, darlin'. And I promise you too that everything will come right. We'll have our music school, and do you know what other promise has been made? Millie promised that we will all be back in Swift's Jam Factory. And I know she can make it happen. So, me darlin', we've to hang on to the hope those three promises give us.'

But even though she sounded sincere, Elsie wondered if any of it would ever happen.

Chapter Eleven

Millie

'Oh, Mama, I'm so worried about Cess and Elsie. I feel as though I've abandoned them.'

'No, you haven't, darling. And they know that. Wilf was right, with you coming here, you have thwarted part of Len's plan to discredit you further. If you were in Southampton he could prove his case that you were involved with Cess, and add to his list of what he thinks is your unsuitability to bring up his son – that is, of course, if he is responsible for what happened.'

'He is, I'm sure of it.'

'You cannot be sure, darling. We have to remember what Wilf said, that this could all be circumstantial. The police are on a mission to clear the streets of prostitution, and it could have been that they were watching the girls. Cess became unwittingly involved in the trick the girls wanted to play to get themselves some freedom to work without harassment for a few days. That's all there might be to this.'

Millie bit into her toast. She didn't believe this theory for one moment, although she did find some hope in it, as Wilf said it would be a simple matter of challenging the prostitute in court – his theory being that liars can always be broken.

She sat back in her chair, feeling the cosiness of its gold velvet cushioned seat and arms, but knew it to be a physical comfort only. Nothing would give her the contentment she really longed for – to be in Cess's arms.

However, she had to admit that everything about this house in Hans Place, Knightsbridge, was comfortable, as well as elegant and beautiful. It stood out from its neighbours, making them look grey and dull against its white, ornate exterior with its carved stone above the entrance, something that none of the others had.

It had six storeys, with the basement being the hub, housing the kitchens and laundry rooms, and the attic rooms being the staff quarters. This breakfast room and another more formal dining room were on the first floor, with French doors opening up onto a balcony overlooking the park opposite. It was truly a lovely house and yet it felt so familiar and like home, housing, as it did, so much of Mama's furniture. Already Wilf had offered it to Millie to rent while he and Mama continued on their travels.

Millie looked out of the window. From her seat she could only see the tops of the trees, but knew that if she stood, she would be given a peaceful landscape of green, with London buildings in the distance. She had to admit that she was tempted and would probably take up the offer. After all, it was only a short drive to where Elsie lived, and in any case Elsie was moving.

Millie knew she wouldn't want to live in The Blue if Elsie didn't, but she had considered moving back to the Burgess Park area, nearer to Cess and where Elsie would be for a time.

'What are you thinking about, darling? You've gone very quiet.'

'Oh, everything, Mama. Should I take the offer of this house mainly?'

'You should, darling. It is right for your needs . . . I know, I don't like all the snobbery here, but it exists and we can only fight any battle with the same, or better, tools than our enemy. Your main battle is to keep little Daniel from the clutches of his father. Taking this house would be a triumph, as Len couldn't possibly have any objection to it being a suitable place for you to bring up his son.'

'I know you're right, Mama. And yes, I think I just needed to come to realize that.'

'Good. Today Wilf will enrol Daniel for a place at Eton and will contact his son's old tutor for a recommendation of a home tutor. He suggests The Hall School as a preparatory school when the time comes, as this is the route through education that he himself took. Not only is The Hall an acceptable school for entry to Eton, but with Wilf being step-grandfather and a former pupil of both schools, Daniel will have a priority placement.'

'Oh, Mama, is this what we really want? I'm not sure that I do. I – I, well, I don't want to bring up the past, as I know you were misguided and have long since regretted what you did to me, but will Daniel experience the same stigma I did? Will he be looked down upon, as I was at my school because I wasn't upper-class but the daughter of a self-made man? I only had the minimum of respect, due to you being of higher birth, but mostly I was ridiculed for trying to be something I wasn't. It was a very unhappy time.'

'Not at all. Daniel's father and paternal grandfather are not upper-class, but they are not self-made, either. They are

134

upper-middle-class, which is more acceptable, whereas we were just rich middle-class . . . Oh, it's all ridiculous, but besides this, Daniel's maternal grandmother came from an upper-class family and so does his step-grandfather, so Daniel will have no such problems.'

'It's just not what I want for him, though. I don't want him to be stuffy and snobbish, but caring and accepting of others who haven't as much as he has.'

'He can be all of those things. Wilf is, as is his son. And so are you, and me. Oh, I know I didn't appear like that when you were a child. I acted like the worst kind of snob, but I had an agenda, darling. I didn't want you to suffer what I had. As it happens, you have suffered more.'

'That isn't down to anything you did or didn't do, Mama. You were a victim. You acted as you thought best, but in the end we sorted everything. Though I still have mixed feelings about my father. I miss him, and yet I want to berate him and hate him, which is what he deserves.'

'Well, I find it best not to talk about him. But, my poor darling, I do want some peace and, above all, happiness for you. Now, please don't worry about Daniel. He will have the influence of us all. We are caring of others, as are his lovely Aunty Elsie and Cess, who can show him the real side of life and community. Besides, you can change your mind on Daniel's schooling once you have legal custody, though I wouldn't advise it.'

This was something Millie felt she would definitely do, because although she agreed with her mama about Daniel's different influences, she felt sure all that top-notch schooling might influence him more than they did.

When Mama left the table, Millie went into the hallway to telephone Elsie. Elsie's voice made her sound as if she was standing next to her. 'Oh, Millie, are you all right, luv?'

'I am. Are you, and how was Cess? I tried to ring several times, but they said you were out. I've been very worried.'

'Sorry, mate. I had a surprise visitor – Jim. Me darling Jim came to see me. He said you'd telephoned him. Ta, Millie. It did me heart good to be with him.'

'Oh, I'm glad, darling. I knew he was going to come, but I didn't ask about his visit, just in case he hadn't managed it. And Cess, is he all right?'

Millie listened to how Cess was. Her heart felt laden with guilt and sorrow. 'He does understand why I had to leave, as Wilf advised, doesn't he?'

'He does. And he's glad something's sorted for you. Oh, Millie, we have to get him out of there.'

'Wilf is on the case, Elsie. Keep holding on to the fact that we have the best person we could to take care of Cess.'

'I will. Anyway I'll have to go. I'm catching the train back today. I should have moved in with Cess and Dai, but I'm going back to Rene's. I need to be with her, and all me stuff's there. I'll check on little Kitty, and I'll hope to bring her and Gertie to mine for the time being. If Gertie agrees and would take care of Bert as well, that would free me up to try to sort out Rene's position.'

'I'm going to Rene's later for just that same purpose. I'll see you there and, together, we'll come up with something. Please try not to worry, darling. We've faced a lot worse than this before and nothing has beaten us. We'll win through, Elsie.'

'Cess will be with us soon, won't he, Millie?'

'He will. I promise. I couldn't live without him now. See you later, my darling sis.'

Feeling heavy-hearted, Millie made her way to the nursery. Rose was finishing bathing Daniel.

'I'll dress him, thank you, Rose. You go and enjoy your breakfast with the rest of the staff.'

'No, Millie, I don't think that I should. I'll have my breakfast sent up to me. It's protocol. As it will be for Daniel's tutor. I'm assuming he will have a tutor?'

'Yes, but between you and me, the rest of the education being put in place for him won't happen. I'll go along with it to prevent Daniel being taken away from me, but then I'll change tack. I want him to be different from the majority of those I know who went to highbrow schools.'

'Oh? I know what you mean, but, well, we were taught as nannies that we should do all we can to encourage our children and prepare them for boarding school. Even to go with them and continue to look after them – make them think this is normal and is expected of them, as our country needs well-educated men to run it, and to be in charge of our armed forces, legal system, banks et cetera.'

Millie sighed. In this mode, Rose would certainly further her cause with any snoopers that Len might send, but she wasn't sure she liked her as much like this.

'Rose, you can be yourself when we're alone. I prefer you to speak in your natural dialect. When you are being the nanny they all say I should have for Daniel, I'm not so comfortable. Though of course I am grateful. But Ruby always ate with the staff, and mucked in with them too. And she never lost her dialect, or the respect that everyone had for her.'

'I know. But if I let the side down, I'd be mortified, Millie. I'd be too familiar, as we've become friends. I don't want to be one of the sticks to beat you with. Maybe, after all is settled, I'll slip back.'

'Oh, damn and blast Len! Why was I ever taken in by his charm?'

'I think that's easily done. Elsie was too, remember?'

This seemed a funny thing for Rose to say. Millie didn't like it, but as she'd just persuaded Rose to be a little less stiff with her, she couldn't pull her up. But in Elsie's defence she said, 'Elsie was taken advantage of. I wasn't, mine was all free will, and I'll live to regret it forever.'

As Millie took Daniel, wrapped in a fluffy towel, Rose asked, 'Will Elsie be back today?'

'Yes, thank goodness. And I'm going to be very busy visiting Rene and seeing if I can help sort something out, as we can't be sure that Cess can continue to do so.' At this, Millie felt a sense of defeat. She knew Cess wasn't out of the woods yet. Wilf had warned her that it wasn't a hundred per cent certain that he could get Cess off, but he was travelling down to see him tomorrow and to see what he thought could be done. *Oh, Cess. Cess, it seems that everyone and everything attached in any way to me, Len has to hurt.*

Snuggling Daniel to her gave Millie comfort, as she filled with love for her son. He turned his head towards her breast. 'You, little man, will get as fat as a porky pig if I give in to you every time you come looking to be fed. You've another hour yet before the milk counter opens.'

Daniel looked up at her. His eyes seemed to be asking questions.

'Yes, I'm your mummy, darling. And I'll never let anyone take you away. I promise.'

Although she knew it was wind, the little smile that lit up his face warmed her heart.

'I truly promise, little one. And I promise to bring you

up among all the *real* people that I have come to know and love.'

Daniel made a noise like a gurgle.

'Ha, I think that he's in agreement with you, lass.'

'Oh, Rose, that's more like you. But I understand. We'll stay with the pretence until all this is over.'

'Aye, it'll be better – oh dear, you see what I mean? One slip and I'm Rose from Leeds again, and not Rose the well-brought-up nanny.'

'The thing is, Rose, Len knows who you are and where you came from, so speaking the King's English may not make much difference, but your qualification will. But yes, it's better you keep up the charade with the staff and the other nannies you may meet on your walks around this area.'

Millie felt much better. For a moment, Rose had seemed alien to her.

With Daniel now dressed in a lovely lemon gown and a cardigan that Ruby had knitted for him, Millie lifted him up in the air. 'There, you're wrapped in the love of Ruby too, now. And one day you will meet her. In the meantime I will need to see to your christening, my darling son.' Then she felt depressed, as she knew that she would have to ask his father and grandfather along.

She handed Daniel to Rose.

'I'll be back up to feed him in about an hour.'

Having made her way to Wilf's office, hoping to find him there, Millie knocked on the door.

'Come in . . . Ah, Millie. How are you, dear? Is there something I can do for you?'

'I'd like to say no, I'm just on a visit to chat, but I'm

139

afraid that I need your services so much of late, it must feel as though you haven't retired.'

'None of it is a problem, my dear. It keeps me from being idle and from longing for my travels.'

'I am sorry, Wilf. I promise I won't always be this much trouble.'

'It's your lovely generous, kind heart that has landed you in most of it – that and marrying a spiteful, philandering man, who only thinks of himself and what he can gain out of life. None of this is your fault. Your father left you exposed to predators by siring children with all and sundry and not leaving you protected. It was easy for Len to trap you.'

'And now the man I really love is from a lower class – you didn't add that, Wilf.'

'Because I don't think of people in classes. I judge them on merit. I don't know Cess, but from what I know *of* him, he's a very decent, hard-working fellow, and that puts him high in my estimation.'

Millie had the urge to hug Wilf, but still felt shy of him and couldn't think of him as anything other than her lawyer.

Wilf must have had the same thought. 'May I give you a hug as a father would a daughter, Millie?'

He stood and Millie went willingly into his arms. 'Two minds think alike, as I had just been longing to hug you.'

As she came out of his arms, a place where she'd felt safe, cared for and given an easy love with no strings, Wilf became something different to her. As he looked down at her he said, 'I will sort everything out for you, Millie. I want you to look on me as a father – one who cares for you and will do his best for you. Sit down, my dear, let us have a chat.'

'Thank you, Wilf. I so need someone like you. I know now that I have never had that dependability.'

'Not with your mama?'

'Mama didn't stand a chance, though she did make a stand over my schooling. Anyway, it is the present that I want to deal with.'

Wilf nodded.

As she took the winged chair opposite his, Millie was reminded of her father's office. She had made it her own in the end, but before that it too had a huge desk, two winged chairs and book-lined walls – although Father's books were for show, whereas the ones here were all legal-orientated and there was a stepladder to access the top shelves, showing that they were used and served a purpose.

'I want you to know that I am really happy to have you in my life, and as a father figure, Wilf. In my father's defence, he always did show me care and love, he just didn't realize that he should also have shown respect to me and Mama. I was shattered to find out who he really was. But I know that I can trust you – and entrust my mama to you – and that you will be an amazing grandfather to Daniel.'

'Thank you, my dear. I'm glad you have good memories of your father too. Hold on to them. You have had so much to contend with, as a consequence of his actions. You are a courageous young lady and stronger than you think. As for me, I would be delighted to have Daniel refer to me as Pops, as my own two grandchildren do, because he is a grandchild to me, in my eyes. By the way, your mama has invited my son and family over – did she tell you?'

'No, she didn't mention it, but it will be wonderful to meet Charles and Sally-Anne and the children again. There wasn't enough time at your and Mama's wedding, but we did chat and we had a laugh, because Charles kept calling me "Step" and his boys found it very funny, but they also

141

wanted it explaining to them – Charles got himself into a tangle trying to. Poor Sally-Anne, though, she was so apologetic that she hadn't been able to dig up any evidence to prove how Len had duped me.'

'It isn't often that daughter-in-law of mine fails, but yes, it will have to remain a very plausible theory forever that Len targeted you at a vulnerable time in your life.'

'I have come to terms with that. He won that round, but I don't want him to win in taking Daniel from me, or discrediting Cess, or holding Jim to ransom, or turfing Rene out of her shop . . . or in stopping me from running my father's factory again.'

'Hmm, you are asking a lot. But let's take one thing at a time. I want you to feel assured that Daniel is safe. I cannot see what possible argument Len could have that would stand up in court, although you will have to agree to him having access to his son.'

'I know. And that depresses me, but then I don't think he will bother much. His only interest in Daniel is to use him as a weapon against me. I won't let that happen, and I will fight him every step of the way if, in the future, he continues along that path.'

'I feel so much for you, Millie. But know that my son and I are on your side, and we are formidable when separate; but together, we are a real force to be reckoned with. However, there are limitations to everything. Now as for Jim, he is taking the right action, so we have to hope he comes up with something. And if he has a case, Len will have to release him. Then it will be up to Jim if he takes it any further. My advice would be to file all the evidence and carry on with his life.

'Cecil's case we are working on, so it's fingers crossed on

that one. I do think like you, though, that this is Len's doing. But how, and who helped him, isn't easy to solve.

'And Rene? Well, you say that Cecil was trying to get her settled elsewhere, with living accommodation for Elsie too?'

'Yes. It's the only solution. He wasn't successful, though. Well, he didn't have enough time really, or I am sure he could have sorted a place out.'

'I can look into that, if you would like me to. I have many property dealers and landlords amongst my friends and on the practice's client list.'

'Oh? Well, if there is anything going for sale, I would like to buy it. Rene is safe renting from me. I could give her a long lease.'

'Yes, and it would be a good investment for you. Enable you to start a new property portfolio. Now, as for your ambitions to buy back the jam factory, that is going to have to be done in the strictest secrecy. If Len gets wind of it, I think he'd rather burn the building to the ground. How many people know about your idea?'

'Oh, I don't know – Elsie and Jim, of course. They may have told Cess, but I haven't discussed it with him . . . Actually we shared the most profound moment of my son's birth, and of his loss and mine of dear Dot, but haven't ever had time together to talk.'

'Well, you have a lot of catching up to do. I know what it is like to love from afar and not be able to share what you most want to. Yours and Cecil's time will come, my dear . . . So, does anyone else know?'

'I may have spoken about it in Rose's presence, I can't remember. Mama, of course and, apart from you, I think that's it.'

'And you trust them all?'

For a reason she couldn't fathom, Millie suddenly had doubts about Rose. She remembered how, when Len called at the flat, Rose had seemed to be on familiar terms with him. Her remark just now about Elsie – not just what she said, but her tone in saying it. And was there a hint of something different in the way she had acted since arriving here, almost as if she had elevated herself. But then that was in their plan, wasn't it?

'Millie?'

'To answer truthfully, I trust Jim, Elsie, Cess and Rene, yes, emphatically. But there's something – a feeling . . . It's unreasonable and unfounded, but suddenly today I'm unsure about Rose.'

'Hmm, well, she is perfectly placed to give information to Len, especially if you say – or, rather, think – that you've discussed some things in front of her that could lead to problems. Does she know Len?'

'Yes, and that's strange too.' She told him about how they seemed familiar to one another, and yet they couldn't have met for many minutes at the wedding.

'Hmm. But then, if they had, you wouldn't be party to it, and you could have played into Len's hands by offering Rose the job as nanny. Let's hope not, but I suggest we lay a trap, so that you can find out if you are being unjust in your suspicions. Make sure Rose has some vital information, and then see if it is acted upon. A ruse. Leave it with me, I will come up with something.'

'Oh dear, I hope I am completely wrong, because I like Rose. I miss Ruby so much – my maid of many years. Rose seemed like a sort of carbon copy, and that helped. Though suddenly I don't look on her like that now. Rose can change herself to someone completely different. Ruby was Ruby, no matter what the situation or the people she had to deal with . . . I feel unsure now.'

'Well, just be careful about everything you say until we have satisfied ourselves one way or another.'

As Millie left his office, she felt as though she was living in a never-ending nightmare. Was she right to suspect Rose? Would Rose do such a thing as betray her? And if so, how did Len get her in his clutches?

Chapter Twelve

Millie and Elsie

It was three in the afternoon when Millie arrived at Rene's. Elsie was already there, having caught a train soon after their conversation that morning.

The two girls hugged and shed tears over Cess, before Rene intervened. 'Come on, you two, give a girl a chance, eh? All these tears and I haven't been able to greet Millie.'

Millie went into Rene's arms. The smell of her cheap lily-of-the-valley perfume gave her the feeling of this being a good place to be, as it gave her the warmth of the Rene she'd got to know through Elsie.

'It's lovely to see you, Millie, girl. And to be able to chat about what's happening. I can't say that I don't believe it all, because while you've that nasty bastard in your life, nothing's ever going to run smoothly for you, luv. You should divorce him, but even then I don't think he'll give up.'

'No. Especially when he finds out who I want to marry, and who will be bringing up our son – although I think he may have wind of that already, from what has happened.'

'Yes, this has his dirty brass-bands all over it. But Elsie told me your and Cess's news and, girl, I have to tell you that though the pair of you are courting trouble, I'm very happy about it. Cess is a lovely lad – a worker, ha, in all senses of the word!' Rene laughed loudly. 'Not yet twenty, married once and with a child, and now thinking of marriage again. You have to hand it to him. Though no one would have wished on him what happened to his Dot.'

Millie smiled. She felt the sting of Dot being mentioned, and the shame of stepping into her shoes so quickly after her death. But even though she acknowledged that the way Rene described Cess was less than kind, she knew Rene wouldn't mean it that way. Rene had a deep love for all of Elsie's family. She was like a mother to them.

'So, Rene, we'd better talk about how we're going to sort out your predicament. I'm sorry this has happened. It's all down to my foolishness in signing over my property portfolio, but we will sort it out.' She told them about the part of her conversation with Wilf that was relevant to Rene's situation. 'So, before you know it, I will be your landlady again, but everything must be kept an absolute secret . . . and I mean secret. Only us three, and Cess when he comes home, and of course Jim, are to know anything about my involvement. As far as anyone – anyone at all – knows, you will have found yourself another property, Rene.'

'Blimey, girl, it sounds like one of them spy stories in the penny dreadfuls. Me and your ma used to read them when we were kids, Elsie. So we can't share this with Dai, Gertrude or Rose?'

'No one. If Len finds out – and it seems, from what has happened to Cess, that he may have eyes everywhere – then we mustn't fully trust anyone, other than those I've mentioned.'

Elsie hadn't spoken, but now asked, 'Do you suspect

anyone in particular of passing on information, Millie, luv? Not Rose, surely, though . . . Oh God, Millie! What if it is her? Everything will be a disaster, as she knows everything . . . all there is to know about us. Even about Jim and his plan. And just when Jim has some hope of changing his situation.'

Millie had been worrying all morning about Jim's position and, if it was Rose betraying them, what that could mean for him.

'The good thing is that she can't know the most recent happenings, Elsie. You only found out yesterday. Is everything all right with him?'

Millie listened to the progress that Jim had made.

'That's good news, and hopeful for the future. If Len knows anything at all, then it can only be that Jim is working towards clearing his name, and not how far he has got.'

'Len may be biding his time. Letting my Jim carry on, for now. Knowing Len, he's probably thinking of getting his new factory up and running first. We can't wait to let that happen. We have to act, Millie. We have to rid ourselves of Rose.'

'I feel the same, but we have to be sure it is Rose who's betrayed us, and be careful of what we talk about in front of her. Wilf is thinking of a way of trapping her, so that we know conclusively. So for the time being, until we are sure, he doesn't want us to treat her any differently. Can you do that, Elsie?'

'I won't want to, but I can see that we have to make sure. But if it is Rose, why? And how has Len got at her?'

'I can only think of it happening at my wedding. Can you remember anything at all, Elsie?'

'No. Oh, Millie, I hate talking about it, mate – I feel me shame every time. All I can remember is Len being with me in the kitchen yard and Rose helping me. But I can't remember them being together. She took me to me bed and left me. But Len had left then to re-join the party, I'm sure of it.'

'Oh, it's all a mystery. I hope we're completely wrong.'

'You can both talk about it till the cows come home, girls, but until you know for sure, there ain't much point. Let's do as Millie says and not talk about anything in front of anyone. Now, Elsie, put the kettle on, mate, and let's have a cuppa. I want to hear all about little Cecil.'

'Well, the first thing, Rene, is that he's no longer called Cecil. You see . . .'

'I'll leave you to it and make the tea upstairs,' Elsie said. 'You can take a break, can't you, Rene, mate? Only I want to check on Bert. I left him unpacking.'

Rene said she could and they'd be up soon. 'With you gone, I can listen to Millie uninterrupted, for once.'

'Cheeky devil!'

Despite her worries, Elsie found herself laughing as she ran up the stairs. 'Where are you, buggerlugs?'

But then she didn't need to ask, as the strains of music came to her. She stood still. Her eyes filled with tears as Bert's angelic voice accompanied the hymn, so poignant, just as he and Jim had rehearsed it together. Bert had said he liked the hymn after it was sung at their mum's funeral, and it had made him feel a little better.

'*Abide with me: fast falls the eventide*
The darkness deepens; Lord, with me abide.'

Elsie took a deep breath and listened to Bert. Poor lost soul. The two men he looked up to, and loved most in the world, had gone from his life. Not forever, but to Bert a short time *was* forever.

Running up the next flight of stairs to the music room, she stood in the doorway. She could see Bert's face. Tears were rolling down his face, and yet he wasn't sobbing as his voice was steady.

Joining in with him, she walked slowly towards him. When he came to the end, he jumped off the stool and into her arms. 'Oh, buggerlugs, you've had to put up with so much for such a young boy. But it will all come right. And you will be the stronger for it. I were like you, as a nipper. I had me troubles, and found comfort in music. Our gran used to sing to us and, like I've told yer many a time, she taught me to play the piano. She'd be so proud of you, mate, especially as you're learning to read music. Gran used to say that was the proper way to play. And yet she was in demand for musical theatre as much as those who could read music.'

'I can't remember having a gran, Else.'

'No, you were very young when she died, but you've heard us all talking about her, haven't yer? Her music-hall days, when she played with all the greats. Her playing piano down the pub and everyone singing along.'

'Yes, and sometimes I feel I knew her. She sounds nice, Else.'

'She was. She did what she could for us.'

'Will everyone leave us, Else? You won't, will you?'

'No. I'll never leave you, buggerlugs. I promise. Now come and help me to make a cup of tea, as Rene and Millie will be with us in a mo and they'll want to know what I've been playing at.'

As they went downstairs together, Bert said, 'I remember the singalongs we used to have, Elsie, with Mum and all of us. Jimmy hadn't gone to heaven then, and he used to love them.'

To hear Bert mention their mum and his little brother – though Jimmy was actually big brother to Bert – cut into Elsie. But she kept her voice light.

'Yes, we had some good times as well as bad.'

'I like to remember the good. Like when Mum would have some money and take me to the matinee, or to buy a new pair of shoes.'

Bert didn't say that she would sell the shoes the next week, as she'd drunk and smoked the money away, but then Elsie didn't want to remember the bad bits about their mum, either. She loved her dearly and missed her so much.

They all crowded onto Elsie's balcony overlooking the streets of Bermondsey to have their cup of tea, with Bert sitting on Elsie's knee on a kitchen chair, and Millie and Rene having grabbed a chair each. Rene sighed. 'I love it here; it makes me heart feel safe amongst all the hustle and bustle.'

'We'll find somewhere just as good for you, Rene.'

'Ta, I know you will. But to be among yer own, you can't put a price on that.'

'Your new place will be. I'll make sure of that. There's quite a few empty properties about, and you've built up your clients and pleased them enough for them to follow you wherever you go.'

'Are you leaving, Rene?' The question sounded fearful.

'We all are, Bert. Hasn't Elsie told yer?'

Elsie closed her eyes. She should have warned Rene to leave it to her to tell Bert.

Bert looked up at her. 'Will Jim and Cess know where we are, Else?'

'Of course they will. But, Bert, you have to keep it our secret that we saw Jim yesterday. No telling anyone – not Dai, not Rose, no one. Promise me, Bert.'

'Why?'

'Never mind why, in this instance. I just want you to do as I ask yer, mate. I never ask favours of yer, do I?'

Bert shook his head.

'Well, I'm asking one of you now. It's important not to tell anyone that you saw Jim.'

'All right, Elsie, I won't. I don't want to be hurt or have something bad happen to you.'

'Hurt? Something bad happening to me? What're you talking about, Bert, mate?'

'Rose said that if I told a secret, something bad would happen to you and I'd be hurt.'

'Oh?' Seeing Bert's frightened look, Elsie shot a quick glance at Millie, who looked just as puzzled as she felt.

'No one can hurt you, Bert, or me. You should always tell me everything.' She giggled then, so as not to upset him further. 'Even if you find out what Jim's got for me when it's me birthday.'

Bert giggled. 'No. I always keep that a secret. I can never tell you that. Jim says it will spoil it for you. Anyway it's not your birthday for ages, and Jim hasn't got you anything yet.'

'Ha, there's no fooling you. But never keep any other secrets from me, Bert. I won't let anyone hurt you. What did Rose ask you not to tell me, eh? That she's stolen the Crown Jewels or something.'

Elsie was desperate not to frighten her little brother or make him feel that he'd done something wrong.

'No. She's Len's girlfr—' Bert suddenly looked in Millie's direction and clammed up.

Millie helped him relax again. She laughed, a laugh that Elsie knew held the same jangled nerves as she was feeling.

'Len has a lot of girlfriends – is that what you were going to say, Bert? Don't worry. I know all about them.'

'You know about Ròse?'

'Mmm. A bit. You tell me what you know and I'll tell you what I know.'

Elsie was grateful to Millie for picking up on her wanting to keep this light-hearted for Bert.

'When Elsie went out with Cess, I didn't know she'd gone, as I was asleep. But I woke and I came through to your bedroom. You were fast asleep, Millie, and Rose was on the telephone. She was whispering. I heard her say, "Promise me, Len, you won't let me down. I can't go on much longer. Tell me I'm not doing this for nowt." I didn't know what "nowt" meant, so I asked her when she came off the telephone. She had tears running down her face, but she wasn't crying. She cuddled me. She told me never to say anything to anyone about what I'd heard. It was a secret and if I did, bad things would happen to you and I would be hurt.'

'Well, sometimes bad things can happen, but not to you, mate, and not to me. But there are consequences for some people. Jim, for instance. If you tell anyone you saw Jim, then he could be in trouble. But just telling us what you heard Rose say in a telephone conversation, no. We can't get hurt then, mate. So if you heard anything else, we should know, right?'

'Well, the only other thing I heard her say was that Cess loved Millie. But we knew that, didn't we? We all love Millie.'

Millie smiled and reached out for Bert, tickling his tummy. 'And I love you, Bert, and I love Elsie and Cess, and Rene.'

Rene pushed Millie on the shoulder. 'Awe, blimey – ta, mate. You ain't so bad yerself.'

Millie laughed at Rene. But again her laugh wasn't an easy one.

Rene kept up the charade. 'And I love yer, Bert, and Elsie and Cess and Millie.'

Bert was laughing at them both. 'And I love yer all, and all the world. All creatures great and small, like in the hymn . . . Only I don't love worms. I hate worms.'

Elsie burst out laughing and hugged him to her. 'You're a card, buggerlugs. Give me a kiss.'

Bert's arms came round her neck and his lips planted a sloppy kiss on her cheek. For a moment Elsie's world seemed well again. But it was short-lived as she thought about Rose's terrible betrayal, although it might be that she was a victim of the evil Len.

'Well, buggerlugs, go upstairs and practise some more. I love to hear you play, and I want Rene and Millie to hear yer. Only something bright and cheerful.'

Always keen to play the piano, Bert scampered off.

Millie spoke first. 'What shall we do?'

'Bleedin' kill her!'

'No, Rene, let's think about it. She ain't the first to be taken in by Len. Me and Millie have been, and Jim too. This is Len's fault. He must have some sort of a hold on Rose.'

'Elsie, luv, you always look for the good in everybody. But I'm bleedin' telling yer, darlin', a lot haven't got an ounce of it in their bleedin' body. Treat people as if they're bad first, and then if the good surfaces, you're a winner. Trust no one other than your own and, even then, you might get bleedin' let down.'

Elsie thought it was this attitude that had probably led Rene down the wrong paths she'd travelled, but she didn't say so. Maybe her own attitude had led her on to her path of often being let down, but she'd rather give everyone the benefit of the doubt, even Rose.

'Maybe we can turn this knowledge against Len. I mean, use Rose to lead him up a false path that ultimately traps him.'

'Blimey, how're you going to do that, Millie, luv?'

'I don't know, but Wilf might. Let's think about it for a while.'

The strains of 'By the Light of the Silvery Moon' came from upstairs – a song that Elsie had taught Bert, much to Jim's annoyance, as he wanted Bert to play to music notes only, and not in the honky-tonk way she did, even though he loved it when she played and they had a sing-song.

Rene began to sing. Suddenly Elsie found that she wanted to too. Millie giggled at them, but after a couple of lines she was singing her heart out with them. A man's voice from street level joined in. Elsie looked down and saw him take a woman with him and twirl her around; the woman hit him with her handbag, but then another man joined in the song. A small crowd gathered. Some of them linked arms and swayed as they sang. Joy entered Elsie. Len could take a lot from her, but he could never take this – her cockney heritage.

Cheers went up as the song finished. The first man who'd joined in cupped his hands and shouted up to them, 'Oi, that made me day, mate. Ta for that.'

Elsie leaned over and waved to him. The crowd all waved back and went on their way.

'That was wonderful, Elsie. For a moment in time we brought happiness to the daily lives of people we don't even know, and whose lives are probably humdrum.'

'Ha, Millie, luv, no bleedin' cockney has a humdrum life – poor maybe, but they've got spirit and a sense of looking out for one another. If they ain't fightin', they're bleedin' singin' or rollin' about drunk, but they're the salt of the earth, luv, and yer won't go far wrong with us.'

Millie smiled, but Elsie latched on to Rene's words. She was a cockney born and bred, and at times she'd let that special spirit of the cockneys die within her. But Elsie could feel it strongly today, and she'd use it to get them all through this latest crisis, which the hateful Len had put them into. He wouldn't win. Not with the might of her cockney spirit to fight him, he wouldn't.

Chapter Thirteen

Elsie

In the end, Millie and Rene had agreed with Elsie that Rose could be just as much a victim of Len as they themselves, and had decided that Elsie should try to talk to her – and maybe persuade her to help them.

Their plan was that Millie was to ring when Rose had taken Daniel out for a walk. Elsie, on the pretence of being on her way to visit Millie, was to bump into Rose and try to talk to her and hopefully get her onside.

It had all seemed so easy when they talked about it, but as Elsie sat on the bus travelling to Knightsbridge she was attacked by doubts. *What if I miss Rose? What if I do meet her and she turns nasty, and that leads her to telling Len about Jim's plans?* A shiver zinged through Elsie's body.

When the bus pulled up halfway down Herbert Crescent, Elsie's legs were shaking as she alighted. Part of her was praying that if she crossed over the green to Millie's house, she would meet Rose out with Daniel, as that was their usual route. And yet part of her wanted Rose to have returned home already, so that this ordeal was removed from her shoulders.

With the shade of the trees as she entered Hans Place Gardens, Elsie felt the chill of the day, which was sunny and yet cloudy. There was only warmth to be had in the direct sunlight. Everything around her looked beautiful, as always happened in the heart of London when a green patch was found, and trees instead of buildings broke the landscape.

Some of Elsie's nerves calmed as she breathed deeply of the fresher air that the trees provided and the peace they brought, as they blocked out the hustle and bustle of the streets. With the increasing number of motorized vehicles belching out stinking fumes, added to the stench of the dollops of horse dung and the constant noise of engines peeping their horns to warn horses and pedestrians, plus horses' hooves clip-clopping along and the carriage wheels grinding over the cobbles, navigating the streets gave her a headache these days.

After a few minutes a group of nannies appeared, pushing large prams. Their uniforms – cloaks flowing behind them, berets holding their hair neat, and long grey frocks showing beneath their cloaks – distinguished them. Rose was with them. Elsie waved. Rose looked surprised, but broke away from the group and came towards her.

As they reached one another the hug they gave each other was spontaneous because, despite everything, Elsie held a lot of affection for Rose.

'Elsie! It's good to see you. Millie said you were coming and might take the route across the green. I thought she might be mistaken, as there's a bus stop closer to the house than the one in Herbert Crescent.'

'I know, but it's rare to get a chance of a bit of greenery and to breathe in the fresh air that the trees give this patch, so I thought I'd come this way when I visited . . . And to tell the truth, I needed to get the courage to go and knock on the door of such a grand place.'

'Oh, I thought you lived in one like this with Millie when I met you?'

'No, it was big and posh, but nothing on the scale that she lives in now. And the area! I almost feel like a trespasser. It ain't known for many cockneys to come up to Knightsbridge. Only the odd barrow-boy, and they're well loved and accepted.'

'Ha, you should learn to talk like me. I went to elocution lessons. No one can tell what background you are from, and they don't even care. As long as you speak the King's English, you're acceptable.'

'You do sound funny. Not like you at all. Don't you drop it for mates?'

'No, once I do that, I let myself down, so I keep to it.'

'Well, you're still Rose, me friend, and oh, I've missed you. It's funny, but from the moment you looked after me at Ruby's wedding, I felt close to you.'

Rose looked down at her hands.

'I know about you and Len, luv.'

This brought Rose's head up with a jolt. Her gasp was audible. She stared at Elsie, her eyes showing her fear. 'I – I, eeh, Elsie. What have I done?'

'Nothing that you can't undo. And you going back into your northern accent brought the real Rose to me – the Rose I love. Did something happen that day, Rose? Did Len get you into his clutches somehow?'

'I love him, Elsie. I can't help meself. I know he ain't a nice person – he's been rotten to me at times – but I believe his promises. Can you understand that? I mean, well, you and Jim, you'd do owt to help Jim, wouldn't you?'

'I would. And yes, I understand.' Although Elsie said this, she didn't really, because she knew that if Jim asked her to hurt others just to help him to gain what he wanted, she wouldn't do it. 'But I still don't get why you've done what yer have. What has Len promised you that has turned a lovely girl like you into someone who can cause such pain?'

A tear plopped onto Rose's cheek. 'I – I'm sorry. I – I couldn't help it. I had naw choice. I didn't knaw the lengths he'd go to. I thought he'd warn Cess off, not make me do what I did.'

'What threat did he have over you, Rose?'

'He . . . I – I let him . . . Oh, Elsie, I'm so ashamed.'

Elsie took her hand. 'Don't be. Just tell me everything, and I promise you, me and Millie will make it all right for you. We need your help, Rose. But that ain't the reason for us helping you. We're both victims of Len too. And when Bert told us the secret you had told him to keep, we both had reservations at first, because of the way you threatened him with harm.'

'I'm sorry, Elsie. I'm so sorry. I love little Bert and would never hurt him. Eeh, I've lived me life in fear these last months.'

Elsie still held Rose's hands. She could feel them trembling in hers. 'I understand that, Rose, and this is what I'm trying to say, mate. Me and Millie understand how Len can get you into his clutches. He took advantage of the feeling that I stupidly had for him. I fell instantly in love with him – well, what I thought was love. But he ended up raping me, Rose. And I fear he may do that again. He's evil, but if we all work together against him, we can beat him. We *can*.'

'I never told him owt about Jim, Elsie, I promise you. I never would've hurt you.'

'But Cess and Millie . . . Oh, Rose. How did yer do it? How could you? Why? There must be more than yer loving him. I wouldn't do what yer've done, for Jim. I wouldn't. Has Len promised to marry yer or something?'

'He has. I – I'm desperate, Elsie.'

Elsie sighed. Rose was obviously really frightened of something, and she knew it wasn't just Len's lies about marrying her that was driving her. 'Tell me, Rose. Tell me everything.'

'It started after I put you to bed that day at Ruby's wedding. I went back into the yard to get the cup I'd given you your tea in. I could smell cigar smoke. Before I could think where it was coming from, the gate swung open and Len stood there.' Rose trembled. 'He threatened me with losing me job if I said owt to anyone about what I'd seen – you knaw, the way he'd been with you. I had me ma to care for at the time. I – I couldn't lose me job. I begged him, and promised him faithfully I'd not tell a soul. He said if I did, he'd see to it that I didn't ever get another job.'

'But you said you gave in to him – you let him . . . Did he try it on with you then, in the yard?'

'Naw, it were later that night. Some of the guests took drinks into the garden and sat around the pond with them. I were sent out to collect the glasses at the end of the party. Len was walking around, it was late and there was only the two of us, and the house was quiet. He . . .'

'I see, well, you don't have to give me the details, mate. I know what he's like.'

'But I – I found I were having a babby after it, Elsie . . .'

Her name came out on a sob. Shocked at hearing this, but with the real reason for Rose's behaviour now becoming clear, Elsie put her arm around Rose. 'Oh, Rose, luv. That swine. What happened to your baby?'

'I went off work, when I showed. I used the excuse that I'd to look after me ma. Len sent me some money, as long as I promised to keep quiet. Me ma died before me babby were born, but she knew . . . Oh, Elsie, the shame finished her off.'

Elsie patted Rose's back, lost for words.

'I don't knaw how no one guessed, but I didn't get very big and I bandaged meself as tightly as I could. Ruby guessed a bit of it, as she said at me ma's funeral that I'd put on weight, but that I'd soon lose it when I got back to work, as me job was still open for me. I was near me time then, and Len had got someone to book me into a convent. So I told Ruby that I had to go away to an aunt who couldn't make it to the funeral, but needed to see me. I told her I needed the break, and then would come back to work.'

'Oh, Rose, I'm so sorry.'

The hug they went into gave Elsie full forgiveness of Rose. Her own tears flowed at this latest unfolding. She longed to have a child herself, and so to hear of a woman being forced to give hers away broke her heart. 'We'll sort this all out – I mean, well, I can't give you your baby back, Rose, and that breaks me heart, but we can help you.'

'How?'

'I'm not sure yet, I still need to understand it all. Tell me, Rose, how – after all of this happening – did you still want to do Len's bidding? And how you can still love him?'

'For me babby, Elsie. I did it for me babby. And the promises. I believed Len. You see, the convent hadn't any families to send me little son to – I named him Ronnie, after me late da; he'll be nearly five months old now. Anyroad, Len said he'd find someone to take him and then, one day, we'd marry and get him back, as he was his heir. But then he married Millie, as planned. He said it was just a temporary thing and that our time would come.'

'Did you see him then? Did he visit?'

'Yes, he did come up to see me. He said he'd told Millie he was on a business trip to his father's bank, and a couple of times he was. We . . . well, we had a good relationship. I fell deeply in love with him. He visited our son, but would never let me do so, or tell me where he was, because he said I wouldn't be able to stop meself from going to him. I loved Len then, Elsie . . . but he stopped coming. I would phone him and he began to threaten me with never seeing me son again. I never stopped loving him, and I did all he asked – not because of the love I had for him, but because I want me son back. The pain of perhaps never seeing him again is so great, Elsie, that I'd do owt. No matter what it is. So, please don't ask me to do owt that would threaten that.'

Elsie felt defeated, but tried one more tack. 'If you could tell me how he did what he did to Cess, that would be enough, Rose. For now it would. Millie will know how to untangle you from all of this without you losing your baby, I'm sure of it. She has Wilf, and he can call on private investigators. They could find your son before Len needs to know that you're not going to help him any more.'

'I don't knaw how we can keep Len from knowing that I helped you. You see . . . well, I had to play a big part. He engaged a private investigator from Southampton, who was able to set up a bribe for him. The bribe went to the top bloke and he arranged everything that happened. Len even had to pay the prostitutes. But, you see, I – I, eeh, Elsie, I had to do the paying. I have a bank account that Len paid money into when I looked after me ma. He put the money for the prostitutes into it, and I had to pass it on to them. I did it when I went out on me walks.'

'Rose, you didn't have any choice. But you do now. If you're asked to testify, please choose to do so.'

'But me babby . . .'

'Is it just your baby, cos I've told you, we will find him and get him back for you. Or . . .'

'Aye, Elsie, it is just me babby. I don't love Len any more. I thought I did, right up until I started to tell you everything. Doing so has opened me eyes. I've been blind, Elsie.'

'You'll get over him. I did. I'm surprised you loved him this long.'

'I don't think I have, really. But he held the key to getting me babby back. You see, I . . . well, when I met Dai I was attracted to him, and that made me think about me feelings for Len. I think I got confused, as I found meself thinking of ways that I could bump into Dai. I don't seem to be able to get him out of me mind. Eeh, I don't knaw. I've messed everything up, Elsie.'

'You have, luv, and it's understandable. Yer even reverting back to you, and then to the posher you – you don't know where yer are, mate, but then you've been battling with a lot.'

'Ta, Elsie. I feel a lot better, but for me shame, because facing it all has shown me just what I've done. And any chance I had with Dai will be gone, when he hears about it all.'

'We'll see. Dai's a decent bloke. He needs time, as it's only just over a year since he lost his wife and son.'

'I can give him that. To be truthful, I'm not ready, either. All I can think of is having me son. But how I'm to look after him, or keep him out of the clutches of Len, I don't knaw.'

'We'll work it through as it happens. But, Rose, promise

me one thing: promise me that you'll stay *you*. The "you" that me and Millie love – the northern lass. Millie needs that. She so misses Ruby. You filled that gap for her. Millie is a strong person, but she was never meant to go through what she has. She needs people around her who love her, and she'll return that love threefold.'

'I knaw. And I have felt it, and it increased me guilt.'

'No more guilt. You're a mother, and what you did any mother would do. Millie will help you get your son back, but you must help her to keep hers. Talking in a posh voice ain't going to do that. Your loyalty to her will.'

'Ta, Elsie. Eeh, come here, lass. You've lifted a great burden off me shoulders, and the love you've talked of, I already feel it for you. Hurting you hurt me more than owt I've done in me life.'

'Well, you're forgiven. Come on, let's get back to Millie and talk all this through with her. Then we need to let Wilf know all the information, as he's gone down to Southampton to defend Cess when he faces the magistrates' court today.'

'Eeh, we're not too late, are we?'

'No. Cess might get remanded for sentencing at the Crown Court, and the information we have isn't in time to stop that. Wilf will need time to sort it all out and make his case. He warned Millie about that, as she told me when she rang me to say that nothing had delayed you from taking your regular morning walk, so I could waylay you.'

'Oh, so you didn't just happen to come this way, then?'

'No. We had to plan it all.'

'Eeh, I'm glad you did. I was of a mind to avoid you as much as I could, as I felt terrible about what I'd done.'

'Well, we've cleared the air now. Anyway, Wilf said that if Cess pleads not guilty, they may elect for him to be tried by jury, and if that's granted, Wilf will ask for bail and propose that Cess resides with him until the Crown Court case.'

Rose gasped at this. 'Eeh, how am I to face him?'

'Don't worry about Cess. He'll understand and he'll be only too glad to see yer get your son back. He'll think it all worth it, for that. He's a family man and must be missing his little Kitty like mad. I am too, and Bert is, but we've had no time to go and see her yet.'

'I've done the same to him, though. I've taken him from his babby and . . . Eeh, Elsie, how am I going to live with meself? How will Millie feel about me, and what will her ma think? I loved working for her ma when I was her maid, and she's always been kindness itself to me. She kept me job open all that while, and didn't have an inkling what the real reason was for me being absent – or how I was going behind her daughter's back, having an affair with Len.'

'Look, luv, none of it will be as bad as yer imagining, I promise yer. They will all understand. They will. Come on. Let's get back, and then you'll see.'

When they stood up, Elsie asked if she could push the pram. She bent over it and pulled down the blanket that had almost completely covered Daniel. His little face looked so peaceful. What would it feel like to have that kind of peace?

As they walked, another question came to her. What would it feel like to have a baby of her own? *Oh, how I long for that to happen.* But she knew it hadn't happened yet, as this morning she'd awoken to find that she'd made a mess in her bed. She'd shed a few tears and then got on with things. *But being brave doesn't always help me. Please God, send me and Jim a baby to love. We deserve that, don't we?*

Chapter Fourteen

Millie and Cess

Millie was shocked to the core as she listened to Elsie and Rose.

'I'm sorry, Millie, I am – I'm sorry to the heart of me.'

'Oh, Rose.'

Millie felt torn in two as she looked over at Rose, who sat in a chair opposite where she and Elsie were sitting on the couch. The room they were in was a small cosy room with a deep-red carpet. The sofa and chair were beige with a leaf pattern woven through, of the same colour. This and the bureau and small occasional table had been bought by Mama especially for the room's purpose, as she intended it to be used for her weekly meetings with the housekeeper.

Part of Millie hated Rose for what she'd done, but a bigger part of her felt pity for what Rose had been through. 'You can put this right, Rose. You can testify for Cess.'

'But me babby!'

'Wilf will find him, I'm sure of that. And before you have to testify, as he told me that waiting for a Crown Court hearing can take up to six months.'

'But, Millie, have you thought on? In all that time Cess

will be here, with you. That'll incense Len. God knaws what he'll do, and then if he sees that I have me babby back . . .'

'Yes, Wilf was worried that having Cess here would jeopardize my case. Oh, it's all such a mess.'

Rose burst into tears. 'Eeh, what have I done? I should have told you the truth in the beginning.'

Elsie made as if to jump up and go to her, but Millie stopped her and went to Rose herself. Holding Rose, she told her that they couldn't undo what was done, only try to deal with it, and that she understood. 'Look, Wilf's ringing before the court case, Rose, as I have already told him about your involvement. He also knew about the plan that we had, to help you open up to us. So he might have more information about what will happen to Cess. Though he might not be able to use anything we tell him today, as investigations would have to happen and evidence be gathered, besides informing the prosecution. But he could start any enquiries that are necessary while he's still down there, which will help him prepare a defence or even get the charges dropped.'

In Southampton the prosecution was outlining the police case against Cess.

To anyone's ears, Cess knew that what they said marked him as a guilty man. Fear gripped him. His hands were cold and yet damp with sweat, and his body trembled.

Wilf, who'd slipped onto the bench next to him, had told him not to worry, saying that he had a few things in place, and how everything could change very quickly.

Cess couldn't take his eyes off the magistrate – a small man, who sat upright, as if trying to make himself taller. Cess thought he looked full of his own importance, and wondered if he was a fair man or wouldn't really listen to the facts and had already made up his mind to send the case to Crown Court, for trial by jury. Something that Wilf had said might happen.

They hadn't had much time together, as Wilf had wanted to get a few things done, but had told Cess that everything was all right at home, and that Dai had been informed of what had happened and would tell Gertie. He had no news of how Kitty was, although this Cess had wanted to know more than anything. *Me little darlin', how long will it be before I see you again?*

As voices droned on around him, Cess pictured his Kitty and felt the pity of her never knowing Dot. He sighed, but then would Dot ever have been well enough to take care of their baby? He thought of Kitty's lovely red hair, so like Elsie's and his late mum's. *If I can't come home, Aunty Elsie will look out for you, me little darlin', and you have Gertie. Gertie loves you.* Tears prickled his eyes.

Wilf's nudging him and saying 'Ah, now we have it' brought Cess back to the present, and he registered that the proceedings had been interrupted. Wilf was smiling as he watched a hasty consultation going on between a court usher and the prosecution's solicitor.

'What's happening, Wilf?'

'Any minute now you will know, young man. I couldn't say anything, but new evidence came in, and a certain witness has probably been instructed to change her lies to the truth. Heads will roll over this. I wonder if the money they were offered will seem worth it then.'

Cess was mystified, but couldn't delve deeper as Wilf hushed him.

The magistrate called the court to order and then adjourned for a recess while he consulted the prosecution and the defence. Before he left him, Wilf told Cess to relax because, if he wasn't mistaken, his ordeal was about to end.

Cess couldn't believe it, nor could he imagine what had happened to change everything, but although he was in the dark about how and why, his heart raced with hope and joy.

When the prosecution solicitor and Wilf returned, Wilf had a smile on his face. Cess felt the trickle of hope inside him soar.

The magistrate followed behind within seconds, giving no time for him to ask questions of Wilf. Everyone stood, then sat as the court clerk bade them to. The magistrate spoke in a grave voice, but to Cess what he said sounded like music. 'Stand up, please, Mr Makin.'

Cess stood. His stomach churned as the possibilities went through his head. Had Wilf persuaded the prostitute to change her story? Had the prosecution been persuaded it was word against word? He didn't have long to wait.

'This case is dismissed. All charges are withdrawn. No criminal record will be recorded against your name, Mr Makin. Your lawyer, whom you have a lot to thank for, will give you the full details. You are free to go.'

Cess felt himself grinning and yet his eyes filled with unshed tears. 'Thank you, Your Honour.'

The magistrate nodded, smiled, then rose. Before leaving he bowed to Wilf. 'My Learned Friend, may I take this opportunity to say what an honour it has been to have you in my court. It has never happened before that this court is graced by the presence of such an eminent lawyer.'

'Thank you, Your Worship, it has been my pleasure.'

As the magistrate bowed again, the clerk called out, 'Court dismissed.'

With this announcement there was a moment of reverence,

as all stood until the magistrate left the room, but almost immediately a hub of noise rose up as local reporters demanded to know what had happened, and why.

The prosecution just told them there was no case to answer. Wilf, though, whetted their appetite and set up a curiosity in Cess as he said, 'In due course a much bigger case will result from what has come to light today. As we speak, I suspect that respected members of your local police force are clearing their desks. I can't tell you any more, except to say that my client was framed.'

This set up a frenzy of questions, but Wilf held up his hand and silenced them.

'Make way for my client, please. He has suffered a terrible injustice, and now wants to get back to his family.'

Once outside, Cess couldn't remember when a gulp of fresh air had felt as good as at this moment.

'Follow me, Cess, my car is just along here, but there is also a nice little tearoom. I think a cup of tea is in order, then I'll drop you off by your car and you can go home.'

Cess couldn't speak, he just did as Wilf bade him to.

The tea scalded his mouth, but tasted like nectar, as did the cream bun that Wilf bought for him.

'Now, Cess, I have a lot to tell you. I took a gamble with some information that Elsie and Millie found out . . .'

As Cess listened to what had come to light, he felt anger and then relief, mixed with love – Elsie and Millie had done all this for him.

His feelings for Rose were ones of hate, until Wilf explained her reasons, and then he understood. He knew that if anyone threatened to take his little Kitty from him, he would commit any vile act to stop it happening.

'Now, the upshot is that I gambled on the information

being enough to set things in motion, and it did. For me, it was a digression from the way I intended to work, as I had thought to let the case go to the Crown Court and then try for bail, but the conditions I was going to put in place suddenly seemed ludicrous, as they would jeopardize Millie's case to keep her child. And so, I took the bull by the horns and went to the chief constable with what I knew. Suspensions of duty were put in place with immediate effect, and an order was given to bring the prostitute in for questioning. And, if everything stacked up, bearing in mind that we had a witness in Rose, then the court would be informed. However, that's not the end of it. The joyful news is that Len is to be arrested and questioned over his involvement, and if all those who took part give evidence, he will be charged with perverting the course of justice – a charge that carries a prison sentence.'

This was the best news Cess had ever heard. 'So Millie will be free of him at last. But what about Rose?'

'Rose is a victim, and I'm sure there is enough evidence to show that she was being blackmailed into doing Len's dirty work. I can't say that she will get off scot-free, but she may be assigned to a probation officer, who will help her to make responsible decisions and assert her own rights. Something of that nature. The service is very new, but it's a much-needed one and already does valuable work.'

Cess had heard of the service, but didn't know much about it. He knew there was shame attached to being assigned an officer, and felt sorry that might be Rose's plight. 'Is there anything I can do to stop that? I mean, if I don't press charges?'

'No, Cess, it won't be up to you. Perverting the course of justice is a very serious offence, and Rose aided and abetted that. I know there are many mitigating circumstances, but I don't think they will let her off from receiving a punishment, only lessen her chances of that being a prison sentence. You see, the case will be very high-profile, and justice has to be seen to be done. A high-ranking officer is involved, as is Len, a respected banker – who, I might add, has a double-barrelled gun at his head, as not only did he commit a crime against you, but he was in the process of doing so against Millie too. Although the custody case hasn't got as far as an actual hearing, papers have been filed. It will be easy to prove that Len was trying to discredit Millie's claim to her child.'

'I hope he rots in jail. Look what he's done to Jim too.'

'Yes, well, I might use that and get Jim released from Len's accusations – aided by his own work in finding a witness. It will be off the record of course, but Len won't know that. I intend to tell him that unless he drops all that he has put in place regarding the fraud against Jim, I will see that it too is taken into consideration. After all, ultimately Len was in the throes of committing a further act of perverting the course of justice by staging a crime and setting up another man to pay for it.'

Cess laughed out loud. He felt like cheering and clapping. 'We've got him! The mighty Len has fallen. He set out a long while ago to hurt Millie – I'm convinced of it. Oh, I wish me little darlin' could get back all he took from her.'

Wilf coughed, and Cess realized what he'd said. He coloured, but then thought, no, the world had to know how he and Millie felt, and he wasn't going to hide it. They loved each other, and everyone had to accept that. *Oh, Millie, Millie, it's over, but for you and me, me darlin', it's only just beginning.*

'Well, we will certainly work on your "little darlin'" getting everything back.' Wilf chuckled, but Cess laughed out loud once more to hear Wilf trying to get his posh tongue around a cockney saying.

'My son will have a few tricks up his sleeve, with what has come to light. He can use blackmail, but in a kind of bending-the-law – not breaking it – way. He can bluff that we have evidence of Len targeting Millie and duping her out of her fortune. He can hint that he will include that in the case against Len. I and Abigail – Millie's mother – can testify to Len's father vowing to have his revenge against her, and I was present when he threatened the same on Richard, Millie's late father, too. I believe that after Richard's death, that need to get even became focused on both Abigail and Millie.'

'Blimey, the world I come from is full of rogues who are out to make a quick shilling, but none of them would go this far! And to think I always respected the toffs.'

'Oh, there's a lot that goes on under the guise of "big business", most of it corrupt. But as far as Millie is concerned, and her rightful ownership of everything her father left her, I think we can safely say it will all come back to her. And I hope that you will make her very happy. And above all, will respect her and her rights. Though I think you will, from what I know of you, Cess.'

'Thanks, I appreciate that, Wilf. Yes, if Millie will do me the honour of marrying me, I will vow to her that she will be a free spirit, to follow whatever path she wants to. I love Millie very much. But yer must be wondering . . . Well, you must know about me and Dot?'

'Yes. It's tragic. I am sorry for what you both went through. But I understand how anyone can love twice, as it happened to me. Not quite so quickly, but then I know it would have done, if I had met Abigail sooner, as I fell for her on sight.

You're lucky. I had to wait years to marry the woman of my dreams.'

Cess felt a great sense of relief at this conversation. He felt for the first time that he wasn't a bad person or disloyal. Falling in love with Millie just happened. He couldn't help it happening when it did.

'It wasn't like that for me. I already loved Dot when I met Millie, and Dot was the only girl for me since we'd been nippers . . . I know this may sound strange, but it seems sometimes as if we lived a lifetime in the short time we had together as a couple. We went through so much. Dot wasn't well for a long time. But I feel at peace in my mind that I did all I could for her, and gave her what happiness I could. I didn't want it to end, but now that it has, I feel I am being given a second chance, and that Dot's with me – cheering me on even.'

'That's very moving, Cess, and I'm happy for you. Now I think we should take you to your car and you can get your journey home under way.' As Cess shook Wilf's hand, Wilf said, 'I'm very happy, Cess. I couldn't have asked for a better outcome. I hope you will find it in your heart to forgive Rose. Now I must get on my way too. I need to hand all this over to my son and then, hopefully, I will soon be able get on with my retirement!'

Cess went straight to his home and was greeted by fourteen-month-old Kitty running into his arms. Her excited call of 'Dada' lasted until she was in his arms and then changed to 'Berdie?', which he knew was her name for Bert.

'Ha, you *will* see Bert, me darlin'. We'll go there now and see him when he comes in from school. Have you been a good girl? Gawd, I've missed you. Daddy loves yer very much.' He kissed her on the cheek.

Kitty nodded. 'Me good, Dadda.'

'Well, we'll see what Gertie has to say.'

Gertie had followed behind Kitty. Cess had seen the tears in her eyes. 'I'm all right, Gertie, luv. A bit of an ordeal, but worth going through for the outcome. Where's Dai? I see his van's out the front.'

'He's not well. He didn't go to work. He's full of cold and said he couldn't face standing around outside today.'

This concerned Cess, as he'd never known Dai not to go to his market stall.

'I'll go up and see him. Stay with Gertie, me darlin'.'

Kitty's bottom lip quivered, but Gertie, Cess's saviour in so many ways, whisked her away. 'We have to get you ready, duckie – you're going to see your Berdie.'

So many times, since meeting Gertie in Carlton Hayes mental institution in Leicestershire, Cecil had asked himself what he would have done without her, or without hearing her Midlands tone punctuated by 'me duck' or 'duckie'. He loved her like a mother. She'd left the hospital to care for Dot during and through her breakdown and had stayed with him after Dot's death, to care for Kitty.

Not that he had lived then in such a grand house as this one on Albany Road, overlooking Burgess Park. Instead he had shared Elsie's flat, and what was now her music room had been his and Kitty's bedroom. Now he was on his feet, having used the grant Millie had made over to Dot, which was then left to him, plus the money he'd saved, to start up a market-trader business with Dai.

A bay-windowed semi-detached, the house wasn't huge, but compared to the tenements on Long Lane where he'd been brought up, and the flat that he and Dot had shared in Leicester, it was a palace, with its three bedrooms and inside bathroom – the latter a real luxury to him.

Knocking on Dai's door, he was met with a nasal-sounding 'Come in.'

Dai shot up from lying on his bed. 'Cess! You're back! What happened? Oh, Cess, I'm so glad to see you. I couldn't bear to think of you going to prison.'

'How are you, Dai? You look a bit rough, mate.'

'I feel it. I seem to have picked up a cold. Never once had one when I lived in Barmouth.'

'Well, that's the price of living among a lot of people and dealing with them every day. As for me, I've a lot to tell you, and some of it affects you – well, it does if you're serious about being sweet on Rose.'

'Oh? Well, I do like her, but how can what happened to you affect that in any way?'

Cess told him what had occurred and the outcome. Dai didn't interrupt, but his expression showed many emotions as Rose's story unfolded. Cess finished with the possible outcome for Len.

'Well, that's good news at least. I've longed for a good while for you all to be rid of him.'

Cess frowned. Dai hadn't mentioned Rose. 'Yer have to feel sorry for poor Rose in all of this too, mate. For a girl to find herself pregnant, and to be made promises that weren't kept and then lose her baby must have been terrible. And yet all anyone saw was her kind and caring side. Anyway, Wilf will put all his resources into finding her child.'

Dai gave a massive sneeze and shivered. 'That in itself is a worry to me, Cess. Is it a genuine person we're dealing with? It seems she can put on any persona she wants to, as no one ever suspected anything amiss. I know I didn't.'

'Blimey, I think you've got a temperature, mate, and it's messing with your thinking. Stay in bed for today. Can I get you anything? I've to go to Elsie's in a mo, but I can see to what you need before I do.'

'No, I'm all right, ta. Gertie brought me some water a while ago, and I'm not hungry. Just tell Millie not to trust Rose fully yet.'

'I will.' But as he said this, Cess thought it a shame that Dai had taken this stance, for he'd thought there was a future for him and Rose.

Before he left the house, Cess telephoned Wilf's house. It seemed an age until he heard Millie's voice. As soon as he did, he was filled with happiness at her joyful cry of, 'Cess. Oh, Cess, my darling, you're free! Are you home?'

'Yes, can you come to Elsie's? I'm just going there now.'

'I can. Oh, Cess, it's all such good news. Wilf telephoned and told us everything. He's not home yet, he went straight to the office. He . . . Oh, Cess, he contacted his son and told him to draw up papers for Len to sign to give me back everything that's rightfully mine. Wilf said he had to act quickly, as he may not have the chance once Len is arrested. They're going to meet Len this afternoon. Oh, I've been so longing to talk to you, to share this with you. Are you all right?'

'I am. Oh, Millie, I'm so glad. Millie, I – I need to see you . . . I—'

'I know, Cess. I feel the same. I love you, Cess.'

Tears pricked his eyes. How could he be so blessed for a second time? 'I love you, Millie, with all my heart.'

A little voice behind him made him jump round. 'Milwie. Milwie.'

Cess didn't answer Kitty. Seeing Gertie staring at him

open-mouthed, he felt bad that she should find out about him and Millie like this. He should have told her, as she was like a mother to him.

'I've got to go, Millie. See you in a few minutes – well, as fast as you can make it, me darlin'.'

Turning to Gertie as he replaced the receiver, he said, 'I was going to tell yer, luv. I was waiting until I'd made me visit and I was sure of Millie. You see, I couldn't believe she could love me. We were going to spend some of the time that I was down there, fetching Elsie and Rose, to be alone together. We both knew how we felt, but we had no time other than on telephone calls to talk about anything – still haven't.'

'Well! It's a bit of a shock, but in the long run, you being happy is all that matters to me, Cess.'

'Ta, Gertie. I know it's soon, and how much yer loved Dot. But I didn't plan it, and I want yer to know that you'll always be with me and Kitty. I promise yer that, luv. Nothing will change that.'

Gertie smiled. 'And it isn't just on the rebound?'

'No. It isn't. I love Millie and she loves me, but none of us will ever forget Dot. My heart still hurts at her loss. Millie isn't a salve for that. She's the woman I want to spend the rest of me life with.'

Gertie nodded. 'That's all that concerned me, when I heard what you said, Cess. Go and be happy, you deserve to be. I won't come with you to Elsie's. I want to make sure Dai is all right.'

Cess laughed. 'You're a mother hen, Gertie, and I don't know what we'd do without you.'

'I hope you'll never have to find out, because you've become like a son to me, Cess.'

Cess had an urge to go to her and to cuddle her, but he didn't want to embarrass her. As he smiled and said 'Ta, Gertie', the thought occurred to him that he wished his own mum had been like her. Then he pulled himself up and felt ashamed, because despite her faults, he'd adored his mum and missed her every day.

'I'll see you later then, Gertie. Don't be fussing round Dai too much – he might get used to it.'

Her laughter followed him through the door. And when Cess got to his car and looked back, she was still on the doorstep. A rounded dumpling of a woman, with a lovely dimply face and twinkling brown eyes, Gertie was a strong woman, a rock he could lean on – dependable, loving, firm, and kind. For her to look upon him as her son had filled him with a warm, good feeling. As he waved to her, the thought came to Cess that everything was about to come right in all their worlds.

Chapter Fifteen

Elsie and Millie

Elsie could hardly contain herself as she picked up the receiver and dialled Jim's office number. When she heard his voice say, 'Lefton's Jam Factory, general manager speaking, how can I help?' her breath caught in her lungs. Excitement gripped her.

'It's me, Jim, luv.'

'Elsie? Is everything all right?'

'It is. It's wonderful—'

'Oh my God, Elsie, you're not . . . Oh, darling, I—'

'No.' Elsie knew that Jim thought she was going to say she was pregnant. For a moment she so wished that was why she was ringing and her heart sank, but then her news lifted her spirits as she told him, 'Something almost as wonderful has happened, darlin'. . . We're free! Free of rotten Len. He's going to jail!'

'What? What are you talking about? I've just put the phone down to him and he said nothing about prison – he was his normal self. What's this all about, Elsie?'

Elsie told him, stumbling over the words as she tried to get everything out as soon as she could, because all of it was amazing. 'And, Jim, you can be free too.' She told him all Wilf had done and planned to do. 'Wilf thinks all this will mean that Len will sign Millie's property back to her, in exchange for her not pressing charges, and will release you, in return for you not going ahead with charges too. We will know later on what Len decides.'

'But that's wonderful. Oh, Elsie, Elsie. I can't believe it. I do have more proof. I was going to let you know later. Another one of my buyers from my father's factory has agreed to testify that he didn't have any personal contact with me, but was told it was me talking when the call was made to him to tout for his custom. He had doubted it, but hadn't taken it further.'

Elsie wasn't sure this was enough, 'Well, let's wait and see what Len says. But, oh, Jim, I cannot believe it all. I will feel like dancing outside the prison gates when he's locked up.'

'Ha! I'll dance with you . . . So, Millie might get the factory back and all her properties? Oh, Elsie, life's going to be wonderful, though I feel sorry for Rose. I hope it turns out that she gets her son back and that she is treated lightly because of the circumstances.'

'I do too, me darlin'. That's the only thing in all of this that upsets me. Ah, there's the doorbell. I thought my days of hearing that were numbered, but now Rene will be able to keep her shop. Anyway that'll be Cess and Kitty, so I'll ring off. I love you, Jim. You'll soon be home, me darlin'.'

Elsie felt a longing to be with Jim as he told her that he loved her more than he could say. But she'd hardly put the phone down when the door burst open. 'Else . . . Else. Me come.'

'Come here, "me". Ooh, give me a squeeze. I love you, me Kitty. I've missed yer so much, me little darlin'.'

Kitty felt huge, after holding Daniel so often, but it was so wonderful as her little chubby arms came round Elsie's neck and she hugged her. 'Else go!'

'I did, but I'm back now, little one.'

Kitty shook her head. 'Else not go.'

'No, me darlin'. Aunty Elsie isn't going anywhere again, I promise.'

Satisfied with this, Kitty asked, 'Berdie?'

'Let's go to the window and watch for him, eh?'

When they got to the window, Kitty decided to wriggle out of Elsie's arms and go back to Cess.

'Well, Daddy can say hello to Aunty Else now, can he?' Cess laughed at Kitty, but didn't pick her up. Instead he held his arms out to Elsie.

'It's over, Cess – truly over.'

'It is, sis.'

They hugged. 'I can't believe it. All the while I was telling Jim, I couldn't take it in. It couldn't have ended in a better way. They say, "How the mighty have fallen", and it hurts more to fall from such heights, but no one deserves this more than Len does. I haven't an ounce of sympathy for him.'

'Me neither. I want to dance on the rooftops. I thought he would have a hold on us forever.' As he released her, he said, 'Millie's coming here too, Elsie. I telephoned her.'

'Oh, I am glad. Would you like me to take Kitty and Bert, when he gets home, to the park and leave you to have some privacy?'

'No, it's all right, mate. I think that would put Millie under pressure. It's too, well . . . intimate, if you know what I mean. I do want to talk to her, though, so we could all go for a walk, but we two will go a different way, tell the kids it's a race to see who can get to the fountain in the park first.'

'That's a good idea, and yes, I understand. You're a good man, Cess, I'm proud to have you as me brovver. So I'll go via the ice-cream cart, and the duck pond – that'll distract them and give you more time. You and Millie can go around the gardens.'

They'd hardly finished planning this when Bert shouted at the top of his voice, 'Cess! Is Cess here? I saw his car.' The door burst open and Bert, red-faced and near to tears, threw himself at Cess.

Cess went down on his haunches and held Bert. 'It's all right, little brovver. Everything's all right. I'm home now.'

'You won't leave again, will you?'

'Berdie cry.' Kitty's bottom lip quivered. She offered her pacifier to Bert.

'It's "Bert", Kittylugs, not "Berdie". And I ain't crying!'

'Lugs,' Kitty giggled. Bert put out his arms and she went to him, gurgling with joy.

To see them hug each other gave Elsie a good feeling. She looked up at Cess. His eyes, like hers, were full of tears, and yet his face was lit with a smile. 'My Kitty will always be looked after by Bert, won't yer, me darlin'?'

'She will, unless she starts that screaming. She could burst your King Lears.'

Elsie and Cess burst out laughing. Cess sobered first. 'That's a good bit of cockney slang, mate.'

'I like it, Cess. Mr Jollop used to teach me cockney slang.'

'D'yer still remember him, Bert? Old Jollop was like a mate to yer. You used to watch for him coming past and he always gave yer a toffee. No other kid got one. Ha, I remember the pair of yer chatting away like two old men.'

Elsie answered, 'He does, Cess. Whenever we go to the

churchyard to visit Mum and Phyliss, we put something on Mr Jollop's grave too.'

'That's nice. I'd like to come with yer next time yer go. I'll take yer in me jam jar.'

This set Bert off giggling. 'Mr Jollop used to say, "Them jam jars ain't as good as a bottle of sauce, and nothing good'll come of them." The first time he said it, I asked Mum what he meant, as jam and sauce ain't the same, so I didn't see how one could be better than the other. She told me then that he meant cars weren't as good as a horse.'

They all laughed with Bert.

Then Cess told him, 'You should have heard your gran. She was a one for using the cockney slang, mate. She sometimes sounded as if she was from a foreign country.'

'I like it. I like to hear Rene when she goes into it. I like to try to work out what it means.'

'Well, it's your heritage, along with the pearly kings and queens. You could become one of them when you're older, Bert. They do a lot of good work, and you've a good heart, like they have.'

Bert grinned and Kitty, who'd been listening to them, put in her pennyworth: 'Jam. Me jam?'

Bert tutted, 'Always thinking of her belly. I'll make us some bread and jam, eh?'

Kitty clapped her hands together.

'Ta, Bert. While you do that, I'll change Kitty's nappy, then Millie should be here and we can all go for a walk. Make me a slice too, will yer?'

Cess put in, 'And me. And I'll have the crust as I'm the man of the family.'

'Well, that won't stop you putting the kettle on, Cess. We can have a Rosy Lee with our jam butties.'

They all nodded and laughed. Elsie picked up Kitty and took her through to the bathroom, feeling contentment for the first time in ages. They were still a family. Her family, and you couldn't put a price on that.

By the time they'd eaten their bread and jam and drunk their tea, Millie was opening the door.

As she looked into the room, Millie had the strange sensation that all but Cess faded into the background. His eyes held hers and she found her body compelled towards him. His arms enclosed her, and to Millie this was her world – all she needed. She clung to him. She heard him say her name and it was as if he was pledging his life to her. She drew back. 'I love you, Cess.' His lovely hazel eyes were misted with tears as she told him, 'We're going to be all right, Cess.'

'I know, luv. Nothing can hurt us ever again.'

'Well, I seem to have lost me sister, then.'

Millie laughed as she turned. 'Elsie! Come here, my darling sis – you'll never, ever lose me or any of us, I promise.' Their hug was special to Millie because to her it held relief, joy and the coming to an end of all they had faced together. 'It's over, Elsie. Truly over. I have more news. I'm delayed because Wilf made it home as I was leaving. Oh, Elsie, Cess, it's all so wonderful.'

'Don't I get a hug, Millie?'

'Oh, Bert, you do. How could I not hug my little brother?'

'But I'm not your real brother, am I? And you told Cess that you love him.'

'I love you too. So much.'

As she bent down to hug him, Bert asked, 'What's over, Millie?'

'All the horrible things, like having to run away to Southampton.'

'Good, because I didn't like that, and not being with Cess, and Cess being arrested.'

'No, we all hated that.' She looked over at Cess, saw the love he had for her and thought, *It isn't all ending, some is just beginning.* A surge of happiness shot through her.

'Miwwie, me?'

For the first time, she registered Kitty's presence. And grinned at her jam-covered face and her chubby little arms stretched towards her. 'Oh, Kitty. You haven't forgotten me! But methinks you need a wash before a cuddle, darling.'

At this, Elsie went to go towards the bathroom. 'I'll do it, Elsie. I want to start being a mother to her now.' There was a silence and Millie felt the tension. She looked around at the almost statue-like Cess and at Elsie. Knowing they'd felt the pain of Dot's loss with her words, she looked up. 'I'll do the best job I can, Dot, my darling sis. But you will always be Kitty's mum. I will just be your substitute. You need to guide me, though.'

Cess smiled. 'No one better, Millie, me darlin'.'

'Me dadda!'

'Ha, yes, I'm your dadda still and you're me number one darlin', Kitty, girl.'

Millie laughed as she went to fetch a flannel. When she came back, the atmosphere was relaxed again. And as she gently wiped the jam from Kitty's face and hands she told them, 'I've brought Daniel with me. I left him downstairs with Rene as he was fast asleep and I wanted to see you all before he woke and gave me what for.'

'Oh, Millie, that's wonderful. I've still got the old pram that I used for Kitty in the basement. We keep a pushchair here for her now. Only we're thinking of going for a walk to the park.'

'I'd love that. I can tell you our news as we walk.'

'No, best tell us now, as we won't all be together.'

Millie looked at Cess, not quite getting his meaning.

He grinned his lovely grin, which she was sure was just for her, as he told her about the race they planned.

'I'd love that. I feel like the winner already.' Again it was as if the others faded and Cess and she were alone, as their eyes held. Millie could feel her heart racing. Cess looked beautiful. His sandy hair was lit like a halo by the sun streaming through the window behind him. But then a sudden shudder ran through her.

'Millie, luv, are yer all right?'

Millie shook the feeling from her. 'I am, Elsie. I'm fine. Never been better.' But she had to force a smile onto her face as the feeling – something she couldn't give a name to – stayed with her.

Kitty demanding her cuddle helped. Kitty had a special way of hugging, holding her face close to Millie's.

Millie now felt ready to tell them the news that would change their lives. 'I own the jam factory again!'

'Oh, Millie!' Elsie rushed at her. Her arms came around her and Kitty, until Kitty said, 'Me jam jar.'

They all laughed. Millie was mystified. Cess explained, 'She means a jam sandwich. It's something Gertie says to her when she squeezes her. She holds her teddy and says, "Let's make a jam sandwich of teddy, eh?" She means hold him tightly between them.'

'Oh, a bit like cockney-speak?'

'Yes, a bit like that, only cockney usually rhymes. We've just been having a laugh about that,' Elsie put in, but then her tone changed to one of wonderment. 'Oh, Millie, has it really happened? You have ownership of the jam factory again?'

'Yes – or I should say *we* do, Elsie, as this time I'm having no arguments. I am going to take you on as a full partner, signed and sealed. Though we have our work cut out. Len has mortgaged it to finance the factory in Kent. So it's deeply in debt. He told Wilf that he would have recouped the money when he'd sold Swift's Jam Factory.'

Cess had moved to be by her side. He put his arm around her. 'I'm really happy for you, Millie. And I won't let Elsie argue with you over ownership – she deserves to be a full partner. You do, Elsie. Yours and Millie's father built that jam-making business up from a tiny corner shop and an old aunt making the jams, and yer've been through a lot because of him. Millie's right. And even though he never acknowledged you, you do have a right to half of the business.'

'Yes, and half of the property portfolio. Wilf agreed with me about this. I have a legacy from my mother now, and from the sale of the house that my father left me, so I am wealthy in my own right. You only have an allowance, which is all you would take. But that isn't right, Elsie. And the other injustice was to Dot . . .'

Cess shook his head. 'No, there was no injustice to Dot, Millie, you gave her a generous allowance from the estate of yer father – well, her father too – and that continued as my legacy from her. That is all that was ever required. I mean, not required, but gratefully received from you. Dot didn't want to know the jam factory ever again, and would never have agreed to work there. Elsie did, as she's dedicated many years of her life to it. Do the right thing by Elsie, and I will be happy on Dot's behalf to continue as I am.'

'At least let me and Elsie sign over a couple of properties

to Dot's estate, Cess. This one, for instance. I know you would look after Rene. And I own a row of cottages in Leeds – well, I did. I don't know what has happened to each individual property until Wilf looks over what I have been given back, and at the state it's all in. But I was planning on having them done up.'

'Well, I'll think about that, but find out first exactly what there is, take advice from Wilf as well. Yer have to stop thinking with your heart, Millie, me darlin'. And me and you need to talk. Let's go on our walk, so we can do that, eh?'

For a moment Cess sounded like Len telling her not to think with her heart, but she knew he didn't mean it in the same way. She knew he was right too. Here she was, having regained her property for five minutes and she was already giving it away. But then again, she had to do the right thing or she couldn't live with herself. And could Cess be happy knowing that his wife was rich, when all he had was a market-stall partnership? Somehow she thought Cess could, but she wasn't so sure that she could. Sharing her father's estate in this way meant that Cess would be wealthy in his own right.

When Millie and Cess met up with Elsie and the children after spending half an hour on a blissful walk, Millie was still tingling from their first kiss, which lit in her a feeling that made her seem alive for the first time – not warily alive, as she had been with Len, always doubting his motives and his fidelity, but beautifully alive and cherished with a humbling love. She and Cess had shared a magical moment that would live with her forever as they stood in the shade of a large oak tree, with the sun dappling the leaves into shadows and seeming to clothe them in a lace blanket of love.

As they had come out of the wondrous kiss, Cess had said,

'I know I ain't of your class, Millie, but love will level us. Will yer marry me? I promise to love yer always and forever, more than I have ever loved before.'

She had answered, 'I will – gladly and with all my heart, I will. And yes, our love will do all we need it to do, but as for levelling us, I could never reach the height of esteem that I hold you in, my beautiful Cess. But I am honoured that you think I can. I'm honoured too to be asked to be your wife, and promise with all my heart always to love you, always to put you first and to love Kitty as my own, giving her a true sense of who she is – my lovely half-sister Dot's daughter – and yet to let her know that she has a mother in me too.'

Cess had looked down on her. 'I promise to love you, and to put yer first and never to dampen yer free spirit, Millie, but to love yer more for the good works you want to carry out and help yer with them. And I promise to love Daniel as me own, and to respect him and his wishes when he is older to make his own decisions on the part his father plays in his life.'

To Millie, this was a fulfilment of her.

After their second kiss she'd told him, 'These promises are all I need. They are part of the exchanging of our vows, Cess. Yes, we will exchange formal vows once my divorce is through, but in the meantime I want these promises to be our bond. I want to be your wife, Cess.'

Cess had taken a deep breath. She'd seen his Adam's apple rise and fall as he'd swallowed hard and knew that he was fighting back tears. But when he'd opened his eyes and looked down on her, he'd whispered, 'I love you, Millie. You are me wife, in me heart.'

'And you are my husband, in mine.'

After holding each other in a blissful silence, they had

chatted about going to the cottage in Barmouth together. They both loved it there. And how they would make it a family haven. They didn't separate the children they already had from this discussion. But they did talk about those they would have once they were married, and Cess had told her that when they came together, he would be careful not to make her pregnant until after they were legally married.

When they had locked together in their final kiss, it had held all the passion they felt for one another. It was then that they laughed and agreed that if they were not to disgrace themselves there and then in the park, they'd better continue with their walk.

Millie was on a high when she reached home, but smiled when told by Campbell, Wilf's butler, that her mother and Wilf were resting. She knew that Mama had missed Wilf so much, even though he'd only been away for one night.

Making her way to Wilf's office – a room he'd made available to her whenever she needed privacy – Millie was tingling with excitement and yet with nerves too. She and Cess had a date that evening. It had been the last thing they had spoken of, just before they had left the privacy of the trees.

He'd thrilled her, when she'd agreed to meet, by saying, 'Shall we make it an overnight date, Millie? I . . . I mean, if you agree?'

'I do, darling,' she'd told him.

His eyes had a veiled look of complete love and desire as he'd looked into hers, but had held a question too.

'I want to, Cess. I want to be yours. This can be our honeymoon night.'

She'd told Cess to leave the arrangements to her and that the venue would be a surprise – her wedding gift to him, as she looked on all that had passed between them as their secret commitment to each other.

'Just be ready by seven, Cess. I will ask Wilf if we can use his driver to take us.'

There was a slight shake to her hand as she picked up the receiver of the telephone. The operator took a while to answer, but put her through fairly quickly once she did.

'The Savoy Hotel.'

With this announcement down the line, Millie's nerves increased and the questions that she should have asked before taking this step crowded in on her: would Cess be all right spending the night in such a prestigious place? Would he think the gesture highlighted the differences between them?

'The Savoy Hotel, are you there, caller?'

The exchange operator interrupted, 'Go ahead, caller, you are connected.'

Millie took a deep breath and booked a room for the night.

Regrets overwhelmed her once she replaced the receiver. Had she done right? What was the best thing for her to do? Should she lower her sights to meet Cess's or ask him to occasionally step up to what she was used to? Suddenly she felt full of doubts, but then decided this night was special. If she saw that Cess was uncomfortable, she would never do anything like it again, but would always leave the arrangements to him.

With this thought, Millie went up to her bedroom and rang for Rose.

She and Cess would work out all the things that could come between them, she was certain of that.

Chapter Sixteen

Millie

Since her confession, Rose always had a look of someone defeated. As she helped Millie to get ready and to collect all she would need for Daniel, she apologized for the umpteenth time.

'I cannot understand why you keep me on, but eeh, I'm grateful, Millie.'

'Because I understand why you did it. I too did wrong things because of Len. I gave away my half-sister's share of the business and left Rene vulnerable. Besides, I think a lot of you, Rose. You are prepared, aren't you, Rose? I – I mean . . . Oh, I hate this, but Wilf warned you what will happen, didn't he? Look, I don't want to frighten you, but you must know that the police could call at any moment to arrest you.'

Rose gasped.

'Oh, Rose, I am sorry. You must prepare yourself for it happening. But rest assured that Wilf is committed to defending you, so if they do come, he will be with you. He has my written statement to that fact that I forgive you and will be keeping your job open for you, and is certain this will lead to a probation order, not a prison sentence, and that he will be able to get you bail until the full hearing.'

'I will try to be brave.'

'You actually had to use bravery to do what you did – even though it was a bad thing, it did take courage, so you have that resource to call on, Rose. Now please run me a bath and then prepare everything I will need for me and Daniel to stay overnight, although, I will choose my own outfits.'

There was still a part of Millie that felt angry with Rose, even though she understood. But she couldn't get out of her mind that everyone has choices. Rose could have spoken to someone about what had happened surely? *But then did I? No, I never sought anyone's advice. I went ahead and signed any papers Len put in front of me. Len is evil. He used that evil on me, and that's what happened to Rose too. I cannot and must not blame her.*

When she came out of the bath, Millie was distraught to find that her breasts were leaking. The hot water had stimulated her milk flow. 'Rose, quick, get me my pads.'

'Eeh, Millie, please let me put it all in a jug, then you can leave Daniel with me. We can ask your mama to take over, if I am taken away.'

'Well, fetch the jug for now and we will see.'

As her milk was expressed, Millie's mind was in turmoil. Could she spend a night away from her son? Would feeding Daniel and seeing to him enhance her time with Cess or take away from it? *It's only one night. And what if I do take him and he is fractious – will the night be spoiled? I'm being stupid. Daniel won't even know that I have gone! I'll do it. I need this one night with Cess. Just the two of us.*

'I think you're right. I'll speak to Mama as soon as you've

finished this. Do you think there will be enough for the night-feed and the morning one?'

'Aye, there'll be plenty – you've allus made enough for two babbies. And as long as you express, more will come in, so I'll take two jugs full.'

With the expressing finished and Millie feeling much more comfortable, she relaxed about her decision. 'Pack my bindings, Rose, in case my milk does come in again. I'll just slip on my underwear and house-frock and go and find Mama, and see that she is all right with the new arrangement.'

There was no opposition to her plan – only congratulations for Millie from Mama and Wilf on the wedding that she planned in the future. And Mama was delighted to agree to the arrangement.

'I am almost praying the police won't come now.'

Wilf spoke up then. 'That won't happen. I have asked to be informed if Rose is to be arrested, and have given my word that I will take her down to Southampton myself. So if they telephone, I will take her tomorrow. But we've talked through the scenario of what might and might not happen to Rose, so let's concentrate on you, Millie.'

Mama clapped her hands, 'Oh yes, let's. I'm so pleased for you, my darling. I just know everything will work out for you and Cess. And I agree too that you should be together as a couple. You're not a young maiden, and Cess has been married before. You can both stay here as often as you like – we'll easily dupe the servants, and in any case, with Len locked up, who will care?'

'Oh, Mama, are you sure? What do you think, Wilf?'

'My dear, you do not need my approval, but you have it. I agree with your mama, but I would also counsel that you get your solicitor on your divorce as soon as Len is arrested.

It is time for you to be happy. Now, go and get ready and enjoy yourself. And don't worry about Daniel, he'll be fine with Rose.'

'Yes, think of it as how it will be when he sleeps through the night. You don't see him then from when he settles till the morning. Tonight won't be any different.'

'Thank you, both. Oh, I do love you.'

They hugged her then. And Wilf whispered, 'Be happy, my dear.'

'I will. And you two enjoy your evening and I will see you in the morning. Oh, by the way, may I borrow one of your bow ties, please, Wilf? I'm not sure Cess will have one.'

'Of course, I'll have one brought down for you. Now off you go or you will be late.'

As she went through the grand hall, Millie saw Rose hurrying up the stairs and called after her, 'Rose? Are you all right?'

Rose turned, and Millie could have sworn she'd been crying. 'Aye . . . I'm sorry, Millie, I was only down here for a moment, and Daniel is in his cot.'

As Millie followed her to the nursery she thought how strange Rose's agitation was. Daniel had been left safely in the nursery on many occasions. It wasn't anything to give her concern, or to stress Rose about.

Once in Rose's sitting room she asked, 'Is something wrong, Rose?'

'No . . . No, I, well, I went down to telephone a friend I've made – another nanny I was going to meet. I – I left a message with the butler of the house. Only, I didn't want them enquiring after me . . . I left a message that I might be going away . . . Oh, Millie, I'm so ashamed.'

Millie crossed the room. 'Rose. Rose, dear, please don't

197

be. We will protect you all we can, I promise. Oh, I hate leaving you like this. Maybe I should take Daniel?'

'No! I mean . . . no, Millie, I'll be fine. I'll swill me face and be back to normal, you'll see. I'll come to your room to help you finish getting ready. I've packed everything.'

'All right, if you're sure. I'll just check on Daniel – one last peep, as I won't see him till tomorrow.'

When the car pulled up outside Cess's house he came out immediately, followed by Gertie holding Kitty. Millie waved to them both.

As Cess slipped in beside her, he took her hand. 'You look beautiful, my darling.'

'Thank you. You do too.'

Cess was wearing a black suit that could easily be passed off as suitable wear for dinner. His white shirt looked immaculate. With it, he wore a black tie. She would advise him to wear the bow tie later, before they went down to dinner.

His kiss was gentle and brief, but enough to make Millie want to grab him and hold him tightly and never have him stop kissing her. But the driver got back in the car at that moment, having loaded Cess's case with hers in the boot box.

'I only brought pyjamas and shaving gear, but I don't think I will use either.' This he whispered in her ear. She felt his warm breath on her neck, sending a delicious tingle down her spine. But she giggled with him, though both of their giggles held a promise – a secret that the world wasn't party to.

'So where are you taking me to then, me fine lady?'

That seemed to suggest that he wouldn't mind where, but so that it wouldn't be a shock, she told him. His reaction was to laugh out loud. 'I'll not open me mouth then – yer'd better do all the talking, Millie, or I'll get us looked down on.'

'You won't, Cess. Oh, tell me you don't mind?'

'Mind? I think it's smashing. Ta, Millie. Ta for classing me as someone who's worthy of such a place, and ta for looking on me as worthy of it – does that make sense?'

'No.' Millie could hardly say the word, such was her happiness and the laughter that bubbled up in her. 'Not one bit. And yet I know what you mean.'

'I meant that you could easily have taken me to a down-market place. If you had, I would have been hurt to think you thought that was all I could be considered worthy of, and it would have widened the divide between us. Now I feel it closing. I'm so happy, Millie.'

'Me too. More than I could possibly tell you. Oh, by the way, I booked us in as Mr and Mrs Makin, so don't forget to write that when you sign us in.'

Once again they laughed. Millie had the impression that they would laugh tonight, no matter what happened. This was to be their night. Nothing could go wrong.

As soon as they entered the beautiful cream-and-blue room, and the porter had been tipped and left them alone, they were in each other's arms and, during a passionate kiss, led each other to the bed.

Everything seemed natural to Millie and she didn't detect any anxiety in Cess. Their love dominated their actions. Millie's fur coat was the first garment to flop on the floor, followed by her pale-green satin gown. As she stepped out of this, Cess held her at arm's length and looked at her, his eyes seeming to drink in every part of her as she stood there in her silk petticoat.

'Oh, Millie, is this really happening?'

'It is, darling. Look.' She pointed to where his jacket seemed curled around her coat in a heap. 'Even our clothes like each other.'

She was back in his arms, his lips kissing her gently as he took the rest of her clothing off. She helped him remove her corset, knickers and liberty bodice, and then stood naked in front of him.

His loving look took away all the unsure thoughts she'd had about how her breasts sagged a little and her nipples were dark and larger than they had been before Daniel was born, and her dismay at the few marks she had on her tummy. Cess caressed every part of her, telling her he'd never seen such beauty.

Millie was stunned by Cess's body, so different from Len's. Cess's body was contoured by muscle – in his neck, arms and chest – and yet his waist and hips were slim, although his legs were powerful and shaped by muscle too. She was reminded of the Farnese statue of Atlas that she'd once seen on a visit to Naples with Bunty and her family – her old school friend that she preferred not to remember.

'Oh, Cess, you're truly, magnificently beautiful.'

She couldn't have said how they landed on the bed, as she drowned in his kisses, his words of love and his urgency as he explored every part of her. She only knew that she was splintered, but then Cess entered her and made her whole again, before shattering her into a million pieces as an exquisite feeling gripped her and took her through waves and waves of almost agonizing bliss.

She cried out his name, grasped his skin with her fingers, felt his flesh submit to her nails digging into it, heard his moans, his gasps, his cries of pleasure. And felt the disappointment of him pulling out of her at the height of this. But he clung on to her and shared with her his ultimate release. When it was over, she curled herself around him again and held him.

They lay in that position, not speaking, just being as one.

And as they were driven home the next morning, they both knew that their lives were entwined forever. They had enjoyed a perfect meal, drunk superb wine and danced.

Millie had felt like a queen in the second gown she'd packed – the first being too crumpled to wear. This one was a ruby-red satin fishtail-style frock, with swathes of matching silk dotted with sequins edging the neckline. With it, she wore matching elbow-length gloves and delicate cream sandals.

Cess had loved his bow tie and wore it with pride. The effect was to make him look debonair – the handsomest man in the room. More than one lady diner gave him an appreciative and inquisitive look. But she didn't recognize any of them as being in her mother's or Len's father's circle, so she felt completely relaxed.

They had made love again later that night, but this time it was truly a giving and receiving of love. They'd taken their time and created a gentle atmosphere of getting to know one another. The urgency was gone on this occasion. This was Millie and Cess joining as one, and carving a beautiful path for their future together.

They had already decided they would both go to her home first. Cess thought it only polite to do so. And then he could talk to her mother and ask formally for her hand, and extend his thanks to Wilf for the open invitation to his home that she'd told him about.

Neither was prepared for what awaited them.

They stood on the steps of Wilf's house, giggling, holding hands and planting little kisses when the door opened sooner than Millie expected. They jumped apart, causing more giggles, but sobered immediately as Campbell bowed and said, 'Mr Hepplethwaite asks that I take you to him immediately you arrive, ma'am.'

His countenance told of a grave situation having arisen. Millie's heart thumped in her chest. She looked up at Cess, and his expression showed that he had detected the same.

Stepping inside, Millie asked, 'Is everything all right, Campbell?'

The butler didn't answer, but bowed at Cess, then addressed Millie. 'I'll take your coat, ma'am, and show you to Mr Hepplethwaite. This way, sir.'

'Is – Is Daniel all right . . . My mama? Has something happened?'

Campbell didn't answer her questions except to say, 'Mr Hepplethwaite wishes to receive you in his office, ma'am.'

She knew the way of course, but followed the butler, feeling that she was being taken to face something dreadful. And this feeling increased when they entered the office to find Mama seated in the fireside chair, weeping into her handkerchief, and Wilf standing next to her, not comforting her, but with his hand on her shoulder, staring towards Millie.

'What . . . what's happened? Wilf?'

Wilf's voice shook as he told her, 'Sit down, my dear. I – I'm so, so sorry, but I have terrible news.'

'Oh God. Not Daniel. Please tell me nothing has happened to Daniel?'

'I – I . . . Oh, my dear, please sit down. I'm afraid it does concern Daniel.'

Millie felt Cess's hand around her waist. With his other hand taking her arm, he gently steered her to sit down opposite Mama.

'Mama . . . Mama, what . . . ?' Millie's body began to tremble. Scenarios taunted her.

'My dear, Rose has taken Daniel—'

'No! Taken him where? Oh God, didn't anyone stop her?' Propelled to stand, Millie looked from her mama to Wilf. 'Tell me! Where has Daniel gone to?'

Cess had been standing beside her, but now bent and held her body tightly to his.

'We don't know. There's a letter – two letters. They were propped up on your dressing table. We think one is from Len, as it has the stamp of his bank on it, and presume the other is from Rose.'

'Oh, no . . . No.' Millie knew her head was shaking from side to side as the horror of different possibilities penetrated her confused mind. 'Not that – please, not that . . . How?'

Cess tightened his grip on her waist.

'All we know, my dear, is that one of the maids saw Rose get into a taxi with Daniel and that she had a heavy bag with her. That was late last night, after we and the rest of the household had retired. The maid said she had left her curtains open and had been reading. When she was ready to settle down, she got up to close her curtains. When she looked down, that is what she saw. She knew it wasn't right and rushed to get my housekeeper up. I'm sorry, my dear, but by the time we were alerted, they were long gone.'

'Oh my God! Mama . . . No, no . . .'

When Mama looked up, she looked like a broken woman. She didn't speak, just shook her head in despair. 'We called the police, but so far they have drawn a blank.'

Cess spoke for the first time, 'Did yer open the letters, Wilf?'

'I did. I took the liberty of doing so, as I thought there might be something in them that might aid the police. I – I, well, I'm sorry, but it seems they may have crossed the English Channel by now. Len says that you will never find him, as he is taking Rose, his son with her, and Daniel across to France in his father's boat. I heard Harold Lefton boasting that his new motor boat can reach speeds of nineteen miles per hour.'

Millie felt her legs crumble beneath her. Cess supported her as he helped to lower her back into the chair. Her stomach churned. Cess sat on the arm of the chair and held her to him, but even though she leaned on him, she felt no comfort from the love she knew that he had for her.

'There's more, Millie. Oh, my dear, I am so dreadfully sorry. I don't know how to tell you the rest.'

'Wilf, order tea. Millie needs a strong cup, with plenty of sugar.' Mama rose as she said this and came to Millie's side and went down on her haunches next to her, taking her hand. 'My darling, you will need to be very strong. You have so much to face.'

To Millie, it seemed the people in the room were somehow detached from her. Mama didn't seem like Mama. Her eyes were red and swollen, her voice dry and cracking. 'I – I can't be strong any more, I can't. I'm crumbling. My heart is shattering into a million pieces. Help me . . . Please help me.'

Cess gripped her. 'I've got you, Millie, me darlin'. I'm here for yer. Hold on, me darlin'. There will be something we can do. Let's get that cup of tea and look at everything that's been said, eh? You can find the strength. For little Daniel, yer can, luv.'

These words helped. She took Cess's hand and felt his strength propping her up. Mama took her other hand. 'We're all here for you, darling. And like Cess says, if you dig deep and find the strength to cope, you will find a way.'

From what seemed like nowhere, a cup of tea was put into her hand. She hadn't really noticed the door opening and a maid entering. Sipping the tea made her shudder. It tasted like treacle, its sweetness so strong. But she did feel a little more able to cope as she sipped more of it.

'Would you like to read the letter, dear, or for me to tell you the general content?'

She wanted neither, but nodded her head. 'Yes, please tell me. Nothing can be worse than Len taking my child.'

'No. I understand that, but please prepare yourself, my dear. Len has played a rotten trick, besides the dreadful kidnapping. He starts by saying that you left him with no choice. You stooped so low as to make him into a criminal on the run, and he says that's what he will be, by the time you read this letter, and that no one will ever find him. What he says after that shows his confidence that he cannot be found, as it is a confession of very serious crimes:

'My poor, stupid Millie,
   My revenge on you is ultimate, in that I will have our son and riches you cannot dream of, as I have taken with me my bank's gold-bullion holdings and all the cash and valuables from the deposit boxes. You will have nothing. I have arranged that my bank forecloses on the loan I secured on the jam factory and the properties in the portfolio. You cannot possibly pay it back. And it is your liability, stupid girl – who thinks she has a top-notch lawyer to make everything right. Well, he

205

*didn't make everything right, because I took the loans in
the name of the company, Swift's Ltd, and Swift's Ltd is
what I signed over to you. You took ownership of a
company that is £500,000 in debt to my bank – a loan
that I secured to enable me to set up the new jam factory
in Kent, but a good portion of which I have now drawn
from the account and have with me . . .'*

The room was silent. Millie felt as if the walls were closing
in on her and her world was coming to an end. She raised
her head, saw the devastation on Wilf's face and knew, even
before he spoke, that this was something he couldn't put
right for her.

On this she was wrong.

'He hasn't won, from the business angle at least, Millie.
I had no time to look into everything. But I am informed
that the Crown Prosecution Service hasn't yet sanctioned
Len's arrest, therefore affording him the time to get away.
However, we do have one saving grace: the papers required
your signature too. None of them were properly drawn up.
What I got Len to sign was more of a promissory note, but
he hasn't realized this. Papers of such magnitude for you to
be the legal and binding owner take time to prepare, as all
aspects have to be looked into. I hadn't wanted to worry
you with this until it was all signed and sealed; neither did
I tell Len that it wasn't as yet a fait accompli. I thought to
get him to face whatever the crimes he had already committed
had in store for him, so that he would realize that any added
charges would be catastrophic, and would therefore sign
everything. I am sorry that I mistakenly allowed you to think
you were the rightful owner of the factory, my dear, but you
are not.'

206

This gave Millie a small amount of relief, as she had envisaged her entire fortune being taken by creditors of the jam factory. But it was short-lived.

'If we weren't dealing with the Leftons, I would say, Millie, that you were in a good position – businesswise, of course, not personally. And I would be advising you to wait for the company to be on the verge of bankruptcy and then put in a rescue bid. However, I can't see Harold Lefton allowing you to get one up on his son, so he will probably do the same, unless we can keep the whole thing from him – something I cannot see happening.'

Millie didn't want to be talking about all of this. She was relieved, of course, though she wondered if Len would ever realize that he'd blundered and would be the one with a bankruptcy order added to his toll of heinous crimes. But all of that faded into insignificance when she thought of her darling Daniel being gone.

Her voice didn't sound like her own as she said, 'Thank you, Wilf.'

The words seemed to float from her as the room spun, and concerned voices shouted and then faded, then merged with the sound as if spoken through water, as blackness descended and she accepted the blessed peace it offered and went into its depths.

Chapter Seventeen

Elsie

Elsie couldn't believe that what Cess was telling her had happened. 'Oh, Cess, I have to go to Millie.'

'You can't yet, mate. Millie came to when we got her to her bed, and the doctor arrived soon after. Millie was hysterical, so he gave her a sedative and said she must be kept very quiet.'

'But I can't bear not to. I would sit by her bed until she woke.'

'I'm going to do that, Else. As her husband – well, sort of – I can't bear to leave her.'

'Her husband?'

She listened as Cess told her of the vow they had made to each other, and how Wilf had said he could stay over at his home whenever he wanted, and that he and Millie's mum would accept him sharing the same room as Millie.

'I'm shocked. That ain't . . . well, I was going to say that ain't right, but thinking of it, it is. Though it still shocks me that they could suggest such a thing. But I'm glad they did, as you and Millie need each other.'

'Ta, Elsie. I wouldn't have liked having you against us.

Me and Millie do need each other. We can't make it legal yet, but we will when we can.'

'And I hope that's soon. But my God, Cess, I can't think how Millie will get over losing Daniel. My heart feels broken . . .'

'Don't cry, Else. Somehow the bottom falls out of me world when yer upset.'

'Oh, Cess, how could things like this happen, and why? Why? How can people be so evil? Rose – I really liked her, Cess. I looked on her as a friend. But this. I hate her with everything I am now. She disgusts me. What did she say in her letter?'

Cess moved towards her and held her as he told her. 'We don't know. Wilf didn't open that one and Millie hasn't yet. But, sis, yer know what Mum used to say, that hate is a destructive thing and can end up destroying yer. Neither Len nor Rose is worth that.'

'But what are we going to do, Cess? How are we going to help Millie? And what about Rene? She will definitely lose the shop now!'

'I don't know yet, but we have Wilf to help us. I've never met two more wonderful people, outside of family, than them two. But Millie still has a small fortune, which will help. She doesn't need the factory, or the property portfolio, to survive. It'll be helping her to come to terms with having lost Daniel that will be the challenge. And as for Rene, Millie will see that she is all right. She told me over dinner last night that she meant it when she said she would buy a property for Rene to rent, but was glad that Rene could stay where she was now. So I am sure she will continue with that plan, even with all this happening.'

'Have they truly all gone, Cess – everything? Is there no hope?'

'I wouldn't say none. I had a cup of tea with Wilf after the doctor left. We were on our own, and he said that he would do his best to get them back. He told me not to say anything to Millie, but that he may still have a legal case with the promissory note, which is legally binding. It may be that the debt isn't Millie's, as it was taken out during the time when she didn't own it, and was called back in before she took full legal possession. And it may be possible that Len is charged with defrauding the company before it was returned to its rightful owner. You see, he didn't invest the complete loan, but put the majority of it into his own bank. Wilf said that if he can prove this, then it is a fraud against the company, and the money is owed by Len personally. But he did say it may be tricky, because whatever Len did with the money, we can't get away from the fact that he used the factory as collateral.'

'Oh, Cess, please let him find a way. For Millie's sake, I hope he does. If it doesn't work out, I don't know what will happen. Yer see, I think the factory could be the saving of her – well, you and the factory. That's if anything can be.'

'Millie is strong. She'll pick herself up. It'll be the hardest thing she has ever done, but I think she will. Rose did, when she lost her son.'

'Don't mention her in the same breath that you mention Millie, Cess. Besides, that scheming bitch had something to fight against – the happiness of me lovely sister.'

Cess sighed. Elsie thought he looked almost defeated, and yet she knew he was fighting a battle against being so. She was proud of this brother of hers. Proud of the strength he had, and the kindness. He was a real gent, in her mind. Changing the subject, she said, 'I need to telephone Jim and let him know what has happened.'

'He'll be shocked, but pleased to get rid of Len, no doubt. What do yer think he'll do – well, what will you both do, if it comes to there being no chance that Millie can get the factory back?'

'Well, for a start, me Jim will come home. He won't stay on, keeping things going now. And going through anything is worth that to me. Then we'll probably pursue our dream and work towards the music-and-arts school we've often talked about. Though even as I say it, I've no enthusiasm in me for it – I am for Jim coming home, but all I can think of is the heartache of losing little Daniel, and what Millie is going through.'

When Cess had gone, Elsie rang Jim. Like them all, he was shocked, but to her great delight, he said he would pack immediately. With Len's disappearance, he felt that the threat against him was lifted.

Elsie wasn't so sure of this. To her, Len was like a snake in the grass, and she would never trust that he didn't have something else up his sleeve. 'Jim, I think we have learned by now to safeguard ourselves. Please carry on gathering evidence and give it all to Wilf. As an insurance policy.'

'Yes, you're right, darling. But I think I have enough now. Did Cess say what will happen next?'

'He didn't know – only that Wilf has hope, but we're not to give that hope to Millie, just in case. Oh, hurry home, me darlin'. I so need a hug. I'm lost without yer, and without being able to go to Millie when she needs me.'

'Darling, I should go to her. Even if you can't see Millie, you will have shown her that you wanted to. She's going to need you. It's wonderful news about her and Cess, but at the end of the day, you're her sister and you have both relied so much on each other over the years. Get you coat on and go, Elsie.'

With this assurance from Jim, Elsie made her mind up. 'I love you, Jim. I will go. Rene will watch out for Bert, if I'm not here when he gets back from school. But please hurry home.'

'I will, darling. And if I can arrange things, I'll be home before Bert is due anyway. I will just walk away and leave the factory. I'll send a telegram to Len's father telling him that the order book is half-full. The last of the machinery is being installed next week, and that's my lot. He can sink or swim. I quit.'

'Oh, I'd like to see his face!'

As they said their goodbyes, Elsie thought that Harold Lefton was another one that she'd love to see get his come-uppance. He'd tried to get revenge on Millie's mum and would have succeeded, but for Wilf.

As Elsie alighted from the bus and walked across the park, the day not long ago when she'd sat with Rose came to her, and she found it hard to believe that Rose could have been so deceitful. How could she do the same to Millie as had happened to her? It didn't fit with the Rose she knew.

Being shown into the withdrawing room by Campbell, who then left to ask if she could be received, reminded Elsie of her days living with Millie in the big house she used to own that overlooked Burgess Park. Campbell seemed to be the double of Millie's old butler, Barridge.

It was all a million miles away from Long Lane. Everything about her life was, and as she sat waiting, she allowed her thoughts to drift to the flat there. She thought about the knocker-up who got her out of the warm bed that she shared with all her brothers, to make sure she got to the jam factory in time; her mum curled up in the bed in the corner, stinking of booze and fags; the living room, bare of furniture, but for an old sofa and a table and chairs. And she thought also of the cold – and of the laughter, the fun, the music-hall-type nights, the love they shared and felt from Rene and poor Phyliss, another of the prostitutes who met a terrible fate. And yes, of the constant hunger and worry as to how to pay the rent – fraught times and good times all mixed up together, but she'd swap all she had in life now for what they had back then.

Not that she would want to go back to the horror that happened after she met Millie. Nor would she ever want to change finding out that Millie was her sister. Millie made up for everything.

The door opening stopped this train of thought. Millie's mum greeted her. 'Oh, my dear Elsie, I am so glad you came.'

Elsie rose and accepted the hug and the kiss on her cheek. She could feel the anguish and fear Millie's mum was going through.

'Millie is awake and has been asking after you. Cess was going to telephone you to ask you to come, as he'd said he'd advised you not to.'

'He meant well, but I couldn't stay away.'

'I know, you and Millie are so close that when one of you hurts, so does the other. Sit down a moment, my dear, and let us talk.'

As Elsie retook her seat, Millie's mum continued, 'All of this is so shocking to me. I cannot comprehend how people can hate someone so much, and want to hurt those who had nothing to do with any of the reasons that fed that hate.

213

What can Harold and Len possibly achieve by carrying on this vendetta against my darling Millie? Nothing they do to her can have any effect on her late father – the one they really wanted to extract revenge upon. My poor Millie. She least deserves all of this. Do you know anything – anything at all – about Rose that will help? I know you became close friends.'

'Nothing. I'm sorry, I wish that I did. It's a mystery to me how she can behave one way and be working away at an evil plan at the same time. I would have said that she was genuinely sorry for what she'd done. But another thing that mystifies me is how she and Len managed to arrange all of this.'

'That must have happened by letter. The staff have their post delivered to the kitchen door. They are asked to tell their family and friends to always write "Staff" after their name, and to put "Kitchen post" on the envelope. I have asked Wilf's housekeeper and there has been a number of letters arrive for Rose, as well as a couple of hand-delivered notes.'

'That bleeder! Oh, I beg yer pardon, Mrs Hepplethwaite. I – I never swear, but Len makes me do things like that.'

'I would use even stronger language, my dear, and I am not offended, so don't upset yourself. You have suffered at his hands too. Oh, there must be something we can do!'

Her despair matched Elsie's own and enhanced it. Elsie wanted to scream out the pain and humiliation that Len had caused her, too. Now it became a raw agony once more. In all of this, the only thing she could hang on to was that Len had gone. He'd left them broken-hearted, devastated and unable to think how to pick up the pieces, but he was finally out of their lives. For that small mercy, she thanked God.

'Have you any ideas of anything we can do, Elsie?'

This deepened Elsie's despair. Millie's mum was married to an eminent lawyer, and yet she was asking her if there was anything they could do.

Elsie shook her head. 'Other than supporting Millie and trying to get her over this, no, I'm at a loss and feel devastated.'

'I had hoped Rose might have said something to you that would give us a clue about where they have gone.'

'No, sadly, but I have thought Len might make for Italy and go to his Italian family. After all, Millie once told me that they are all gangsters, and that makes me think they will help him in whatever action he takes to lose himself, to protect himself from being arrested and to get his gold bullion changed to cash.'

'Now why didn't we think of that? I must go and talk to Wilf about it. But first I'll take you up to Millie, Elsie, and pray that you can help her.'

As she followed Mrs Hepplethwaite up the stairs, Elsie had no idea how anyone could help poor Millie. Although she registered the grand staircase carpeted in a deep red, and the cream-and-gold patterned walls, none of it made any impact on Elsie, as her heart beat loudly in her chest at the prospect of facing Millie's anguish and trying to bring comfort to her. There was no comfort that anyone could possibly give in such a situation, but somehow she had to try.

Millie seemed to have shrunk and looked like a little lost soul, propped up against a mound of pillows.

'Oh, Millie. Millie, I can't believe this has happened, luv.' Elsie ran towards the bed and climbed onto it. Cess was sitting on the other side, holding Millie's hand, but he let go as Elsie took Millie into her arms. Holding her close, she rocked Millie backwards and forwards.

'When will it all end, Elsie?'

Elsie looked into Millie's white, strained face. 'I don't know, Millie, luv. I don't know how yer going to cope with this, but somehow we've got to find a way, or Len will have won. We can't let him, Millie, we can't.'

'He has won. He's taken the most precious thing in my life from me . . . He's destroyed me, Elsie.' Her head pressed into Elsie's breast. Her sobs vibrated through Elsie's body.

'No, Millie, not destroyed, luv. Yes, he's rocked your world off its axle, but don't let him win. Find the strength to cope, Millie, and then to fight back. There will be a way. Cess will help yer, and so will I. Remember, yer son is still alive. He ain't with yer, but he is alive, and that means there's hope that one day you will see him again. I don't know how at this moment, but something could happen. The law won't let this go. Len is a wanted man and has added to his crimes now.'

'I can't feel any hope, Elsie. Daniel is lost to me.'

'For now he is, luv, but we don't know what will happen in the future. But we can make some things happen. We can fight back. I was telling your mum that I reckon Len will make for Italy to get help from his family. You know where they all live, Millie. If we went there, we might be able to kidnap Daniel and bring him home.'

Millie sat up. For a moment there was hope in her face, but then the despair won as she said that to beat Len's family would be impossible. 'From what Len told me, they are ruthless, and I could detect that while I was there. Only . . . well, it seems impossible now, but I was so happy that none of it mattered to me and I didn't take much of it in. I know where they live, Elsie, but we would never get within a mile of it. They would know. Len spoke with pride about their

216

goings-on. He told me many things that they do, and of how everyone is afraid of them. No one would dare to help us, and the minute we ask any questions concerning them, we will be found out. We can't do it, Elsie . . . There's nothing we can do – nothing.'

Cess reached out for Millie's hand once more. 'Millie. Millie, luv, me and Elsie are by your side. We can help yer. Don't give in, Millie, please don't give in.'

Poor Cess, he must think he was looking at Millie becoming like Dot, in the way she had a mental breakdown. He must feel that he was losing Millie to that too.

'She'll be all right, Cess. Millie's strong.'

Cess shook his head. 'We were so happy, Else. How could this happen?' He lowered his head and sobbed.

This seemed a turning point for Millie. She put out her hand and stroked Cess's bent head. 'Stay strong for me, Cess. Without you and Elsie, I won't be able to cope. With your help, I will.'

Cess lifted his head and then rose. He leaned over and took Millie into his arms. 'Oh, Millie, Millie, I'm here for yer, luv, and always will be. We'll never get over this, but we can find a way to live with it while we work towards getting Daniel back. I vow to you now that we will, me darlin'. You will get your Daniel back. But if you crumble, Len will have won on every score, because no doubt his father will feed him information about what this has done to you. If he can tell Len that this broke you, then Len will feel great satisfaction.'

Millie didn't answer for a moment, but Elsie was in awe of her young brother.

'You're right, my darling, I know you are. I feel that, given time, I will be able to cope. Will you take me to my cottage in Wales? I want to be there with you. Just for a few days. I feel I can heal a little there, and it will help me get to a place where I can cope – I will never accept it, though. If it takes me to my dying day to find Daniel, I will.'

'Of course I will. I'll need to go to see Dai and make a few arrangements.'

'Cess, Jim and I can look after your stall, if that's what you are worrying about. You show us the ropes and we'll take care of everything.'

'Jim?'

'Yes. He's coming home, Millie. He has enough evidence to prove his innocence and, with Len gone, he is free. And if Len's father tries to bring charges, he'll fall flat on his face.'

'That's good news, Elsie, my dear. I am so happy for you. You are an example to me.'

'Well, that's really good of you, ta, Else. I was worrying. You see, Dai isn't well – oh, it's a heavy cold, that's all, but it's taken him off his pins and means that none of us would be bringing in money if I go away.'

'It isn't a problem. It will keep Jim and me out of trouble. I've always fancied being on a stall. "Cam on, you lavely people, grab yersen a bargain. You, luv, this length of pure silk'll make yer a perfect frock – it really goes with yer hair. Only threepence a yard, luv, where can yer get it cheaper, eh?"'

Cess burst out laughing. 'I tell you what, yer can take Millie's mum with yer, she can bawl out the cockney as good as that and always wanted to work on me stall.'

'I might just do that.'

A giggle came from Millie. The sound was so wonderful that both Elsie and Cess fell silent and looked at her. 'Oh, Elsie, do ask Mama. And if she says yes, we have to go and see her at work before we leave, Cess.'

Their giggle was spontaneous, as Elsie lowered herself into a kneeling position. 'Cam 'ere, me darlin's.' She took them both in her arms. 'Cockney humour can always blow the blues away.'

'It can. I feel better, Elsie, darling.'

It was a tap on the door that pulled them apart, though Cess remained with his arm around Millie as her mum popped her head around the door. 'Well, well, that's a good sound – can I share the joke?'

'More than that, Mrs Hepplethwaite, I need to ask yer a favour.'

Millie's mum clapped her hands together at Elsie voicing what they had been laughing at. 'Really? It isn't just a joke? Can I work at the Petticoat Lane stall? Oh, please say yes, as it has been my dream for a long time to be shouting out, "Lavely trinklets 'ere."'

This undid them all. The laughter was something Elsie had thought she would never hear again and it reaffirmed to her how resilient and brave Millie was.

'Oh, and wouldn't it be wonderful if one of the snobs appeared wanting to sell a necklace or something? I would look at it and shake my head and tell them, "There ain't much call for this kind of stuff, lady, but I'll take it off your 'ands for a capple o' bob."'

When the laughter died down after this, Elsie said, 'Well, that's settled then. So how about you show me and Jim the ropes tomorrow, Cess, and then you and Millie can get away soon after? We'll leave Jim to look after your stall outside Rene's, and me and Mrs Hepplethwaite will do the Petticoat Lane bric-a-brac one.'

'Please call me Abigail, Elsie – and you too, Cess. And if you tell me where the stall is, I'll get a taxi to bring me, as

Wilf's driver would have a heart attack if he was asked to deliver his master's wife to a market stall.'

By the time Elsie arrived home she felt cheered by the fun they'd had and excited that soon she would be in Jim's arms, but she still held a worry inside her concerning Millie. Cheering her up for an hour wasn't the solution, but then what more could they do?

Rene greeted her. 'Hello, darlin', how did it go? How's Millie, luv? I'm at me wits' end for news of her.'

'Put the kettle on, Rene. I'm dying for a cuppa. One thing you don't get offered at them posh houses is a decent cup of tea. It's as delicate as the china it's served in.'

'Ha, they wouldn't know a Rosy Lee if they saw one. Though chance would be a fine thing. I'm not like you, hobnobbing with the wealthy, girl.'

'Well, I sometimes wish that I wasn't like me, and life was as uncomplicated as it used to be, luv.'

'Yes, I miss the old days – well, parts of it. I don't miss opening me legs for all and sundry, though sometimes I wouldn't mind opening them for someone nice and loving and kind.'

Though Elsie laughed at Rene's coarseness, she had an inkling that the last sentence was heartfelt.

'Maybe it will happen one of these days, Rene. You deserve a good man to take care of you.'

'I wouldn't want him to take care of me, girl – just give me a bit of real loving. And I have me eye on someone.'

'Oh? Who?'

'He owns the warehouse that I deal with on the dockside. He's not a bad-looking bloke – a bit of a paunch on him, but nice teeth. I like nice teeth.'

Elsie burst out laughing. 'Teeth! Yer make him sound like a horse. I used to talk to one of the cabbies and stroke his horse and he used to say, "Look at his teeth, girl, that's the sign of a healthy horse."'

'I wouldn't mind him being built like one!'

'Rene!' But despite the crudeness, she couldn't help laughing. 'The kettle's boiling, go and busy yourself and cool off.'

Rene laughed, but when she came back she sounded serious. 'What do yer really think, Elsie? Am I too old to want to be loved? Could anyone love me and forgive me past?'

'Oh, Rene, I don't think that love counts ages, and real love doesn't set conditions. You and Mum did what you had to do. There weren't many choices for yer. Has this bloke said anything or given you some encouraging looks?'

'Lusty looks, more like, but I could start off like that – being his floozy – and then let him see another side of me.'

'No, Rene, I wouldn't do that or you'll never be certain what he wants you for. Rene, well, don't take this the wrong way, but if you're serious about finding someone . . . Oh, never mind.'

'Out with it, girl. I can take it. 'Ere, get yer throat around a decent cuppa and tell me what's on yer mind.'

Elsie took a sip, hoping it would give her the courage to speak her mind. Taking a deep breath after swallowing the hot tea, she said, 'Well, luv, you know when you first had the shop and you wore that lovely navy-blue frock with the high collar and lace trim? You looked lovely, and nothing about you told of – well . . .'

'Me former life? I know what yer mean, girl. But I've slipped back, haven't I?'

'A bit. You still look lovely. You always look lovely, darlin', but not so as . . . Well, the lust this bloke looks at you with is all you'll ever get, if you look like that's what you are about. Oh, I feel awful now – sorry, Rene.'

'Come 'ere, girl, and give me a hug. Yer right, I know that, and it needed saying. And who better to say it than yer best mate in all the world, who's like a daughter to me, eh?'

Putting her cup down, Elsie stood and went into Rene's arms. 'I love you, Rene, yer everything to me – mum, friend and the person I rely on most in the world.'

Rene's body shook and the sound of a sob came from her.

'Oh, Rene, I didn't want to make you cry, luv.'

'These are happy tears, darlin'. Happy cos I have you in me life, and yet a little sad cos yer mum ain't 'ere to see what a wonderful daughter yer are.'

Elsie swallowed. She didn't want to revisit the emotions of her deep loss. 'Come on, yer daft thing. We've got each other, Rene, and that's all Mum would want for us.'

'Yer'll always have me by yer side, girl.'

'I know. Drink yer tea.'

'Yer right, though, I have slipped back. I just feel more like "me" in me working clothes.'

'But that's not the "you" that you are now, Rene. You need to put that behind yer. Yer a businesswoman. Yer need to get yerself out of thinking you're what yer always were, and think more of yerself. And I think you'd attract a clientele that would pay well, if they thought they were dealing with a businesswoman, and not a . . . Oh, well, yer know what I mean.'

'I do, and I needed a good talking to. I may act as if I know it all, and can take on the world and beat it to a pulp if it angers me, but I'm not really that person. It's me brassy look that gives me confidence.'

'You don't need it, Rene – yer not fighting the world any longer, luv. I sometimes feel that I am, with an enemy like Len Lefton, but though we'll never forget our roots, we don't have to live them, day in and day out. We've come a long way, Rene. We've other challenges to tackle, luv.'

'Yer right, luv. And I'm going to start right now. Watch the shop a mo.'

Rene disappeared behind the curtain that covered the door to her kitchen and back door. Elsie hoped she wouldn't be long, as she didn't fancy dealing with a customer – but then it would be good practice for tomorrow.

With this thought, a small nerve tickled her stomach. She wasn't a natural sales lady – and never thought she'd ever run a market stall. But oh dear, that's exactly what she would be doing tomorrow and with, of all people, a lady! *Sometimes my life beggars belief! But facing tomorrow is nothing compared to all of the tomorrows. How am I to get Millie through them, and how will me and Jim fare?*

After a few minutes a transformed Rene came back through the curtain looking lovely in her navy 'business' frock.

'That looks lovely, Rene.'

'But it ain't *me*, girl.'

'Oh, it is. It's the new *you*. The you who'll attract all the decent men with a bit of a paunch and nice teeth that you want, darlin' Rene.'

They laughed together and Elsie knew she would get through everything with Rene by her side to keep her going.

Chapter Eighteen

Millie and Cess

With everyone gone but Cess, Millie lay quietly, thinking.

The laughter she'd joined in, caused by the arranging of Elsie and her mama to run Cess's stalls, hadn't lifted her heart. Nor had the pieces it had shattered into been joined together.

Rose's letter loomed large in her mind and she knew she had to face its contents. But could she? Could she stomach reading the excuses she was sure it would contain, when she felt sick to her stomach at the action Rose had taken. Despite these feelings, she decided that she must find the courage to do so.

'Cess.'

'Yes, me darlin'?'

'Pass me Rose's letter, please.'

'Are yer sure? Wouldn't yer like to wait a while until you feel stronger?'

'No. I need to see what she has to say about what she's done.'

Cess went to the dressing table and picked up the letter. 'Shall I read it through first, eh, just in case?'

Millie nodded. She liked how Cess wanted to take care of her, and she didn't want to thwart him in that. She so needed taking care of. So needed Cess by her side.

As he sliced open the envelope, Millie felt her lungs squeezed into a painful knot, making it hard to breathe. She couldn't take her eyes off Cess's face as he read, steeling herself to withstand the agony of Rose's possible mirth at having won the day, or her excuses as to why she had to do it, or her apologies – anything at all that the letter might contain.

'Well!'

'What? Oh, Cess, is there any hope contained in the letter?'

'There is, me darlin'. Here, you'd better read it, as I think it is what yer'd want to hear.'

Millie took the letter, eager to see what Cess had seen, and yet still shaking with apprehension. This dissipated as she read:

Dear Millie,

I know that by the time you read this your heart will be broken and you'll hate me, but I were left with no other choice. I wanted to tell you of Len's plans, but was afraid that even Wilf doesn't seem able to stop him, and that Len would carry out his threat to take me babby away from me forever.

I'm not asking you to forgive me, as I know I couldn't forgive such a thing, but I promise you, Millie, that wherever Len takes me, I'll find a way of letting you know where we are. I'll care for Daniel as if he were me own, as I love him, and I'll do all I can to escape with both babbies.

Rose x

The letter gave Millie hope.

'Oh, Cess!'

'Rose has come up trumps after all, luv.'

But although this was so, a small part of her still felt so very angry and let down by Rose. To find anything like forgiveness for her, she had to ask herself, *Would I sacrifice another's happiness and cause extreme pain to another person, if it meant getting Daniel back?*

The answer came to her: yes, she would. She'd do anything asked of her to be able to hold Daniel and put him to suckle at her breast, and never have him taken from her again. This was all that Rose had done.

Cess held her to him. 'This opens up a way to get Daniel back, me darlin'. The only thing is that we have to wait, and that will be hard to do. But we'll try to enjoy our time at the cottage, and we have our future to look forward to. We'll be all right, luv, I promise.'

With the hope that was beating in her heart, Millie felt she could look ahead to better times. She put her face up to Cess and found his lips with hers. The kiss was a gentle, everything-will-be-all-right type of kiss, but soon deepened to a passionate need.

Millie couldn't believe that she could feel this way when her heart was breaking, and yet she wanted to be taken out of herself. Wanted to be loved by Cess. Taken to the heights she knew that he could take her to, and drown in his love. She didn't resist as he gently pressed her to a lying position. She couldn't object as every part of her became alive and full of her love for him, and her hope that all was going to come right in the future.

*

Not wanting to leave Millie, having loved her with his whole being, Cess decided he must make his way home. He'd telephoned earlier to make sure that Kitty was all right and to ask how Dai was, and Gertie had reported that Dai was well on the mend and that Kitty was missing him.

She was looking out of the front window as his car pulled up. He felt the tug on his heart as he saw her, her red hair catching the light of the late-afternoon sun. She lifted her little hands in joy when he pulled up outside his house. He'd been neglecting her lately and would do so again as he headed off to Barmouth the day after tomorrow. But he promised himself that this would be the last time he arranged anything without her in the daytime hours when he wasn't working. They were a family – him, Kitty and Gertie, and they all needed time together.

As soon as he opened the door, Kitty ran into his arms. He held her close. Gertie wasn't far behind.

'Well, for someone who should be glowing with his new-found love, you look like you had a rough night – not the best in your life, as you were expecting, duckie. Didn't it go well?'

'It did, we had a lovely evening and everything was perfect, but then . . .'

Dai appeared, looking a lot better, though still weak on his legs, as he held on to the hand-rail to help him down the stairs. They shook hands.

'Good to see you up and about, Dai, though you look washed out.'

'I could say the same about you, man. Has something gone on?'

He told them both what had happened.

'That man is evil! So Rose has gone?'

'Yes, sorry, mate, but—'

'I'm all right. It isn't as if I feel ready to start another relationship, as you do, and I didn't get to know her well – there was no time to. But I'm not surprised. I did say to tell Millie to be wary of her. I'm only sorry to have been proven right, as this is awful.'

Kitty, not to be left out, took herself from sitting on Cess's lap to kneeling on it and pulling his face towards her. She stroked his cheek in a gesture that said she knew something was wrong and she wanted to comfort him. Cess decided to lighten the mood. 'But apart from all of that, Daddy's going to fetch you, little lady, a stick of Barmouth rock, and a teddy bear from the beach shop, as I'm going to Barmouth for a few days, and yer going to spend time with Aunty Elsie and Bert!'

Kitty brightened. 'Berdie?'

'Yes, and guess who else? Uncle Jimbo! He's home by now and not going away again. So won't that be something, eh?'

'Wimbo! Wimbo!' Kitty clapped her hands together.

'Ha, that's made you happy, me darlin'. Now, Gertie will get you ready and I'll take you round to Aunty Elsie's to see your Wimbo, eh?'

Kitty scrambled off his knee and went off excitedly with Gertie.

Cess was laughing as he turned his attention to Dai. 'Now, Dai, I've something to tell you and to make *you* laugh.'

When he'd finished his tale, Dai looked incredulous. 'What, Millie's mum and Elsie, have you gone mad, man?'

They laughed together, but Dai sobered first.

'Will they be all right? I was worried about losing trade, as we were just picking up after the winter months, but I thought my stall would be all right, with yours ticking over. Now, with you going away again – and I don't blame you one bit – and with me not up to doing it, I suppose we have no choice.'

'You need to take yourself to a doctor, Dai. You need a pick-me-up, some sort of tonic.'

'Aye, but more than that, I need my wife and baby. Will you visit their grave for me when you're in Barmouth, Cess?'

'I will, mate. Theirs and our little Jimmy's. I'll see that they're nice and tidy and put some flowers on each.'

Dai lowered his head. An immense sorrow seemed to weigh on his shoulders. Cess wished with all his heart that things had worked out with Rose and him.

'Dai, why don't you dress and come to Elsie's with us, eh? It'll do you good to get out for a bit.'

'I haven't the energy, Cess, but thanks. I think I'll go and lie down again.'

For all that Dai was dismissing Rose from his life, Cess had a sneaky feeling that her being found to be working against Millie, and the truth coming out about her having a child, had hit Dai hard – and now he'd had to learn that she was gone. Yes, he was dismissive of her, but Cess felt sure that underneath he was hurting. And probably feeling guilty at doing so, as if he was being unfaithful to his late wife's memory. A feeling that Cess knew only too well.

However, he had to admit that his guilt over Dot was fading, and that making love to Millie hadn't in any way felt wrong. Anything but wrong, as it felt to him as if he'd been waiting all his life to feel the way he did now. He was coming to the conclusion that he and Dot had had an adoring relationship, fuelled by their deep need of someone to love and be loved by, from the time they were nippers. They were good for one another, they fulfilled a need in each other, but what they had was more of a brother–sister love than the all-consuming, earth-shattering love he felt for Millie.

These thoughts gave him no shame, just an amazing feeling of being blessed to have been loved by two of the most wonderful women he'd ever met.

He wanted that for Dai, but knew it might be a long way off.

Elsie was glowing with happiness when they arrived at her flat. After the greetings, hugs and handshakes were over, Cess felt that although a lot was still sad in their lives, a lot was being sorted, and happiness awaited them all.

Kitty asked at once where Bertie was. 'Oh, so Aunty Elsie and Uncle Jimbo ain't good enough then?'

Kitty looked shyly at Jim.

'Come on, don't I deserve a hug after being away so long.'

Kitty immediately went into Jim's arms. When he lifted her, she grabbed his moustache and pulled it. They all laughed at him faking extreme pain.

Bert thumping up the staircase and bursting in stopped their laughter. He didn't look at any of them, but flung himself at Jim, who handed Kitty to Elsie, then bent and picked Bert up. To see them together was very moving for Cess. *Me little brovver has a father – and a good one*. This thought settled his mind.

Kitty wasn't to be left out. She outstretched her arms and bent so far forward that Elsie struggled to hold her. 'Berdie, Berdie!'

Bert smiled at her, then said, 'You'd better let me down, Jim, so that I can see to Kitty.' In that one sentence Bert seemed to get back into the skin of an older-than-his-age lad. 'Come on then, Kitty. I'd better give you a hug.'

The two giggled as they hugged.

'What about me, buggerlugs?'

At Elsie asking this, Bert went into her arms and then turned to Cess and hugged him.

'Take Kitty up to your room for a bit, Bert, or to the music room, eh? I need to talk to Jim and Elsie.'

'All right, Cess. Come on, Kitty.'

With the children out of the way, Jim asked, 'So, Cess, you and Millie, eh? Lucky fellow.'

'I am, Jim. And a happy one. But am I glad to see you home at last, mate. Yer've already put a smile back on Elsie's face. I reckon this time we've beaten the evil Len.'

'Well, almost, though he still holds one trump card – Daniel.'

'I know, but there is hope.' Cess told them about Rose's letter.

'Oh, Cess.' Elsie sounded relieved. 'I am glad. I like Rose, like her a lot. And I believe her. She's found herself being used by that rotten pig and although she's causing hurt, she didn't have a lot of choice but to go along with him.'

'You're right, Else, but I can't help thinking that if she had told any of us, we might have been able to do something.'

'So what do we all do now?' Jim looked at each of them. 'You can't marry Millie, Cess, and I'm out of a job and have no prospects of getting one. And it looks like we'll lose our home soon too, as no doubt the bank will take possession with Len's other assets.'

Elsie put her arm through Jim's. 'We'll be all right, Jim. We're together, that's the main thing, and we have all the evidence we need, in the event that Len's dad tries to pick up where Len left off. But I don't think he will. He'll be too concerned with covering Len's criminal tracks, as he's up to his neck in trouble.'

Jim patted Elsie's hand, but although it was a gesture that tried to convey that he agreed, Cess could see he was still very worried.

'Look, there is more news, but Millie mustn't get a hint of it until Wilf has had a chance to look into it. But he thinks there is a possibility that the promissory note Len signed will stand . . .'

'And the debt?'

'It will be put down to Len, because he used it fraudulently – he admitted to taking the majority of it for his own use, and in writing.'

As he spoke, Cess could see the hope coming back into both of them, but mostly into Jim.

'Cess, this is wonderful news – very hopeful. Please tell Wilf that I will go to the factory at a moment's notice and get it up and running again. And hopefully he can get this sorted before it's closed completely. Len didn't do that, did he?'

'I bet he did. I can't see him going and leaving it hanging. He'd take great pleasure in telling them all that the factory was closed.'

'Not necessarily, Else. Wilf wasn't so sure. He was of the opinion that Len wouldn't want anyone but Rose to know anything. If he shut the factory, there'd be a big hullabaloo from the workers and Len wouldn't want that. It probably opened and ticked over as usual today.'

'Well, usual was nothing like it had been, he was getting ready to close it, and the workers all knew that.'

'Why don't we go for a walk, Jim? We could go near to where Ada works now and drop in on her – we might learn a lot.'

Jim agreed with Elsie, saying it might be useful to do that, so that they could find out all they could. 'Are you coming, Cess?'

'No, I'll ring you later, Jim. I want to pop back up to Knightsbridge to see if Millie's all right, and then get back to Dai, as he isn't very well.'

'We'll take Kitty with us, Cess, and bring her back to yer later on, after she's had her tea. Then we can make arrangements for tomorrow, mate.'

'Right-o, Else. It'll do Kitty good to be with Bert a bit longer. She don't have enough time with any kids. They're a stuffy lot around our way.'

When Cess arrived back at Millie's he found Millie was up and dressed. She came running down the stairs to greet him, having seen him from her window.

Campbell had hardly shown him in before she was in his arms. There was a distinct tut from Campbell, and as he walked away and left them to it, an air of disgust seemed to clothe him, but they ignored it.

'I feel much better now, Cess. Mama and I have been talking it through and she has made me see all the positives. She thinks we will hear from Rose in a very short time, as she told me what Elsie's theory is, about Len making for his family.'

'Didn't you say once that they lived fairly remotely on a farm?'

'Yes, but it will take days to get there, and Rose should have plenty of chance on the way to get a message to us.

My worry now is how Len will treat Rose. He may use her like a maid and yet . . .'

'Well, Rose isn't out of the woods yet, and Len is going to be watching her. He ain't daft.'

'I've been thinking about that. Let's go into the withdrawing room – there's no one in there.'

Cess followed Millie through. As soon as the door closed on them, she turned to him. He held her lovingly, knowing that for all her renewed courage and strength, she was still fragile.

'Don't worry too much, me darlin', we've a lot of hope now.'

She moved out of his arms. 'I keep thinking what a brilliant actress Rose is.'

As she said this, Millie led him to the sofa and they sat down.

'Look how she was able to carry on, knowing what was planned, and how she can turn herself almost instantly from a northern girl to seeming to be a well-educated one. I think she will find a way to contact me without Len knowing. I have to believe that.'

Cess could see that this tiny thread of hope was all Millie was hanging on to. 'So do yer still want to go to the cottage, or hang on here to see if anything comes from Rose.'

'Yes, I need to go to the cottage, Cess. I need to be with you. To walk and talk and . . . well, just be together. I need that more than anything. How long will it take to show Elsie and Jim what to do tomorrow?'

'Not long. I need to give them the keys to me lock-up and me van, and show them the ropes of setting up the stall, sort a float out for them and take them to Dai's stall, which doesn't need setting up, as it can be secured overnight. They'll just need to check the stock and take more from the lock-up if it's a bit low. Being a bric-a-brac stall, it don't matter what they choose to stock it with, and Dai's got loads of stuff.'

On Millie asking how Dai was, Cess told her what he'd surmised, as to Dai feeling the hurt of finding out about Rose's past and about her present actions.

'Maybe things will work out between him and Rose when all this is over. So Dai had an inkling that everything wasn't as it should be with Rose?'

'He did, which is telling. I hadn't a clue. But when there was something wrong with you, I knew immediately. Anyway he'll be all right. He just needs a few days to get himself back on track. I might drag him out for a pint tonight and let him talk.'

'Oh, you're going home, then?'

'I have to, Millie, luv. I don't want to, but I have to think of Kitty too. I've promised meself to give her a bath and put her to bed. I can see she's suffering from me being away so much.'

'Bring her with you to Barmouth, Cess. She won't be any trouble; we can be a fam— I mean . . .'

'Oh, me darlin', we will be, I promise you – me, you, Kitty and Danny, we will be a family. Keep hoping.'

Once more he held Millie to him, and knew that what he'd thought earlier was true: she was like a small twig and could snap at any time. 'I think just you and me, luv, as Kitty'll be all right with Gertie. Don't worry about her – we'll only be away a few days. I think we need time on our own.'

'Are you sure, Cess? I don't want her to suffer. Or to get the idea that I'm taking you from her.'

'Yes, I'm sure. She has her routine and that's good for her. But it was the loveliest thing yer did by asking her along.'

'She is part of you, Cess, and therefore a part of me. Although I am her half-aunty already, I want to become like a mother to her. I love her very much.'

Cess felt a warm glow fill him as Millie said this.

They sat for a moment in the shadows that the crackling fire in the hearth threw around the room. Cess was reminded of his childhood home and of himself and Elsie, poor Jimmy and Bert watching the last embers of the fire die, while their bellies rumbled and they prayed that Mum would have had a customer and would bring home some bread for them to eat.

'Huh, you know, Millie, me memory often goes down a lane to the past. How it can – as I sit here in this luxury, a million miles away from the tenements – I don't know. But when I do, it makes me determined never to let me own children suffer in the same way we did.'

Millie didn't speak, she just squeezed his hand and snuggled further into him.

'Well, me little darlin', I've to make tracks.'

'Don't go, Cess. I feel safe with you with me.'

'I have to. I don't want to, but I must be home for Kitty, and I need to see Dai. Look, why don't we get off to Wales tomorrow and not wait any longer? We could go as soon as Jim and Elsie feel confident – especially Else, as she has to be clued up before Abigail arrives. Do yer still think she will go and help Elsie?'

'You try to stop her! Do you know what she's done? She's only sent one of the maids to the market to buy her a serge frock and a pinny with big pockets. She told the maid she was thinking of holding a party where the staff dress as the ladies, and we all dress as the staff and wait on them! Ha, though it was a ploy, I think she will arrange it one day.'

'She's a card. An adopted cockney!'

'I know and yet, as I grew up, I never saw that side of her. She always pushed me.'

'She's explained that to yer, Millie. She did what she thought best to help yer future. No parent can do more than that.'

'I know. I don't hold any grudge, I just wish, that's all.'

'Well, you know what wishing can do – it can't change the past, but it can have a bearing on the future, as wishes can be dreams, and dreams can be achieved.'

'Quite the philosopher, Mr Makin. But so true. I wish to do more to change things – the rights of women mainly. I was going to go to the Derby races tomorrow. I was contacted by a woman who is in the National Federation of Women Workers that I belong to, but is also a suffragette. She heard that there may be a spectacular protest taking place. No doubt by Emily Davison. I have never met a braver woman than her.'

'Yer've met her? Isn't she, well . . . You won't do as she does, will yer, Millie? I couldn't bear for yer to be arrested.'

'No. I feel strongly that we should be able to vote, but more strongly about what women suffer by being considered . . . well, sort of goods and chattels of the men. No matter what our standing in life is, there is so much we're not allowed to do. Nor can we even protest about our treatment. And the working conditions for poorer women are appalling, as is the abuse they suffer, which goes unpunished. I—'

'Hey, hold on. Much as I'm fascinated by this, and agree with what yer saying, I have to leave. We'll discuss it all as we stroll along the beach. But one thing, Millie, I am one man who will never make yer do anything yer don't want to, nor will I ever hurt yer, or demand me goods and chattels, so you're safe now.'

'Will you support me, Cess? I mean if I want to march, or go to poor areas to offer help?'

'With all me heart, and I'll be beside yer every step of the way. Change is needed, me darlin', and I can help you identify where. We'll make a formidable team.'

'Like Ada Salter and her husband. As you will be my husband one day, Cess.'

'I feel that I am already, Millie, me darlin'.'

As he left the house, Cess thought to himself that he couldn't wait to be Millie's husband in the proper sense. For them not to have to be careful, and to have children of their own. He'd be the happiest man alive – he didn't doubt that. But at this moment he wondered if it would ever happen that they could marry.

Chapter Nineteen

Elsie

By the time Jim pulled the car up outside Ada's, Kitty was asleep in the back, her head leaning on Bert. Ada stood on her step, looking forlorn, and this came over as she called out when Elsie alighted, "Ello, Elsie, girl. Am I glad to see yer.'

'Oh, Ada, you look so tired. Are you unwell?'

'Oh, it's me usual. I tell yer, I'm glad to see it. Nothing's as welcome in this 'ouse as that is, once a month, even if it does make me feel like sh— Well, you know what I'm talking about.'

Elsie didn't want to pursue this, with Jim almost alongside her now, and so she changed the subject, 'I do. But how's things otherwise with you?'

'Don't ask.' Ada wiped a tear from her eye with her sleeve. The baby on her hip put his hand up to her. 'It's all right, Teddie. Mum's just 'aving a moment.' Clutching her baby's hand, Ada took a deep breath. 'To tell the truth, we're starving, Elsie. And it won't be long before we're evicted, mate.'

'Oh, Ada, I'm sorry, luv.'

Jim spoke then. 'Ada, you won't starve. We'll bring you some food later, after we have dropped Kitty off at Cess's.'

'Yer a good 'un, Jim. Nice to see yer 'ome, mate. We all knew yer hadn't gone of yer own free will. Not leave Elsie, yer wouldn't, or 'ave allowed the factory to close, if yer could do anything to stop it.'

'I wasn't sure it was closed, as I wasn't informed. But no, I was left with no choice.'

'No, well, it's only 'appened a week ago, but before then and while yer were there, one or two of us saw things and weren't sure that yer wouldn't get the blame.'

'What things, Ada? Me and Jim need information. We can't tell you all that's gone on, but we might need yer help.'

'Well, it wasn't anything specific – just that certain boxes of jams weren't there in the morning when we returned to work and yet you didn't notice, so none of us rocked the boat, so to speak. And then Beatie telling us her old man had come into money. Well, me mate who lives in the tenements and does a bit on the streets now and then, she told me that she saw a truck being loaded in the middle of the night. She said she saw it a few times, and one night one of the drivers became a punter. He took her into his cab and had her. And she said he were going up to the Leeds area. She said he were that good that—'

Jim cut in, 'Yes, well, thanks, Ada. That might be very useful information, but . . .'

Elsie laughed out loud at how Jim's face had coloured. 'He's been working with a posh lot in Kent, Ada – he's gone soft.'

Ada joined in Elsie's laughter. And after a slight pause, so did Jim. This pleased Elsie, because if ever the factory got up and running again, she knew he'd hear many a crude joke and would be the subject of one or two himself. He always used to take it in his stride, and she didn't want that to change. These cockney women were her family and always would be; their ways were hers, and Jim must adapt to that.

Changing the subject once more, she asked Ada if there was anyone she knew that might need help.

'Florence might. And Betty, but I ain't seen either.'

'We'll call on them later and see how they are, but we'll have to go now, Ada. But, like Jim says, we'll be back. We'll fill Kitty's old pram with stuff, so if yer can think of anyone who might want something, let us know when we call back.'

'Ta, Elsie, mate. I will. Though you'd be best served by going to the tenements after yer've been to me.'

'I'll do that. I'll ring Millie and see if she can help. See yer later, luv.'

When they reached Cess's house, Cess was waiting for them. Elsie told him about Ada's plight. 'Do yer think Millie would help us distribute some stuff, Cess? Only it might take her out of herself for a bit.'

'I think she might. She's very tired, but she's been on about doing good works. This might be exactly what she needs.'

Elsie used Cess's phone and gave the operator Wilf's number. As she waited to be put through, she heard a sarcastic remark from the operator: 'It's that girl again from Bermondsey, wanting to talk to someone in Knightsbridge. She sounds a right cockney, so I wonder how she got her foot in with that posh lot?'

Elsie seethed. 'Just put me through, will yer?'

'Hold the line a moment, madam.'

This was followed by muffled giggles. Then Elsie heard

the phone being answered by Wilf's butler, whose 'Oh?', on being asked if he would take a call from Bermondsey, sounded just as snobbish.

It seemed to take an age for Millie to come to the telephone. On hearing that it was Elsie, Millie's voice took on a worried note: 'Is everything all right, Elsie, darling?'

'It is, luv. Well, it is with all of us, but Ada is suffering.'

As soon as she heard what Elsie had to say, Millie came alive once more. 'I'd love to help. Wilf's waiting for me in his office and, once I have seen what he wants, I'll ask him if I can raid the kitchen and the vegetable garden. Cook and the gardener won't like it, no doubt, but if Wilf is all right with it, then I will bring all that I can. I'll borrow Wilf's car and driver to bring me and to take us around.'

'Bringing you is fine, Millie, but we can't have him taking us around – it'll scare the living daylights out of those we're going to. What we could do is put whatever we have with yours, and he can drive to the end of the street. We'll then fill Kitty's old pram with produce and walk it to the houses. We'll go to Ada's first, as she's going to compile a list of those whose needs are greatest. But I also have a good idea, knowing the women and how most only scraped by when they had a wage coming in.'

'Oh, Elsie, I feel that by running away we neglected them all, as they had to face the factory closure on their own. But we're here now and it'll be wonderful to be able to help them.'

Elsie was smiling as she put the phone down. 'Well, that's Millie being Millie.' As she said this, she let out a sigh of relief.

Cess's face lit up with happiness. 'That's good to hear, mate. I was so worried about her. I'm only sorry I can't help out too, but I need to put Kitty to bed and spend time with Dai. I'll see you in the morning around seven a.m.?'

'Eek, seven! Ha, I've not been getting out of bed till half past, and that's only on school days.'

'You're going soft. Good job that Jim's here now – he'll sort you out.'

She laughed with them both, and then felt a tingling of anticipation as Jim caught hold of her when Cess had closed the door behind them and whispered, 'In more ways than one, my love.'

Elsie looked up into his loving eyes and read the promise they held. Bert's sigh brought them down to earth.

Jim winked at Elsie. 'Right, young man, when this job's done, I want to hear that you've not slid back with your piano practice while I haven't been here.'

Bert's whole demeanour changed. 'I think you'll be surprised, Jim, though I ain't had a lot of chance, with being in Southampton. I didn't let it stop me, though, and I've been practising all I can since we got back.'

'Good boy. Well, things have been tough, I know that, but we'll soon get back into our routine.'

When they reached home, Elsie told Bert to go up and practise while she and Jim got everything ready.

Bert clucked his tongue. 'Well, when we get back, me and Jim have got work to do, you know, Else.'

When he closed the door, Elsie burst out laughing. Jim caught hold of her and stopped her laugh with a gentle kiss. Responding with a kiss of her own that held a promise, Elsie felt a calming of all the turmoil of the last weeks.

As the kiss ended, she pleaded with him, 'Never leave me again, Jim. I can't live without you.'

His husky tone told her he'd always be by her side. But there was no time to pursue the longing they had for one another.

'We'd better get on – we've things to do, luv.'

Jim smiled. 'For now, but later we can seal our reunion, my darling.'

'We will, luv, but can I ask a huge favour, Jim? Would you tell Bert about Daniel? I think coming from you, as a man-to-man chat, it might help him to cope with it.'

'Of course, darling. I wondered why you hadn't told him. It won't be easy for him, but at least we have the hope that Rose gave us. I think I'll use that approach. Tell him not that Rose took Daniel, but that Len did and Rose went along to take care of him and to work out how she could get him home again. What do you think?'

'Yes, that's a good idea. Otherwise, when she's back and forgiven, Bert could get the idea that you can do something really bad and get away with it. He's too young to absorb the whole story all at once. The main thing is that he feels that Daniel will come back.'

'I'll go up now – can you manage?'

'Yes. Good luck.'

A few minutes after Jim left her, Elsie heard them both playing. She hummed to their tunes as she sorted out some food from her larder. Luckily she'd had a grocery order delivered that afternoon, so she had plenty to choose from.

Once she'd refilled the brown paper bags that her order had been delivered in, she grabbed a box that had held potatoes and that she hadn't yet crushed and ran down to Rene with it.

Rene greeted her with a surprised look on her face. 'Well, love, I didn't expect to see yer today, with Jim coming home. Let me just shut up shop.'

With the bolts all in place, Rene turned back to Elsie. 'Well, what's so important to drag yer from Jim's side, then? Yer wouldn't catch me leaving a bloke like Jim for a second – he must be over-brimming.'

Elsie laughed. 'I shall find out later, but I won't be telling you. Now, to change the subject, I'm here with me begging bowl . . . well, cardboard box. But I have to say, you look lovely, mate. Have yer made that frock?'

Rene was wearing a modest, long grey frock with a white collar.

'Yes, and loved doing it. I made a green one too. They're going to be me work frocks. I put pockets in the side for me tape measure, instead of looking for it when I have a customer waiting. I'm sure the mice eat them, as I can never put me bleedin' 'ands on one when I need it. Oh, and I can fit in a little box of pins, too.'

'Ha, yer've to remember to put them in your pocket in the first place. Anyway I've come to beg for anything yer can spare, Rene.' Elsie told her the plans they had.

'Always the do-gooders, you and Millie. Well, I've been living on fish and chips and pie and mash lately, so me pantry ain't been touched. I know I've got some cans of fruit and meat. And I've a bag of spuds with eyes growing out of them, but they might have gone over too far.'

'No, the women these are going to will soon boil them up. I'll take them. Have yer any tea, luv?'

'I've a couple of packets, as it happens, and some cocoa – at least two tins of that. And me sugar tin's full, though it might be a bit damp. You could fill a few bowls with that as yer go round.'

'Ta, Rene. With what Millie brings, we'll have a good lot to give out.'

'You're a good 'un, luv. Just like yer mum.'

Before Rene could get nostalgic, as she had earlier, Elsie said, 'Well, we were always taught to help others and to accept help, and God knows we had to do the latter often enough. But it was Millie who first took me round the poor houses a few months ago. She's got a heart of gold.'

'She has. I hope she sorts something out and can be happy.'

'I think she can, but I doubt it'll be total happiness until she gets Daniel back.'

'I still can't believe the bastard has done that. Yer should 'ave let me get him beaten up when he did what he did to you, Elsie.'

Elsie smiled. Getting her contacts to beat people up if she thought they needed it was Rene's trademark.

With all that Rene gave her and what she'd gathered herself, Elsie filled the pram and was sweating from her efforts by the time Jim came down the stairs with Bert. He was a little cross with her for lugging it all down the stairs herself, but pleased with what she'd got together.

'It'll be pie and mash for our supper tonight, though, Jim, as I've got all our suppers for next week in this pram.'

'That'll be brilliant. I've not forgotten the wonderful taste of that cockney speciality.'

As they manoeuvred the pram out of the door, Millie pulled up. Her cheeks were glowing. As she stepped out of the car, with the door opened for her by the driver, she said breathlessly, 'I've such wonderful news.'

Elsie held her breath, hoping that somehow Len had been stopped and that Daniel was home. She didn't expect what Millie said.

'The jam factory is truly mine after all, and it isn't encumbered with any debt!'

'What? That's amazing – whoopee!' Elsie did a little jig, sending the pram wobbling.

Millie laughed at her antics, but Jim just stood there with an expression that told of his relief and yet his disbelief, all at the same time.

'That's incredible. So Wilf has managed to sort out the bank in this short time.'

'You knew? How?'

Jim coughed. Elsie rescued him, as Cess had told them in the strictest confidence. 'No, we didn't know, but this is wonderful! Yer know what Jim's like, wanting all the t's dotting and the i's crossing.'

When Millie and Jim burst out laughing and Bert joined in, Elsie felt bemused. It was Bert who put her in the picture. 'You mean the other way around, Else.'

Elsie realized what she'd said and laughed with them.

Millie became serious first. 'Anyway, yes, Wilf has sorted everything out. The factory is now mine, and I want to open it up again as soon as I come back from Barmouth.'

'Well, why don't we become messengers tonight? That's if you can afford to take me back on, Millie, and for me to have a team of the workforce in for a week, to get the place ready?'

'I can, Jim. I'm going to invest quite a bit of my money into getting the factory up and running again. When can you start?'

'Well, is next week soon enough? Just as soon as you and Cess come home, or sooner if Dai's health improves.'

'He'd start tonight if you'd let him,' Elsie said, 'but I'm with you, Jim. And as you say, if Dai improves and can take over from me, then I can come here and take over Cess's stall from you. By then Millie's mum may be able to manage on her own, which will mean that I can come to the office to ring round our old customers and see how things lie with them.'

Jim beamed a wide smile. 'It'll all fit in well. We're back in business. Swift's Jam Factory will be getting ready to be up and running by the end of next week – that is, if you will still call it that, and if we can get the fruit ordered in time. We have a lot to do, though.'

'I don't know about the name. I will have to ask my partner. What do you think, Elsie?'

Elsie's smile widened. 'Just as soon as I sign on the dotted line, we can have a meeting about it all. But how on earth did Wilf sort this all out?'

'Wilf knows a great deal about the dealings of the Leftons – more than he is telling – but he says a lot of it stood him in good stead as bargaining tools. Besides, there was Len's confession in his letter to me, telling me he was taking with him the money he'd borrowed against the business. As Len's father is a director/owner of the bank that the money is owed to, it was a simple matter to get him to agree to honour the promissory note of sale to me, pending full ownership papers being drawn up. And to write off the debt owed on the business. In exchange, Wilf wouldn't inform the share-holders of Len's theft.'

'So Wilf was only going to tell the bank's shareholders? Aren't the police going to be involved?'

'They are, of course, Jim. Wilf found Len's father in a frenzy, trying to cover Len's tracks. But all of that will incriminate him too, and will be added to the file of evidence that Wilf has compiled. Wilf has many contacts at Scotland

Yard and he has already informed them of the letter from Len, confessing all.'

'Thank goodness for that. My own position wouldn't be so safe if Len was let off scot-free.'

'That won't happen. It can't, and Wilf wouldn't want it to. But as for all the legal stuff about the factory still being mine, it's a maze to me, but as long as it is clear-cut to Wilf, then I trust it's all as it should be. Wilf told me to leave everything with him and to go away and enjoy myself, then come back and throw myself into building up the jam factory to its former glory. In the meantime he will work on finding Daniel, and as the police will work on finding Len, even if Rose doesn't get a chance to contact me, Wilf is sure I won't be parted from Daniel for long.'

'Oh, Millie, I'm glad.'

'Yes, and I believe it and am able to get back to something like my old self. And it's good to know too that when all is settled, Wilf and Mama can complete their world tour.'

'I feel full of hope for you, Millie. It will work out, luv, it will. And though yer'll have bad moments, you hang on to that fact. Wilf seems to me as if he can move mountains.'

'I know, I just wish . . . But, you're right, Elsie. I might cry on your shoulder a few times, but I'll be strong most of the time, I promise. Doing work like we're doing this evening will help, as then I get to see how much worse off these poor people are.'

'And the work at the factory too, as we'll have that cut out for us. That'll help yer, luv. But I'm here for you, Millie luv. Always and forever, I'm here.'

They hugged in solidarity. Hard times bound folk together, more than good times could.

*

They were to have that demonstrated as they began with Ada and her list of folk.

'Crikey, Ada, do yer know everyone in Bermondsey, mate?'

'Ha, them as are suffering, as you do too, Elsie.'

'Well, they won't be suffering long. Get the word out, Ada. Me, Millie and Jim are the owners of the jam factory once more, and all those who worked there when we were there before will get their jobs back. We want as many as can to start next Monday or even sooner, but we'll let you know. Eight o'clock sharp, mind. But there'll be no clocking in. There'll be a breakfast waiting for them, and the work will be cleaning and organizing – all sorts, but not jam-making for a while, till we see how the land lies. Can yer do that, luv? Only give us time to tell Peggy. She deserves to be asked formally by us to work for us again. We're going there first, so warn everyone that if Peggy says yes, they'll get her wrath as forelady if they're late.'

'I won't steal yer thunder, mate. I'm going to feed me kids and meself before I go anywhere. We ain't ate properly for a week. Our last meal was boiled-spud peelings that the lads fetched from behind the pie-shop.'

'Oh, Ada, luv. Yer know where I live, why didn't yer come to me?'

'Because yer've done so much for me – getting me this house, and away from Salisbury Street – and I knew yer were missing your Jim. I didn't like to intrude.'

'Well, never do that again, mate. What I've got, you can all have half of.'

'And the same goes for me, Ada.'

At Millie saying this, Ada retorted, 'Oh, right, I'll take half of the factory then.'

Ada's cackling laughter started her kids off. And despite

feeling the painful tug on her heart at the sight of the poor, half-starved ragamuffins with their torn clothes, dirty faces and bare feet, Elsie thought it was a sound to gladden anyone's world. She joined in the laughter as she turned away with Jim and the pram, and called to Millie that she'd see her on Long Lane at the tenements.

Millie stopped her as she called back, 'Hey, hold on – I'm walking with you. I've brought that pushchair that I took to the zoo, do you remember it? Cess had fetched it, amongst other things, from my flat. Now, there's an idea . . . Yes, I will see you on Long Lane, Elsie, as I'll get the driver to take me to my flat. I left a lot of food there. He can help me load it all into the car.'

As they said their goodbyes and set off, Jim held Elsie's elbow. 'Did you mean to say that I was one of the owners, Elsie?'

'I did, Jim. I intend to sign most of my half over to you, my husband. I'm old-fashioned and I want my husband to own more than I do. It's how it always was, and it never affected me or folk of my standing, as it did Millie's class, but it will if I own half of the factory and you have nothing – that won't feel right to me.'

'Oh, my darling, thank you. But please don't tell Millie you feel like that, as she would have a fit. She'd join the suffragettes if she could, I'm sure of it. And I agree with what they are fighting for too, so less of this about me "having the biggest share". We will be equal partners of the share that's coming to you.'

Elsie didn't argue. None of it was what she'd ever known, and she doubted if anything the suffragettes were fighting for would ever have an effect on her and her kind, so it was of no consequence. But whatever made Jim happy was.

Going back to the tenements on Long Lane gave Elsie mixed feelings. Seeing her own and Dot's old flats was heart-wrenching and brought back many memories of their childhood friendship, lived in such hardship. And in some ways it wasn't easy to return as a benefactor, but she was reminded that the folk from around here had long accepted her as such and were all pleased to see her.

They called on Peggy first.

Peggy couldn't contain her emotions. 'Well, well, and I thought me life was over. You can rely on me, Miss Hawkesfield . . . I mean, Mrs— Oh, blimey, I don't know what to call yer, luv.'

'You can call me Millie. But I won't be your only boss . . .'

'No, Jim and I will be too, so watch out, Peggy!'

Millie smiled. But then said something that almost floored Elsie.

'Peggy, there have been a lot of changes and there will be many more. I am no longer married to Mr Lefton – well, I am formally, but that will be sorted soon and then you will be introduced to my new husband, Cess.'

Elsie couldn't believe Millie was broadcasting this fact, but then she knew Millie well and her open, honest ways. Hadn't she stood in front of the whole workforce and told them the truth about her father, and how his infidelity meant that she and Dot were Millie's half-sisters, and so stopping all speculation and snide remarks? Millie's philosophy was that if they knew the truth, they had nothing to gossip about.

Peggy's jaw dropped.

'This is privileged information for now, Peggy, as we hold you in high esteem as our forelady, but please don't broad-cast my new status. It is only fair on everyone that they too

252

are told directly by me, and I shall do so, just as soon as I get back to work.'

'Yer can count on me, luv – me lips are sealed. Now don't yer be leaving any of that food with me, I'm all right. I've a good husband who's worked overtime to keep me table loaded, and I've seen to 'elping many in the flats, though all of them could still do with something from yer pram, so I won't 'old yer up. And I'll see yer on Monday. And you tell them all, if anyone's late, they'll 'ear about it.'

Peggy looked bemused when Elsie burst out laughing, but she didn't say that those had been their very words to Ada. 'We'll see yer then, Peggy, luv. And don't ever change. You're one in a million.'

Peggy grinned and waved them off. The last thing they heard her mutter was, 'Cess? Blimey, whatever next.'

Chapter Twenty

Elsie

As the sun dappled through the curtains the next morning, memories of their lovemaking trickled into Elsie and awoke feelings that she wanted to visit again, but a tap on the door stopped all such thoughts. It opening and seeing Bert there, precariously balancing a tray of tea and cups, had her sitting up in surprise.

'Bert! How lovely.' His bottom lip quivered. 'Are you all right, buggerlugs?'

The sound of the cups rattling told her that his hands were shaking. Her worry for him deepened.

'Hold on a minute, mate, I'll take the tray off you.'

Jim stirred as Elsie turned her body and slipped her feet out of bed, feeling glad that she'd put her nightie back on during the night, when the flushing heat of their lovemaking subsided and she'd felt the night chill.

Taking the tray, she spoke softly to Bert. 'Jump up and get into bed between us, luv.'

The tea looked like ditch-water, but she was more worried about Bert having handled the kettle, though the lack of steam told of him not waiting for it to boil.

Elsie poured the tea, grimacing at Jim as she passed him his. She was glad to see that he had also donned his night-shirt at some time during the night. The tea tasted as bad as it looked.

'Now then, young fellow, have you had a bad dream?'

Bert nodded. 'A man came to take me away, Jim.'

Jim put his arm around Bert. 'That's not going to happen, Bert. We will always protect you. And Daniel has Rose protecting him. Len is Daniel's daddy – he won't hurt Daniel, either. But as I explained to you yesterday, he has done wrong in taking Daniel away, and Rose will make sure that she gets him home again, don't you remember?'

'Yes, but in me dream Len came for me, only he had a horrible face.'

Jim took a sip of his tea. 'Ugh! As horrible as this tea?' With this, he put down his cup and turned and tickled Bert's tummy.

Bert creased up into a ball. 'No, no . . .' He couldn't catch his breath for giggling.

'I won't stop until you promise never to make another pot of tea until I say that you can.'

'I – I . . . promise, Jim! Stop!'

Lifting a hopeless ball of little boy over onto his knee, Jim cuddled Bert to him. 'I'm serious now, Bert. Promise never to touch the kettle again. It was a lovely thought, but when you're old enough, we will show you how to handle it safely and how to make a proper cup of tea. And then you will be our slave and will have to bring us one in bed every morning.'

Bert snuggled into Jim and put his thumb into his mouth. 'I promise. I was scared, so I didn't let it boil properly. It didn't whistle.'

'You needn't ever be scared, my little soldier. Me and Elsie will always protect you. And you can come to us any time – you don't have to come under the pretence of making us a cup of tea.'

Bert's eyes were closing. Elsie's were full of tears. She knew that the love Jim gave to her little brother was that a father should give to a son – something both Jim and Bert had missed out on, as had Cess. She didn't count herself, as she always thought girls needed a mum more than a dad, and they had all had the very best mum.

And she knew too that Jim got comfort from Bert, as he was able to give Bert the love that he was deprived of giving his beloved late brother.

Looking at the ticking clock, she saw that it was just on six o'clock. Another hour until she had to be up for the market. Sliding back down the bed, she turned towards her two boys and put her arms around them both.

The alarm going off woke her with a start. Sitting up, Elsie saw that Jim still held a sleepy Bert.

'You're wide awake, Jim!'

'Yes. I've had the most wonderful half an hour, watching the two people I love most in the world sleeping peacefully. I had a beautiful feeling that I had contributed to the peace you've both found, and it made me feel proud and determined to beat Len. To triumph over him and show him that he cannot use me ever again. I am loved. I am needed. Something he will never know the feeling of.'

'Oh, Jim, that's lovely to hear, me darlin'. I do love you.'

'I know. It took you a while, but like everything, when you do it, you do it with all your heart. So I'll forgive you for wanting to be just friends in the first place.'

'Forgive me, ha! You've shown me what real love is. I

forgive you for that. For taking my heart, I forgive you. For making me feel like jelly. For taking me to wondrous places . . . and—'

Bert woke. 'Can I go with yer to wondrous places next time, Else?'

Elsie coloured. Jim burst out laughing. 'Come on little fella, the only wondrous place you're going to is the bathroom. Then the kitchen for your breakfast, then getting dressed to go and spend the day with Gertie and Kitty!'

Bert jumped up. 'Yes! I forgot it wasn't a school day.'

'It's Epsom Derby Day, son. The day the horses run a famous race, and I need to get my bet on. I'm hoping your brother will know of a bookies runner, as I don't know where the one who used to come to the factory lives.'

'Cess will know. We girls used to love to have a sweepstake and, well . . .'

Elsie saw Jim look expectantly at her. Taking her courage in her hands, and telling her memory to leave her alone, she finished her sentence, 'Well, Chambers used to allow us to have the radio on and listen to the race.'

Jim gave her a pitying smile. She knew that he knew what had prompted her hesitation. She turned away. *When will I ever get over what Chambers did to me – to us, as a family?* The memory of Chambers forcing himself upon her caused Elsie to tremble.

But then Jim's arms came round her and he pulled her to him. Turning to Bert, he said, 'Scarper to the bathroom, son, and don't take long, as we all have to get ready.'

Bert obeyed.

Jim lifted Elsie's chin. He went to speak, but instead he kissed her. The kiss said more to her than any meaningless words could. The memories faded and she melted into Jim's strong, loving body, before he scrambled out of bed and pushed the washstand across the door.

She didn't have to ask why. She just thrilled when he took hold of her again and gently laid her back down on the bed. The wondrous place that Elsie had spoken of was within reach when the door handle rattled and Bert's voice came loud and clear, 'I can't get back in, Jim.'

Jim turned his pleasurable moan into a cough. 'No, son, Elsie dropped something and I had to move the washstand – it's blocking the door. Go and get your breakfast, there's a good lad.'

'All right, but don't be long. Cess'll be here soon.'

Their giggling calmed the embarrassment of the moment. 'I feel like a naughty boy being told off.'

'You *are* a naughty boy, but I love you when you are.'

With Jim's movement, the wondrous place took Elsie into its depths. A place where she forgot the terrible things of the past, forgot the Lens of this world and filled herself with the love of her beautiful Jim.

'You look hot, Elsie, and you didn't half make a fuss shifting that washstand. I heard yer down here.'

'Oh, I've been hurrying, that's all. And you had better too, Bert. Have you got everything you'll need?'

Jim sniggered at Bert's words. Elsie didn't dare to look at him.

'I don't need anything, Else. Cess has everything for me at his. He says it's me second home. I like the toy train he got me best. I build all the track and then take the animals to market. I've got sheep and cows. But sometimes Kitty grabs them and makes me train come off the track. Then she breaks the track apart.'

258

This was said with a deep sigh.

Jim told him, 'She's probably jealous of it because it takes your attention, son. If you involve her in the game, she will be a lot happier and then she won't do that.'

Bert bit into his toast and nodded his head. Elsie didn't think for a minute that he liked this idea. But he was back to his old self, and that was all that mattered. She knew that he and Kitty would always have their falling-outs, but at the heart of it all, they adored one another. Anyway, kids soon forgot things, as Bert showed when Cess arrived. No one would guess that he'd had a bad night of fearful dreams as he jumped for joy and ran into his brother's arms.

Petticoat Lane was alive when they arrived. Stallholders were setting up and calling out to one another, as goods of all shapes and sizes and a rainbow of colours spilled out of their vans and cases. Hot, steaming mugs of tea were passed around from a huge urn set on an open fireplace.

Seeing that they were new, the vendor called out, 'Best tea on the planet served 'ere, mate. And when I get me sausages going, you won't have tasted nothin' like 'em, I can guarantee.'

Elsie felt a surge of excitement course through her. The atmosphere, the comradeship – all of it was wonderful, as she answered many of those setting up nearby who asked after Dai.

She looked with pride on her own selection of goods to set up, as Cess had left her to choose from the huge stock in his and Dai's lock-up, having been told by Dai that they did need to take some stock to his stall. Amongst her choice were antique clocks, trinkets, jewellery boxes – said to be made in the Orient, and patterned with beads of all colours

– as well as silver candlesticks, and three velvet cushions on which she was displaying the most exquisite necklaces and rings, which she'd chosen as those she liked the most. Picking through them, she told Cess, 'These must be worth a small fortune, Cess.'

'They are, so keep your eye out for pickpockets, they work the people and the stalls. Dai keeps a walking stick – ah, there it is in the corner of the van. He has it next to him and then he can reach out and rap thieving fingers, when they think they can half-inch what he has on display and shift themselves before he can get to them.'

'Oh dear. I think I'll change me mind and put the jewellery in the middle of the stall, not on the end then.'

As she was doing this, a voice called out, 'I've found you! Hello, Elsie. Hello, Cess. Well, where do you want me?'

Abigail wasn't recognizable in her long, grey serge frock and her red apron with its frilly bib and huge pocket at the front. The only thing that spoke of this being a lady was her sunshade, held as only a lady can, at a dainty angle; her bonnet, which was more a wedding affair than market trader; and her short white gloves.

'You made it, then? Good to see you. You can help me display the jewellery, if you like. But would you like a mug of tea first?'

'I would love one.'

''Ere yer go, then, missus. Get your lips around that, it'll put 'airs on yer chest.'

Elsie held her breath, but Abigail burst out laughing. 'Thanks, duckie.'

It was the turn of the vendor to look astonished now.

'Oh, and served in your very best tin mug – excellent.' Abigail gave him a huge smile.

'Grantham, ma'am, at yer service. I can tell yer quality, but yer a good sort. Welcome to the market traders of Petticoat Lane, mate.'

Abigail beamed. 'This tea is rather good, sir. I'm glad you're set up next to us. Now, Elsie, show me the ropes. And you, Cess, had better make your way to Millie, as she's practically sitting on her valise on the pavement outside the house.'

Cess laughed. 'Are yer sure you'll be all right, sis?'

'Yes, off you go, you've to set Jim up yet. He'll be waiting for you, and then get off on your holiday – and, Cess, enjoy every minute, mate. Despite everything, give Millie a good time.'

'I will.'

When he'd gone, Elsie had a moment of feeling awkward with Abigail, but it didn't last long.

'There, how does that look, Elsie?'

Elsie looked at the display and thought it beautiful. 'You have a way with it. I think we should up the prices, don't you? They seem very cheap, now they are laid out like that.'

'They are cheap. This piece here is an heirloom. I know the young lady who parted with it and she is a particularly nice girl, a lady, but she married a scoundrel who was not of her choosing. A lord who was considered the best catch of all, but then girls can't choose. Or those of her standing can't. I am going to buy it, and give it back to her and help her out.'

Elsie was shocked. She'd never got used to finding out that the rich toffs had their problems just as much as the poor did. Until she'd met Millie, she'd thought all rich people were blissfully happy and didn't care a jot about anyone. But Millie was an eye-opener – a girl suffering because she was forced to attend schools with those of a higher class than her. And Abigail, her own mother, had been responsible.

As if she'd read Elsie's thoughts, Abigail said, 'I am so ashamed that I wanted such a marriage for Millie. You see, I was so unhappy. I was the daughter of an aristocrat and married wilfully a man who was not of my father's choosing. But how I suffered from his infidelity . . . Oh, of course you know that. I'm sorry to have mentioned it, my dear.'

'Don't be. I like that we are talking about it. I want to understand.'

'Well, you see, although these girls, like the one I have mentioned, aren't happy, they do have each other. They are like a band of comrades, they can take tea together, and chat and cry even, if they are so inclined, and they gain strength from each other.'

'Very much like the cockneys do.'

'Yes, very like that. And I wanted that for Millie. I wanted her well taken care of, but with a large group of friends who understood, and to whom she could turn. I never had that. I had broken the code and married new money – well, a self-made man who made good because of my inheritance. Anyway, I was ostracized by the women I should have been able to turn to, and yet my stupid husband was only accepted in the circles he wanted to move in because of me being who I was. It's all daft. But I was so lonely. I realize now, though, that they are not the only circles that offer love and friendship. And I am glad that Millie has broken free from her husband and is marrying Cess. But will she be accepted, Elsie?'

'She is already, and has been for a long time. You should have seen the folk welcoming her with open arms yesterday evening, and not just as a benefactor, but as a friend. They love and trust her, and her getting the factory up and running again has made their day – their lives. They'll always look out for her, don't you worry. And Cess adores her, he'll make her very happy. He'll never be unfaithful to her or hurt her in any way.'

'She's a lucky girl, and so am I. Not only in having Wilf, but in having all of you as my friends. Now, shall we start to be market traders?'

With this, Abigail turned and yelled, 'Lavely jewellery, grace any occasion – came from the toffs, it did. Fallen on 'ard times, they 'ave – cam on, make their folly your gain . . . 'Ere you are, duckie, try that for size.'

Elsie burst out laughing as a young woman, who was of obvious means, came over and picked up a bracelet.

'Now then, duckie, two florins is the price, but I can do it for three shilling to you, luv.'

'I'll take it, thank you.'

Elsie couldn't believe it. The bracelet was pretty, but was priced at only ninepence. She saw Abigail quickly snip the price tag off before handing it to the young lady. 'It'll look lavely on yer, madam. Ta very much. Good day to yer.'

When the lady had left, Elsie doubled over.

'There.' Abigail rubbed the florin piece and the shilling between her hands, before dropping them into the pocket of her pinny. 'That's the way to do it. And do you know, that was such fun! Let's have a competition, see who can sell the most!'

The rest of the day went along in a similar way. Elsie couldn't have said when she'd laughed so much. Abigail was a card, and Elsie loved her. During quiet times they chatted more about their lives. Elsie found it difficult talking about hers.

'Tell me, Elsie, don't be embarrassed. I'd like to understand more fully. I only know that you and your friend Dot were

263

fathered by my late husband. But what was it like for you, not knowing who your father was all those years and then finding out? And, well, how did your mother come to be my husband's mistress? Did he pick her up when she was working the streets?'

'No. He was the cause of her going down that path. He was her boss. He promised her a lot . . . Look, I don't want to hurt you more than yer have been, and . . . well, it's all in the past.'

'I won't be hurt. I have long lost any love that I had for my husband, and that happened a good many years before I learned about you, my dear. I just feel that I am missing some details. And I don't know why they are important to me.'

Elsie suspected that Abigail wasn't completely over Hawkesfield, and maybe hearing the really bad side of him – which she had been denied by his guilty plea stopping the need for a trial – might help her to rid herself of the last thread of any doubt she had.

When she began her story, Elsie found it easier to relate than she had thought she would. She was helped by the interruptions of the stall having a busy flurry every now and again, which gave her a breather and allowed her to gather her emotions, until at last she got through it.

'Thank you, my dear. It seems I was married to a monster. A man who craved riches and stood on anyone to get them. A user, and an abuser, of women. Even me. Oh, he never physically abused me, but he did abuse me in the same way that Len tried to do to Millie. How tragic that she fell for a man who is almost a replica of her father's character. It's very difficult to watch her suffer.'

'I'm glad I've helped yer. We have a saying that it is better to put ghosts to rest.'

'You have done that. Richard was like a ghost. It was as if he was still trying to spoil things for me. You telling me everything has finally stripped me of every thread of feeling I had for him. I apologize to you for what he did, and I so wish I could apologize to your mother too.'

'Ta, but you have no need to. You accepting me, and all the help you gave me when you engaged Wilf to help me, even though you didn't know me then, is more than enough.'

'You have my Millie to thank for that – as it is, we all have a lot to thank Millie for. Her social conscience has often been at odds with my views in the past, but she has changed me. She has lessened the class divide and brought the most lovely people, like you and Cess, into my life.'

Elsie blushed, but enjoyed the warm glow that these words gave her, and even more so when Abigail asked, 'Can I hug you, Elsie?'

The hug was like that of a mother and brought tears to Elsie's eyes.

When they parted Abigail said, 'Well, after all that soul-searching and visiting the past, I'm hungry. Have you ever eaten a sausage, Elsie?'

The question showed the differences between them. 'Yes, many times – they're delicious. I'll go and get us one each, and tomorrow I'll introduce you to pie and mash, the best tea ever.'

'Oh? You don't have cakes for tea, then?'

'Ha, I was forgetting, you posh lot call your tea your dinner, and your dinner your lunch. Tea, to you, is some fancy thing yer have in the afternoon.'

Abigail laughed with her. 'Them posh lot get on yer nerves.'

They both laughed out loud at this and, to Elsie, it sealed their friendship.

Chapter Twenty-One

Cess

When Cess and Millie arrived at the cottage in Barmouth, the church clock was chiming eight o'clock. They were exhausted, but exhilarated to finally be at the cottage. Even the brisk wind that blew off the sea and fanned them with the spray of the full tide, dampening their faces, failed to daunt them as they made their way down the steps to the cottage.

'I'll soon have a fire going, me darlin'. Yer know, I love this place – it's a sanctuary.'

Memories of the time just after Dot died assailed Cess as he went outside to gather wood from the log pile. A sad pain tugged at him. Poor Dot, she didn't have much of a life with that mother and stepfather of hers, but he knew he'd made her happy and that was the main thing.

Coming here after her death and meeting Dai had been a turning point for him, and yet it should be a sad place, as Barmouth was where little Jimmy died, away from all his family except Bert, as the two of them had been put into an orphanage here. This thought hurt more than his memory of Dot, causing Cess to stop what he was doing and catch

266

his breath. When he carried on stacking logs into the log box, he marvelled at how he could find such peace here with such a memory, but was determined that Millie would do so too.

Millie had owned the cottage for a few years now and loved it. It had been willed to her by her father. Cess didn't want to change her feelings about the place by dwelling on his own memories, as he wanted to be able to come here throughout the rest of their lives whenever they needed a break.

'Are you all right, Cess?'

'Yes, coming, luv.'

Millie stood framed in the doorway of the cottage, her outline picked out by the light of oil lamps that she'd lit, as the cottage didn't get a lot of natural light through its small leaded windows. To him, she was the most beautiful he'd ever seen her.

Once the fire was going and the kettle whistling on the gas stove, Cess thought he'd landed in heaven. 'I could live here, Millie, luv.'

'Ha, it wouldn't be very practical. Let me make the tea, and then I'll listen to your dreaming.'

Cess sat down in the high-backed wooden chair and looked around him. The low ceilings flickered with the dancing light of the fire and the lamps. This living room was small, with walls that looked as if they were made of cobblestones. Off it led three doors, one to the scullery and the others to the two bedrooms. There was no bathroom, and the lav was a trip up the yard – something Millie had talked of changing, but hadn't yet got round to.

Cess was a little worried about sleeping in the double bedroom with Millie because of the million tears he'd shed in that room when he'd stayed here on his own. But then with Millie lying next to him, he was sure his heart would be settled.

After a loving night, which sealed his dreams of the life they wanted together, they had mapped out the day ahead while they had lain in bed with the sunlight splashing across them.

Breakfast, then a visit to the convent where Bert and Jimmy had been cared for, and where Millie was now a patron. And then they planned to visit the churchyard – Jimmy's grave, as well as Dai's wife's and baby's.

'I'm not going to find the convent visit easy, Millie. I've seen it from the outside, but that's all, and I've never wanted to talk to Elsie about it. Is it a loving place – are the nuns kind?'

'They are. They used to have a very strict one, but Elsie and I sorted that out and hopefully her treatment, which was verging on cruelty, has long been stamped out. I won't stand for it. And to make sure it isn't still going on, I try to have a chat with the children on their own. This gives me a true picture, as my visits are always impromptu, making it impossible for the children to have been prepared or rehearsed. But I want you to know, Cess, that they did all they could for Jimmy, darling.'

'I know – Elsie told me that much. But I'm still not sure, because of the tales Bert sometimes comes out with. Mind, poor little Jimmy was never for this world. He was always sick, poor chap. I've always wished I could have stopped the boys being taken away, but I was only a lad.'

'Oh, darling, I hate to see you hurting.'

He went into her open arms and hugged her to him. 'None of my pain hurts when I hold you, me darlin' Millie. I love you so much.'

Millie smiled up at him. 'And I love you with all my heart, you're my everything, Cess. Together we can cope with all they throw at us. Oh, Cess, I so want to be your wife. I so want to.'

'You are, remember? We made our own vows to each other.'

Millie put her head down on his shoulder, and happiness burned through him. He would never forget the smell of her hair, the feel of her in his arms or the taste of her kisses as long as he lived, and he hoped with all his heart that they never became a memory but remained a reality, always and forever.

'We'd better go, luv, or I'll be taking you back into that bed, and I had the devil's own job to get you out of it, as it is.'

They both giggled and the moment lifted.

At the convent, a nun who seemed to be in charge greeted them. 'How lovely it is to see you, Millie. Come in – go along, children, and go about your business.' The crowd of children who'd gathered to see who the visitor was went obediently through doors that Cess assumed led to classrooms.

It was all very different from what Cess had imagined. Happy giggles filled the space around them, and the place was brightly decorated, with its many windows giving a light, welcoming feel. Cess felt his heart rest easier than it had done.

Millie smiled as she took her hands from the nun's. 'We'll have a chat in a while, Reverend Mother. I want to show Cess around – he is Bert and the late Jimmy's brother – and I want to show him how lovely it is here, and how well his little brothers were cared for.'

'Very well, Millie. How nice to meet you, Cess. I'll have

tea served in my room for you as soon as you are ready. Oh, and I have a favour to ask you. I was going to write, but you're here now, so God must have sent you.'

Millie smiled. 'This way, Cess, I'll show you where Bert and Jimmy slept first, then the gardens and then the play-rooms and classrooms.'

Cess was impressed with the cleanliness, and loved the smell of polish as they toured around and the happy sounds of the children too. It was when they entered the dormitory that shivers ran down his spine, making him feel cold and strangely afraid.

'What is it, darling? You've gone pale.'

'I don't know. I feel that something happened in this room.'

'It did, my dear Cess. This is the boys' dormitory, where little Jimmy died. Bert was holding his hand at the time. Which is a nice memory for us, but I have often wondered if it will have a lasting effect on Bert.'

A sound made them both jump round. For the first time they noticed a mound in one of the beds. Millie walked towards it. The sobbing got louder.

'Are you all right. Can we help you?'

There was no answer. Millie had reached the bed and had her hand on the mound, although nothing could be seen but the shape of a body.

'Let us help you, my dear. Don't cry – nothing is as bad as it seems.'

Cess thought that this was an older boy than Jimmy and Bert had been. From the size of him, he looked as though he could be around fourteen or fifteen.

Millie pulled the cover back and then gasped. 'Oh, my dear, what happened to you? My poor boy.'

Cess stepped forward and saw the terrible scars that almost covered the boy's face. 'Tell us your name, son.'

'Jack.'

'How old are you, Jack?'

'I'm thirteen. I shouldn't be 'ere, but no one'll 'ave me. They say I'm trouble, but I only defend meself.'

'You sound like a Londoner, lad. Sit up and tell us what happened, eh?'

'Maybe we can help you, Jack. I'm Millie. I'm a patron of this convent.'

Jack sat up. Now that they could see him, they saw that the scars were only covering one side of his face and weren't as bad as they first thought.

'Come on, mate, stop crying, eh? Here, take me handkerchief and give yer nose a good blow. We men have to square our shoulders sometimes and be brave.'

'I – I used to be brave. I used to stand up to me dad.'

'Well then, yer can be brave again. We all get knock-backs, but it is how we deal with them that's important. Start by telling us what happened to yer face.'

Jack blew his nose loudly, then wiped his eyes. 'Me dad was drunk. He had one of his temper rages. He hit me young brovver, then me mum. He knocked her out . . .' His tears flowed again, only this time no sobs accompanied them.

'Go on, mate.'

'I went for him, but he was too strong for me. We had a paraffin heater. It got knocked over and . . . it set light to me mam. Me dad wouldn't . . . He 'eld me. I – I couldn't . . . The fire spread – the smoke . . . choking me. I – I kicked me dad in his bollocks. I tried to get to me mum, but the heat stopped me and I couldn't see me brovver. The smoke . . . the flames . . . I don't know any more. I

271

woke in 'ospital, and me family were gone – all gone, and so had me 'ome.'

'Oh, my dear boy. How terrible.' Millie took Jack into her arms.

Cess looked on, unsure of what to do. His eyes filled with tears at the sight of Millie rocking the kid backwards and forwards and saying, 'We'll take care of you, Jack. We will. You'll be all right. Have you any other relatives?'

'Me gran. She's me dad's mum. I went to her, but she couldn't 'andle me. I just kept wanting to run and not stop. I ran away a few times and wouldn't go to school. I – I'm sorry. I don't know why I did it. It caused her a lot of worry, she couldn't cope. I – I love me gran.'

'You were in shock. If you went back to your gran with our support, do you think you could stop running away?'

'I'd never upset her again, but she won't 'ave me. I wrote to her, but she didn't reply.'

'Look, mate, what yer did were only natural. I've had times like that, when I've just wanted to run and run and not stop running, and what I've been through is nothing to what you have.'

'I'd 'elp me gran now. I'd take care of her.'

'Of course yer would. But yer still suffering and still need to get stronger.'

'Not 'ere. Please don't make me stay 'ere. Everyone's younger than me, and they make fun of me. I've no mates. I 'ad mates back in Wapping.'

'That's just across the river from us – we're from Bermondsey.'

'Yer don't sound like yer are, miss, but you do, mister.'

'Well, there are all different kinds of people in all areas. And we are Millie and Cecil – Cess for short. Look, Jack, let me talk to the Reverend Mother. We'll find a way of helping you, I promise.'

'We will, Jack. Yer've been through enough, mate. Yer need to be back amongst yer own. But we ain't promising it will be with yer gran. We have to see what she wants, and what is best for you, but we'll do something for yer.'

'Ta. Ta ever so much. I'd never play up again if I were back in Wapping – me mates'd look out for me. They won't care about me scars.'

'Get yourself washed and dressed, Jack, and we'll see what we can do.'

'Ta, Millie. I'd always be good, I'd never play up again.'

'You don't have to keep telling us that, mate. Everyone deserves a second chance and, besides, there were reasons why yer did. So forget as much as you can about all that, and let this be a new beginning for yer, eh?'

Outside the room, Millie said, 'It might not be that easy, Cess. He may have to be assigned to the custody of one or the other of us. Elsie and I had a procedure to go through before we could take Bert, despite her being Bert's sister, although my solicitor soon sorted that out.'

'Blimey, the poor lad – he has the impression we can do it right now.'

'Well, we may be able to. Let's seek out the Reverend Mother.'

Cess was getting used to posh china, so the tea being served in dainty bone-china cups didn't bother him, though he felt he could down a good enamel mugful right now. This place disturbed him – not just because of what happened to Jimmy here, but because he knew what it was like to be in the shoes of these kids. And, but for Elsie keeping them together until it was taken out of her hands, he would have been subjected to the same thing. He couldn't bear to think of how it was for Jimmy and Bert.

'Well now, dear Millie, it is always a pleasure to see you.'

'Thank you, Matron. You said you had a favour to ask?'

'Yes, it is concerning a young boy.'

'Not Jack, by any chance?'

'Yes, did you meet him? He usually keeps well out of the way.'

'We did and we have already made up our minds to help him. What did you have in mind, Reverend Mother?'

'A job. He is far too old to be here and, if we could find him a job, we could release him to a Christian Fellowship Hostel. Or something of that nature. The Salvation Army even, as they have hostels too. But I am at a loss as to how to get him sorted.'

'Yes, I can give him a job. When is he fourteen?'

'I would have to look at his records, but he has been here a couple of months and I remember calculating then that he was thirteen and four months old.'

'Oh, six months to go . . . Reverend Mother, if we could give him a home with a job when he is old enough, could you release him to us to care for him?'

'I could, and I would be glad to. He doesn't come under the strict rules of the convent guidelines, as we only have those in place from infancy to twelve years. And I know of no law that would prevent this. We only took Jack out of kindness, because of what he has been through, but I fear we aren't helping him in any way – only adding to his problems.'

'Well, we'd be very willing to take him back with us and see that he is cared for. And we would try to establish a rapport with his grandmother and see if we can build bridges between them.'

'And a job won't be a problem, as I could do with help on me market stall.'

'Well then, that's settled. Now, may I ask how Bert is, Cess? Such a little character. And may I extend my condolences to you over poor Jimmy. There was nothing we could do for him, but we gave him the best care we could.'

'Ta. Bert's doing all right. He's living with me sister and he enjoys school, but mostly he enjoys his music. He can play the piano and he's learning to read music.'

'Oh, that's such good news.'

Before they left, they chatted with Jack and told him they would come and collect him for a couple of hours most days while they were here, so that he could get to know them, and that they would take him with them when they left. Jack was elated. He turned into a different boy, although Cess knew he had a long way to go to recover.

At the churchyard Cess visited the grave of Dai's wife, Blodwyn, as he had promised he would. He told her that Dai would come soon himself, but that he still missed her very much.

Millie held his hand but didn't speak. At Jimmy's grave she shed a tear with him and then surprised him by asking, 'Did none of you ever know who your father was, Cess?'

'Well, as yer know, Elsie found out hers. And Jimmy, well, we think it were the bloke at the corner shop – Jimmy had the look of him, and there were rumours. Besides, he used to treat Jimmy in a special way. Me? Mine were some bloke who used to come round the streets sharpening knives and scissors. Bert, well, we have no idea.'

'Could it possibly be my father?'

'What? Why do yer ask that, luv?'

'Well, I know Bert was very fair when he was young, but his hair is going dark now and his eyes are blue, but so were my paternal grandmother's. But every now and then – oh, I don't know, it can be a look or a grin, or anything – I'm immediately reminded of my father, and even more so of a sister he had who died when she was young. There was a photo of her up in our house when I was growing up.'

'Well, it isn't impossible. Let's face it, your father was in me mum's life for a long time. Well, coming and going. You know, I don't want you to think badly of me mum, as she was a good person at the heart of it.'

'I don't – I know that everything was my father's fault.'

Cess put his arm around her. 'Whoever was to blame, it wasn't you or Elsie, or me and me brovvers – we are all the victims of it.' He looked at the statue of an angel on Jimmy's grave and then kneeled on one knee. 'Well, little man, I've news for you. I'm going to marry Millie. So what do yer think of that, eh?'

A nice feeling came to him, and he closed his eyes.

'I think he's very pleased for us, Millie, me darlin'.'

Millie put her hand on his shoulder. 'I know he is, Cess. Jimmy would want anything that made you happy.'

Cess wiped away the tears that misted his eyes. 'He would. He were a lovely lad.' They walked back to the car in silence and were nearly at the cottage when Cess said, 'Well, it's been a funny day. How about we walk along the beach and blow the remnants of it away?'

As they walked, Millie talked. She spoke of her plans for the jam factory, and of how she had decided that she would rent Wilf's house. 'You see, I will need to have a nanny for Daniel, so that I can work at the factory; and for us to be taken care of, as you will be busy working and—'

'Us?'

'Yes, I want you to live there with me, Cess.'

'Well, that will take a bit of thinking about, Millie. I don't know how I would take to all the grandness of the place, and having maids, and . . . all of it.'

'I understand. Well, for now do as Wilf suggested and stay over a few times, to see if you could adapt. The maids are very discreet – you'll hardly notice them.'

'I know. I found that when me and Dot stayed with you at Burgess Place . . . All right, I'll give it a twirl. In fact I'll give you a twirl too. Come here.' With this, Cess picked Millie up and swung her around. She was as light as a feather, but his many years of weight training, which he'd first under-taken as a lad with a heartfelt wish to sort out Dot's violent stepfather one day, and to take care of his family, had made him strong.

Millie squealed to be put down, but her laughter overrode her squeals. It was a lovely sound that Cess hoped he would hear more of, as his biggest wish in all the world was for Millie's happiness.

The next day they were surprised at how resilient Jack was, as they chatted while they walked along the beach, with him in tow this time.

Cess had warned Millie that Jack might be hard to handle, that he himself as a lad had had patches of such resentment and had at times become moody and uncooperative.

'So, Jack, how are you today, son?'

'I'm cock-a-hoop, Cess, ta.'

'Oh? Well that's good news. So you're ready to start a new life then, mate?'

'I am, Cess. And I'll do anything yer ask of me. But where will I live, as I've no 'ome?'

'You'll live with me, just off the Old Kent Road, near Burgess Park. Do yer know the area?'

'No, but I 'eard that it's the posh end of Bermondsey.'

'Well, it is a nice area, but I'm from Long Lane originally. I just had some good fortune, that's all.' Cess didn't go into how his fortunes had changed, but told him about Dai and Kitty, and how he ran a market stall. 'So you can work with me – how does that suit yer?'

'I'd like that. I used to 'ang around the Wapping market, 'elping the stall 'olders and shifting rubbish for them at the end of the day. Some gave me a few pennies, but I liked it when the veg stall 'olders gave me stuff to take 'ome. Then I knew me . . . me brovver were getting some goodness in him.'

'That's a good memory to have, Jack,' Millie told him. 'Hold on to the good memories, as they will help you.'

Jack went quiet for a while, and they allowed this.

Cess broke the silence. 'When you're ready to, I'd love to hear more about your brovver. I lost a brovver, so I know the pain you're feeling. I like talking about Jimmy. What was your brovver's name?'

'Ben. He could be a pain at times, but I – I loved him all the same. He . . . he was only eight. There was a big gap between us.'

'That's like me and me brovvers. I have another one, and he's only seven. His name's Bert. You can be an older brovver to him, mate – he'd love that.'

Cess held his breath, knowing that this was a huge thing for Jack. No one could take the place of his Ben, and it might be difficult for him to accept another boy as part of the family he was joining. But he needn't have worried.

'Does he like footie?'

'Huh, do you know, I have no idea. He and our Jimmy used to kick a ball about, but Bert used to get fed up quickly, so maybe not. He likes music, but hey, he might love footie with an older boy who's interested in showing him the game again. Meself, I was more into boxing as a lad.'

'I support The Hammers. I ain't ever been to a game, but I've stood outside West Ham stadium and heard the crowd cheering. I tried to guess which side was winning.'

'Well, we'll put that right, shall we? We'll go to a game and take Bert. I might even become a fan meself.'

Cess had an overwhelming feeling of being with Jimmy, as Jimmy used to love to kick a ball with the lads in the street. But then it came to him how he could never do so for long without having a fit of coughing. Cess's eyes misted with tears at the memory, and he felt a sudden urge to put his arms around Jack and give him the love he missed giving to Jimmy.

He resisted because he realized he might frighten and embarrass the boy, but he did put his arm around his shoulder as Jack said, 'Do yer mean it, Cess? Would yer really take me to see West Ham play?'

'I mean it, son.'

Jack's smile, though hampered by his scars, which tightened the skin on his left cheek, lit up his face. He freed himself from Cess's arm and punched the air.

Millie laughed. 'I've heard how passionate you West Ham supporters are. I might just come along with you all.'

Jack laughed. 'There ain't no women go, Millie. Well, not many. It's a man's game.'

'Oh, well, I'll leave it to you men then.' She gave an exaggerated sigh. 'I'll just have to wait for Kitty to grow up and we'll find a pastime that you men can't join in.'

Cess laughed out loud. 'Knowing you, Millie, you'll soon have a gang of suffragettes marching outside the football stadium, shouting, "Football for women".'

They all laughed. Cess thought to himself that they were like a family. Something told him that's what they would become one day. He looked at Millie and saw a longing in her eyes. She was so brave, so strong. Yes, she'd wept in his arms last night when her milk had leaked from her breasts, but today – despite the pain of missing Daniel – she was cheerful and bright, for Jack's sake.

A surge of love for her gripped him and Cess vowed that he would personally fetch Daniel home as soon as they knew where he had been taken.

Chapter Twenty-Two

Millie

When they arrived back at the cottage, having dropped Jack off at the convent and promising him faithfully that they would pick him up the next day, Millie set about making Cess a cup of tea, and peeling potatoes and carrots to go with the ham she'd bought earlier.

She loved looking after him in this way. Loved being like a 'proper' wife to him – the kind he was used to. A woman in the kitchen, tidying the cottage, making the bed and cooking the meals, although Cess wasn't the conventional man of the day and helped all he could.

Not that she wanted him to. To her, this was all a new experience and she wanted to do everything – though she stopped short of getting in the wood, lighting the fires and swilling down the outside lav. Cess said she was a posh housewife, and if she'd lived as the women in his life had, she'd be doing it all. He'd laughed at the thought of her lugging the wood basket a few inches, let alone from the wood pile to the hearth.

Cess had bought a newspaper earlier and sat unfolding it. The fire was beginning to come to life. These old walls didn't warm up in the weak sunshine of early June, which had been covered by cloud for the most part.

'Oh dear, Millie, that poor Emily Wilding Davison.'

'Why? What's happened to her?'

'She's gone a bit far this time. She only jumped in front of the King's horse at Epsom. The very one that Jim was going to put a bet on.'

'Oh no!' Millie took the tray of tea through to where Cess sat next to the fireplace. 'Is she badly hurt?'

'She is. It says here that she is very seriously injured and is believed to be in a coma.'

'Oh dear, why does she go to such extreme lengths? The movement doesn't ask that of its members. Just to attend protest rallies, which I haven't done yet, and hand out leaflets – that sort of thing.'

'Well, you always get them as will go that bit further.'

'What about the jockey and the horse?'

'Both all right. The jockey is injured, but not badly. If you do take up a more active role in these protests, you won't be doing anything that could put you in danger, will you, Millie?'

'No. I'm not militant, but as you know, I do believe passionately in women's rights.'

'Ha, I saw that with the strike back in 1911. You were a powerhouse, even against your own father. All of you did well, especially that Lucy . . . What was her name?'

'Lucy Dalton. She's very big in the National Federation of Women Workers now. I'm planning on contacting her and asking her to advise me on all the aspects of putting into place safety measures, as well as welfare measures, for my workers. Oh, I'm so excited about getting the factory going again . . . it, well, it's helping me, having that to think about.'

'Come here, luv.' Cess patted his knee.

A shyness came over Millie. She hadn't sat on any man's knee since she'd been a little girl and sat on her father's – a time when she'd adored him, and felt nothing but annoyance at her mother. A time when he and she were like conspirators against Mama.

'Come on, me darlin', I won't bite.'

Millie rose and went to Cess. His arms reached out and pulled her down. When they enclosed her, her body shook with emotion.

'Millie. Millie, me luv, don't cry.'

Her sobs racked her body. They took all her strength and left her limp with pain. The pain of yesterday – of her deceitful, hateful father, of not seeing the love her mama had for her, of finding out all her father really was and what harm he'd done to people. And the pain of today, of what Len had done to Elsie and to herself. But most of all she cried for her son. Her darling baby, who'd left her arms empty, her breasts weeping milk that he could no longer drink, and her heart broken.

Cess held her, rocking her gently, making soothing noises, and promising her over and over again that he would get Daniel back for her. For himself too, as he loved the little chap with all his heart. 'He's our son, Millie. He'll always be ours. And has been since the moment we brought him into the world together and he brought our love for each other to our notice. Because I believe now that we have always loved each other. We thought it was in a brother–sister way, even though we aren't related. But we were both distracted: me with me childhood sweetheart, and you with all that was going on, and then being charmed by the rotten Len.'

'Yes, I – I didn't know it then, but I did feel a . . . a special bond with you, Cess.'

'And now it is a deep love, and it matches the love I have for you. We'll be a match for anyone together, Millie. No Lens of this world will ever hurt yer again, me little darling. You're safe now. And free. You can be the Millie yer want to be. Yer've no boundaries tying yer to convention – ha, I wouldn't know a convention if I saw one!'

Millie felt a giggle rising up inside her. It burst from her in a loud laugh that was almost verging on hysterical.

Cess held her tighter. 'I've got you, Millie, luv. I'm holding on to you. Don't give in, Millie. We can get through this. We can.'

Controlling the urge to laugh, scream and cry all at once, Millie turned her face to his and kissed him. It was a kiss hampered by her rebound sobs, but she put her heart into it.

'Oh, Millie, Millie. I want to love yer better.'

Millie rose and took his hand. She wanted him like never before.

When they reached the bedroom, they became frantic in their efforts to join together and once more seal their love.

Though hurried, the love Cess gave her filled Millie with joy and a sense of really yearning to be his. She didn't want him to leave her – wanted him to be careful, but to fill her with himself and join them in a way that only staying together as he climaxed could. Wrapping her legs around him, she held him as if in a vice. Heard him call out in an agony of trying to stop the inevitable, and then knew the exquisite feeling of him releasing himself inside her. Now she was truly his.

They lay quietly afterwards.

Cess spoke first. 'Millie, it was what you wanted, wasn't it?'

'Yes, Cess, my darling. I wanted to be totally yours, and now I am. Thank you, my beloved.'

'And if it means—'

'Then that will be the happiest moment in my life, darling. A brother for Daniel and Kitty – only truly ours together, my darling.'

'Oh, Millie.' Cess rolled over and looked down into her face. 'You are the most amazing woman. I want to have dozens of babies with you. Dozens of brothers and sisters for our Kitty and Daniel.'

Millie smiled through her tears. 'We'll be the happiest family on earth. Oh, Cess, please say that you and Kitty will move in with me when Mama and Wilf leave.'

'We will. I promise . . . Huh, will that be me going against convention?'

'It will. How bad are you?'

They both laughed.

When they were dressed and Millie had made a fresh cup of tea, Cess became serious. 'You know, Millie, living together without being married isn't easy. It does take a toll on yer. Me Dot suffered terribly because we were forced into that state.'

'I know she did, darling, and I felt so sorry for her. Her status as, well, "living in sin" is really looked down on by cockney folk. That's the real meaning of convention – the rules put in place by our own people. Dot hated every minute of being thought of as a . . . oh, I don't know. What do they say about women who have a child and aren't married?'

'They call them a lot of names – fallen woman is the polite term, slag, loose woman, trollop or a scrubber. Poor Dot.

She so wanted us to be married, but for that bigoted mother of hers.'

'You married her in the end, darling. She was so happy.'

'She was. But, Millie, you won't suffer like she did by what we do, will yer?'

'No. I have always been a lonely girl, Cess. No real friends until I met Elsie and Dot. There's no one who will care what I do. I mean, Elsie, you, Jim, Dai and Rene do, but I have no one else. And all of them will be happy for us, as will Mama and Wilf. My solicitor will be surprised, but he is very modern in his outlook. So no, we have no one to worry about . . . Oh, except the servants. Ha, they'll be very snooty about it, but I won't tolerate them being disrespectful to you, or to Kitty.'

'Kitty worries me. I don't want her brought up a snob. Oh, Millie. We will be able to make this work, won't we?'

'We will, with compromise, darling. Both on your side and mine. We will have Len and his father as a thorn in our sides, but we will just have to be strong.'

'I can't see Len ever setting foot in this country again.'

'Don't underestimate him, Cess.'

'Millie? Are you worried about him?'

'I always will be. It seems his father is covering for him, which means it may be very difficult for the police to expose the fraud, although Wilf feels certain they will. But it's funny how there hasn't been a trial, or any suggestion of one taking place of the prostitutes who were involved in what Len did to you.'

'Well, true, I haven't been called to bear witness, but these things take time.'

'Yes, and money talks fast. Len's father can offer the earth, and big money can sway the most honest of people to do the bidding of another – and that includes members of the police force.'

'Well, we can't alter things now, so you have to have faith in what Wilf is telling you. I trust him, and I know he will sort it all out. So let's enjoy our evening. It started with a blip and then improved greatly, so let's continue it that way, eh?'

Millie had to laugh at the way Cess winked when he said 'improved greatly'.

'Honestly, Millie, I'd rather talk about all those kids we're going to make than that soon-to-be ex-husband of yours.'

The telephone ringing stopped this conversation. Wilf was on the line, but it was hard to hear as there was a crackle that seemed to drown out every third or fourth word.

'All finalized . . . end, dear. I have the . . . to the factory.'

'You have the keys? That's wonderful. Can Jim pick them up? He's ready to get started.'

'Yes, and there is . . . on Len. Not good I'm . . . to say.'

It was as Millie had suspected. All hint of a fraud had been eradicated. Her heart sank. 'And the charge in Southampton?'

'No one will stop . . . I have filed my papers. But all is not lost . . . delayed. One thing Harold didn't bargain for . . . being prosecution lawyer. I wangled it . . . I . . . bargaining power.'

Millie knew that Wilf had a lot of bargaining power – not to mention the magistrate being in awe of him – and that he had been able to substantiate everything before Len's father could do his dirty work.

'And my divorce?'

'Papers filed. I . . . your solicitor. Nice chap. He got on to it. He is . . . abandonment. We may need to use Rose . . . where she tells of her and Len's son. But it will . . . time.'

'Yes, we have the letter, and Elsie is witness to Rose telling us that her child was Len's. How much time will it take?'

'Could be a year, or more.'

'Oh?'

'Sorry. But these things cannot be rushed. Be easier if you were the man seeking to divorce your wife.'

Millie seethed at this.

'Is there a problem, Millie? You knew there would be a wait.'

'I . . . I, no. Only, could Len counteract and use Cess?'

'Possibly. But would that matter, as long as you are free?'

'No. Only, well, for my child and the financial side of things.'

'Don't worry – Len can't claim anything. And I still have a lot up my sleeve. Let's hope that Rose contacts us soon. Are you enjoying yourselves?'

When the conversation ended, Millie had the sensation that her world was still very rocky, and not at all a safe place.

'So is everything all right, Millie? One moment I understood it to be, and the next . . .'

'Yes, as right as it can be. There are a lot of pitfalls, but I just want to get on with the positives. I have the factory keys!'

'That's great – I'm happy for yer, luv. I heard you mention Jim starting work. I'll ring Dai and see if he's up to releasing Elsie to my stall, so that Jim is free.'

'Cess, can I ask something of you? Please say no if you don't agree. But can we go home?'

Cess looked taken aback. She knew he was so happy here. They could be a proper couple – she hadn't yet had the courage to tell him of them possibly having to change their 'living together' plans until the divorce was finalized. And although he thought he had that promise to come, she knew it wasn't going to be like being here in Barmouth, and so did Cess.

'Well, it's disappointing, luv, but if yer think it best, of course we can. I just hope that your mama and Wilf don't have to leave it too long before they can go.'

It was all a bit rushed the next day, but now they were on the road, conscious of their extra passenger, an excited Jack, who of all things seemed to suffer from motion sickness, making their progress very slow and worrying, as he looked really poorly. They tried everything, from lying him down across the back seat to letting him sit in the front, but nothing helped.

'I think we should stop and get help, Cess. I'm really worried about Jack.'

Cess pulled up outside a Tudor building and looked back at Jack. 'Good God, you're right, Millie . . . Jack? Jack, lad. Are yer awake? Have yer got any pain?'

A weak and sleepy Jack nodded. 'Me ears.'

'Cover them up, with the blanket over yer, son. We're taking yer to a doctor. We won't be long – there's bound to be a dozen of them in this place.' He turned back to Millie. 'Hereford Cattle Market's just over the road there, look. And there's loads of people, so someone should be able to help us.'

As Cess got out, Millie did too and slipped into the back seat with Jack. 'Lean on me, Jack. That's right, put your head on my lap, dear.'

Jack did as she said, crying out with pain as he moved.

'Have you had this before, Jack?'

He nodded, but grimaced against the agony that the

movement caused him. His voice was a whisper as he said, 'Since the fire. It's me ear, and the side of me face – it makes me be sick and feel dizzy.'

'So, not just when you travel?'

'No.'

'All right, don't try to talk any more. I just wanted to make sure it wasn't car sickness.'

The doctor was an attentive man and most concerned about Jack. 'I think he should see a specialist in the subject of ears, nose and throat. I can see there has been damage to his left ear, and it may be that an operation would help the young man.'

'Can you give him anything for the pain until we can get home?'

'Yes, I can give him a sedative too, so that he'll sleep through it.'

For the rest of the journey Millie sat with Jack in the back, as she had done, with his head across her lap. He slept all the way, but not peacefully. Her heart went out to him as he muttered in anguish, fought against the horror that was replaying in his mind and cried tears.

When they reached home, his condition had greatly deteriorated. Millie had no time to explain who he was, or why he was with her, but implored Wilf to call the best doctor he knew.

Hours later Millie looked across the hospital bed at Cess. Jack now lay in a deep sleep, his head swathed in bandages, but resting peacefully following an operation on his ear.

'It's a good job you decided that we'd come home today, Millie, luv. Otherwise we might not have found the kind of help for Jack that we have.'

'No. I dread to think how much he has suffered, poor boy.'

Jack stirred. 'Millie . . . Cess?'

'We're here, mate.'

Millie rose. 'How are you feeling, dear?'

'Strange. Are . . . is it you, Millie?'

'Yes, dear, it truly is me. You have had an anaesthetic and will feel odd, but you shouldn't suffer any more pain, once you've healed from the operation you've had.'

'Millie?'

'Yes?'

'I love you, Millie.'

Millie swallowed hard. 'Thank you, Jack, and I love you. You are always going to be a part of our family, isn't he, Cess?'

'You are, mate. You're all right now.'

'Ta, Cess. I love yer as well – yer like the big brother I never had.'

'Ha! They say that stuff you've had makes yer talk a lot. But I like what you're saying, son. Like Millie says, yer've no need to worry any more. Now I'll have to send Millie home, as she's exhausted and she has business to see to tomorrow. But I'll stay with you. How will that be?'

'But you're tired too. I'll be all right, Cess. I'll just sleep. Ta for everything.'

Convinced by Jack that he'd be all right if they left, they told him they would ring the hospital later and make sure he was; and if not, then they would come straight back to him. Then Cess and Millie made their way home.

They held hands on the way. 'What a lovely lad Jack is, Cess. I feel as though I want to rescue all children who suffer.'

'There are a lot of them, Millie. Places like that convent, and Barnardo's, do a good job . . . Well, we hope they do, but a lot of children are ill-treated or are still in workhouse orphanages. You can't save them all, luv.'

'I know. But I wish I could do more.'

'Oh, Millie, luv, you carry the world on yer shoulders. I luv that about you. We'll see. Maybe in the future we can do something together.'

'I'm afraid of the future, Cess. Afraid of all that could happen, and of the uncertainty.'

They'd pulled up outside her home. 'Don't be, luv. All will come right, you'll see. I'll see you tomorrow, eh? I've to get home now. It's work for me tomorrow, as I want Elsie to be able to come to the factory with you. Dai will be all right to look after his own stall.'

'Yes, Mama was really upset about that, when I telephoned her to say I was coming back and what was happening. She's loved it – and loved being with Elsie too.'

'I know. According to Dai, the takings that they have dropped off are far more than he takes – he's thinking of employing her.'

Despite her tiredness and all that had happened, Millie laughed at this. 'Well, I'll get in. I'll no doubt face a lot of questions about Jack, and how we came to have him . . . Wasn't it lovely how he said that he loved us?'

'It was, me darlin'.' With this, Cess kissed her on the cheek as the car door was opened by Campbell, who stood waiting for Millie to alight.

An hour later, having enjoyed a lovely bath, some hot milk and having chatted with her mama and Wilf, bringing them up to date on everything, Millie lay in her bed. She'd asked the maid to leave her curtains open, and now she gazed upon the stars. Her thoughts were with Daniel, wondering how and where he was, and her heart felt heavy.

The feeling she'd had earlier about the future wouldn't leave her. It was as if she was heading for a cloud of doom. And yet so much was hopeful. Rose might write or ring any day, and the factory was to open again. And more than all that, she had Cess's love. His beautiful, unconditional love. *Why, then, do I feel that I'm heading for an awful event?*

Sighing, she closed her eyes. The action squeezed out the tears that had been brimming and sent cold trickles down her cheek. She brushed them away and told herself, 'Be strong. Don't give in, Millie, girl. You must never give in.'

Chapter Twenty-Three

Rose

Rose ached all over as she stared out at the passing terrain. They'd gone through the Italian border with no problems. Len had seen to everything and had all the papers he needed for himself, her and the children.

She couldn't enjoy the scenery, but only noted that it wasn't dissimilar to Britain. And she couldn't relax, because apart from the stiffness of her body from sitting for hours, she felt disgust at herself, which she couldn't come to terms with. Len was using her, night after night. His coming to her bed and taking her was no more than rape, even though she had shown her willingness to lie with him.

It wasn't what she wanted to do, as she hated Len with every fibre of her being, but she wished to do everything he said so as not to upset him. And it wasn't as if she was travelling with him as his equal because, at all times, she had to dress in the nanny uniform that he'd presented her with.

They had travelled for days on trains, boats and more trains. Which, although first-class, still made it very difficult for her to cope with two babies, even though she had the help of two wet nurses. Neither spoke English, but even so, it seemed to her that they had been warned not to communicate with her, as both were cold and unfriendly towards her.

Len had told her that her child had been registered as Ronald Harold Lefton, and he had dampened some of her joy at being reunited with him by telling her that Ronnie was his son, and his alone, as he had formally adopted him.

In his over-pompous, egotistical way, Len assumed that she did everything asked of her because she was in love with him. And he seemed to think he was taunting her by telling her that Ronnie had so far been brought up by his mistress, but Rose hadn't cared. She'd only cared that her son was well, had been looked after and that she was reunited with him. Her love for her child surpassed any she'd experienced, and although she loved Daniel too, so very much, the love she had for him didn't come near to that she had for Ronnie.

Her mind left these thoughts and drifted to the ever-present longing to escape, and how she could possibly accomplish it. Len had told her that they were going to his mother's family farm, and that this side of his family were even more powerful than he and his father were, as they were highly regarded and feared Mafia.

This had put a terror into Rose. She had read about the way the Mafia conducted themselves and she wondered what Len had in mind for her when they arrived. It was this fear that prompted her to be compliant and to behave like no more than a lapdog.

A cry brought her out of her thoughts. Daniel had woken up. A quiet, undemanding child, his crying wasn't the loud, persistent kind, just a gentle letting you know that he was either uncomfortable or hungry, whilst Ronnie was quite the opposite – God help your ears if he needed anything. This made her smile indulgently, as she would give him the earth if he needed it.

The babies were sleeping in a little hammock slung from the luggage rack, the gentle rocking motion of the train swaying them and keeping them content for hours.

'What is it, little one? Are you hungry?'

Pulling the covers back, Rose stared in horror. Daniel's cheeks were glowing and beads of sweat stood out on his hot, red cheeks.

'Oh, my little darling, what's the matter, eh?'

Daniel whimpered, the sound seeming all too much for him as he looked back at her through half-closed eyes.

Lifting him out of the hammock gave Rose a shock, as his body felt hot through the swathes of sheet that bound him, making him appear like an Egyptian mummy, but for his face being uncovered. She had never agreed with this method of wrapping a baby and had indicated to the wet nurses not to restrict the babies in this way. But they just shrugged as if they didn't understand, and did it anyway.

Unwrapping Daniel she hoped would cool him, but as the layers unravelled, his body heat became more apparent, and the dampness of the sheet he'd sweated in deepened her worry as she realized that he must have a high temperature.

Taking him to the closet, Rose stripped him of all his clothes and, holding him over the bowl provided, she lifted the jug of cold water and gently poured it over him in an effort to bring his temperature down. His cries became croaking sounds that told her his throat must be sore.

'My poor little one – it's all right, don't fret. Rose will make you better.' But all her efforts were in vain. Daniel remained hot, though now he was shivering uncontrollably.

Wrapping him in a towel, Rose went through the first

carriage and then another one, frantic to find Len. She knew he'd be playing cards with some cronies he'd met on this leg of the journey, but wasn't sure which carriage he would be in. The train seemed endless as she ran along the corridor, looking into every carriage she passed. Some had their curtains pulled across and she dared not knock on them, fearing to disturb someone's privacy.

Daniel lay limp in her arms, increasing her fear. At last she came to the dining carriage and heard laughter. A group of men sat around a table laden with wine bottles. Most of them were laughing, but Len was slumped back on the bench in a drunken stupor.

Just as she was about to call out to the others to wake him the train began to slow. Rose turned and hurried back the way she had come, pushing past the people beginning to emerge from their carriages, frantic to get back to Ronnie. This was her chance!

But trying to get past the luggage and the hordes of people hampered her. The train stopped and the doors opened. Taking a huge risk, Rose jumped down onto the platform and ran as fast as she could. At last she came to her carriage. The door was open. Beckoning to a porter, she indicated the suitcase she wanted. Her head swivelled as she searched the windows, hoping that the wet nurses – always curious whenever the train stopped – hadn't poked their heads out to watch the goings-on, but the coast was clear.

Remembering the Italian for 'Just a second', which was said often by the stewards on the train, she commanded, '*Un momento*.'

Jumping on the train, she pulled a small valise from under the seat and her handbag, which lay next to it, and handed them to the porter, before scooping a sleeping Ronnie from his hammock and following the porter off the train. Hoping that he understood, she told the porter, '*Taxi, per favore.*'

Then she followed him, not daring to look back. When she reached the barrier, she felt relieved that she'd picked up her handbag, as her ticket was inside. Len had given it to her – a sign that he didn't think it would matter. Besides, in a small hole that she'd made in the lining, she'd stuffed money that she'd stolen from Len's coat whenever she had the chance, a little at a time. But, she hoped, enough to get by, if she needed it. Now all she had to do was to change some of it into lire.

She looked back, frantic to see if she was being followed. But these worries faded as the shrill sound of a whistle sounded and the train slowly chugged out of the station.

Getting to a bank was easier than she'd anticipated, because on asking the taxi driver, he just confirmed by asking, '*Banca?*'

This was near enough for Rose, and she nodded.

Everything she did was a struggle while juggling two babies, but somehow she managed to buy some lire and was very pleased with the amount she got for the remaining twelve pounds she had, leaving her a few oddments of change in English money.

Luckily she found it easy to make the taxi driver understand that she needed a hotel. But by the time she was in a room with twin beds and had lain the boys down, her arms burned from holding them. Even finding the money to tip the hotel porter gave her pain. But nothing could daunt the elation she felt.

Daniel had cooled down and was now sleeping. She gently checked him over. Whatever had ailed him had gone as he didn't stir whilst she did this, and she found nothing to worry her about his condition. Thanking God for this, Rose picked up the decanter of water laid out on the dressing table and poured herself a glass. As she sat in the chair near the window, overlooking the busy street below, she realized that she was overwhelmed with problems. The only thing she knew was that she was in Turin, as she'd seen the sign at the station. But other than that, she was lost. She couldn't speak the language and didn't have a clue what she was going to do next.

Looking around her, her anxiety didn't allow her to appreciate the grandeur of the room and only registered that the main colours were royal blues and creams, as she opened the suitcase and checked the contents.

To her relief, the two unopened tins of Cow & Gate baby milk and two feeding bottles that she'd advised Millie to buy were there. Millie had been adamant that she didn't want a wet nurse to feed her child, in the event of not being able to do so herself. At this thought, Rose felt her anguish rise. *Oh, Millie, I'm so sorry. I just had no say in the matter.*

Shaking herself mentally and trying to keep strong, Rose was reassured too by there being an adequate supply of nappies and clothes for the two boys, which had all been worn and laundered during the journey. For herself she had a change of underwear and one frock. She didn't care about this, as long as she had what she needed for the boys.

The locked valise sat next to the suitcase and, though small, it contained all her fears – inside was the mountain of notes and valuable jewellery that Len had shown her and boasted he'd taken from his bank. He saw no wrong in doing so, as he needed it and that was justification enough for him.

Her fear stemmed from knowing he would stop at nothing to get it back. Panic threatened to strangle her, as she now regretted taking it. Looking around the room, trying to think what to do next, she spotted an elegant desk in the bay window, equipped with writing paper, a pen and ink, and knew that her next action should be to write to Millie:

My dear Millie,

By now you will have read my letter, and will know why I did such a terrible thing. I hope you will now know that I meant what I said, as I have managed to escape with our babies. I am frantic with worry, though, as to what to do next.

She went on to tell Millie how she had escaped and where she was, and then wrote of her fears:

My concern is that if Turin is the only stop before the train reaches whatever destination it is heading for, then Len will know that this is where I am. And as I have stolen his money, he will be desperate to find me.

I have taken the precaution of not using my own name to register in the hotel. I am Mrs Raven, after the house in Leeds where I was so happy. But despite this precaution, I am still afraid and must find a way of moving on.

Not speaking the language will make it very difficult. But I want you to know that at least I have got this far, that I will protect our children with my life, and that I will do all I can to get us safely home to England. I will contact you when I can.

Your true friend, Rose
P.S. My love to Elsie x

With this done, Rose made her way to the bed and the two sleeping babies. Sitting in the chair next to them, she wrung her hands together. *How will I protect you? I don't even know how to ask for hot water for your bottles.*

As if in protest to this, Ronnie woke and yelled at the top of his voice, increasing her distress. There was nothing more to do but ring the pull-cord situated next to the door and hope that, by gesturing her need to whoever attended, she could make them understand her.

When the tap on the door came, a flustered Rose, cradling her baby, ran to answer it. The bellboy, who was more of a young man, bowed.

'I . . . need . . . hot . . . water . . . *Per favore.*'

The young man grinned. 'Of course, madam. Is it for the *bambini*?'

'Oh, you speak English?' Tears of relief filled Rose's eyes.

'Yes, madam, I have an English *madre*, who insists on being called Mama and that I speak English at all times in front of her. She has been in Italy for twenty years, but still cannot speak Italian well. My *padre* – Papa – also speaks English, as they met when he worked in England. But what Mama doesn't know is that we have many conversations in our own language.'

He laughed then and Rose, her astonishment at being told so much mixing with her relief, giggled with him. 'Oh, I am so glad to meet you. I so need the help of someone who can speak my language.'

'What can I help you with, madam?'

'I need to begin my journey back to England, but I don't know the times of the trains or how to buy tickets, or the route I will need to take. I know I got here via Paris, as we stopped there for two nights, while my . . . my husband enjoyed . . . Oh, I mean—'

'Are you running away?'

Rose sighed. She'd talked herself into a muddle. The truth, or near to it, now seemed her only option. 'Yes – from a very brutal husband who forced me to leave England.'

'Where is this husband?'

Rose explained how she had jumped from the train while he was in a drunken stupor. 'I am afraid that he may come here and find me, so I must leave as soon as possible.'

The young man was silent for a moment, but then became her saviour. 'I will take you to my mama, she will help you. Firstly, I will get your hot water, and bring more so that you have enough to wash your babies. I have never seen twins before.' He leaned forward over the surprisingly quiet Ronnie. 'A beautiful *bambino*. But I am no good at telling if babies are boys or girls . . . Oh, I thought twins were identical, but this one is so much bigger than that one.'

'They are boys. Yes, I – I . . . well, you see, my sons had different starts in life. Ronnie, the bigger boy, thrived from the beginning, but Daniel was very poorly. The doctors assured me that he would catch up . . . Oh, I can't tell you how grateful I am. Thank you so much.' Just before he left, Rose handed him her letter. 'And can you see that this is posted, please?'

'I will hand it in to reception. All post is collected from there.'

As the door closed on him, Rose danced around the room. 'We're safe, little ones . . . safe.'

*

By the time the young man returned, Rose had changed both boys, and had the milk powder ready in the jug she'd brought with her. She was having a job to stop the babies being in competition with each other, as they both cried out for food. When he entered the room, he had all she needed on a trolley.

'Thank you. I am so grateful. So will you take me to your mama when you finish work?'

'Yes, I am going home in an hour. I walk, but you cannot do so, with all you have to carry. I can get a taxi for us, but I cannot pay for it.'

'That isn't a problem. Here, this is for you.'

He unrolled the money and gasped. 'But this is too much.'

'No, it isn't near enough. I want you to help me further, by getting me out of this hotel without me having to check out, and by trying to arrange it so that no one knows I have gone with you.'

'Are you in that much danger?'

'I might be. But I don't want anyone to be able to tell my husband where I went, if he calls. It is better that they all think I am in this room.'

The young man looked fearful.

'Please. I promise that if I can get away somewhere safe tonight, I will leave your house tomorrow and no one will ever know I was there.'

'I think I can manage it. We have a back staircase. I can take your baggage down that way and take care not to be seen. I can then send it to my house in a taxi, with a note for my mama. When I am ready to go, I will come for you and take you that way also.'

'Thank you so much. I am so sorry to put you in this position.'

The young man smiled. 'I am enjoying it. My job is boring. I only do it while I wait to go to *università* . . . I mean, university. I want to study law. This is excitement. I will come back for your cases shortly.'

Rose didn't have time to concentrate on how it would all work out as she set about feeding the boys, with them both on the bed, so that she could sit and hold both bottles. Her love for them overwhelmed her. But so did her fear. If it was true that Len's family was the Mafia, then they would hunt her down.

She trembled at this thought, but then dismissed it. They, like Len, would be wanted for their crimes and probably felt safer staying where they were. And she felt sure that Len could never go home to England, as he would face years in prison.

'No, we will be safe, I'm sure of it. We just need to get our feet back on British soil, my little ones.'

The hour until the young man returned seemed like ten.

The route out of the hotel, though dark and dingy, posed no problems, and yet as Rose sat back in the taxi cab, her body trembled as she watched the Grand Hotel di Torino disappear.

The open horse-drawn carriage left her exposed to the warm breeze and as she pushed the stray dark curls back off her face, she couldn't shake the feeling of being afraid, despite the soothing clip-clop of the horse's hooves.

Alongside this feeling she had an overwhelming sense of being alone in the world but for the boys, and the responsibility of them hung heavily on her shoulders. On top of this, she hadn't a clue where the young man was taking her. Was she right to trust him? She didn't know, but at the moment he was her only hope.

When the carriage came to a halt just a few streets away, in a cobbled road lined with white brick buildings, the driver turned and shouted, 'Po Strada.'

Rose realized, from a sign, that this was the name of the street.

'Our apartment is through here and up a flight of steps. I won't be a minute, I'll just pay the driver, as I can now thanks to how generous you were.'

Rose put down the valise containing Len's money between her legs and took some money from her bag. 'No, you keep that, I'll see to it.'

'That valise is very precious to you. You have struggled to hold on to it. I am thinking that it may contain something very important?'

This shocked Rose, as she hadn't realized she'd drawn attention to the valise. 'My . . . my papers. I must not lose it.'

'Oh, I see. Come along, then, follow me.'

As she followed him, she told him, 'I don't know your name. I have been so anxious that I forgot to ask you.'

'Lorenzo, but I am known as Lori.'

'I am Rosalind, known as Rose. Rose Raven.'

'That is a nice name. It is a lovely flower, and you are lovely, like a rose.'

She blushed.

A woman appeared at that moment. 'Ha! I heard that. My Lori is learning to flirt. And who is this you are flirting with?'

Rose introduced herself, wondering if she should have changed her first name, but it was too late now.

'You're English! How wonderful. But . . . how did you get here? Where did you come from?'

'Mama, Rose is in trouble . . .'

Rose watched Lori's mother's face take on many expressions as she listened.

'I told her you would help her, Mama.'

'But of course I will. My poor dear. I am sorry you and your twins have been through so much. *Casa mia è casa tua* – my home is your home. Now, let me take one of the babies. Come on through. You may have to sleep on the settee, and we will have to push two chairs together to make a cot for the boys, but you are very welcome. And oh, we have so much to talk about.'

Though not Italian, Lori's mother could be taken for one, as the sun had darkened her skin. This, along with her dark hair and large brown eyes, didn't give you the impression of a British lady until she spoke.

'You are very kind. After all, I am a complete stranger to you.'

'No, not a stranger – a caller from home – and I am very happy to have you here. I want to hear everything about London while I cook tea. Whether it has changed in the last twenty years. You see, I left there then and have never been back. My name is Jenny.'

Everything turned out to be a series of questions as to whether this statue and that park was still there.

'I am so sorry, Jenny, but I am from the North and haven't been in London long. I think everything is the same as it always has been, though.'

'You don't speak like a northerner.'

'No, I had to unlearn my northern dialect in order to become a nanny.'

'I see, a nanny who married well but fell flat on her face?'

'Yes. I – I thought I was a lucky girl. I married a man of

means. I – I didn't know he could be violent until I was pregnant, I just had to get away. We were on a trip to see his parents.' Rose never thought that the experience with her real husband would one day give her part of a cover story that had the ring of truth.

'Oh? Where do they live?'

'It is in Italy, but I can't remember the name of the place.'

'Well, no matter. You're here now.'

'Mama, while you talk, I am going to go to the station to sort out Rose's passage home tomorrow.'

'She can stay here a few days. I can look after her. I need some English company.'

'No, I cannot stay! . . . I'm sorry, but I must leave as soon as possible. My – my husband has links to the Mafia. If they find me . . .'

'Oh my God! The Mafia?'

'Yes. I'm sorry, I shouldn't have come, but I didn't know what else to do. When your son offered that I could come here, I only thought of how safe me and the children would be.'

'He did right. But I do think, under the circumstances, that you should leave. I know the times of all the trains. I have so longed to travel back to England myself that I take an interest. There is an overnight train, on which you have to make a few changes along the way to get to Paris – it will get you there tomorrow night. Then from there you can board a train the next morning to Calais, and then it is a matter of getting a boat. They depend on the tide, but by then you will be well away from here. I am sorry, my dear, but now you have told us about the Mafia connection, I cannot offer for you to stay here.'

Rose knew the journey only too well, and she knew that

it would take at least three days – more if they had to wait for high tide. It had taken them longer to get here, with the stopover in Paris.

'Please don't worry. Although I feel exhausted, I want to get on my way as soon as possible. I don't want you to be afraid.'

'I will go with you to the station, Rose. I will see that you get on the right train and help you to buy your tickets. I can write down for you how to ask for your ongoing tickets too, as I can speak French.'

'Thank you, Lori.' An idea occurred to Rose as she said this, 'Lori, when do you go to university?'

'In September.'

'Please say no if this doesn't appeal to you, but would you consider coming with me? I will pay you, and all expenses. And for you to stay in London for a week and see the sights. I will look after you.'

Lori turned to his mother. 'Oh, Mama, can I?'

'I think it would be wonderful, my dear. I only wish that I could come with you, but Papa wouldn't allow it . . . Thinking about it, he wouldn't allow you to go either, so go now before he comes in from work. Hurry, Lori – get what you'll need together.'

The next few minutes were a flurry of activity. Rose felt a mixture of feelings: excitement as the possibility of getting home became real, and fear that, with the hours passing, Len might be on his way back to find her. Plus worry over how she was going to manage to feed the boys.

They were peaceful now, but in a couple of hours they would be hungry again. Her only option was to take two bottles, ready prepared. Cold milk was better than none.

Jenny expressed her surprise, but accepted it when Rose

told her that she hadn't produced enough milk to feed them both.

'Oh? I have never seen that method, as the Italian women are natural breeders – they can feed a dozen babies. It is all the good, fresh food they eat. Anyway, I already have a kettle boiling. But, my dear, how will you feed them afterwards?'

'I have been thinking about that . . . You don't happen to own a Thermos flask, do you? I could fill it with boiling water and it would be enough to get us through the night, and then I can keep getting it refilled.'

'I do. Well, it is my husband's. He goes fishing a lot, sometimes camps out and he bought one recently . . . Oh, but it is his pride and joy and was so expensive. You see, none of his friends have one, and he is so proud to pour them a cup of coffee from it. I cannot let it go. But, well, for the babies . . .'

'I will pay for it. Then you can buy another one. Oh, please, Jenny, it will be a lifesaver for my boys.'

'I'll get it. What am I thinking? How could I even have considered saying "no"? But if you don't mind buying it, that will help me with my husband's temper.'

As Rose got the money out of her handbag, she felt a tinge of guilt. She hadn't meant to spend so much. She might be forced to prise open the valise somehow, when she had hoped to return that money, intact, to the bank – or what was left of it, which was a great deal. But she might have no choice. She had to do all that she could to get home to safety. But then would she ever be safe again while Len was alive?

Chapter Twenty-Four

Elsie

Elsie felt so many emotions assail her as she walked into the empty jam factory – years of toil, since she was a thirteen-year-old, flashed before her.

When Jim had turned the car into Staple Street, for a brief moment she'd felt the same dread as she had then. As it had to her young self, gazing along that same cobbled street, the factory had looked foreboding as it loomed large in the early-morning smog. But then she would hear the clatter of the wooden-soled shoes, and the laughter of the women calling out to one another as they surged towards the gates – a sound that always cheered her and made her remember how she was part of the lovely cockney community.

How different it appeared now, and yet all that had changed was her own perception of it, as it had gone from being a place of drudgery to a place of fear, with the actions of Chambers, the then-foreman, and of her boss – Hawkesfield, the man who had fathered her – into becoming a place of hope, with happy vibes, sustaining those very same women instead of dragging them into the gutter. She, Millie and Jim had done that, and now they would do it again.

Jim had held her hand as they'd stood outside for a moment, gazing up at its now-rusted sign proclaiming 'Swift's – Manufacturers of Fine Preserves', before entering the building. It was then that the excitement in Elsie had died a little and been replaced by the feelings that took her now, as she gazed across what felt like a hollow space to the spot where Dot's memorial plaque used to hang.

'Len took it down?'

'Yes. I didn't want to tell you at the time and then, with all the excitement, I forgot, darling. I'm so sorry.' Jim squeezed her hand. 'But the good thing is that I have the plaque safe. I removed it myself after work, as I couldn't bear the shame of what would have happened if I'd done it in front of the women.'

'They would have lynched you.'

'I think they felt like that at times, as I had no way of telling them that I had to do Len's bidding. It was a relief to me when he sent me to Kent – from that point of view, I mean.'

'I know, me darlin'. But I put them all straight by telling Ada, and she's like the *News of the World*. I didn't say the real reason, just that you were forced to do as you had done.'

'Well, they know the reason now, and they are willing to help us. Come on, let's make putting the plaque back up our first job. Then we can assess what will need to be done to get this place up and running.'

'Can we make it an early job to get the sign outside changed?'

'Yes, we'll see what we all come up with as a name for the new factory, or whether we decide on keeping it as it is. I hope it is agreed that we name it something completely different from Swift's or Lefton's. Both have a bad reputation, and we want this to be a new start. We can let all our old and faithful customers know that we are back and hope they will support us again.'

'We may have to put on a few deals to begin with, as our business will have been replaced by others.'

'Yes, you're right. Ah, here's Millie.'

'You two beat me to it – haven't you slept?'

'Not very much. Welcome back, luv.' Elsie held her arms open to Millie. As they hugged, they both shed a tear. But both dismissed the emotion quickly. 'We need to be strong, Millie. And I have enough strength to prop you up. And yet I will be a shoulder to cry on if yer need it, luv.'

Millie smiled as she pulled away. 'Join the queue. Ha, I've a mountain of them, but I need your strength, Elsie, and I need you to keep me from crying. Bully me along, if you have to. I have to get on with life.'

'Well, with that speech, mate, I'd say you have a mountain of strength too!'

They both smiled at this.

'So, what's the plan?'

'I'm just going to fetch the first task, and then we both thought that we need to come up with a name, as one of us needs to begin to contact all our suppliers.'

'Right, I think a board meeting first, after whatever it is you are planning, Jim.'

Elsie explained to Millie while Jim disappeared.

'A fitting new opening for us, to have Dot back in place, Elsie.'

When Jim returned, they made rehanging the plaque a jolly event, avoiding all the sadness that Elsie felt in her heart. They laughed at some funny memories of Dot. Elsie told them about how it would take her a while to master a job, and what happened when she'd been put on hulling the fruit. 'Oh, dear, did she get it in the neck! She chopped half the berries away, to get the stalk out, and was put on cleaning duties for a week. When she came back, I made her hand each berry to me to hull. We were a great team and used to giggle a lot. Always we found something to amuse us . . . Dot was so lovely.'

Near to breaking her's and Millie's pact not to cry, Elsie was grateful when Jim jumped in with, 'Well, we can continue to remember – to relate tales, and to honour Dot now, as she is back in her rightful place.' This made her burst out laughing. 'She's probably fuming at us.' She told them how Dot wanted nothing more than to get out of the factory.

They laughed with her. Millie looked up at the plaque. 'Sorry, Dot, love, but we're not a full team without you, so you're here to stay.'

This pleased Elsie. Not just what Millie said, but because she knew that where Dot's memory was concerned, Millie did feel a prickling of her conscience now and again, but this showed that she was coping. She tucked her arm into Millie's.

'Well, this won't get the washing done, girl. Let's get a pot of tea on the go and start our chinwag.'

Millie laughed and went along with her. Elsie knew that Millie was by now familiar with all her cockney sayings and didn't question the meaning of them, or take them literally any longer.

With a mug of hot tea in front of them, they chatted through their options and came up with renaming the factory something a world away from any family connection. This took time and dissolved them in fits of laughter, as suggestions were made along the lines of 'Jumping Jam' and 'Jam Buttie'.

'Can you girls be serious for once? We have a lot to do.'

'Oooh, 'ark at the boss.'

'Sorry, darling, but as much as I am enjoying this process, we do need to assess the factory and get a flier off to all our past customers.'

Elsie grinned at him. 'Don't apologize – I like it when you're masterful.'

'None of that, you two. Jim's right, we do have to be serious about this, but I'm at a loss as to what to suggest.'

'How about something to do with nature? After all, our produce all comes from the earth.'

'Hmm, yes, I like that, Jim. What's everyone's favourite flower? I think we should avoid fruits.'

None of the flowers they came up with suited. 'Trees, then?'

'Willow?'

'Yes, I like that, Jim.'

'But, Millie, it will remind us of sorrow.'

'No, Elsie, I know they call it the weeping willow because it is always dripping water, but the tears can be happy tears too. We will think of it as crying happy tears that we are all reunited where we are meant to be – here, in our jam factory.'

'Put like that, yes, I love it. And I love that you came up with it, Jim, as they can be happy tears to signify you becoming a director and shareholder.' Elsie told Millie that they wanted her to arrange this for them.

'I will, and gladly. I think it's a wonderful gift that you are giving Jim – and none more worthy of it. Welcome on board officially, Jim. I will ring my solicitor now to get the ball rolling. It will only be a matter of you both signing papers.'

'So, "Willow Jams" or "Willow Tree Jams"?'

They all liked 'Willow Tree Jams' and signed it off. Their logo was easily sorted, as Jim drew a willow tree shielding a jar of jam. The jam pot he drew was like the preserve jars that housewives stored their home-made jam in and, like them, he added a square of checked linen tied around the neck of the jar with ribbon and a bow. On the front of the jar he sketched a willow tree and, now on a roll with his creativity, a slogan: 'Taste the fruits of Mother Nature.'

Millie clapped her hands. 'I love it!'

Elsie felt a surge of pride in her Jim.

Looking pleased with himself, Jim suggested, 'Now, I think we should delegate what has to be done, so that we are ready to receive the workers tomorrow and have jobs for each of them to do.'

Elsie stood and went to the office window. She looked down at the empty factory floor – from down there, the office looked as though it was suspended in the air, but she thought it a really good design, as it gave them a bird's-eye view of all that was happening on the factory floor. Often she'd stood here and looked down at the women that she had worked alongside, and marvelled at how they didn't resent her having risen in the world. And she loved that she was still treated as one of them because, at the heart of her, she would always be a cockney girl.

'From here, there seems such a lot to do,' she told Millie and Jim. 'Some of the machinery looks rusted. We always had a problem with the pulping machine, and now it looks in an even worse state.'

'Yes. We do need a more modern one, but we need the money to invest.'

With this, the discussion turned to funding, and it was

decided that Millie would loan capital to the business and would be repaid from the profit.

One thing really pleased Elsie, and that was that Jim and Millie readily agreed that she would take up her old position of welfare officer and that they would look into employing a nurse to take care of the workers' health.

With all the loose ends tied up, they set about sorting out what to do next.

Millie stood. 'Well, for me, there's the minutes of the meeting to file and telephone calls to make.'

'We'll leave you to it, as Elsie and I need to inspect the factory floor and come up with a list of prioritized jobs.'

Elsie was dismayed to find the neglect there. And she knew that all of it couldn't have happened in the weeks since the closure, but had been allowed to slide over the year that Len had owned the factory. It seemed he had done his best to run it into the ground. It took several hours to come up with a plan of action.

The next day everyone turned up. The banter between the women brought life back to the factory, which erupted into laughter as Peggy called out, 'Come on, you lot, show what scrubbers you are!'

'Ha, Peggy, luv, I've always been the best scrubber in the business!' This from Irene – who in the past had been a bit of a thorn in Peggy's side, due to her tending to her nails when she should have been working – really set them off.

When they calmed, Peggy said, 'Ha, the Willow Tree Scrubbers: we ought to have a prize for the best one.'

Nancy's cackling laugh showed her mouth empty of teeth, save for one brown and decayed front tooth, confirming to

Elsie that they really did need to put some sort of care in place for the workers.

The work kept this jolly feeling as the banter went back and forth.

It was the appearance of Millie that brought it to a halt. She clapped her hands to get their attention. Elsie pushed through the women as they gathered round, knowing what Millie's intention was and wanting to stand by her side, thinking how brave she was to face everyone, when she was going through life-changing events that she knew would cause a lot of gossip and might lead to ill feeling.

But these women, hardened by difficult times themselves, appreciated Millie's approach, as there was no one more honest and open than they were. Elsie chuckled to herself at this thought and added: *when it suits them*. But she sobered as, beside her, Millie took a deep breath and began to address them all.

'Firstly, welcome back. It has been a long haul to get us here, and a lot has happened – much of it to me personally, and to Jim and Elsie.

'I want to start our new working relationship by informing you of as much as I can. I cannot tell you everything, though, because some of it is subject to a police investigation, which we mustn't divulge – but which doesn't concern the three of us, I hasten to add.

'However, I feel it is only fair to tell you that once I am divorced, I will be marrying Elsie's brother, Cess.'

There was a gasp from all but Peggy, proving that she hadn't broken Millie's confidence.

Elsie stepped in. 'I think this calls for a round of applause of congratulations to Millie.'

Before she could start to clap, Peggy shouted, 'Three

cheers for the three of yer, as in my mind, we could have none better as our bosses. And I, for one, am very 'appy for yer, Millie. Cess is a good bloke, and it's good to 'ave yer all back where yer belong. Hip, hip . . . !'

The cheers resounded around the factory, with the sound no longer echoing, as all sounds had the day before.

Millie, with tears in her eyes, clapped her hands together. 'And we applaud you all. You have worked under unsure and regressed conditions while we were unable to be here, but you have all turned up today. Thank you.'

At this, Elsie joined her applause to Jim's and Millie's.

When that came to an end, Peggy shouted, 'Right, show over: get back to work, everyone. We've to find out who the Willow Tree Scrubber is.'

Millie looked bemusedly at Elsie, as the women filed back to their positions.

'Ha, I'll tell yer about it in the office, as I want to talk some more about the women's welfare with you both.'

They were all tired when they left the factory that evening. Elsie and Millie stood outside the gates, while Jim gave George's dad the rundown of his duties as the new night-watchman. George was a school friend of Bert's. They'd taken him with them on a trip to the zoo last year and they'd all fallen in love with him.

They'd found out that George was one of a large family living in the slum area of Salisbury Street, and that Mick, his dad, was out of work. The family was one of those that she and Millie visited regularly and helped out. It had seemed a natural choice to offer Mick the job after they'd got rid of Reg Riley.

Thinking of Reg brought Beatrice to her mind. 'Millie,

I wonder how Beatrice will fare now? I mean with Reg out of work, and them living in an area where the rent is high.'

'Do you want to ask her to come back to the factory?'

'Yes, after all I don't think it was any of her doing. I'm convinced that she believed Reg.'

'Well, I won't object, but I think it is up to Jim. I know that you both suffered, but Jim's whole reputation and future were on the line, with what Reg was a party to.'

'You're right, but I know he will agree, so I needed to know that you would too. Beatrice is one of the best operators of the filling machine there are, and we're all thinking that we need more machines to cope, so she could train the others. Even now the machine is the cleanest one in the factory because of how she left it, and that's before the women got to work.'

'Yes, Jim has often remarked on her excellent work rate. Well, I'll leave it with you.'

Suddenly Elsie wanted to celebrate all they had achieved, and there was only one way in her mind. 'Millie, how about we all meet for pie and mash tonight, and then go and swill it down with a pint of ale in the Blue Anchor?'

Millie burst out laughing. 'A pint of ale? Oh, Elsie, I couldn't drink a whole pint!'

'Well, half then. Ha, we could share a pint and see who drinks the most.'

'I'm game for that. And I've never forgotten the pie and mash we had on the Old Kent Road – shall we go there?'

Elsie sighed inwardly. She knew that was one of the best places, and Millie had loved it. But she didn't want reminding of anything connected with Len, and she held a secret within her concerning that night.

Millie seemed to cotton on to her thinking. 'Or perhaps not. Have you tried the one just down from us . . . ? I mean, from where I used to live?'

'Yes, me and Jim did go there, and the liquor – the most important part – is every bit as good as the place on the Old Kent Road.'

'That's settled then.'

'Millie, have yer thought about what yer going to do with your flat yet?'

'No, not yet.'

Elsie listened as Millie told her what her reasons were for continuing to live in Wilf's house.

'I think you're right. If Len gets away with everything this time, he won't give up on getting Daniel back. Oh, I wish we could hear from Rose.'

'I try not to think about it. I think of, and long for, Daniel my every waking hour, but if I looked for a message from Rose as often, or longed for the telephone to ring and for it to be her, it would drive me insane.'

Elsie understood this. 'Well, here's Jim now. Oh, and your driver, so I'll see yer later, Millie. In about an hour – is that all right?'

'It will have to be later, as I'm going straight to the hospital to see Jack.'

Millie had told them about Jack, in her telephone call to them before they'd left Wales. 'Oh, of course, I was forgetting. I hope he's all right, Millie, luv. I'm looking forward to meeting him.'

On being reminded, a niggling worry entered Elsie.

'Look, why don't we forgo the pub, and I'll bring Bert. Ask Cess to bring Kitty and then, if it's still nice after we've eaten, we'll take them to the park instead. It'll be good for

Bert to be with Cess. He wasn't too sure, when he heard about Jack.'

'Oh dear. Poor Bert. Well, that might be best, as that'll give Cess a chance to reassure him before he gets to meet Jack. But in any case, I like that idea much better. I've never been in a pub. They seem to be men-only places.'

'They are mainly, but women can go in, accompanied by a man. Once they are in there, most women are left in the snug while the men go to the men's-only bar room, but the women don't mind – they love a good gossip. They do get a bit raunchy, though, so it's probably a good idea not to introduce yer to that.'

Elsie could see the relief on Millie's face and smiled.

'See yer later, luv.'

When they arrived at the M. Manze Pie Shop, they hugged all round. Cess hugged Bert the longest, twirling him round and making him giggle. Kitty became jealous and demanded attention by screaming out, 'My dada!'

'Well, Dada is Bert's big brother, me little darling, and I wanted to thank him for helping to take care of yer. Besides, you were having a cuddle from Aunt Elsie.'

With this, Kitty turned to Elsie and hugged her again. Elsie felt Kitty's little body shake with a sob, so clung on to her, though she was getting too heavy for such treats to last long. So Elsie lifted her and tickled her tummy with the top of her head.

With the crisis between the children over, they piled into the pie-and-mash shop and were lucky to find a big enough table for them all to sit round. Elsie looked at all the faces she loved dearly. *This is my family*. Warmth filled her at the thought.

As they all chatted about how Jack was improving and might come home, and what the children had been doing while Cess and Millie were away, and then laughed out loud as Elsie recounted Abigail's antics at the market, she knew that although her family had changed beyond all recognition from how it had been three years ago, they all loved each other and had each other's back. No cockney family could ask for more.

Chapter Twenty-Five

Millie

Millie tore open the letter that had been brought to her as she sat with her mama in her sitting room.

'The stamp shows it's from Italy, Mama. Oh, please let it be from Rose.'

'You will soon see, darling.'

'It is!' Millie caught her breath, and her hand went to her breast in a gesture to steady her beating heart.

'Read it out, Millie, please. I can't bear the suspense.'

As she read the letter out loud, tears ran down Millie's face.

Mama didn't sympathize with her – something Millie was glad of, as she felt she would break altogether if a kind word was spoken. Instead Mama clapped her hands. 'Well done, Rose – we knew she'd come good.'

Millie smiled secretly at this, as Mama had doubted Rose meant what she'd said in the note she left.

'It's dated a week ago, so that could mean she is nearly home or . . . Oh, Mama, what if Len did catch up with her?'

'Now don't be thinking the worst, darling. I think she is

probably nearly back in Dover and will ring you, once she is.'

'But she says that she has no idea what she is going to do.'

'She may not have, but she will have figured it out. She probably just got in touch as soon as she could, knowing how long letters can take, coming from abroad. No doubt she will ring very soon. Or at least as soon as she is able to.'

As if by magic, the telephone rang. Millie looked at her mama, and neither spoke. Millie could hardly breathe.

Mama's tension showed in her voice as she responded to the tap on the door and bade the butler enter.

'Telephone for Mrs Lefton, ma'am. The caller is Miss—'

As Millie stood, Mama surprised her and cut into her joy by snapping, 'Please refer to my daughter as Miss Millie. She is no longer married to Mr Lefton!'

The butler scurried out.

'Mama?'

'Oh, my dear, I know that you are, but it gets on my nerves to hear that name. Now hurry and answer the telephone. Rose must have made it to England, my darling.'

Millie's hand trembled as she picked up the receiver. 'Rose? Oh, Rose, are you safe? Is Daniel safe? Oh, my darling child, please tell me he is all right, and your own child – are you all safe?'

'He is . . . We are, Millie. We're in Dover. I'm going to buy train tickets to get us home. But, eeh, Millie, we're exhausted.'

'We? You said the babies are all right?'

'Aye, they are. I have them both, mine and your son, with me. They know no different, as they've had the best care I could give them, but I were referring to me and the young

324

man with me, who has helped me. He's poorly with seasickness, so I've booked us into a hotel. The babbies need to be bathed and fed, and we all need to rest, so I won't continue me journey till tomorrow.'

'We'll come and fetch you, Rose. Give me the name of the hotel. Do you need anything bringing?'

'Aye, more clothes for the babbies and me. I had to leave a lot behind on the train. And we're in the Dover Stagecoach Hotel on Camden Crescent.'

'We'll find it, but oh, Rose, thank you. Thank you, from the bottom of my heart, for taking the chance you did.'

'You do understand, then – I mean, why I did it . . . ? I'm sorry, Millie, really sorry. Nowt excuses using your child so that I can be reunited with mine, but I were desperate.'

'I do understand, my dear. It hurt. It hurt badly, and that will take a while to heal, but you've earned my forgiveness. And yes, I fully understand.'

The pips that signalled the end of the time allowed for the call sounded.

'I'll have to go. I'm still using the name, Mrs Ra—'

The line went dead. Millie turned and flew back towards the sitting room and into her mama's arms.

'Oh, my dear, is everything all right? Is Daniel . . . ? She has got Daniel, hasn't she?'

'Yes. Oh, Mama, he's coming home.'

She told her mama what Rose had said.

'A young man? That sounds strange.'

'I suppose it does, but I think he has been some kind of help. Rose would need help with two little ones, and the language barrier – not to mention the cases. I'm sure that's all it is. But the main thing is that Daniel is fine, as are Rose and her child. I must get ready. I have to pack some things for them, and I'll need an overnight bag. And . . .'

'Slow down, darling. Get ready for what?'

'I'm going to go down to Dover to pick them up. Rose is exhausted. I don't want Daniel travelling on trains to get here. Well, none of them to: they deserve to come home in comfort. Besides, I can't wait another moment. I have to do something. Oh, I wish Cess wasn't working.'

'Well, that's soon solved. Elsie lives opposite where Cess has his stall, doesn't she?'

'Yes, bu—'

'No buts. Wilf is busy today. Oh, I know, it's Saturday and he is meant to be retired, but he wants to finalize things where Len is concerned, before that father of his can interfere more and stop justice from happening. And, of course, your divorce. He has taken that over from your solicitor. Anyway that leaves me out on a limb, now that you are heading to Dover. I'll just go and get my market clothes on.'

Millie stood in the empty room, shaking her head. Where did this mama come from? *Why didn't I know her like this all my life?* But then Mama had been a suppressed woman, and now she was free and could be herself. *I only wish that could happen for all women. Goodness knows what we might achieve.*

As she passed through the hall on her way to do her packing, Millie decided she'd better try to warn Cess.

Rene answered the telephone. 'Millie! Are yer all right, mate?'

'More than all right – I'm more all right than I've ever been. Rose has brought my baby back.'

'That's the best news I've 'eard in a long time, luv. Made me day. 'Ow can I 'elp yer?'

'I need to contact Cess, only I can't get an answer from Elsie.'

'Oh, she popped out a few minutes ago with Bert, and Jim decided to go into the factory for a couple of hours, so he's not about, either.'

Millie smiled. Jim was so anxious to get the factory ready that she wasn't surprised he'd forgone his Saturday off.

'Elsie shouldn't be long; she said she needed a few bits from the corner shop. I can nip over to Cess . . . Ha, I can 'ear him from here, shouting his wares. I bought a nice swathe of silk from 'im meself this morning.'

'Thanks, Rene. He doesn't know about Daniel, as I have only just received the call . . .' Millie explained to Rene what she and her mother had planned. 'I want to know if it is all right with Cess, and to tell him that we'll pick him up, if it is, and take him to fetch his overnight things.'

'Can you 'old on, or do yer want to ring back, luv, as I can find out the answers for yer?'

'I'll hold on. Oh and, Rene, tell Cess that if he can come with me, we'll call in at the hospital and see Jack first.'

'Is that the lad you brought back with you? 'Ow's he doing?'

'Really well. He'll be home by Monday.'

'Well, he's fallen on his feet now. 'Ang on a mo.'

When Rene came back, Millie was relieved to know that Cess had agreed.

'He's over the moon for yer, luv. He suggested that yer take Elsie and Bert up to the 'ospital with yer to meet Jack, so if the lad needs anything while yer away, the 'ospital can ring Elsie. He also said that Elsie could visit the lad tonight, and then he won't feel abandoned.'

This relieved Millie of the only worry she'd had about

suddenly taking flight. 'That's a good idea. So can you tell Elsie, when she gets back, Rene . . . Oh and, Rene, we must get you a new contract in place, now I am the rightful owner again. I haven't done anything about it yet, but you will need everything in writing.'

'Ta, luv. Good luck with everything, mate.'

'Thanks, Rene.'

'Oh, and don't yer worry about yer mother, girl. I'll make sure she gets regular cups of tea, and me and Elsie will support her, as and when we can.'

'That relieves my mind, thank you. Well, I must go, Rene – see you in a little while, my dear.'

As she ran up the stairs to the nursery, Millie's excitement mounted. *Oh, Daniel, Mummy's coming to get you, and I'll never let anything happen to you again, little one.*

Cess, she could tell, was more than pleased. He grinned at her when the car pulled up and gave her a wink that sent shivers through her. She smiled back, trying to contain herself from flinging her arms around him, as she knew that even though her mama had turned into a market-trader, she still wouldn't like such a public display of affection.

Once she left them engrossed in what Mama needed to know, Millie ran across the road to Rene's shop.

Rene opened her arms to her. As they hugged, Rene told her, 'Yer going to be all right now, luv. Yer've been through something – and a lot is because of yer love for us lot, and that makes me sad. But everything seems to be slotting into place now for yer.'

'It's not your fault, Rene – or any of you. You are all among the best things in my life. Now, let me look at you:

I've been told about the new you . . . You look lovely. Every inch the business lady.'

'Well, I 'ave to admit, I've 'ad a few who were recommended to give me dressmaking a try turn their noses up at dealing with me. That hasn't happened since Elsie took me in 'and. Yer see, I was lost for a while. Me life changed beyond anything I dreamed of, and yet a part of me still 'ankered for me old life – not the prostituting, but . . . I were just comfortable in me old skin. Am I making any sense, girl?'

'You are. I felt like that when Elsie said we should go to the pub for a beer. It was so natural for her to celebrate an occasion in that way, but for me, I feel more comfortable in a hotel sipping a cocktail. But . . . well, I don't want there to be those differences, or to highlight them.'

'Well, we can all learn, and then find that we like the new us more than the old one. I'm beginning to feel more like the me that I was always meant to be. Life takes yer down paths that yer might not have chosen, if the circumstances 'ad been different.'

'It does. If my father had stayed as a corner-shop owner, I would have had a very different life.'

'Well, our paths are there to be trodden. It's the way we tread them that matters. And you, girl, are a shining example of how we can change – and make good changes for others. I've never told yer, Millie, but I love yer with all me 'eart.'

'Oh, Rene.' They hugged. 'And I love you. You're like a favourite aunt that I never had. I'll always look out for yer, mate.'

As they came out of the hug, laughing at Millie mimicking the cockney way of speaking, Rene said 'Soppy cows' as Elsie came down the stairs. She halted her progress and stared at them. This made them giggle even more.

'Did you just call Millie a "soppy cow", Rene?'

'Ha, that's for me to know and you to wonder over.'

Elsie laughed with them. Then she came down the rest of the stairs, her arms wide and tears brimming in her eyes. 'Oh, Millie, I can't believe it. I'm so happy for you. And for me. Me little nephew is coming home.'

Elsie's hug was full of love, and brought tears to Millie's own eyes.

'Ha, look who's being a soppy cow now. The pair of yer cry at the drop of an 'at.'

This lightened the moment and had them giggling again.

'I'm all ready. I'll just give Bert a shout. He's been hopping for joy and singing at the top of his voice, "Daniel's coming home, Daniel's coming home." Everything's a song to him lately.'

'Ah. How does he feel about going to see Jack?'

'Oh, he's fine. He's had loads of reassurance and been made to see that he has to accept Cess will love others, but that none of them can take his place. Once this had sunk in, he asked, "What about Millie? Will she love Jack more than me?" What goes on in his head, I don't know, but we managed to make him understand in the end.'

Before Millie could answer, the door at the top of the stairs opened.

'MILLIE!' Bert raced down the stairs and jumped into her arms. He kissed her cheek and hugged her, filling her with a feeling towards Bert that she'd experienced many times. A feeling that always made her wonder if he was her half-brother – she would never know, but she could call him that.

She hugged him to her. 'My little brother. I love you.'

He kissed her again. 'I love you too, Millie. And I'm going to meet your Jack.'

'Oh, he isn't my Jack. Jack's from the same convent you stayed in. Do you remember what it was like for you in the convent?'

'Yes. I dream about it sometimes and think I'm back there.'

'Well, Jack was sad there too. Like you, he wasn't being treated unkindly – though I know the Sisters are strict – but he missed his family. Only he can never go back to them, so we must become his family. You will make a lovely brother to him, and we will all be his aunties.'

'That should make him happy. You know, no one can be your mum, but everyone can love you and take care of yer, can't they?'

'They can. Now, I must be a mum to Daniel and go and fetch him, so if you are ready, we'd better get going!'

Bert nodded. 'I love Daniel.'

Millie smiled. This was a happy and settled Bert, and she was so glad. She'd never want him to feel that others were taking his place.

At the hospital Jack was feeling much better, if a little overwhelmed. He and Bert were shy of each other in a wary kind of way. But as Elsie saw Millie and Cess off, she told them not to worry. She and Bert would come back later to the hospital and she'd find a way of leaving the two boys alone.

'We'll buy a present for Jack, and Bert can give it to him. Something of his own for when he gets to Cess's house.'

'Oh, I never thought. I'll do the same – I'll bring them both something back with me. Bye, Elsie.'

'Bye, luv. Go and bring our lovely Daniel home. Oh, and tell Rose that we can't wait to see her and meet her Ronnie.'

In the car Millie sat in the back with Cess. He took her hand and smiled at her. 'Did you bring that contraption that passes for a pushchair?'

'Ha, you remember it? We put Kitty in it at the zoo, and she loved it. Yes, I did. I used it recently when we took the food parcels round, and I thought it might be useful today.'

'Well, it will. We can take Daniel and Ronnie for a walk in it. I've been thinking: I wonder who this young man is that Rose has with her?'

'I don't know. But I think Rose has been the bravest of women. What she has done has taken so much courage, and though it will always hurt that she took such a chance with my son, I forgive her and will look after her. What did Dai say about it all? Is he looking forward to Rose returning?'

'Dai's still in a bad place. He's taking a lot longer to get over his wife and child's death. He was very angry with Rose and hasn't forgiven her for what she put you through. He knows the pain of losing a child.'

'Oh, Cess. We must include him more. Why didn't we invite him the other evening? I feel guilty now, but I didn't think.'

'I did – and I did invite him, but Dai said it would be too painful for him to be with couples. I really don't know how to help him.'

'Well, you won't have to. Not on your own. We'll all help. It's just that we didn't know. He is always there, kind and gentle and nice to know, but I haven't ever thought any more about him. I will now. As your special friend, he'll be mine too. We'll make it our mission to make him happy.'

'Oh, that means yer'll be in your element trying to match-make him. Go easy. I don't think he's ready.'

'We'll see.'

Cess sighed.

Millie burst out laughing. 'I'm only having a bit of fun, dafty! Of course I'll be careful not to push him. But as he will be your best man, I have to do something for him. Maybe I could ask Rose to be a bridesmaid.'

'Millie! Anyway, I'll have two best men. Dai and Bert.'

'Oh, Cess, that will be wonderful. If only there was such a thing as a quick divorce, although Wilf has hinted there might be such a path.'

'If there is one, Wilf will find it.' He squeezed her hand and lowered his voice. 'In the meantime, we have our own vows to live by, me darlin'.'

When they reached the hotel three hours later, Millie told Cess to ask for a Mrs Raven. 'I hadn't said, but that was the name Rose told me she was using in her letter, and when she phoned – she was trying to tell me that she was still using it, when she got cut off.'

The five minutes they waited while a bellboy went to ask if Rose would receive them seemed like a lifetime to Millie. But at last Rose came downstairs, carrying Daniel.

Millie jumped up and ran to her. 'Daniel, Daniel. Oh, my darling son.' Holding a sleeping Daniel close, she looked down into his beloved face. 'Hello, little man.' Her tears wet his face as she bent to kiss him. His eyes opened. His expression looked cross at having been woken, but then changed to wonderment as he focused on her. His little hand poked out of his shawl. Millie took it. 'You're safe now, my darling. You're safe.'

Cess's arm came round her. 'He is, Millie . . .' He took Daniel. 'Hey, little fella. Remember me? I was the first person yer saw in the whole world, and I'll always watch out for yer, mate.'

A smile, probably prompted by wind, crossed Daniel's face, and Millie saw a tear trickle down Cess's cheek. She wanted to keep this picture in her mind forever – her Cess and her son bonding through a look of love.

'Millie?'

'Oh, Rose, thank you. Come here.'

They hugged. 'I'm sorry, Millie.'

'I know, but I also know that most mothers would have done what you did—'

Cess interrupted them. 'Millie, I'll just go and see if they have a room for us. Here, take Daniel, luv.'

'Thank you, darling. Would you ask for a service room for our driver, and for them to book all his expenses to us?'

As Cess left them, Millie turned back to Rose. 'I can't wait to meet Ronnie. Oh, and your mysterious young man.'

As they all went up the stairs, Rose explained about Lori.

'Well, we owe a great debt to him for getting you both here safely.'

'Particularly as I told him about Len's family. His mother was terrified at the mention of the Mafia.'

'I felt that myself when I met Len's family. I had a second wedding day in Italy with them, and although they were lovely to me, there was an atmosphere of fear coming from a lot of the guests. They all seemed to vie with each other for attention from Len's uncles, and their gifts were elaborate, as if they were in competition with one another. Len loved and admired them. So now he will probably become one of them. But how can we repay our debt to Lori? He helped to save our children.'

Millie listened as Rose told her how she had promised to give Lori enough money to pay for him to go to university. 'But the only money I have is what I stole from Len, whenever he got drunk. I do have the valise with all the money that he stole from the bank, but . . .'

'You have that? All of it? When you said you'd stolen his money, I didn't dream it was everything.'

'Yes, but I haven't touched any of it . . . I can't even open the valise anyway. Though if I had to, I would have found a way of prising it open.'

'Oh, Rose, Rose. No wonder you are so afraid.' The thought struck Millie then that Rose could so easily have used that money to take her anywhere in the world. Somewhere Len would never have found her. 'My dear Rose. You are such an honest person, and so very, very brave.'

'I don't feel honest, or brave. I deceived you, and I was terrified the whole time. I still am.'

'Don't be, Rose – we will protect you. And this could mean that we can prove Len defrauded the bank, despite his father having covered up for him. With the letter he wrote to me and your testimony . . . That is, if you are prepared to testify, Rose?'

'I'll do anything. Anything you ask of me. Oh, here we are.'

Rose opened the door to her room to a squeal, which seemed too loud and strong to have come from a baby. Millie jumped and Daniel let out a cry of fright.

'My Ronnie can be very demanding, like his father, but I'll teach him different ways.'

'Oh, I'm sure that's just a cry of hunger, don't worry

about it. Poor little mite has been pulled from pillar to post.'

'Yes, and fed on demand by wet nurses who were afraid to let him cry, so he is impatient.'

'Was Daniel fed by one of them?'

Rose nodded.

This hurt Millie. Her own milk had dried up now, but to her, putting her baby to her breast had been the most intimate of experiences, which had bound her to her son.

'I couldn't do anything to stop it, Millie. He is weaned onto bottle-feeding now.'

'The main thing is that he is well. Thank you for taking care of him, Rose. Now you'd better pick Ronnie up before he deafens us.'

'No, he can wait. It won't hurt him. I am trying to get him into a routine. He's safe in his cot. Nothing can harm him. He has to learn that there is a time for feeding, and it isn't whenever he demands it.'

Millie saw the nanny in Rose and yet, although this sounded harsh, a loving mother too. One who cared about her baby and his well-being and upbringing. 'At least let me hold him, as I haven't got acquainted with him yet. He can learn his lessons later.'

As she handed Daniel to Cess once more and held Ronnie, while Rose made the bottles for the two babies, Millie was struck by how like Len the child was in his looks. This highlighted for her how she hadn't seen this resemblance as strongly in Daniel – something that had pleased her. Daniel did have some of his father's features, but he was more like her, as was his colouring because he hadn't Len's dark, tanned Italian look.

But despite Ronnie's likeness to his father and the constant reminder that would bring, she felt a love for him as she looked down at him and he gazed back. He seemed to be asking if he could trust her. She held his hand. 'Hello, Ronnie.'

He frowned, but then clung to her hand and turned his head to try to suck her finger.

'He's certainly hungry for life, Rose. A fine boy. It will be lovely for him and Daniel to grow up together.'

'You mean you'll have me back, Millie? I can carry on working as your nanny?'

'Yes, of course. Ronnie is Daniel's half-brother and should be cared for in the same way that Daniel is. I couldn't bear to set you and him adrift. I would only be repeating what my father did. I know it isn't quite the same, but if my father had done the right thing by Elsie and Dot, they wouldn't have suffered so much – none of us would. I am not going to let that happen to Ronnie. None of this is his fault. You made a mistake by falling for Len's charms, Rose, but that was no more than I did, and we have both paid dearly for it.'

'Thanks, Millie. I don't deserve any of this. I'll never let you down again, and I promise I will do whatever it takes to get Len convicted. With him out of our lives, we can have a proper life. No more blackmail, and no more having to do . . . his bidding.'

From this Millie knew that Rose had been subjected to far more than she was saying, and her heart ached for her, but she thought it best not to broach the subject.

'Well, Rose, if you don't mind, I think we'll go along to our room to feed Daniel and get freshened up after the long journey. We'll meet Lori later, if he feels well enough.'

Rose smiled. 'Poor chap, he's not much of a traveller, and I think he's missing home. It wasn't a pleasant journey.'

'He's a very brave young man. And we will thank him by taking care of him and making sure he can realize his dreams.'

Cess propped Daniel up on one arm and took Millie's hand with his free one. 'Everything will come right, Millie, me darlin'.'

How often he'd said that to her, and she knew that if he could make it do so, he would. She smiled up at him and had the feeling that yes, everything would come right one day. And then she told herself that a lot had already.

Chapter Twenty-Six

Millie

When they got back to London the next day, Millie was pleased to see that her mama had invited Elsie and Jim over. The excitement around their return filled her with happiness, as she was enclosed in her mama's arms and saw Elsie open her arms to Rose, telling her, 'Oh, Rose, thank you for bringing Daniel back.'

When they'd all finished greeting each other, Mama said, 'So, this is Lori. Millie told me about you. Thank you so much for what you have done to bring my grandson, and Rose and her child, back to us. Please will you do us the honour of staying with us until your return trip?'

Lori blushed. He was such a lovely young man, Millie had liked him instantly.

'Thank you, ma'am. Your home is beautiful and is right in the area my mama told me is the heart of London. I would be very grateful to you if I could stay. I hope to see a lot of London, as my boat doesn't go back to France until next week.'

'Well, we'll do our very best to show you around. There's a lot of London to see.'

'Oh, you have no need. I will enjoy finding my way around using your Underground. I cannot wait. My mama quickly drew me a map of what she remembers, and instructed me to visit each part to tell her how it is now.'

'I'm told it's like travelling a maze on the Underground, but as long as you remember the name of each station where you get off, then you should be all right. Oh, and take our address written down, as you can always stop a cab that will bring you back here.'

Millie saw Rose smiling at this. But she knew she was fearful for Lori and his family, as it would be a simple matter for Len to find out that Lori had helped her, and where he lived. He only had to find the hotel that Rose had stayed at.

Not letting this worry take hold of her for the moment, she turned to Wilf. 'Wilf, we have to speak to you as soon as possible. I'm sorry, as I know it is Sunday and you worked all day yesterday, but it is very important.'

'I know, and I have a lot to tell you. Jim and I had a short meeting before you came home. Jim has a lot of evidence that will help me get a case together against Len and make sure nothing can ever stick to Jim. I am guessing that Rose will have too?'

'She has. A great deal, besides having brought something home that I think will greatly assist you.'

'That's good. Very good. I have been in touch with a contact that I have at Scotland Yard. If I can get enough evidence to warrant it, he has promised a massive investigation. With the Yard involved, no stone will be left unturned, as they can gain access to all bank transactions.'

'But won't Len's father have altered them?'

'More than likely, but me saying that didn't faze my friend. He said they have their methods, and that nothing gets past them. Besides, Harold Lefton will think that I have no more than the letter Len sent to you, and he thinks that can be passed off as an idle threat by his desperate son. So he won't have gone to elaborate methods to cover Len's tracks. Yes, he will have balanced the books at the bank, and seen to it that the money was paid back, but that will leave a lot of holes that Scotland Yard can detect.'

Millie's sprits lifted. With Len under the threat of arrest, he wouldn't want ever to set foot on British soil again. They would be free of him.

As they sat in the garden a little while later, Rose having taken the two boys to the nursery, Millie felt impatient to get a chance to talk to Wilf, but at the moment he was engaged in conversation with Lori. She'd heard Lori asking him about a career in law. Wilf had gone into a lot of detail and had finished by saying, 'If you do take law and would like to have a British law apprenticeship at any time, then I can sort that out for you. A lot of crimes are international, and at this moment we haven't a good international law system that covers them. We can only have the criminals arrested if they come back to this country, but I sense that changes are afoot, with it becoming easier to travel, and all countries may get together eventually and make treaties that allow for extradition. To be able to practise in Britain might be a great advantage to you.'

Lori said that he was very interested and excited to think of such an opportunity.

'Well, my boy, you will find that your work is never done. Here I am retired, which is laughable and, it being a Sunday, I still have work to do.'

With this, and to her relief, Wilf turned to Millie.

'Are you ready to come to my office so that we can talk, dear?'

'More than ready, Wilf. I have such a lot to tell you.'

Once they reached his office, Wilf's tone as he asked her to sit down sounded very formal and set up a worry inside her.

'My dear, I want to tell you firstly how far we have got, in looking at the possibilities of you divorcing Len. I'm afraid it isn't all good news, as I want you to understand that it is very difficult for a woman to divorce a man, because her grounds for doing so are limited. We will have to go to the High Court, but both my son, Charles, and I feel that we could have a case, if Elsie and Rose are prepared to testify to the fact that Len raped them. But it is their word against his, and the man who is being accused isn't here to defend himself, although Rose's testimony will go a long way, as she has a child by him. I will need more evidence from her – some proof that the child is Len's. Is that possible?'

'I don't know. Maybe, if she could find the woman who has been looking after Ronnie. She might know something. I mean, Len may have told her who the mother is.'

'Hmm, it's highly unlikely that he would let Rose know who his mistress was.'

'So is there no chance?'

'Yes, there is a chance, but it's not a certainty. And not without the risk of damaging your reputation – in business as well as in public. And if we do lose, we could jeopardize everything that we hope to achieve in having Len accused of fraud. The reason for this is that all divorce cases are made public, and the newspapers love everything about a divorce – in particular when it is a woman who has brought the proceedings. They most often make the man out to be the wronged party and he gains the sympathy of the public.'

Millie didn't know what to say. The news was devastating to her hopes and dreams. It seemed that, even though he was in the wrong, Len could be the winner.

'Now, if we concentrate on Len's indictment for fraud, it could all change, as you are definitely the wronged party – and will be, in everyone's eyes. We could even get the divorce through without citing anything more than his unacceptable behaviour and desertion. So, my dear, I hope that all you have to tell me makes that more of a probability than a possibility.'

Millie told him everything.

Wilf gasped. 'Where is the money?'

'In my bedroom. We haven't opened the valise yet.'

'Well done, Millie – or, rather, Rose. This makes a huge difference. And you say that Rose is willing to testify?'

'She is. She will tell everything she knows and has been told. So how will the money help?'

'Rose's testimony that she took the money from Len's possession proves that he had it. But besides that, all bank notes are numbered. The bank would have recorded the numbers of the notes put into the vaults. And if the jewellery that Len stole is from safe-deposit boxes, then they can be identified by their owners. Let's get that valise open and see what we have.'

Millie fetched the valise and, not for the first time, wondered how Rose had managed to lug it all the way across Italy and France, as it wasn't light.

When it was opened, Millie gasped. She had never seen so much money. And the necklaces, brooches and bracelets in the bottom of the bag dazzled her, encrusted as they were with diamonds, rubies and other precious stones.

Wilf sounded triumphant. 'Got him! I am certain of it. And Len will know it, so there is a danger that he will do something drastic to prevent Rose from being a witness. Not him personally, but Harold Lefton is quite capable of doing something on his son's behalf. However, he has no way of knowing that Rose has made it home. Len may have written, but we could be really lucky and the letter has not yet arrived.

'I must act quickly and go to Scotland Yard tomorrow. In the meantime, Rose is not to leave this house and garden. Please fetch her here at once, Millie, and then go and join the others as if nothing has happened. Just warn them, so that they are on the lookout for anything amiss. No one must breathe a word of this to anyone, although our biggest problem is the servants. They can always be bought. I will have to find a way of handling them.'

Millie fetched Rose and then, finding the boys were asleep, hurried downstairs and into the garden, doing everything as calmly as she could, so as not to set the staff speculating. She checked there were none of them around the garden, before she told all the others how Rose was in danger.

Each looked at her with alarm on their faces. 'Please make this look like any other conversation we have had all afternoon. We mustn't alert the staff that there is anything for them to be nosy about.'

'But if Rose is in danger, am I in danger too, Millie?'

'No, Lori. We are taking precautions against anything that Len's father might do. But he doesn't have anything to do with the Mafia.' She explained to him how Len wouldn't have had time to contact his father, and the precautions Wilf was taking about that eventuality. 'He most probably doesn't even know you exist. So please don't worry.'

As he still looked concerned, Millie told him, 'Perhaps

you would feel more comfortable staying in a hotel? That way, no one can connect you with us, or Rose.'

'Yes, if you say this man who may harm Rose doesn't know about me, then I would feel safer if he never found out about me and what I did to help Rose – safer for my family too, as we know what the Mafia are capable of.'

'We will see to that for you, Lori. And we will pay all your expenses. I think you have made the right choice, but keep in touch, and I will keep my promise to help you through university. And then one day, when all this is over, we would love to welcome you to our home again.'

'Thank you – you are so kind.'

'You deserve much more. Without you, we know we would not have got Daniel back, or Rose and Ronnie home safely.'

With all that Rose had been able to tell Wilf, he now felt confident that they had a case, and that his contact at Scotland Yard would be able to make it substantial enough to prosecute not only Len, but his father too.

Millie had mixed feelings about it all, as she sat talking to Cess in his garden later, while Gertrude was getting the children ready.

They'd been to see Jack, who would be able to come home the next day, and had then gone on to Cess's house, as he was worried about being away from Kitty. Elsie and Jim had been there too, with the intention of picking up Bert, as they'd left him with Gertrude and Kitty while they'd come to greet Millie's homecoming. But Bert had other ideas and had begged to be allowed to stay, when he heard that Millie and Cess were planning to take Kitty for an early dinner in Rodle's restaurant, a popular eating house nearby that welcomed families. They'd readily agreed to take Bert too.

'I don't know what to think of it all. I feel afraid, and disappointed about our own position, and yet elated to have Daniel back. I didn't want to leave him this evening.'

'No, thinking about it, we shouldn't have. Why don't we go back and collect him?'

'That wouldn't be fair on him – he's been travelling for a week, he's in a strange place . . . No, no, he'll be fine with Rose. And Mama asked for another young maid to sit in the nursery and watch the boys while Rose rested. Poor Rose, she was distraught.'

'What do yer think will happen – will she have to go into hiding?'

'Yes . . . Wait a minute . . . my cottage! It would be ideal. None of the Leftons know exactly where it is, and it has a telephone, so we can keep in touch with Rose.'

'Yes, no one would think of looking in Wales.'

'May I ask what anyone might be looking for in Wales?'

'Dai!' Millie stood up from the bench they had been sitting on and greeted Dai with a peck on the cheek. 'How nice to see you.'

'You too, Millie. Though I'm surprised too. Does this mean you didn't find your son?' He shook hands with Cess. 'Good to have you back, Cess – you've become like the roving wanderer lately.'

'Ha, you're only jealous. Besides, Abigail did well on the stalls for us, so we should employ her full-time.'

They all chuckled at this.

'So, you were talking about Wales?'

They told Dai what had happened.

'Well, well, Rose is a hero, and yet she is in danger?'

'Yes. We were talking about how much safer she would be at Millie's cottage in Wales.'

346

'Oh? I'll take her there, if it would help. I'd like to go back for a couple of days. I could stay at a guest house and make sure she's settled in.'

'That would be so kind, Dai.'

'It would. And it would do yer good too, mate.'

Millie agreed. 'Dai, I know we don't know one another really well, but may I be bold and say something that might ease what is on your mind, regarding Rose? You see, Cess has told me how upset you were that she did what she did.'

Dai looked shocked, as did Cess.

'I'm sorry, maybe it isn't my place, but if you're going to take her to Wales, and you are staying a while, I'd like to think that you can be friends. You could be a help to each other. What Rose did hurt me so very much, and is a pain that I know you can relate to, but she did it for a reason no woman could ever condemn – to be reunited with her own child. She's been through a lot. When Len took advantage of her, she'd suffered the loss of her husband and was vulnerable.'

Millie didn't feel it was her place to say that Rose's marriage wasn't a happy one; besides, troubles or not, it couldn't have been easy to face the world again as a single woman. 'Forgive me for saying this, Dai, as I don't want to hurt you, but try to think like her, and what you would do to get your child back into your arms.'

Dai looked shocked. Tears came to his eyes. 'I've misjudged her, haven't I?'

'Yes, you have, Dai. I am so sorry for upsetting you, but I wanted you to see that.'

Dai trembled. Cess stood and took hold of him. 'Sit down, mate.'

As Dai sat down, he crumbled. Sobs racked his body.

'Oh, Dai, I am so sorry, please forgive me.' Millie felt distraught to have triggered this reaction, and at a loss as to what to do. She did the only thing she could think of. She put her arms around him and held him. Cess did the same as he perched on the arm of the bench on the other side of Dai.

'It's all right, mate, let it out.'

Between sobs, Dai said, 'I'm sorry. I shouldn't have been so judgemental.'

'Don't worry about it, mate. After what you've been through, it's understandable.'

'But you're not like that, Cess. You've gone forward with your life and found happiness. I can't.'

'Guilt can hold yer back, Dai. It is a powerful emotion. Try to latch on to how your wife would feel about your unhappiness. She wouldn't want this for you. I know my Dot wouldn't, as she only ever wanted me to be happy.'

'But I miss Blodwyn so much and . . . our baby didn't have a chance at life.'

'Of course you do, Dai. And yer always will, mate, but yer have to find a way to live with that.'

'You need to let other people into your life, Dai – and women too, not just men. I have never got to know you properly, even though you're the best friend of the man I love. Women can be your friends too. I know men don't look on us in that way, but we're not all about whether you fancy us or not, or being a threat to the love that you have for your wife. The day that men, in general, stop looking at women as someone they can use will be a liberating day for women. Rose will be an excellent teacher of her son, in this thinking. He is demanding, but she doesn't pamper him, as most mothers do. A mother is usually the very person who gives her son the knowledge that he can manipulate and use women. I am going to learn from her and make sure that Daniel doesn't get that idea from me.'

'Ha, you've got Millie on her bandstand now, Dai. Beware: never trigger a woman who has suffragette leanings. I don't – I toe the line. You'll learn, mate.'

Dai smiled. 'Thanks, both of you. You've made me see a lot more clearly and I feel better. Blodwyn wouldn't want me to be unhappy. She'd never want me to forget her, and she would want me to hold her memory dear, but she was a good, kind and loving girl and wanted nothing but the best for me.' He took a deep breath. 'I'm going to sound like a school kid now, but will you be my friend, Millie?'

Millie giggled. 'I will, Dai. You can talk to me any time, and you can ring me up to go out with you for a walk, tea and a bun or anything, whenever you need to chat – I'll even have a beer with you, even though I hate the taste and have never been in a pub!'

'Hey, watch out – yer'll have to get past me first.'

They all laughed at Cess.

'Look, mate, go and swill your face, then come and have dinner with us and the kids, eh?'

'I'd like that. Thanks, Cess.'

Dai was like a new man as they ate their meal: chatting to the children and playing with Bert, although Kitty seemed to think that Dai belonged to her and nestled in on the fun Dai and Bert were having, making a pretend train out of the knives and forks. She jumped on his knee, took his chin in both of her hands and turned his face towards her before planting kisses all over it.

Millie laughed, 'Now that's a woman at her worst, manipulating a man.'

*

349

When Millie got home it was still only six-thirty in the evening. Without greeting anyone, she ran upstairs to the nursery.

Finding that Daniel was just about to have his bath, and that she was in time to do this for him, lifted the loneliness and heartache that had assailed her at having to be parted from Cess. *How long will I have to endure not having Cess by my side at all times? Please don't let it be forever.*

With the babies bathed and settled, Millie sat with Rose in the nursery sitting room, which had a lovely view across the park. 'Rose, I am so sorry about the turn of events. You deserve to be free now, after all you have been through.'

'Will any of us be free while Len lives, Millie?'

'Yes, we will, I promise. We have to believe that Wilf and his son can use the evidence you brought back, and your testimony, to thwart Len forever.'

'But in the meantime I am to live my life in fear?'

'No, Rose, we will protect you. I have had an idea.' She told Rose about the cottage in Wales, and how Dai would take her and Ronnie there. 'But only if you want to, Rose.'

'Oh, I do. I do. I have thought and thought about how I can feel safe. And you say that Len doesn't know where it is?'

'I am almost certain he doesn't. At some point I may have mentioned it in a conversation, but not its precise location – I feel certain of that. You see, Len was never interested in it. If he had been, he would have noted for sure where it was and visited it. So please don't worry. And you will have Dai to take care of you. He won't stay at the cottage, but will be on hand.'

'I really like Dai. I – I, well, I more than liked him when we went to that cafe when I first met him. Is he all right?'

They chatted for a moment about Dai and his grief. 'But I think you could help him, Rose. I really do.'

'Poor chap, I will try. I won't ask anything of him, just support him. Millie, I know I'll feel very safe at the cottage – do you think Wilf will let me go there?'

'I do. Or at least he will if Scotland Yard agrees. But we'll tell him that Dai will bring you back the moment you are needed. Or if Dai has returned by then, we can make sure you get back safely, if you're needed.'

'Can we go and speak to Wilf now? Then, if it is all right, I can get packed and ready.'

Wilf was in agreement and welcomed the idea. He admitted that he was worried about Rose staying in his home, as it had implications for him being seen to influence a witness in what he thought would be a high-profile case. 'Once the press begins to make insinuations, they can influence opinion. So yes, I think it is an excellent idea, for more reasons than one. Oh, and Lori has gone to a small but comfortable bed-and-breakfast. I thought it best for him not to go to a well-known hotel. I made sure he has all he needs, and told him that we hope he will enjoy himself. I also took his address in Italy, so that we can send him a money order at a later date when he is ready to start university. But I'm still concerned about him and his family. I have read a lot about the Mafia and how they operate.'

Wilf told them then how the Mafia started in Sicily because the people there wanted to fight against oppression. 'But the irony is that they have evolved quickly into the oppressors, using violent methods and extortion.'

'But what can we do? Rose has unwittingly involved them.'

Rose looked fearful. 'We have to help Lori and his family.

I wouldn't be here, and neither would Daniel and Ronnie, without their help.'

'I will talk to the boy. Maybe he can persuade his parents to come to England.' Wilf sighed. 'Whoever would have thought, my dear Millie, that all of this would happen because of a chance meeting you had with Lefton in a little-known park off Long Lane in Bermondsey?'

'But that's it, Wilf: was it chance? I think the theory of Len having planned it all is the true version of what happened. He knew everything about me and my family, and had a grudge to settle with my father. He saw a way of doing that through me, and made a play for me. I fell for it, hook, line and sinker. But oh, I have lived to regret it. All my family and friends have suffered so much because of it.'

'Yes, my dear, I truly believe that is what happened. Well, you are fighting back, with the help of us all, and we will win in the end, I am sure. But we must protect everyone that we can from the consequences.'

As Millie went back to the nursery with Rose to help her pack, she tried to reassure her that everything would be fine. 'Everything will work out, I promise. We have right on our side and, from tomorrow, the might of Scotland Yard, as well as Wilf. They will win – the likes of Len and his father never will.'

But will they? Please God, I implore you to help them bring Len and his father down and to keep us all safe.

As she gazed down on her sleeping son, Millie thought that he was the single good thing to have come from her knowing Len, and she would fight to the death to protect him from his father's clutches.

Chapter Twenty-Seven

Rose

As soon as she sat beside Dai in his car, Rose felt safe. Dai had greeted her in a friendly, if reserved way, but knowing what she knew about how he was suffering, Rose understood and didn't press him. This journey back, she knew, would be an ordeal for him, because she understood that although he had stayed on in Barmouth for quite a while after he lost his wife, once he'd left, he had no intention of returning.

They chatted about this and that on the journey, but Dai was distracted and it wasn't until they had to stop to feed Ronnie that she felt she made a breakthrough with him. 'Can you hold him while I get everything ready, please, Dai? He'll only scream the place down if not.'

'Yes, of course. I heard that he was a demanding little fellow, but that you are working to curb that trait in him. Is it a harder job than you thought?'

'No. He's doing really well. This is a hungry cry – he's long overdue. I think the motion of the car kept him sleeping. But yes, he still has his moments.'

'I understand your concerns but, you know, babies don't realize that you are going to respond to their needs. Maybe he is just assertive. Hand him to me. There, little fellow, what's all this fuss, then?'

Ronnie quietened and gazed up trustingly at Dai.

'Well now, that's better. You don't give a good impression when you bawl the place down, and yet I can see you're a reasonable fellow. You just don't know what's happening, do you? You're with your mummy now – and none better, lad – and any minute you'll have your tea. And, by the smell of you, you need changing too . . . Ugh, I didn't know babies could make such a stink.'

'Ha, they can. You should try changing them.'

'I never got the chance.'

'Oh, Dai, I'm sorry. That was a thoughtless thing to say.'

'No. No, Rose, I was being thoughtless and self-pitying. I didn't mean to wrong-foot you like that. I will try to stop this wallowing in my self-pity, Rose. You must tell me off if I do.'

Rose smiled. She thought this was a step in the right direction. 'Well, when something really traumatic happens to us, we can take two paths. We can get on with life, like Cess does, even though it doesn't mean he isn't suffering, or we can cling on to our sadness and make it the focus of our lives. Cess's way is the best, Dai.'

Dai nodded. 'I will try. And I think being with you and Ronnie will help me. Rose, I haven't said anything, but you speak differently to when I met you.'

She explained to him why, and how she had to learn to speak this way because of the position she had. 'I dropped back into it, for the sake of the staff. "Eeh, but Millie don't like it, and don't want me to talk all posh, but I had to, you see, lad."'

Dai burst out laughing. 'That's more you. I felt uncomfortable with the new you.'

'I knaw, and if feels good to be natural. But, you knaw, everyone's going to end up confused, as there's them as have never heard me speak me natural way. Millie, Elsie, Cess and Millie's mam have. Bert just accepts me however I speak. Wilf will think I'm someone different, though.'

'You must do as you want to. I prefer you being your natural self. Everyone will understand why you changed.'

Rose screwed the top back onto the Thermos from which she'd filled Ronnie's bottle. 'By, I can't tell you what a relief it will be. Now, hand me babby to me and I can change him while his bottle cools, and then feed him as we carry on our journey.'

'I think I'll get out of the car while you tackle his nappy.'

Rose laughed at this. She really liked Dai. She felt a protectiveness towards him . . . No. What she'd said to Millie was true: she more than liked him and looked forward to spending a few days with him.

As she changed Ronnie and cleaned him up, wrapping his dirty nappy in reams of newspaper that she'd brought with her for the purpose, then tipping water from a bottle over her hands to clean them, she felt herself relaxing inside as all the pent-up fear released her from its shackles.

The cottage was adorable. Tiny, but so cosy, especially when Dai lit the fire while Rose unpacked the box of food.

'Oh, Dai, this is a dream. I feel so safe.'

'Good. You are, Rose. And you'll love Barmouth. Would you like to go for a walk before we part? We could walk to a guest house that I know and book me in, and then go to the beach.'

'Aye, I'd love that. I'll need that pushchair that Millie insisted we bring.'

'I think we're best to put Ronnie in it when we all get to the car, as it will be difficult to lug it up the steps.'

The walk to the guest house wasn't far and, with Dai's accommodation sorted and his case dropped off, they walked along the promenade. Rose loved the views and the feeling of space. She breathed in the fresh air. 'It's grand here, Dai. Look at those hills in the background. It's so picturesque.'

'There's some wonderful drives, and Snowdon isn't far away. It's the highest mountain in England and Wales, though it doesn't come near to Scotland's Ben Nevis, or to many others that Scotland can boast of having.'

'Eeh, it sounds grand. And I don't know about you, but I'm getting hungry. Will you come back to have dinner with me? By, I have got meself some posh ways. In the past I'd have had me dinner by now and would ask you to come to tea.'

'I know – it took me a while to get used to it being called dinner. Millie's having an influence on us all, because even Cess calls it dinner now. But, yes, I'd love to come.'

'Well, I brought some pork chops with me and veg, and Millie keeps a store cupboard, so I'll find sommat to rustle up for pud. A jam tart or some such. I'll take Ronnie back now and get him settled and see you later, eh? Shall we say seven? Then hopefully Ronnie'll be asleep.'

When they parted, Dai didn't go towards the guest house, but turned to walk up a street that led towards the church that looked down on the promenade. She guessed this was where his wife and child were buried. She watched him go, head down, shoulders bent, and for all the world wanted to run after him, but carried on and left him to make his own way.

As time went on and Dai would soon arrive for dinner, Rose found her heart fluttering. *I'm a daft ha'p'orth. Dai ain't ready to take on the likes of me and me little Ronnie.* But telling herself this didn't stop her hoping that he felt the same way.

The meal went well and tasted delicious. Their chatter flowed and so did the laughter, as Rose mimicked some of the people she'd trained with and related some of the antics of the kitchen staff at Raven Hall in Leeds.

'I've heard of Millie's old maid, Ruby, but never met her.'

'She's expecting a babby. I'll have to ask Millie how she is. I miss her. She's a good sort.'

'You're a good sort too, Rose. I feel so relaxed in your company.'

'Ta. And I do in yours, an' all.'

'Ha, you're so like the girl I met back in March now. I'm sorry for all you've been through and have yet to face.'

His eyes held hers. Rose didn't know why she did it, but she had a sudden urge to hold his hand. She slid hers across the table towards him.

'Oh! Um, no . . . I mean, I'm sorry, Rose, I . . . I'd better go.'

'No, please don't, Dai. I'm sorry. It were just me being friendly. I didn't mean owt.'

Dai coughed. 'Well, I'd better go anyway. It's been a lovely evening.'

Rose coloured. She knew he'd seen through her. Knew he didn't believe the friendship thing. *Oh, why did I do it? Dai needs time. I meant to give him that.*

'Thank you for dinner, Rose. I'll see you sometime tomorrow.'

'Naw, don't do that. I've spoiled it now. I'll be all right. You have your few days with your memories. There's naw point in embarrassing us both by trying to carry on as if it didn't happen.'

'But, Rose . . . Forgive me, Rose. Please try to understand.'

Rose didn't sleep well. When she woke up, after having at last dropped off following Ronnie's night-feed, she felt stiff and had a feeling lying heavily in her chest of having lost something.

Somehow she went through the motions, but the incident at dinner kept coming back to haunt her. *Dai stole me heart from the beginning, but I'm soiled goods, as the northerners call fallen women. How can I expect him – or any man – to want to be with me?* Wiping away the tears before they had a chance to fall, she squared her shoulders. 'Well, if this is me lot, then it is, so I'd better get on with it.'

Ronnie was surprisingly calm and good. He didn't complain once as she bathed him, fed him and dressed him for a walk.

The wind was blowing and held droplets of rain in its blustery gusts, but she didn't care. She needed to walk and to think. Ronnie was wrapped up against the elements, so she didn't have to worry about him.

Without realizing it, Rose found herself at the bottom of the same street that Dai had walked up the day before. Turning into it, she found it hard going, propelling the pushchair up the narrow street. When she reached the church, she was struck by how neat the graves looked.

Ronnie stirred, and a hand escaped from his cover. As she

bent to tuck it in, a voice startled her, as she hadn't seen anyone.

'Rose?' Looking up, she saw Dai staring at her as if she was trespassing. His tone shocked her. 'I told you, Rose, I'm not ready . . . Oh, I should never have come here with you.'

'Dai, I haven't followed you here. I did see you come up here yesterday, but I didn't knaw you were here today. I were just curious. I understood and accepted what you said.'

'Curious about what exactly? What a grave looks like? Well, it looks like a barren place – a place that has buried your heart in its cold, damp earth. A place that holds all that was yours, but has now been claimed by the earth, and a place that rots the flesh off the beautiful bones of someone you loved dearly.' He sank to his knees. His head bent, his body crumbled.

'Dai, Dai. Oh, my poor Dai.'

Rose lodged the pushchair on the grass, where it couldn't move, and ran towards him. She kneeled beside him, taking his sobbing body in her arms.

'Don't think of it like that, Dai. Think of it as a resting place for Blodwyn's body, but she isn't in there. Not the Blodwyn you knew. She's in heaven. She's happy and at peace. She has your babby in her arms, and he's happy an' all. Just think of this as the place where you can visit to be near her, as this is her last resting place on earth. She is trying to heal your heart, Dai. And you have to let her. You have to trust folk, and let them do her work for you and help you.'

Dai leaned his head on her. 'Help me, Rose. Help me. I'm so afraid. So guilty.'

'Get up, Dai. The grass is damp. Stand up and let's go inside the church, out of the wind. I can get Ronnie's pram inside.'

Inside the church they left the pram at the back and sat side-by-side. 'Tell me why you feel guilty, Dai.'

'Because . . . well, if I hadn't loved Blodwyn and made her pregnant, she wouldn't have died.'

'Oh, Dai. If you hadn't have loved her, she wouldn't have lived.'

Dai lifted his bent head from his hands and looked up at her. 'Really? I never thought of it like that. But yes, I lived – I mean, properly – and knew such happiness because Blodwyn loved me.'

'We can all help each other in that way, Dai. I've only ever known one love – that of me ma.'

'Not your husband?'

'You know about that?'

'Yes, but you never speak about him. Is it too painful?

'Not in the way you think, Dai. Well . . . I haven't told anyone else, though Ruby and most of them up in Leeds knew, but I was glad when he died. He treated me badly – beat me. I knew what his temper was like, we'd known each other a long time, but he never hit me until after we were wed, then he said he had a right to now I was his wife.'

'I'm sorry, Rose.'

'Me ma was me saviour. When she died, my world folded. But then I came to look on it that she was having her time again. She deserved that. Some don't have as long as she had. Little Jimmy, for instance. I didn't see his grave, but from what I've heard of him, he didn't have much of a crack of the whip at all – no real happiness, only sickness, poverty and then death. Blodwyn suffered none of those things until her time came, or at least I haven't heard that she did.'

'No, she had a good life. She was a good baker, you know. Her cakes were delicious. And work – she'd work all day and night trying to get our guest house ready.'

He talked and talked. At some point he'd taken her hand. She remained still, letting him say and do as he wished. She knew tears were running down her face as she imagined the beautiful Blodwyn, through the pictures of her that Dai was painting.

When he came to a funny story about them and laughed, he looked at her with shock. 'That's the first time I've laughed over anything to do with Blodwyn.'

'That's a good thing to do, Dai.'

'You know, I find it so soothing sitting with you – well, just being with you. I wish . . . but I'm not ready yet. Do you think . . . ? I mean . . .'

'Aye. I do think one day. But, you knaw, I have to heal an' all. I reached out to you in the way you're reaching out to me. I think we need each other, Dai.'

'I think you're right. I'm so sorry for the way I spoke to you.'

'Don't think about it. You need help. I heard that you gave that help to Cess, when he was lost.'

'Yes, I did. I don't know how, but I felt stronger then. But now Cess is coping better than me.'

'That's because he hasn't tried to do it on his own. He's allowed others in. He hasn't just functioned, but has lived, and now he can see a way forward.'

'You're very wise, Rose. You do know that I was trying to ask if you would give me time, don't you?'

'Aye, I know. And I can. I think you knaw how I feel.

Well, knowing that, you'll knaw that I'll never desert you. But I need time an' all. I need all of this business with Len to go away. I need to forget how he used me. And the things he did to me, but . . . Dai, I – I haven't told a soul, but I'm scared. I think I may be pregnant again.'

Dai looked shocked.

'I had naw choice, Dai. With someone like Len, you do his bidding. He allus has sommat that he can hold over you. In my case, it was his threats to abandon me, and to take my son.'

'Oh, Rose, Rose. Don't cry.'

'But I feel so lonely. So dirty and afraid.'

'Don't. Please don't.' Dai's arms enclosed her. 'I'll . . . we'll all look after you, Rose. None of this is your doing.'

She longed for him to say that he would take care of her, but now he'd probably never be ready to.

'Are you sure – I mean about the baby?'

'No. It's just that Len didn't take care. Oh, Dai, I don't knaw what I'd do.'

'Please don't think like that, as you have me, and Cess and Millie, and Elsie and Jim. You don't have to feel despair. And it may not happen. Oh, Rose . . . Rose.'

His hold on her tightened. Her heart beat faster. But still he held a large part of himself back, and the hug became only that: the hug that a friend would give her.

Ronnie stirred, giving her an excuse to release herself from the hold, which had started as one that had lifted her, but changed to one that had become almost torture.

She dried her eyes. 'Are you ready to walk for a while, Dai?'

'Yes, I am.'

Outside in the fresh air he led her to Jimmy's grave.

She stood gazing at it. 'Poor little chap.'

Next to the grave a rose bush was in full flower. Glad that she had her gloves on, Rose snapped off two flowers. One resisted and she had to twist its stem. She placed one on Jimmy's grave and muttered, 'Rest in peace, little lad.' And then she went to Blodwyn's grave. 'Dai'll be all right, Blodwyn. I'm his friend and I will help him.'

Dai's arm came around her waist. 'Thank you, on Blodwyn's behalf, Rose. I think she would have loved you.'

As they walked, they fell into an easy conversation. Dai said he felt as though he'd been cleansed, and that his heart felt lighter than it had for a long time. He didn't resist when she held his hand.

'That's good, Dai. I just knaw it's what Blodwyn wants for you. You'll never forget her, or stop loving her, but you'll live with her memory.'

'Can a woman accept that? I mean, if . . . well, wouldn't it come between us?'

Rose would have liked to think he meant between her and him, but knew he was speaking generally. 'I think some could. Millie does. I knaw she knew Dot and was related to her, but in some ways that's worse, because she must feel like she stepped into Dot's shoes. But she copes with it, and I think she and Cess are going to be very happy.'

'Could you cope with it, Rose?'

She felt her pulse race. 'Yes, I could. I am learning to love Blodwyn through your eyes. I haven't seen a picture of her, but I can imagine her, and I think we would have been friends.'

'Would you be willing to try?'

They'd reached the promenade and, for late August, the

wind was blustery. Here on the coastal path it had become stronger. It whipped Rose's bonnet off and left it tied loosely around her neck. She battled with her hair, but kept her eyes on Dai's. 'If you could cope with all you'd have to – with me and me past – then I would, Dai.'

He didn't speak, but looked deep into her eyes. 'You don't have to ask that. But I am asking you to accept me, knowing that a big part of me belongs to another. If you can, then I will be a good husband to you.'

This shocked Rose. The hand that she had on the pushchair gripped the handle so hard it hurt. 'I don't want you to take me on only because of what might result from what Len did to me. I want you to love me, Dai.'

'I can learn to.'

Rose turned away and her soaring heart crashed inside her. 'Dai, let's just be friends. The support you are talking about can be mine, as a friend. You don't have to marry me. Come on, let's get moving – it's suddenly feels cold.'

'I'm sorry, Rose . . . Rose, wait.'

'Dai, you can spend your life being sorry, lad, but there's no need to be. What you just did, you did out of kindness. But it's not what I want. I do want the friendship you offered earlier, so let's leave it at that, eh?'

Rose didn't ask Dai back to dinner that evening. She sat by the fire, hoping he would call round. He didn't and she ended the evening in tears, praying to God that she wasn't with child, and that one day He would make Dai fall in love with her.

Chapter Twenty-Eight

Millie

Already it was November. Millie stared out of the window of her bedroom and wondered, for the umpteenth time, why the wheels of the law ground so slowly. Investigations had continued and reports were that a breakthrough was expected. It seemed there was one piece of crucial evidence still needed, and it wasn't proving easy – to find the bank clerk who it was believed was in cahoots with Len and who, it was thought, had received a huge pay-off. He seemed to have disappeared off the face of the earth.

It wasn't that Millie was unhappy – unsettled was more the word, and worried too. She worried about Rose stuck in Wales on her own, even though Rose insisted that she was well. No one but Dai dared to visit her, for fear of giving her whereabouts away.

Although Rose had seemed happy enough in her letters and when she telephoned, Dai had dropped a bombshell when he'd returned from his last visit at the weekend. Rose was pregnant with her second child, and Len was the father. He said that Rose was devastated, but was being very brave and getting on with things.

But when Millie had telephoned her, Rose had sobbed her heart out. She'd felt her life was over. She told of her love for Dai, and how she now thought any chance of him returning that love, which she admitted had only been slim in the first place, was seeming impossible. Millie had felt at a loss to know what to do for her.

Another niggling worry Millie had was for Lori's family, as his father had refused to move to somewhere they might have been safer. At least, though, this had eased on Lori asking if Wilf could get him a place at university in England. And since September he had been happily studying at Leeds University and reported that he was enjoying his time there and his studies.

Millie coped well most of the time. The jam factory was now up and running, and was beginning to get former clients back. It already had a healthy-looking order book, thanks to Jim's efforts. He'd managed to supply many of the customers from the Kent factory when it was almost out of stock, due to closing down. It wasn't even for sale now, as it formed part of the fraud case against Len. But always the threat hung over Millie that Len would suddenly, somehow, cause her heartache.

And there was another complication. She'd missed her monthly twice. To her, this was a double-edged sword. She was ecstatic to be carrying Cess's child and yet so frightened of it causing a counter divorce claim from Len.

The voice of one of the maids cut into her thoughts. 'Would you like me to pack this coat, madam?'

Turning, Millie saw that the coat the maid held up was the flared one she'd worn last winter, when carrying Daniel.

Millie felt her colour rise. Had the maid heard her morning sickness? For a moment she didn't know how to react, but then saw a kindly, concerned look on the maid's face.

'I don't think it is cold enough yet, thank you, Jean . . . though of course it will be colder in Leeds. Perhaps you'd better put my long red coat with the Astrakhan collar and cuffs into the car, where I can get at it when we arrive.'

'You're going to see the maid who attended you before you were married, aren't you, madam?'

'Yes.'

'Well, may I be so bold as to ask if you can give her a message from me and tell her that I am doing my best to step into her shoes.'

This shocked Millie. She hadn't taken much notice of Jean before. She hadn't been unfriendly towards her, but she hadn't formed the same bond that she had with Ruby or Rose.

'Ruby's had a baby, ain't she, madam?'

'She has – a little girl.' How the staff knew everything that went on always bemused Millie. But she didn't dwell on it. She found it nice to chat with the girl, instead of keeping her at arm's length.

'I would have taken you with me, Jean, but I am staying in a hotel, so I won't need your services. But I wanted to say that you serve me well, thank you.'

'Nice of you to say so, madam. And yer can count on me – I don't gossip with the others. I hear what they say, and I know things, but they get nothing out of me concerning you and your life.'

'Thank you, Jean, that's very comforting. I expect they are curious about everything?'

'Oh, they just love to speculate – and to make two and two make five, as me mum says.'

Millie smiled. She found that she liked Jean. A girl of about twenty, she was plain-looking and very thin, almost gangly, but she had a lovely smile and a quiet way about her.

'Jean, I've never stood on ceremony, and my maids have always called me Millie in private, but have given me a title in front of everyone else. I'd like you to do that.'

'It'll take a bit of getting used to, but thank you, ma— I mean, Millie.' Jean did a little bob.

Millie smiled. She liked the thought of having a maid she could trust, but would tread warily for a time until she was sure.

Whenever they travelled now, she and Cess had decided to do so as a family – both of them had hated leaving their children behind, so she sat with an excited Kitty on one side of her and Daniel on her lap in the back of Cess's car. Bert was coming with them on this trip too. He sat up in front, as if he was much older than his years, showing pride at sitting with his brother.

They'd been waved off by Elsie, Jim and Jack. Jack had the huge responsibility of taking care of Cess's stall for the couple of days. It was his first time on his own, but since recovering from his operation he had been working alongside Cess every day. It was as if he'd been born to be a market trader. He loved the work, and Cess had told her how good he was at getting those who were hesitating to make a purchase. 'He has the gift of the gab, Millie. The compliments that roll off his tongue make me laugh, but the ladies fall for it. They don't seem to notice his scars, or be repulsed by them. Mind, he has a way of turning his head, or positioning himself so that his good side is much more visible, poor lad.'

Millie always felt pity at Jack being so scarred, as he would

368

have been a very handsome young man. But what he lacked in looks, he made up for in charm, good manners and a lovely nature. Her matchmaking heart told her that one day a nice girl would fall for him.

Dai stood with Jack. He'd helped him to set up the stall, so that Cess hadn't needed to. It was good to see how much better and able to cope Dai was lately. He hadn't shown any depression and seemed to enjoy his trips to Wales. Millie just wished he'd see Rose in a different light, as she so needed his support – and not just as a friend.

'That was a big sigh, love, and not a happy one. Are yer all right?'

'I am, darling. It's just that I've been thinking things over a lot this morning.' She couldn't wait to tell Cess her suspicions. She nearly had when she'd missed the first period, but hadn't wanted to worry him. They'd both spoken of their concern over her getting pregnant before everything was settled and they could marry, but still had times when they couldn't part when they should.

But now, she knew she would have no choice but to share her news, as Cess would guess in the morning if she was sick. However, she doubted there would be any 'if' about it.

'I think things over a lot too, luv, but it doesn't help. The main thing is that we're very close now to it all being resolved – we have to keep hanging on. And we've two nights in a hotel to look forward to, and the christening of Ruby's baby.'

Millie grinned. 'I cannot wait to meet little Millicent. How lovely that Ruby named her after me and asked me to be her godmother too. I'm honoured.'

'It'll be strange for yer to go back to Raven Hall. Nice of

the new owners to allow the christening party to be held there, though.'

They'd spoken of this before and Millie had expressed her concern, but as she told Cess now, she'd got over the feeling that it would seem as if she was a stranger in what used to be a second home to her, when her mama owned it. 'Well, at least I don't hold any bad memories of the place. And according to Ruby, the family are lovely and all the staff love them, so I've come to think of this as a nice experience – a chance to see the house as a happy place. And that will settle my mind about my enforced sale of Mama's home.'

'That's good, luv. We've a long journey ahead of us, so try to relax and we'll take a break every hour or so, or when I see a wayside inn, and then we can feed the kids.'

After three such breaks – two for toileting – they finally arrived at their hotel at three in the afternoon and were shown to a comfortable family suite with adjoining bedrooms and a bathroom. Decorated in creams and greens, the hotel was on the outskirts of the city. Their room had a pleasant outlook overlooking the hilly countryside and a garden, which the children were loving.

Millie stood with Cess looking down on them playing a catch-me game in the increasing dusk, wrapped up in thick woolly coats, hats and scarves. Kitty was running after Bert, who kept slowing his pace and then speeding up when she caught up with him.

'Uh-oh, she'll only stand that for so long. Any minute now she'll stand still and scream at him.'

Millie laughed. 'I don't blame her. I'd find that frustrating in the extreme.'

Cess laughed as he tightened his hold on her waist.

She looked up at him. 'I have something to tell you, Cess.'

'Oh? That sounds ominous, me darlin'. Is something wrong?'

'Well, not wrong exactly, but I don't know what you'll think. I – I think I'm pregnant, darling.'

'What! Really? Oh, Millie. Millie, me little darlin'.' He turned her towards him and looked deeply into her eyes. His own filled with tears.

'You're not worried?'

'No! I'm a very happy man, and I love yer, me Millie. I know it ain't what we planned, and we both had our worries concerning the divorce and what – if anything – Len could do with the news, as it's proof that you've committed adultery . . . Not that we feel like that, and I don't think God does, either. I think He understands. But I wouldn't worry, luv. I think we'll hear soon, and we can keep this a secret until after it is all over and we're wed. I love yer so much, my Millie.'

'Oh, Cess.'

She went into his arms and allowed his love to dispel her worries, until he asked, 'You haven't told anyone, have yer, Millie?'

'No, darling. I wanted you to be the first to know . . . Only, well, something funny happened this morning when I was getting ready.' She told him about Jean asking if she should pack the flared coat. 'It was almost as if she was telling me that she knew . . . I suppose she may have heard me being sick this morning.'

'That's maids for yer: nosy so-an'-sos.'

Millie wasn't so sure. Yes, it was a way that the maid could get her to take her into her confidence, but it seemed a funny way of doing it, because the coat was so obvious and Millie was nowhere near the stage when she needed to wear it.

Cess lifted her chin. 'Stop worrying. Let's celebrate, eh? Let's get all the children settled and then we can order dinner to be served up here.' He nodded towards a small round table and two chairs standing in the second bay window in the room. 'Then we'll have a romantic dinner for two, and leave all our worries and cares where they should be.'

Millie agreed and accepted his kiss, feeling it deepen to match the passion she felt and enjoying Cess's caressing of her, until an almighty scream caught their attention. Just as Cess had predicted, Kitty was standing in the middle of the lawn, bent over and screaming for all she was worth.

'Uh-oh, saved by the kids! I'd better get down there. Blimey, it's almost dark. It might be the sudden realization she is somewhere strange that has upset her. I won't be long, me darlin'.'

Once the children were all settled, they both felt exhausted after the long drive and coping with their baths and feeding, but enjoyed their dinner of lamb cutlets and sautéed potatoes.

When she awoke the next morning Millie stretched, remembering their lovemaking and the joy of abandoning all precautions, as they had done many weeks ago. She marvelled at how their few times of throwing caution to the wind had resulted in her becoming pregnant.

Her thoughts went to Elsie, and how she longed for a baby and yet nothing happened. It was a mystery to Millie. But the now-familiar feeling of her stomach churning gave her no time to dwell on it, as she leapt out of bed and made for the bathroom.

Cess wasn't many steps behind her and stood rubbing her

back, until her being sick set him off and he hurriedly moved her to one side and joined her.

When it was over, they both laughed. 'Oh dear, Cess, we're not both carrying this baby, are we?'

Cess giggled as he wiped his mouth. 'I hope not. I don't fancy the birth, with my equipment.'

This really set them off and woke the kids.

Bert and Kitty came running through to them, Kitty clapping her hands and Bert smiling. Kitty jumped into Cess's waiting arms, and Bert ran to Millie. She cuddled him to her.

'Well, did you sleep all right, Bert? I heard you snoring.'

Bert giggled some more and made a noise like a pig. Kitty demanded to be put down and came over to Millie, holding her arms up to her.

The glance from Cess told of the same thought that Millie had: Kitty was jealous of Bert having attention from either of them – something she would have to handle and curb. She didn't want any of them feeling jealous of the others. But it wasn't anything she'd noticed Kitty do when she held Daniel, so she was glad of that.

Swinging the light-as-a-feather Kitty around, she bounced her onto the soft bed. 'We've an exciting day, little one. You have to have your breakfast and then dress in your pretty new frock. And, Bert, you need to dress in your suit. We're going to a new-baby christening!'

There were questions as to what a christening was, from Kitty, and general chatter, which relaxed the atmosphere between the children.

When they reached Ruby's cottage, they found it crowded with people. But despite the crush, Millie was greeted by a joyful Ruby pushing her way through everyone.

'Eeh, Millie – me Millie!'

The two of them hugged and laughed and cried.

'It's good to see you, Millie, lass. By, I've missed you.'

'And I've missed you, darling Ruby. I so could have done with you by my side. But getting your letters and your words of wisdom helped me.'

'Me an' all, when yours came. But to hear of the goings-on – by, I could kill that Len. How's Rose?'

'She's doing all right . . . but there's an added complication. We'll talk later.'

'You should have sent her up here to me, lass. I'd have taken care of her.'

'I know, but it isn't that simple. We need to make sure she, and everyone else, is safe. Anyway we won't talk of our worries. Where is little Millie? I cannot wait to hold her.'

'She's through here. Where's Daniel?'

'Cess will bring him and the children in.'

'Right. Eeh, you lot, move for me special guest, will you?'

The other guests, laughing and giggling, parted, and Millie saw Ruby's ma sitting with a tiny bundle on her knee. The joy of holding Ruby's baby almost came up to the feeling of holding her own – only now Daniel looked gigantic in Ruby's arms, where Cess had placed him.

The christening itself was lovely and little Millie was really good, only crying out in astonishment when the cold water trickled over her head.

Millie felt a great love for her, and a feeling that at least Ruby was settled, when she glanced over at her as she stood linking arms with her Tom and they both beamed.

It wasn't until they reached Raven Hall that Millie experienced any feelings of sorrow or anxiety, but returning there did that to her. Although she was happy to be greeted by the lovely new owners, and could feel the happiness that the house was now enveloped in, it was the thought of what had happened to Rose here, and how Len had begun his pursuit of Elsie here too. And the memories of her father, which would always visit her when she was in a place she associated with him – though, thankfully, they no longer did so at the jam factory, because since losing it and gaining it back, it now felt like a different place.

By three o'clock they were back at the hotel. Kitty and Bert were both tired out. They'd had a lovely time running around the grounds, but their journey yesterday was telling on them.

'Why don't you both have a nap?'

'Good idea. Come on, Kitty, me little luv. Daddy will take yer through and sit with yer till yer fall asleep.'

Bert was a little more reluctant, saying he wasn't a nipper any more and didn't want to go to bed in the afternoon – until Millie found a copy of *The Tale of Peter Rabbit* on the shelf of books next to the dining table.

'There you are, Bert, you needn't go to sleep, but can have a quiet hour reading. I love to do that. It gives your brain a change from all the things it has to do on a minute-by-minute basis.'

She had to bat away a few questions about what his brain did, but he eventually went through and lay on his bed.

Millie felt exhausted and was glad to kick off her boots, and to change into a house-frock, leaving her corset off and feeling that at last she could breathe. She'd made sure that her light-blue cotton frock had been packed for her. It fell to her ankles in a loose style from under her bust and caused no constrictions, because even its sleeves were bell-shaped.

She sighed as she sat in the easy chair by the window and

then jumped as the telephone rang. 'This is the hotel switchboard. You have an external call, ma'am. It's from a Mr Hepplethwaite: would you like me to connect him to your room?'

Millie swallowed. 'Yes, please. Thank you.'

She heard the familiar 'You're now connected' that went with all telephone calls and then heard Wilf's voice as clearly as if he was sitting next to her.

'Good news, Millie. We've truly got Len. The person who aided and abetted him has at last been located and has squealed like a baby!'

'Squealed? Is he hurt?'

Wilf laughed. 'No, it's a term for someone who tells all. Anyway there is a warrant out for Len's arrest, the squealer and your father-in-law are both in custody, and your papers, asking for a divorce, are ready to be rubber-stamped. I'll have no problem getting them granted on Monday morning. I had a few favours to call in, to speed everything up for you, my dear.'

'Oh, Wilf . . . Oh . . .'

'Don't cry, my dear. I know this is a huge weight off your shoulders.'

'I – I'm all right. I . . . Oh, Wilf, thank you so very much.'

'My dear—' Wilf's voice broke for a moment. 'My dear Millie, I love you like a daughter and couldn't be more relieved to have been of service to you, or happier for you.'

'And you have acted more like a father to me than my own father ever did. I love you, Wilf, and owe my life to you. As do so many people. Will you wait a while before you and Mama resume your touring, as I want you to be the one to give me away on my wedding day.'

Wilf didn't speak for a moment. She heard him blow his

nose loudly. 'Well, my dear, dear Millie, you have just made me a happy man. Hurry home: your mother and I need to hug you. You'll be safe from now on, my dear. You and Cess can make a proper home together, as Len cannot touch you or your child ever again . . . Oh, hold on, your mother is pestering me to hand her the telephone.'

Millie heard him laugh and then her mama's beloved voice. 'Millie! Oh, Millie, it's over.'

'It is, Mama. I'm so happy.'

'Now, my dear, we have a wedding to plan.'

Millie laughed. 'Yes, we do. Start as soon as you like, Mama. I know Cess will agree.'

'Agree with what, me darlin'?'

'Oh, Mama, I have to go – I have to tell Cess everything!'

Cess's delight had him waltzing her around the room, before holding her closely to him. Millie thought she would drown in his love. Happiness burst from her every pore.

Chapter Twenty-Nine

Millie

Christmas, two days ago, had been a magical affair, with everyone invited. Today, though – a dry, crisp day – was the one everyone had been waiting for: Millie's wedding day.

The atmosphere in her crowded bedroom was one of laughter, as Rene put a final stitch into the side of Millie's ivory organza gown. 'Now don't put any more weight on in the next hour. I ain't got time to undo and do any more stitches. I ain't even got me hat on yet!'

Mama looked at Millie. 'Weight, dear?'

'Yes, Mama. I am having Cess's child. I think I am three months.'

'Well, you kept that quiet! But, oh, it's wonderful news.'

The room filled with gasps of delight. Elsie pushed her way through everyone and put her arms out to Millie. 'Oh, luv, this is the icing on the cake.' Her eyes were full of tears.

'No crying today, darling sis . . . not even happy tears. Not yet, anyway, or my face will be all puffy.'

'You're beautiful, Millie. So beautiful, and there ain't a soul can match yer.'

'Thank you, Elsie. I love you so much.' They hugged

again. 'And you look beautiful in that blue, darling,' Millie told her. 'I know green is meant to be the colour for redheads, but you couldn't look more beautiful. And you too, dear Rose. How clever Rene is to make your dress in that gathered style – you can hardly tell.'

She gently patted Rose's stomach, which was surprisingly small. But then she felt a tinge of worry as she looked into Rose's pale face.

'Are you feeling all right, Rose?'

'Aye, don't worry about me. Ruby's promised to stay by me side all day and take care of me. You just enjoy your day, it's going to be grand.'

'Aye, it is, lass. Now you go and sit down, Rose, and let me near to Millie.'

Millie gasped when she saw Ruby. She looked so lovely in her bridesmaid's frock. 'Oh, Ruby, it's one of the happiest days of my life.'

'I knaw, lass. And mine too, as to see you happy makes me happy. Mind, it feels funny having a nanny looking after me little Millie, but I'm going to enjoy the day.'

They hugged. 'I know. I would love my Daniel to be there, and your Millie and Ronnie too, but better they are kept warm and cared for here . . . Ah, look at you, Kitty, and you, Bert. Oh, Kitty, you look like a princess. And you look so smart in your breeches, Bert. You'll be a fine best man.'

Elsie cut in, 'Yes, and you'd better hurry, young man. Dai is waiting for yer, it's time for yer carriage to take yer to the church.'

When Millie's carriage pulled up outside the beautiful Church of St Saviour's in Walton Place, Knightsbridge, she thought she would die from the excitement coursing through her.

379

She didn't notice that Rose wasn't among the bridesmaids as they fell in behind her. But she did notice that only Bert was by Cess's side as she walked into the church. Her happiness became tinged with worry as she sensed something wasn't quite right.

When Cess turned and smiled at her, she forgot this worry and gasped at the beauty of him, as the winter sun shone through the stained-glass window above the altar and lit up his sandy hair.

The service went without a hitch, and it wasn't until afterwards, as they were being taken back to the house and Cess had kissed her, that the niggling worry re-entered her.

'Millie – Mrs Makin – I love you. Thank you for marrying me.'

'Oh, Cess, I'm so happy.'

He held her hand. 'Millie, something happened. I'm so sorry, but just before the bridesmaids left the house and you and Wilf came downstairs, Rose fainted.'

'Oh, Cess. Is she all right – the baby?'

'I don't know. I only know that when the rest of the bridesmaids arrived, Elsie told us, and Dai said he was sorry, but he had to go to her.'

This little bit of news softened the awful news that Rose wasn't well.

'We'll find out as soon as we get home. But my first job is to delay the reception. Your mama said that I was to tell Campbell to assemble everyone in the withdrawing room until you were ready for us to receive them all in the dining room.'

When they arrived, Jean met them. She bobbed a curtsy and then told them that Rose had lost her baby. 'The doctor and a gentleman are with her. She's all right. Do you want me to ask if you can go in to see her, ma'am?'

'Yes, Jean, thank you.'

'Oh, and congratulations, Mill— I mean, ma'am.'

'"Millie," Jean. From now on, it is all right to call me Millie in front of Cess. But avoid doing so at times that would get you into trouble with the butler or housekeeper. And thank you, that's very kind of you. I will come into the kitchens later to see the staff.'

They found Rose propped up in bed. Dai was perched on the bed and was holding her hand.

'Oh, Rose, Rose, I'm so sorry, my dear.'

'Ta, Millie. I'll be all right. It's a shock, and I missed being yer bridesmaid an' all. But, well, good has come out of it . . . Me and Dai . . .'

'We're going to be married, Millie.' Dai said this in a shaky voice that was full of emotion.

'Oh, Rose, I am so happy for you. And for you, Dai.'

'Well, mate, yer took your time, didn't yer? Congratulations!'

Dai grinned at Cess. 'Yes, I did, Cess. I – I don't think I knew my own mind, but the minute we were told that Rose was unwell, I knew in a flash. I was so terrified I was going to lose her.'

Millie watched as he put Rose's hand to his lips and kissed it. A tear flowed down his cheeks.

'I couldn't bear to lose you, my darling Rose. And I will help you to get over this terrible loss.'

That Dai thought of Rose losing her baby, not as a blessing for their future together, but as a tragedy, showed what a lovely man he was. One who had been lost for a long time, but was capable of great love.

'Mate, we have to go. I'm sorry for your loss, Rose. But really happy for you and Dai, girl.'

'Ta, Cess. I'm going to be all right.'

'I know you are.'

'We'll have something sent up for you both. Rest now, Rose.'

'Ta, Millie.'

The smile that Rose gave Millie spoke of a happiness she'd so wanted for her lovely friend.

Chapter Thirty

Millie

JUNE 1914

Six months passed in blissful happiness, with Millie only occasionally wondering about Len and whether he could ever do them any harm again. Yes, Wilf had said not, but then she knew Len and couldn't quite believe it.

Dispelling these thoughts as she lay back on her pillows with her newborn baby son, James Cecil Bert – to be known as Jimmy, after the uncle he would never know – cradled in her arms, she allowed her love for Cess, and her children, to fill her with a warm glow of happiness.

She looked around. All her loved ones except Wilf, whom Mama had said would be up in a moment, and Rene, who couldn't get away, were with her. Though tired, happiness at having them there to greet little James was keeping her going.

Cess lay on the bed with his head next to hers on the pillow, cradling Daniel. Bert and Kitty sat on the end of the bed with Elsie. Jim stood next to Elsie with his hand on her shoulder, and Mama, Jack and the newly married Rose and Dai stood on the other side. In his arms Dai held Ronnie. All were cooing over Millie's baby and congratulating her and Cess, when the door burst open and Wilf came in.

His face alerted her to something being wrong. She held her breath, then saw everyone turn and stare at him as he told them, 'There's bad news, I'm afraid . . . Well, to be honest, for us it's good news, but I don't like calling it that.'

'Wilf, not now, darling. Greet our new grandson first. Whatever you have read can wait.'

'Oh, I do apologize. Dear Millie, what must you think of me? Well done, my dear. So this is the fruit of your labour, eh? Hello, little chap.'

'Fruit of her labour! Wilf, you could have chosen better words, darling.'

Millie laughed. 'Leave him alone, Mama. It was labour, and jolly hard.'

They all chuckled, but Millie could tell they really wanted, as she did, to hear the news Wilf had spoken of.

'Now, tell us what's happened, Wilf? Is it something bad or good?'

'Oh, my dear, I am so sorry to barge in like that. I was very distracted. You see, I have just had a telephone call. Len is dead.'

There was a collective gasp, but no one spoke.

In the face of each person in the room Millie saw a conflict of emotions, and she knew that no matter the relief this brought to her, and to them, it didn't seem right to do what she wanted to do – and felt sure they all wanted to do – and cheer.

Everyone looked at her.

All she could say was, 'How?'

'It isn't clear, but it's thought he took his own life. His father was informed this morning, and his solicitor has just rung me.'

Millie sighed. 'I have this strange sensation that I want to thank him. This is the least selfish act he has committed since I have known him. In some ways it exonerates him, as he has given himself the ultimate punishment. I hope that he rests in peace.'

All nodded their agreement.

'Wilf, will you get a message to Len's father for me?'

'Of course, dear.'

'I just want to offer my condolences, and to tell him that as far as I am concerned, it's over. That I will write to him in prison with news of his grandson, and that he will be welcome to have visits with him when he is free.'

Wilf nodded.

'But, Wilf, he won't ever be Daniel's main grandfather. That will always be you. As you are to James.'

Wilf gave her a lovely smile that held his relief and gratitude. She could see that he was overcome, so she didn't say any more.

Millie looked at Cess. 'I love you, Cess, with all my heart. Thank you for being by my side. And all of you. You got me, Cess, Elsie and Jim through everything that we've been through. You are my family, and the very best anyone could wish for.'

She smiled at her beautiful family – for each person, whether related to her or not, had become that, as had Rene. And Jack even more so, because to her and Cess, he'd become like a son.

Mama sighed. It was a sound that held her happiness and relief. 'Well, we have to celebrate, my darling. Where's the champagne? You promised to order some to be sent up, Wilf?'

'I did order it, but I asked them to wait a moment. I think now, though, that we are all ready. You're nearest, my darling, so will you pull the bell cord? The housekeeper will know what you want.'

Mama giggled as she crossed the room.

Elsie got up and came nearer. 'Oh, Millie, he's a real smasher. Can I hold him?'

'Yes, Elsie. Here you are, darling.'

Elsie gingerly took little James. Millie saw her face flood with love and sent up a silent prayer that one day she would see Elsie holding her own baby. She turned her head to Cess. 'I'll hold Daniel while Elsie has James, darling.'

As he passed her Daniel his smile lit up his face. 'We have two sons, Millie . . . I can't stop saying it to meself. Ta, me darlin'. The best present you could ever give me.'

As she took Daniel Millie told him, 'Actually you have two brothers, Daniel.'

'Yer have, mate.' Cess looked up at Jack. 'Jack's yer brovver too. At this rate, we'll soon have a football team for yer, lad – you can be a trainer, and I know you'll look after them as if they're your real brothers.'

Jack grinned. 'I've enough on me plate with the stall, Bert, and now three nippers, as it is. Not to mention when Ronnie visits.'

Everyone laughed.

Millie watched little Daniel chuckle his baby-laugh with them. Holding him tighter, she looked once more around the room. She'd made many promises in the last twelve months. All she'd been able to keep, and now she promised herself that nothing was ever going to spoil her happiness again.

Just as she thought this, Elsie bent towards her and whispered, 'I have something to tell you, luv. Not even Jim must hear.' Elsie looked around. Everyone was chatting and not taking any notice. Jim was in deep conversation with Wilf.

'Is everything all right, Elsie?'

'More than all right. I've missed two of me monthlies, and then this morning I were sick the minute I put me feet on the bedroom floor – well, not there and then, but I had to run for the lav.'

'Oh, Elsie!'

'Shush, luv. I'm not ready to tell anyone yet. I want the doctor to say it's true, and then we can tell the world.'

Millie caught hold of her hand. 'It's true, darling – it's true and the very best news in all the world. Things are going to be different from now on, darling sister. No more threats hanging over our heads. The jam factory will go from strength to strength, and the future will be wonderful. We fought back, Elsie. We fought back and we won.'

Millie couldn't stop smiling and, it seemed, neither could Elsie. They clung to the babies and to each other's hands, and Millie knew that the same peace and happiness that engulfed her filled her beloved sister too.

Letter to Readers

Hello all,

Well, here we are at the end of another trilogy. I hope you have all enjoyed the journey with Millie, Elsie and Dot, and I hope you liked how the story finally concluded and are happy to know that the girls have found the love and peace they were seeking and can once more make others' lives better too.

But don't worry if you have missed the first two books, *The Jam Factory Girls* and *Secrets of the Jam Factory Girls*, as all of the books are stand-alone too. If you do want to find out how the girls got to where they are you can order copies from bookshops or online.

And so, as one door (or in our case 'page') closes, another one opens. For me that means a brand new series to tackle, and I have been busy writing the first two books for release next year.

This series is to be called The Orphanage Girls. Set in Bethnal Green, London, we will once again meet three 'salt of the earth' cockney girls as we follow the lives of Ruth, Ellen and Amy who are desperate to leave the confines of the orphanage and all the unhappiness and despair it holds for them.

Each of their stories are told in separate books but are interwoven, starting with Ruth's story – as yet untitled.

In the second book, as the First World War breaks out, we will see them take up the challenge and become the strong young women they were destined to be, able to support each other as tragedy strikes.

The third in the series will bind them in a way they could not have imagined and bring a special someone into their lives. I have loved writing the first two and am itching to begin the third. Look out for the first one hitting the shops in May.

To get further news on my books and to interact with me I would love to meet you on my Facebook page: www.facebook.com/MaryWoodAuthor

Follow me on Twitter: @Authormary

And subscribe to my webpage to receive three monthly newsletters, interact through email and keep up with all that is happening in my book world: www.authormarywood.com

Best of all – when our lives return to normal – look out for me visiting your area for a book signing, when we can meet in person and have a chat.

Thank you all for the support you give to me.

Take care everyone. Much love,

Mary x

Acknowledgements

My heartfelt thanks to:

Bonne Maman, manufacturers of fine jams with the lovely, distinctive gingham lids and of preserves and confectionery, for their wonderful support in joining with Pan Macmillan to put on a competition for *Secrets of The Jam Factory Girls*.

And to all these wonderful people who helped my book on its way:

My adored editor, Wayne Brookes, and my best-in-the-business agent, Judith Murdoch. Both are always by my side encouraging me on and keeping me smiling.

Victoria Hughes-Williams for her insightful structural edit and Samantha Fletcher for her dedication in guiding me through the line edit, bringing clarity to where I may have muddied the waters and checking my research.

To Philippa McEwan and Becky Lushy, my publicists, who have made exciting things happen for my books.

To my son James, who helps me in so many ways, reading the first draft, going through edits to highlight where I need to give most attention to changes suggested and finding all the tiny faults in the final proofread.

My love and thanks to you all.

And a special thank you to my darling family: my dearest husband, Roy; my children, Christine, Julie, Rachel and James; and my grandchildren and great-grandchildren. Thank you for the beautiful love that you give to me. You help me to climb my mountain. x

Their adventure begins in

The Jam Factory Girls

by Mary Wood

Whatever life throws at them, they will face it together

Life for Elsie is difficult as she struggles to cope with her alcoholic mother. Caring for her siblings and working long hours at Swift's Jam Factory in London's Bermondsey is exhausting. Thankfully her lifelong friendship with Dot helps to smooth over life's rough edges.

When Elsie and Dot meet Millie Hawkesfield, the boss's daughter, they are nervous to be in her presence. Over time, they are surprised to feel so drawn to her, but should two cockney girls be socializing in such circles?

When disaster strikes, it binds the women in ways they could never have imagined. And long-held secrets are revealed that will change all their lives . . .

Available now

This historical saga of friendship continues in
book two of the Jam Factory Girls series

Secrets of the Jam Factory Girls

by Mary Wood

Can the jam factory girls
create the future they all deserve?

Elsie's worked her way up at Swift's Jam Factory from the
shop floor to the top, and now it's her time to shine. But
when she's involved in an incident involving her half-sister
Millie's new husband, she is forced to keep it secret – the
truth could threaten their sisterly bond.

Dot is dogged by fear, coming to terms with her mother's
rejection of her. She should be enjoying the happiness she
craves with her beloved Cess; instead, she's trapped in an
asylum, haunted by the horrifying cries of inmates. All she
wants is to get married, but what chance is there for her if
she's locked away?

Millie is trying to build a life with her new husband. But
the man she loves is not all he seems . . .

Available now

The Forgotten Daughter

by Mary Wood

Book one in
The Girls Who Went to War series

From a tender age, Flora felt unloved and unwanted by her parents, but she finds safety in the arms of caring Nanny Pru. But when Pru is cast out of the family home, under a shadow of secrets and with a baby boy of her own on the way, it shatters little Flora.

Over the years, however, Flora and Pru meet in secret – unbeknown to Flora's parents. Pru becomes the mother she never had, and Flora grows into a fine young woman. When she signs up as a volunteer with St John Ambulance, she begins to shape her life. But the drum of war beats loudly and her world is turned upside down when she receives a letter asking her to join the Red Cross in Belgium.

With the fate of the country in the balance, it is a time for bravery. Flora's determined to be the strong woman she was destined to be. But with horror, loss and heartache on her horizon, there's a lot for young Flora to learn . . .

Available now